# The Hampton Court Murders

DEAR NANCY,
I HOPE YOU TAKE
PLEASURE IN THIS
TUDOR TALE!
MEET YOU AT
LOUISA'S.
ALL THE BEST,
DAVID.
FALL 2010

## Also by David Hoekenga

Santa Fe Solo
*A Death in the Shadow of the Sangre de Cristo Mountains*

Placitas Particular
*A Death in the Rind of the Sandia Mountains*

# The Hampton Court Murders

## Death by Design

David Hoekenga

**To order additional copies of this book, contact:**
Xlibris Corporation
1-888-795-4274
www.Xlibris.com
Orders@Xlibris.com
52097

To
Earl Nelson Hoekenga

"Practice being relaxed"

Why come you not to court?
To which court?
To the king's court?
Or to Hampton Court?
Nay, to the king's court!
The king's court
Should have the excellence
But Hampton Court
Hath the pre-eminence!

John Skelton 1523

# FOREWORD

This book, set in the sixteenth century, was much more challenging than my first two books, *Santa Fe Solo* and *Placitas Particular*. While all three are mysteries, writing about times long past with some semblance of verisimilitude proved a challenge. I will confess right now that there are a series of anachronisms in the story, mostly because I believe it made the texture of the story richer. You might want to see how many you can spot (you can compare your list to my list at the end of the book). While more unstable in 1530, the English language was richer then. I have chosen to use many of the words of those times. For example, I used 'amanuensis' which is, to my mind, one of the most melodious words in the language in place of 'secretary.' In the endnotes you will find definitions of the many unfamiliar terms such as an 'hermaphrodite brig.' When there was a choice I adhered to the English spelling as in 'grey' rather than the American version 'gray.'

I wanted the pile of soft red bricks built by those energetic and farsighted builders, Cardinal Thomas Wolsey and Henry VIII, to be like a character in the book. Therefore you will find the parts of the Palace, such as the Great Waiting Chamber, capitalized and described in some detail. Fortunately for all of us, this warm, majestic, and beautifully balanced structure still exists, little changed on the banks of the Thames. When you stand in the largest courtyard, Base Court, two-thirds the length of a football field on a side, it is easy to imagine Cardinal Wolsey in his red silk cassock walking there, or King Henry and the flirtatious Anne Boleyn alighting from an ornate carriage pulled by four white stallions. For a map of the convoluted Hampton

Court Palace drawn in 1530, as a reading aid, go to my web site-www. BooksbyHooks.com.

Step back with me, now, to a time when England was young. The country had a smart, handsome, vigorous monarch who at six feet six inches tall, was half again as big as most of his loyal subjects.

# PART 1

# CHAPTER 1

A dense, wet fog drifted off the Thames River and invested every garden and courtyard of Hampton Court. The Thames curved nearby in the shape of a horse's muzzle with the Palace sitting where the bit would reside. During the previous night, a tall middle-aged man had ridden west in a hansom from London. The Thames undulated upstream from London like a long, slender grass snake. The highway the traveler took followed a more direct route from Southwark to the village of Hampton where the Thames and the Mole River meet. From the iron gate on the highway he glimpsed the five-story Great Gatehouse. After crossing the lawn, he arrived weary and bone-sore, and entered the servant's door into Lord Chamberlain's Court on the left side of the palace.

A serving gentleman took his two heavy brocaded suitcases and ushered him down the broad hallway of the North Cloisters, and then left through a broad door into the Kitchen. A nervous older man in guard's livery approached the traveler. The older man was short and portly with long grey hair and kind grey eyes. His face, usually clean shaven, had stubble on it this morning.

"My name is Warder Peter Chertsey, sir," the guard began in a nervous voice. "I am master of the guards at Hampton Court."

"And are you responsible for calling me out on a matter of some urgency on this rainy night?" the traveler replied in an irritated tone, as water continued to drip off his greatcoat. "Why am I here? Spit it out, man!"

"There has been a murder!"

"What, pray tell, makes you say so?"

Wordlessly, Warder Chertsey led the traveler across the large high-ceilinged kitchen. Despite a fire in a fireplace large enough to spit and roast a whole ox, the room was dark and smoky. Oak branches were stacked seven feet high beside the brick-lined fireplace. A faint light came through a mullioned window on the south wall. Lying on a long, heavy, trestle table was the body of a young man.

The irritated traveler was Seamus Scott Weatherby, MB. As he approached the body, his demeanor changed perceptibly. His irascible, agitated state changed to one of intense concentration as his eyes focused on the corpse. A helpful servant girl placed a silver candelabrum by the dead man's head. Sir Weatherby was still for many minutes as he studied the body in total, and catalogued what he saw in his mind. Warder Chertsey shifted nervously from foot to foot, expecting more criticism from the arrogant stranger. He didn't have to wait long.

"Who placed the body like this, or was he dispatched right here in the bloody kitchen?" Sir Weatherby fumed.

"Of course not, sir. I moved him out of respect for the dead, sir."

"He was already deceased, my man. His soul is already in heaven, if you believe in that sort of thing."

The warder clearly did, because his crossed himself involuntarily.

"You have made my job infinitely harder by disturbing the *corpus delecti*. I suppose you'll claim this is your first suspicious death in this vast palace, but if it ever happens again, don't lay a *hand* on the body!"

It was two-hundred and fifty years before Scotland Yard was founded on Sir Weatherby's principles and he knew, for his time, his request was extremely unreasonable.

Sir Weatherby began a focused and detailed examination. First he checked for the four *mortises*, or signs of death, that he learned in medical school so that he might estimate the time the murder. He noted *pallor mortis*, a marked paleness of the skin. Next he looked for *algor mortis*, a time related cooling of the body in dead and noted the body was close to the ambient temperature in the kitchen. Next he rolled the body on its side with Warder Chertsey's help and looked for *livor mortis*, the purple discoloration of the dependent part of the body. Each of these signs suggested death occurred at least ten to fourteen hours earlier. Finally, he checked for *rigor mortis*, which he felt to be the most valuable of the four signs for timing a person's demise. The victim's muscles were rigid, and Sir Weatherby, applying his full strength, could not bend the corpse's forearm. He knew that full rigor was apparent twelve hours after death and then all stiffness resolved thirty-six hours after death. So death most likely occurred the previous evening.

Sir Weatherby called for more candles. He removed a large magnifying glass with a brass handle from his great coat. He examined the victim's head in some detail. He noted that the occipital bone and temporal bones were crushed on the right side of the skull. He picked through the clotted blood and hair and removed a piece of wood and two thin slivers of metal with silver tweezers that he kept in his pocket, which he placed carefully in a folded parchment.

Next he removed a shiny metal disc with a hole in the center from his coat. He affixed it to his head with a leather strap and positioned it so that the hole was over his eye. He used the disc to focus a concentrated beam of candle light on the victim's body. Warder Chertsey had never seen anything like it. Sir Weatherby examined the victim's boots carefully; next he studied the dead man's arms and hands minutely finding several small cuts and abrasions over the knuckles. He used a small knife to remove material from under the victim's finger nails which he placed in another folded parchment.

Suddenly he was very tired and hungry. Turning to the buxom serving girl who had brought the candles, Sir Weatherby said, "Bring me porridge, a chunk of ham and black tea." Then glaring again at the warder he said, "Call for the man who found the body, and while he is coming, sit down and tell me everything you saw when you were brought to the body, down to the smallest mote or mite."

"The guard was in such an agitated state that he nearly ran from the Great Kitchen back to the Closets. He was talking rapidly when he got here and not making a lot of sense. He said that the body was lying in a pool of blood in the Council Chamber near the Chapel. It's an area of new construction ordered by the King. Some carpenter's tool lay about, but there was no sign of another human other than the guard who found him."

"But the light in the Closet must have been very poor."

"Yes. He had but one lantern, and there was no moon due to the rainy night."

Sir Weatherby ate the food that was set before him with the delicate manners of someone at a royal banquet. He patted his mouth frequently with a cloth napkin and placed his utensils precisely next to his china plate after each bite.

Then after a large swallow of tea, he said, "What killed him?"

Warder Chertsey led Sir Weatherby toward the room where the body was found. They conversed as they walked.

"The right side of his head was stove in," the warder replied in a slightly exasperated tone.

"Yes. I could see that, but what instrument was used to strike the blow?"

"I saw nothing near the body that was heavy and hard enough to do it, Your Grace."

"Who was the victim?"

"I'm told he was a young architect named William Suffolk."

Once in the Council Chamber, Sir Weatherby knelt on the new wooden floor marred by a large irregular circle of blood that had become dark maroon. Sir Weatherby searched the corners of the nearly finished room assiduously for clues and slid one small item into his pocket. After checking the room while standing, he knelt down in several spots to change the play of light on the objects in the room. A short way down the hall, a faint bloody boot print could be seen when Sir Weatherby lowered his eyes to floor level. He took a folded piece of parchment from an inside pocket carefully opened it and then removed a crude round wooden pencil with writing material secured in the center. Warder Chertsey, who wrote with a slender rod of zinc when he wasn't using a quill, had never seen such an instrument. As he sketched the outline of the boot print, Sir Weatherby continued to question the warder.

"Not the son of Lord Suffolk, I trust?"

"I'm afraid he is the Lord's fifth son, and therefore of no account. As you well know, Sir, the first son will inherit everything, the second will enter the military and the third becomes a prelate. No one cares what happens to the rest, least of all the Lord."

"How long has he worked here?"

"Henry VIII ordered work to begin on New Years Day 1529, so I suppose he has been living and working here since then."

"I'll need a list of his friends and colleagues here. Had he been in any altercations?"

"He had a public disagreement with the King's Master Carpenter, Humphrey Coke, in the base court last winter. I didn't witness it, but I heard tell of it."

As the two walked back toward the Great Kitchen, Weatherby reflected on his life. For the past five years he had worked solely for the King of England. His charge was to solve crimes against persons and properties that belonged to his monarch.

# CHAPTER 2

"I need to speak with the witnesses to the altercation. Where is the watchman who discovered the body?" Sir Weatherby said.

"He lives in the village. I sent someone to rouse him and bring him to the kitchen," the Warder replied.

Warder Chertsey led the way back through the vast palace from the Council Chambers, past the Gallery and down the stairs to the Great Kitchen. The night watchman, Tobias, was hunched over a bowl of porridge.

"I need you to tell me about the body you found last night, young man," Sir Weatherby began as he sat down across from Tobias. "Mind you, no detail is too small."

"I don't know much," Tobias said with a quizzical look as he placed his spoon on the worn planks of the table. "By my count, the palace contains three hundred ninety-seven rooms on three floors, and they are often connected by long galleries. It takes me six hours to inspect each room and the surrounding grounds. On moonless nights it's hard to see. I have only the light from the candle in my lantern. Some of the new rooms are piled with lumber, stone and building tools."

"Could someone hide in the palace without your noticing them?" Sir Weatherby asked.

After a moment's reflection, Tobias said, "A gang of men could hide in one of the larger rooms or behind a pile of lumber. If they were still, I wouldn't know of their presence. The palace is very dark and shadowy at night. The timbers and windows make noise even when the wind isn't blowing, like it was last night. If I had an imagination, I could see gargoyles, dragons and ghosts at every corner. It's a lonely, solitary employment."

"I see you think you have a hard lot. Tell me about your encounter with the body last night."

"I had already checked the ground floor and found nothing untoward. On the first floor I started on the north side and ambled through the newly constructed Great Hall. I opened the doors to the Great Watching Chamber and cut diagonally across it to the gallery. Then I opened the door into the Royal Closets and turned toward the Chapel. In the dim light, as I entered the Council Chamber, I tripped on something, which is not unusual during my rounds. However, it didn't feel hard like iron or stone or even wood; no, it felt soft and yielding. I swung around and lowered my lantern toward the floor. There was the body, lying in a pool of bright red blood. It gave me a terrible start. I grabbed the whistle around my neck and blew it, almost involuntarily. Then I remembered that no person was within earshot. In fact, I suspected no person was within one hundred yards of me."

"What next?"

"Me heart was racing. I didna' tarry. I ran, stumblin' and lurchin' to this very room, the Great Kitchen."

"Thinking back, was there anything else that you saw or heard?"

"No, Sir," Tobias answered as he pushed his now cold porridge toward the center of the broad, rough table.

"You have been very little help, young man," Sir Weatherby shot back. "Either you are not intelligent, or not observant, or perhaps you committed this crime. Can you tell me which it is?"

"I never murdered no one! I didn't go to school because my parents were too poor. I am hardworking and honest, Sir."

"That's all for now. However, I may call you back later for more questioning or drag you to London if I find out you have lied to me. Be gone."

Tobias got up hastily and left the kitchen.

Sir Weatherby turned his piercing gaze back to Warder Chertsey after he called for more hot tea.

"I want a plan of the Palace, a list of all your employees, including the stonecutters and carpenters, and an interview with the man in charge of the construction," Sir Weatherby said as he stifled a yawn.

"The last would be Sir John Moulton, Surveyor of the King's Works," Warder Chertsey replied. "He has an office near the old part of the Palace. We can go there now."

"No. First I want to sleep some." Weatherby replied.

"Very good sir. I will have the kitchen girl show you to an apartment."

The serving girl led the way through galleries and halls to a two-room apartment on the first floor of the Base Gallery. Cardinal Thomas Wolsey had constructed dozens of two-room apartments for important personages just before Henry VIII took Hampton Court from him. The entrance was off a long gallery. The main room had a large fireplace and two large windows each containing ten small, leaded panes of glass. Glass was very expensive and therefore large windows such as these were a rarity in the sixteenth century. Weatherby deduced that Wolsey and the King both had ample funds to squander on glass. The smaller room contained a tall narrow bed and a private toilet called a garderobe. Originally there was a simple chute from the garderobe that went to the outside wall of the castle or manor house around the country. Waste fell into the moat, creating a smelly mess outside the structure. Wolsey's architects, for the first time, built the chutes as well as the chimneys within the walls of the Palace, smoothing the outside wall and reducing the smell, even though the excrement still ended up in the moat. Clothing was always stored in the garderobe because the pungent smells deterred moths. It gave origin to the later word, "wardrobe," Weatherby had heard.

Sir Weatherby noted that the floors were plastered over oak planks and the wooden walls whitewashed. The ceiling was chamfered wood beams left a natural brown color. Cardinal Wolsey was a voracious and extravagant collector of tapestries, and examples from his collection hung on every wall of his apartment. A high, narrow bed rested against a wall of the smaller room. The kitchen girl turned the bed covers back and then helped Sir Weatherby remove his boots, great coat, doublet and waistcoat, hanging them on hooks in the garderobe. When she left she took his tall leather boots with her to clean the mud from them. Weatherby fell onto the bed and was asleep in minutes.

He was awakened three hours later by the cold. The small fire in the stone rimmed fireplace had died, but as he drifted into consciousness he remembered the nightmare. Perhaps that was what had awakened him. In fact, it was a blood-curdling apparition that woke him in a cold heavy sweat. In the dream he was riding a white horse across the foggy fens on a dark, moonless night. The horse was galloping fast into a stiff wind. He was chased by three tall wraiths dressed in black robes on foaming black stallions. One carried a sword, one a trident, and the third a long-handled scythe. The trail narrowed between tall twisting trees as his horse went up a small hillock. Just as Weatherby reached the top, a small child in a long white gown crawled suddenly into the middle of the trail, directly in front of his horse. Just at that instant, he always awoke in a panic. When he had some time, he would sit and ponder the deeper meaning of the nightmare.

Sir Weatherby retrieved his boots from the door and pulled his clothing on. He walked purposefully from his suite on the Base Court and east toward the Great Kitchen. His confident sense of direction helped him through the maze of the galleries, rooms and great halls. When he reached the Kitchen he called for a cup of tea and sat down at the long trestle table. Warder Chertsey had summoned all his guards to the Kitchen and sent them off to look for anything untoward in the Castle.

"I need to speak with the director of construction, Warder," Sir Weatherby said abruptly.

"That would be Sir John Moulton, Surveyor of the King's Work, Sir," Chertsey replied. "He has a temporary office in the Clock Court and starts work early. I will summon him or I can lead you there."

Gulping the rest of his tea, Sir Weatherby said, "Take me there. I will learn more of the man if I see him in his own surroundings."

Warder Chertsey strode out of the kitchen with Sir Weatherby at his side. The portly Warder cut through back passageways, down narrow stairs and into a large area of new construction. Bright red bricks and distinctive black bricks lay in disorderly piles in the courtyard. The black bricks created the distinctive diaper-work or diamond pattern in the stories tall curtain walls.

"The workers set up kilns in nearby Home Park and have made more than sixteen million bricks," Warder Chertsey said. "They still needed ten million more from other kilns in the county."

A small temporary wooden building stood in the far corner of the Clock Court. As Sir Weatherby approached the building, he smelled the strong tannin aroma of freshly sawn oak timbers. It was a familiar smell that he always enjoyed. Inside the building a large scale, very detailed, wooden model of Hampton Court was balanced on two saw horses. In another corner, a draftsman wearing an eyeshade sat hunched over an architectural drawing.

# CHAPTER 3

A tall white-haired man stood in the middle of the room smoking a clay pipe.

"Sir Weatherby, this is Sir John Moulton," Chertsey said obsequiously.

"I understand, Sir, that you are the director of the construction here at Hampton Court," Sir Weatherby began.

"I am, Sir," Sir Moulton replied. "In fact, I am in charge of all of the King's works. I am supervising remodeling at Somerset House and Windsor Castle but the work here is by far the most extensive and demanding."

"William Suffolk was murdered here last night, Sir," Weatherby replied sharply. "What do you know about this?"

Sir Moulton expected deference from almost everyone he encountered and he took umbrage at Sir Weatherby's brusque remarks. He stared and slowly removed the pipe from his lips without speaking.

"I was sent here by His Majesty, King Henry VIII, Sir Moulton," Sir Weatherby replied without backing down. "I believe we work for the same monarch and I am calling for—no, I'm demanding—your help right now."

Sir Moulton threw his pipe on the floor shattering the pipe into a hundred pieces and started toward the door. Warder Chertsey, afraid of getting caught between the large egos of these two powerful men, half-blocked the door of the construction hut. He hoped Sir Moulton would have a chance to think for a moment and quell his anger before he left the building. The Surveyor of the King's Works was forced to pause, and rather than pushing past the Warder, he turned and took a deep breath.

"William Suffolk worked at Hampton Court for the past year and a half," Sir Moulton said in a voice laced with controlled anger. "The King ordered far-reaching new construction and remodeling on the Palace in 1528. William began work here with me, on New Year's Day 1529. He was a junior architect who had studied at Cambridge. He was responsible for the design of windows and doors at the Palace."

"Thank you for that information, Sir Moulton," Sir Weatherby replied. "Did you work closely with the victim?"

"He had a desk here in the construction shed, but he was often absent."

"Working on the scaffolds of the Castle?"

"Sometimes, but often he would be missing for several days."

"Where did he go and what did he do?"

"I couldn't tell you. He often came back disheveled and fatigued."

"Did you question and reprimand him about his absences?"

"No, I did not. William worked here by order of the King. I presumed he was employed here as a favor to his father, the Earl of Suffolk. He was a fifth son, so of little use to the Earl. The King has granted me a lot of authority, but William, as the son of an Earl, I was told was beyond reproof."

"Did the two of you speak?"

"Seldom. We were cordially to each other, but had little in common. His designs for mullions and oriel windows were superb and gradually I gave him more and more latitude."

"Did he have any enemies?"

"Last summer, after a hot spell he had a very public disagreement in the Base Court with the King's Master Carpenter, Humphrey Coke. I spoke with both of them after the incident."

"What was the disagreement about?"

"Humphrey said that he suspected William of purloining glass from the window shop and that William took offense and punched him. Humphrey was so surprised by the blow that he fell down. After he got back up, and the two were squaring off with their fists up, other workers restrained them both."

"Were there any further incidents between the two?"

"Not to my knowledge. They were both in the vicinity of the Base Court nearly every day. When they meet, they are icily polite with each other."

"Thank you for talking with me, Sir Moulton," Sir Weatherby replied. "May I say how much I admire the quality and elegance of the work you are doing here?"

"You may. Thank you. I hope I never lay eyes on you again, Sir," Sir Moulton replied vehemently.

"You will not be that fortunate, Sir. I shall reside here at Hampton Court until this murder is solved, even if it takes a millennium."

Sir Weatherby stormed out of the construction shack, slamming the door behind him.

"I would like a tour of the castle," Sir Weatherby said to the Warder.

"It would be my pleasure, Sir," Warder Chertsey replied with a slight bow of his head. "However, it is a very large Palace extending over two hectares with twenty-four hectares of outbuildings and gardens. There are an additional three hundred hectares of farm land. A careful tour would take many days. May we do half today and perhaps half tomorrow?"

"That's an excellent suggestion," Sir Weatherby replied.

"I will show you the building starting with the oldest parts first. I've studied the history of Hampton Court Palace for the past thirty years. This site was recorded in the Domesday Book, the land survey of William the Conqueror done in 1086. A Sir Walter de St. Valery, a prominent Norman, owned Hampton. His land was poor but he introduced sheep and gradually increased its value. His grandson Reginald went on the Second Crusade in 1149. Jerusalem was captured and Reginald de St. Valery became Baron of Jerusalem. In the holy city, the Knights Hospitallers provided visiting knights with succor and hospitality. Reginald became acquainted with the Hospitallers while in Jerusalem, and when they expanded to other countries, Reginald rented Hampton to them."

Warder Chertsey walked Sir Weatherby across the Base Court to the Great Kitchen.

"Initially the building consisted of a chamber block and a great hall surrounded by a rectangular moat," Chertsey continued. "It was located where the Clock Court is now situated. Some of the foundations were found in the building process."

"I'm sure that other crimes were committed in this Palace," Sir Weatherby queried.

"Robberies and assaults yes, but never murder," Chertsey replied. "I have never heard of a fatality. This Great Kitchen was the site of an assault by one of the cooks five years ago."

Sir Weatherby looked across the flagstone floor of the kitchen toward the cavernous fireplace where a fire blazed. The upper walls of the twenty-foot-tall room were whitewashed. However, the front of the fireplace was stained black-brown from the smoke of hundreds of fires. The eighteen-foot-long trestle table was dwarfed by the size of the room.

"The only other parts of the Palace built in medieval times were the Dressers area, Serving Place and the North Cloister," Chertsey continued.

"This area is a long way from where the body was found."

"Yes. We are on the far north side of the Palace up against the outside wall and over two hundred feet and down a floor from where the body was found.

"The next large construction phase was began by Cardinal Thomas Wolsey in 1514 and lasted for fifteen years. The Palace grew to ten times its former size while he was master of the property. During that time Cardinal Wolsey was the most powerful man in England except for the King."

As the Warder talked, he led Sir Weatherby to the grand Base Course that Wolsey had constructed. To the front and south of the medieval rooms the Base Course was a large elegant square. The entrance was through an imposing five stories tall, red, brick Great Gatehouse. The soft red bricks were painted bright red and the mortar painted a contrasting white, which made the tower even more imposing.

As he walked Sir Weatherby out through the Gatehouse he turned and stopped to speak. "This is the most recognizable part of the Palace."

"It's an imposing façade," Sir Weatherby replied. "Suitable for a very powerful and ostentatious man, such as Cardinal Wolsey."

"The red brick towers on each side are five-stories tall making it the tallest structure in the county."

"Those four large ornate lead turrets with their eight smaller turrets set off the whole grand entrance."

"For me, it's all humanized by the double limestone bay window over the central arch with the frieze beneath it."

"It is a most pleasing portal."

"As I stand here at the Great Gatehouse looking eastward into the Palace I see it as divided into two natural halves," Warder Chertsey said. "On my left hand, toward the north is the servant's part of the Palace with storerooms, kitchens, laundry, wine cellar, and servant's quarters. To my right, on the south side, is the royal part of the Palace with the Wolsey Apartment, the Bayne Tower and the Princesses' Chambers."

"What a clever construct!"

"Yes I was worked here for almost twenty years when the dichotomy occurred to me," Chertsey said with pride in his voice.

As the two walked through the grand portal of the Base Court, a man in leather breeches with a loose white cotton shirt walked across the courtyard carrying a small carved beam. The man glanced at the two sightseers.

"Humphrey, could we talk for a minute?" Warder Chertsey called out.

"Of course," the man called back, placing his beam on a pile of bricks.

"Sir Weatherby, this is the King's Master Carpenter, Humphrey Coke."

"I imagine you are here about the murder, Sir," Humphrey Coke replied cheerily.

"You don't seem very upset about the death of your colleague," Sir Weatherby noted. "Did you see him yesterday?"

"No. I'm not upset about William's death. He was an arrogant, dishonest, self-important man," Coke replied. "And I'm glad he's dead. He won't be missed."

"You had a very public fight with him last summer and he knocked you down," Sir Weatherby said. "Did you have any fights or disagreements before or after that?"

"No that was our only altercation," Humphrey Coke replied a little too quickly.

"I think something else happened between you two."

"From our very first meeting, we didn't get along. He was an aristocratic supernumerary. He didn't respect anyone who wasn't from the aristocracy, he talked down to his co-workers, and he treated everyone badly. We had words right from the beginning. I outranked him, and he wasn't taking orders from me or respecting my authority. Everything was a battle between us."

"How was your conflict resolved?"

"It wasn't, sir. I simply gave orders to my assistants who gave William Suffolk his orders. Despite his recalcitrance he was an excellent and original architect, and we used his designs for windows and archways all over the Palace."

"Tell me about the fight."

"Starting last spring, panes of rare, colored glass started disappearing from our shops. It was occasional at first, but then it became more frequent. I had the guards pay special attention to the glazier's shop, but they came up with nothing. We got a shipment of valuable Chartres blue glass for the chapel. I staked out the glazier's shop myself and started sleeping nearby. On the third night I heard a noise and then saw someone leave with a pane of glass in his hand. I followed at a distance but then lost him in a nearby copse. Just before he ducked into the small trees he turned his head and it looked like William Suffolk to me."

"Hence, you confronted him?" Sir Weatherby interjected.

"Yes. When I saw him the next day. I accused him of stealing the blue glass. Without saying a word in reply, he hit me in the face."

"Did he deny the theft?"

"He never did."

"Thank you for talking with me. You have been most cooperative. I may ask you some additional questions as the investigation proceeds."

Lifting the carved beam back onto his shoulder, Humphrey Coke said, "Any time, your grace."

# CHAPTER 4

"It's time for supper, Sir," Warder Chertsey said, glancing at the large clock in the nearby tower. "I had a table set for us in Cardinal Wolsey's old apartment."

Chertsey led the way across the Base Court to the right toward Wolsey's rooms. A small table, with a linen tablecloth, had been set near the fireplace, as the night was getting quite cold. Servants brought silver bowls filled with green beans and root vegetables complementing a joint of mutton on a large platter. Each diner was given a large tankard of ale.

After sating his hunger, Sir Weatherby turned to the Warder and said, "Tell me about the Cardinal."

"He resides now in North Yorkshire, in much reduced circumstance, stripped of all of his titles except Archbishop of York," Chertsey began.

"Do you know him well?"

"I should say so! He obtained Hampton Court as a residence, for it was not yet a Palace, in 1514. I started working for him that very day and continued until he left in 1528. I saw him daily. He was a religious man, but also a venal man with appetites. He overate to corpulence, displayed his ostentatious wealth with expensive clothes and jewelry, collected prohibitively expensive tapestries, and frequently engaged in sexual congress even though he was a priest."

"While you may not have approved of everything he did, I sense that you liked him," Sir Weatherby replied.

"I did indeed. He lived life to its fullest and never denied himself, but he was also generous to those that worked for him. He had a humble origin. His father was a butcher. He managed to go to college and was ordained as a priest when he was in his mid twenties. He became personal chaplain to the governor of Calais and met Henry VII, our King's father, there."

"When Henry VIII became king in 1509, Wolsey prospered. He was made Bishop of Lincoln, then Bishop of York, and then made a Cardinal in 1515 by the Pope. For the next thirteen years he was the most powerful man in England, save the King. He negotiated treaties, reformed the courts and changed the tax so that taxes paid were based on income for the first time. All the while he added new properties and grew more and more ostentatious. When foreign dignitaries or high churchmen visited he had lavish feasts and fêtes. We served fifteen-course meals, had jousting, tennis, bowling and other games, fireworks and dancing all night. I'll never forget the excitement of those visits."

"As you know, his fall was sudden and complete. The King wanted his marriage to Catherine of Aragon annulled, so that he could marry his new love, Anne Boleyn. Henry VIII was in a fever about it. When Cardinal Wolsey couldn't arrange it, he was stripped of his vast property and government offices. He lost two palaces, York and Hampton Court, and several lavish houses, as well."

"I saw the Cardinal once when he visited London," Sir Weatherby mused. "He always had a large retinue of richly dressed servants and was draped in yards and yards of red silk adorned with gold and sapphires. The Cardinal openly visited the King at Whitehall with his 'wife' Joan Larke, which always astonished me. He publicly violated every tenet of his very Catholic religion."

The servants poured another tankard of ale for the two diners.

Warder Chertsey, with a faraway look in his eyes said, "He was larger than life."

Sir Weatherby excused himself from the dinner table and walked out of the Palace to gaze at the Thames, before turning back to his apartment. The river was a broad band of sparkling silver highlights in the light from a half moon. He slept hard and avoided his recurring nightmare. Early in the morning, Sir Weatherby heard a sharp knock on his door. He threw on a dressing gown and stumbled to the entrance. When he opened the door, a young but misshapened chap barely four and a half feet tall stood before him.

"Welcome Bradford," Sir Weatherby called out in a cheery voice. "Won't you come in?"

"I took the liberty of ordering tea, butter and crumpets from the young woman who showed me here, Your Grace," Bradford Dredge replied. "It should be here anytime."

Bradford Dredge was in Sir Weatherby's employ as an amanuensis. He kept all of his master's correspondence, wrote letters from dictation and catalogued all the copious and sundry items Sir Weatherby collected during his investigations. Bradford Dredge had been born in a poor village north of London and malnourished as a child. He had developed a severe case of rickets and the bones of his arms and especially legs were bowed like the sides of a beamy sailing ship. His gait was wide-based and slow and his height reduced to that of a ten-year-old. However, his mind was unaffected and he wrote with a beautiful smooth flowing hand. Sir Weatherby was absentminded and before he hired Dredge, he would spend hours looking for a misplaced piece of paper before flying into a rage of frustration and throwing objects around his library or laboratory. Since hiring his amanuensis things were catalogued, recorded and easily recovered.

Sir Weatherby emptied his many pockets of the scraps of evidence, folded parchments, and hand written notes that he had collected during the first day of the investigation, and handed them to his amanuensis.

"Thank you, Sir," Dredge replied. "I have a small room in the old servant's quarters, but more importantly there is a large workroom nearby. I have asked for a large table and shelves which should be moved in today to accommodate several trunks of chemicals and glassware I brought from our laboratory. I also brought several volumes from your library. Just before I left a messenger brought the new microscope you ordered from the Netherlands. I took the liberty of bringing it with me. It contains a long letter from Professor Anton van Leeuwenhoek."

The tea and crumpets were brought in on a tray by a serving girl who had knocked softly on the apartment door. Both ate hungrily for several minutes before resuming their dialog.

"I learned a lot about the small animalcules you can see with the microscope," Sir Weatherby remarked, "when I visited van Leeuwenhoek in Amsterdam last year. His main interest is in studying creatures so small that they can't be seen by the naked eye. He has already classified over three hundred new animals. Leeuwenhoek has also written several papers about structure in copepods and other fresh water crustaceans. I think the microscope can be used in criminal investigation, an application he hadn't thought of. That is why I had you make slides of various hairs and fibers and classify them by size, shape and other distinctive features."

"I brought the collection with me," Dredge replied. "I will go and organize your investigative laboratory."

In addition to his severely deformed limbs, Bradford Dredge had a series of swellings over his sternum known as a "rickety rosary," from his childhood illness. He also had a "square headed" appearance from the osteomalacia, but with regular features and a shock of brown hair his overall appearance was handsome. His most memorable feature was his large, intelligent green eyes.

"Once you are settled, track the body down. It is being kept cool in the Undercroft. Make some drawings of the victim. I also want a drawing of his skull showing the missing occipital and temporal bones."

"Yes, sir," Dredge said as he turned to leave the room.

"I will resume my introductory tour of Hampton Court Palace with Warder Chertsey," Sir Weatherby replied.

Sir Weatherby found the Warder in his small office on the ground floor.

"Have you solved the murder yet, Sir Weatherby?" the Warder said in a cheery voice.

Sir Weatherby scowled and then said, "Of course it isn't solved. You have given me little to work with. May we continue the tour?"

"At your service, sir. Let's head back to the Base Court where we were interrupted by running into Humphrey Coke."

Chertsey led them into the south side of the Base Court opposite Sir Weatherby's apartment. As they examined the elegant rooms, the warder resumed his dialog.

"Cardinal Wolsey began his revolutionary expansion in the fall of 1514. You'll recall from the thumbnail history of his life that I gave you yesterday he was already Bishop of Lincoln and York and large sums of money given to the Church were diverted to him. His goal was to make Hampton Court Palace the largest and most elegant residence in England, and to do that he had to increase its size by ten times. But he couldn't just add rooms. He had to create an original, extensive and elegant plan. He hired John Lebons, a very talented designer and craftsman, and appointed him as Master Mason. The Cardinal and Lebons pored over the plans rearranging the parts for almost a year before a single brick was laid."

"The design has a wholeness that I haven't seen in any of Henry's other castles," Sir Weatherby replied.

"This elegant court, the Base Court, is one hundred and eighty feet on a side to give it a majestic scale. The rich red bricks were made here on the grounds. The architect found that the bricks closest to the fire turned a shiny black. He used those shiny black bricks to make a stylish diamond, or diaper pattern, in the red brick walls. After going through the tall Gatehouse, a visitor would be led next into this imposing court. Just beyond is the Clock Court named for the large clock high in one of the walls that could be seen from many parts of the Palace."

Warder Chertsey led Sir Weatherby across the Clock Court and into the Royal Chapel.

"This glorious Royal Chapel was completed in 1528 at a cost of twelve thousand angels or six thousand pounds. As you can see, it is over one hundred feet long and fifty feet high. It is a very impressive space for what began as a cardinal's residence."

"The rich blue ceiling with gold stars and ornamental decorations of wood projecting down from the ceiling is truly spectacular," Weatherby gasped. "It is the most beautiful ceiling I have ever seen!"

"The two stairways to the balcony suggest that Wolsey planned on having the King and Queen visit frequently. I stop by here every day to pray. I will show you some other parts of the Palace as time allows, but now you've seen the major elements."

Thank you for the tour, Warder," Sir Weatherby replied. "Now I need to get on with my work."

# CHAPTER 5

Sir Weatherby cut across the Clock Court to the servant quarters to check on his amanuensis. He found Dredge standing on a sturdy stool busily putting glassware on shelves.

"It looks as though you should be fully functional by tomorrow, Dredge," Sir Weatherby said.

"I'll have most of it done tonight, Sir. I'll need to pick up some additional chemicals from the apothecary in Hampton tomorrow, but by noon we should be fully operational."

"It's a nuisance to have to bring the whole laboratory here from London," Sir Weatherby replied.

"Yes, but taking samples to our quarters in London wouldn't be practical either."

"Particularly if the case takes several weeks to solve and given the paucity of clues and suspects that may well be the case. I'm going to interview several of William Suffolk's coworkers. Do you have a sharp pencil?"

Dredge handed Sir Weatherby a newly sharpened wood pencil as he walked out the door of the laboratory. A small office for Sir Weatherby was set up in Wolsey Apartment where he had a series of interviews scheduled. The first interview was with William Suffolk's assistant, Clyde Lawrence. Warder Chertsey showed Clyde Lawrence in and made the introductions.

"How long had you worked with the victim, Mr. Lawrence?" Sir Weatherby began.

"Why, ever since he came here, Sir."

"Did you get along well?"

"Yes, Sir. It was my job to."

"So he wasn't easy to work with?"

"I'd say he wasn't, Sir, but most of it wasn't his fault. He was aloof, overbearing and demanding, but I think most of that was because he was the son of the Duke of Suffolk. He was taught to think he was better than others, certainly me."

"Did you two ever clash?"

"No, Sir. I never allowed it. I knew my place."

"He must have made you angry at times."

"Not really, Sir. I didn't allow myself to feel angry."

"What did you think of his work?"

"It was exceptional. His arches were ornamented with just enough detail and his windows were inspired. His designs were used throughout the Palace, so we were both very busy."

"So, he was a good worker?"

"Yes and no. When he came to work he was very diligent and worked long hours, but then with no warning, he would disappear for several days. When he returned, he was always unkempt and distracted."

"Do you know where he went or what he did?"

"I have no idea, Sir. I know he had a small lodging in the town of Hampton, but I don't think he went there often. I always had the feeling he had traveled during his absences, perhaps a great distance."

"Did he have any unusual religious or political beliefs?"

"Not that I know of. He was a Catholic and attended church in the village irregularly. I never heard him espouse any political views."

"Who killed him?"

"I've puzzled over that, Sir, since I heard of his death. I can't honestly think who the killer was. Perhaps Lord Suffolk was simply in the wrong place at the wrong time and saw something he shouldn't have."

"Thank you for your time and your candor. Would you ask the next workman to come in?"

"Yes, Sir."

An uneasy man named Webb came in next. He had a burly build and wore rough leather pants and a loose jerkin. Sir Weatherby motioned him to a chair.

Once the man was seated, Sir Weatherby began questioning him, "Did you know the dead man, William Suffolk?"

"I did indeed. He was an arrogant aristocrat with no use for the likes of me."

"Do you know a reason why someone would want to kill him?"

"He treated commoners like dirt, but that's normal at Hampton Court Palace. It's no reason to kill a man."

Sir Weatherby felt his anger rising and in a sarcastic tone said, "Yet he is dead. You would agree?"

"I do indeed, Sir. Suffolk fought quite publicly with Humphrey Coke last summer. Perhaps he is the murderer."

"Be gone, you cannot help me. You have nothing new to tell me. Speaking with you is like visiting with a hedgehog. Get out of my sight."

The workman scrambled to his feet and left.

"Warder Chertsey come in here now," Sir Weatherby bellowed.

"Yes, Your Grace."

"These interviews are a damnable waste of valuable time. This isn't getting me any closer to the killer. Cancel the rest! I'll go to my laboratory to see if my assistant's analysis is of more use."

Sir Weatherby stormed out of the apartment, slamming the door behind him. He found Dredge hunched over a desk, with an eye shade on examining fibers with a magnifying glass. When Sir Weatherby entered, Dredge looked up.

"What have you found?" Sir Weatherby demanded.

"I'm examining some fibers I found on the body that don't belong to the victim's clothing. I need some more time to identify their origin."

"What else?"

"You gave me two fragments of a grey hard metal. The label on the parchment said that they came from the head wound. I analyzed one in a base solution and the other in an acid one. When I added chromate to the acid, the solution turned orange. This led me to conclude that the sample was unrefined iron that might be used in the head of a mallet or as the head of an adze."

"That could help in narrowing the search for the murder weapon. I will pass that on to Warder Chertsey."

"I haven't had a chance to work on the reconstruction of the skull."

"All in good time, Dredge. But, right now, let's go look at the crime scene again while the light is good."

Sir Weatherby led the way out of the servant's quarters and up a broad stairway to the Council Chamber. Dredge brought a small knapsack of tools and folded pieces of parchment. He got down on his hands and knees and brushed small amounts of material from the floor onto pieces of parchment. Bits of wood, mud and scrapings of blood were collected. Sir Weatherby examined the walls and window sills of the room which had recently been painted a dark brown. After carefully inspecting the walls for thirty minutes, Sir Weatherby noted blood spatter near where the body was found. He hadn't seen the small pattern of spots at first because the color of the dried blood was very similar to the dark brown color of the wall.

"Dredge, come here. There are drops of blood here that came from the blow which killed our victim. We talked last week about how we might use such evidence to determine the direction of the blow and even the height of the killer. I will need a detailed drawing of whole field of drops. Then we can do a reconstruction."

"I will need a larger piece of parchment, Sir. I'll return to lab and get it."

"While you are doing that I'll check the three ways of getting in and out of the Council Chamber and draw a diagram. I assumed how the killer left because of the bloody boot print I found, but perhaps there is other evidence on the stairways."

Sir Weatherby had several candelabras brought to the area and they both worked until midnight. After they had packed up their drawings and specimens and extinguished most of the candles, Sir Weatherby turned to Dredge.

"I find Warder Chertsey a little smug in his position here at the Palace. He's held the same job for almost thirty years. He sees the murder and the murderer as having very little to do with him. I'd like to shake him out of his complacency. Let's pay him an unannounced visit."

Dredge nodded his assent and Sir Weatherby led the way to the Warder's quarters. Sir Weatherby burst into the dark, quiet room without knocking, approached the sleeping man's bed and started yelling imprecations.

"The devil, Sir," Sir Weatherby roared. "You know more about this murder than you are letting on. I want some answers and I want them right now."

Warder Chertsey started from a deep sleep and sat up in bed while rubbing his eyes. Dredge could see in the dim light that the Warder had a look of astonishment and dread on his face.

"What? Who is it and what do you want?" Warder Chertsey said in a tremulous voice.

"It's Weatherby and I want the whole truth about the murder, now."

"I've told you everything I know, Sir," Chertsey said his voice steadying.

"That's not true. I can sense that there is something going on here at the Palace that you aren't telling me about."

"I swear by all that is holy, that there isn't."

Sir Weatherby grabbed the Warder by his night shirt with both of his long-fingered hands and dragged him up out of bed.

"Yes, there is! Now start talking."

"All right, all right. We had an amicable community amongst the three hundred servants and construction workers that lived and labored in the Palace until a year ago. Now the community is riven in two by acrimony and hate."

"What precipitated this sudden change?"

"Hampton Court Palace is the property of Henry the VIII and his wife the very Catholic and very Spanish Catherine of Aragon. The King cares about the Catholic religion. However, now the King is in a fever of desire for Anne Boleyn, the Queen's raven-haired lady-in-waiting. He has had many liaisons, but after bedding the woman he desires he soon tires of her. It happened to Mary Boleyn, Anne's older sister. The servants at Whitehall Castle report that Anne Boleyn flaunts her body in expensive gowns, bats her eyes and wets her lips in front of the King. He is mad with wanting her. However, the courtiers say she will not satisfy his desire unless and until he marries her."

"Do you take me for a bloody fool? I am aware of all of that. Whatever does this have to do with the problems at Hampton Court Palace, pray tell?" Sir Weatherby asked.

"Then you know that Anne Boleyn is a Protestant and has a deep hatred of priests and all things Catholic. She wants all Catholic monasteries, cathedrals and schools confiscated and destroyed. The religious hatred and fear came to Hampton Court with the influx of workers a year and a half ago. Now we have deep revulsion and animosity between persons who were previously friends."

"And you think the murder is related to this spiritual enmity?"

"Yes, but I don't know precisely how."

Sir Weatherby turned on his heels and strode out of the dark Warder's room with Dredge just behind him.

# CHAPTER 6

Sir Weatherby and his disabled assistant fell into bed at one a.m., but both awoke at first light the next morning. Sir Weatherby had awoken in the middle of the night in a cold sweat after having his recurring nightmare of the three galloping horsemen. For some inexplicable reason he had been able to return to sleep after changing his sodden nightshirt.

After breakfast Dredge had the body of William Suffolk brought to the laboratory from the coldest cellar of the Palace. The body was laid out naked on a long wooden table that was covered with a thin layer of zinc. Dredge had already sharpened the scalpels and saws and laid them out in an evenly spaced row. He would assist Sir Weatherby in the performance of the autopsy. Weatherby made his incisions quickly and precisely as he had learned in medical school. The internal organs appeared to be in good shape: a maroon colored heart, grey-blue lungs and orange-red liver. Dredge adjusted the light from the windows to increase the illumination. As each organ was removed, Sir Weatherby examined it and handed it to Dredge to be weighed.

Sir Weatherby sliced open the stomach along its greater curvature and picked through the contents with a long-handled forceps. He picked up several samples and placed them on a porcelain rectangle for further analysis.

"I believe it's just undigested food," Sir Weatherby said. "But please analyze it for tinctures of plants and other possible sedatives or poisons."

"Yes, Sir."

"For many years I had to perform these useful examinations hurriedly and in secret because of the Catholic Church," Sir Weatherby mused. "Even though their value to medicine and forensics is incalculable. Then Pope Sixtus the Fourth issued an edict permitting dissection of the human body. It took Cardinal Wolsey twelve years to issue such a decree for our islands."

Sir Weatherby turned his attention to the decedent's skull. As already knew the occipital lobe and temporal lobe of the brain had been crushed and mixed with fragments of bone. After collecting some samples, Sir Weatherby washed his hands while Dredge sewed the body closed with a long sinew.

While Sir Weatherby wrote his findings in a note book, Dredge set up an exhibit based on the blood-spatter pattern he had obtained the night before. He used the victim's height of five feet, nine inches as a vital measurement in his calculation. Once everything was in place, Dredge sought out Sir Weatherby and brought him to their workroom. Dredge had erected a straw dummy of William Suffolk's size with a cloth-wrapped head. He assumed the victim fell straight down from such an overwhelming blow. He then measured the distance from the pool of blood in the Council Chambers to the blood spatter on the wall and placed his dummy at the appropriate spot. He affixed a thin, long strip of wood to blood spatter and then to the dummy's head.

Following the strip of wood backward Sir Weatherby could deduce the location of the metal object just before it began its fatal descent. Both investigators assumed that only a blow from a fully raised arm could cause such severe damage to the victim's skull. A simple calculation revealed the height of the murderer from the length of an average arm. Sir Weatherby's measurements suggested that the killer was five feet, eleven inches tall. His employer Henry VIII was six feet, six inches tall, a veritable giant. The average man in the British Isles was only five-three and the average woman only four-eleven. Both Sir Weatherby and Dredge assumed the killer was a man. Sir Weatherby turned to his assistant.

"Find Warder Chertsey and get a list of all the tall people living and working in the Palace," Sir Weatherby ordered. "I also need the religious affiliation of every member of the staff and of the construction crew."

"Very good, Sir." Dredge replied.

Sir Weatherby walked across the Base Court and out into the gardens on the south side of the Palace to think about his case. The minute he stepped outside, he realized that Cardinal Wolsey had broken with the traditional medieval plan of having a gatehouse and great hall across from each other on opposite sides of an entrance court. The new Base Court changed the entrance of the Palace from the south to the west. Sir Weatherby thought that the Cardinal's architect had done this to create a large south garden. As he walked into the gardens, he saw drifts of golden daffodils in full bloom, gently swaying in the breeze. The tulips were a little behind them and had already swollen to red globules with prominent green veins. Beyond the bulbs were beds of elegant primroses with ripply green leaves and flat low growing flowers in intense yellows and purples. Next to the flower beds a large walled orchard was just beginning to bloom. The white flowered apple trees were ahead of the pink flowering cherry trees. When the breeze blew, white petals like large cupped snowflakes drifted lazily to the ground.

As Sir Weatherby walked further from the Palace, lost in thought about who might have murdered Suffolk, he came across a very formal garden in a square shape. The plants were herbs and other aromatics woven into a complex interlacing design. It was a knot garden, he realized, the new fashion among the royalty. The edge was a low box hedge with paths throughout of fine raked gravel. The center of the garden consisted of slender low rows of lemon balm, marjoram, hyssop, chamomile and mallow.

A servant rushed up to Sir Weatherby in the knot garden and said while panting hands on knees, "At last I've found you."

"What is it, man? Spit it out."

"There has been another murder, sir and Warder Chertsey sent me to find you. I've been looking for you for over thirty minutes."

"Take me to the body immediately," Sir Weatherby said, as he worried that the crime scene had been disturbed again.

The porter led the way from the knot garden to the west toward a nearby area of new construction called the Bayne Tower. It was meant as new quarters for the King and named for the bath contained in it. The three story tower was almost three-quarters completed. The timber frame work was finished and the brick walls were recently finished to the third floor. The porter entered the ground floor where Sir Weatherby knew the Office of the Privy Chamber was located. Next door was the Wardrobe of the Robes where the King's clothes were stored, repaired and cleaned.

The porter ascended the stairs to the first floor where the King's new bedchamber was located. A complete bathroom was also located on this floor. It featured hot running water supplied by a small boiler behind the bathroom that Sir Weatherby had seen. The bathtub itself was circular and made of wood like the bottom half of a very large wine barrel.

Next to the bathtub lay the body of a young woman with raven black hair and pure white skin. She was dressed in a long blue velvet gown and looked deeply asleep except for her wide open sapphire blue eyes. Sir Weatherby glanced around the room. He noted the frescos by the Italian painter Toto del Nunziata, a few pieces of wood and scattered tools. The ceiling was of elegant gilded battens with a white ground. Nothing seemed disturbed, Sir Weatherby noted with satisfaction.

"Fetch my assistant Bradford Dredge from his work room, immediately!"

Sir Weatherby roared. "Tell him what has been found so he knows what equipment to bring. Hurry, man."

Sir Weatherby knelt by the body and gently checked it for a pulse and for *rigor mortis*. He noticed an unusual odor that he had never smelled before, like bitter roses. Dredge arrived quickly. The porter carried two large canvas bags filled with investigating tools.

"Measure the body, Dredge," Sir Weatherby ordered and then turning to the porter said, "Fetch Warder Chertsey, now."

After his recent tongue-lashing by Sir Weatherby, Warder Chertsey was lurking nearby. When he was summoned he ascended the broad stairs to the first floor two at a time and burst into the King's bathroom.

"Thank you for not disturbing the body," Sir Weatherby began. "Who found this unfortunate young woman?"

"A workman came to Bayne Tower to install a molding one hours ago and he discovered the remains."

"Who is it?"

"Her name is Anna Maria Wimbledon and she was employed at Hampton Court as a librarian."

"Has she resided here for long?"

"Oh, yes, Your Grace. She came here as a girl. She was an orphan from the West Country and Cardinal Wolsey took pity on her."

"Who would want to kill her?"

"No one would. She was beautiful, kind and gentle and every member of the staff adored her," Chertsey replied. "She looks so peaceful perhaps she died of natural causes. Maybe her heart simply stopped and God took her to heaven to be an angel. After William Suffolk was killed, I told you I had never heard of murder at Hampton Court Palace. I looked in all our dusty old history books last night and there was a murder. A Hospitaller was killed in a knife fight over money in 1338. The murder took place in the undercroft, the vaulted stone compartment, under their chamber block, the first large series of rooms built on the property. That structure is part of the foundation of the east wall of the Clock Tower now."

"Perhaps you are right and this was a natural death, Warder," Sir Weatherby replied thoughtfully. "Our analysis will give us the answer."

# CHAPTER 7

Dredge had completed the measurements of the body and had set up an easel five feet from the body so that Sir Weatherby could sketch the body before it was moved. Dredge collected small bits of fiber and wood from the King's bathroom and noted that two inches of warm water remained in the large wooden tub. When Sir Weatherby was done drawing the corpse he turned to Warder Chertsey.

"I want you to seal the door," Sir Weatherby instructed. "And return in one hour with two men to transport the body to our laboratory."

"Yes, Sir." The Warder backed out the door.

Dredge and Sir Weatherby removed the victim's clothing slowly, looking for stains and marks. The blue velvet dress seemed in good condition. Dredge carefully folded the garment and set it aside. The victim wore a long muslin slip with buttons in the back and a pink chemise. The two men removed both garments, clumsily fumbling with the buttons.

"Where is Amarantha when we need her?" Sir Weatherby said in an exasperated voice.

"You sent her to visit her family in Wales, sir," Dredge replied. "And I have sent a messenger on horseback with a note asking her to come to Hampton Court with all possible speed."

Anna Maria's neck was free of bruises. As they rolled her gently on her side they found no muscle rigidity, but her back showed long fine linear cuts that were scabbed over.

"Perhaps those cuts are a sign of abuse," Sir Weatherby observed. "But more likely they are signs of self-flagellation if she was Catholic."

Dredge spoke suddenly in an excited tone, "There is fluid on the inside of her right thigh."

40

"It could be very important," Sir Weatherby replied. "Collect it in a glass vial and rush it to the lab. Perchance she was assaulted. As you know, van Leeuwenhoek reported being able to see spermatozoa with his new more powerful microscopes, but the sample will spoil quickly."

After Dredge left, Sir Weatherby wrapped the victim's body in a clean white sheet. He motioned for the two men at the door to come and carry the body down the stairs.

Sir Weatherby hurried ahead of the two men to his laboratory on the ground floor. Dredge had already prepared a sample of the fluid and placed it under the microscope. Sir Weatherby applied his eye to the compound lens and saw many black-headed sperm with their motile tails propelling them forward.

"This poor woman was raped before she was murdered or alternately had consensual intercourse shortly before her demise," Sir Weatherby said. "We must prove which is true, Dredge."

Dredge took some time to organize and catalogue all the material he had collected from the two bodies.

"I must speak with the man that found the body." Sir Weatherby said as he walked out of the lab.

Weatherby sent a servant to bring the workman and Anna Maria's closest friend to his office. While he waited he unpacked the satchel of books he had brought with him. He placed Chaucer's *A Canterbury Tale, A Book of Common Praier,* Dante Alighieri's *Divine Comedy,* and *Utopia* by Sir Thomas More on a shelf. Sir Weatherby had paid a large sum for each volume, but he truly enjoyed owning them. The workman who discovered the body knocked at the door. Sir Weatherby wasn't hopeful about the upcoming interview. So far his interrogations with the guard, the warder and workmen had been a complete waste of time.

"Come in."

"I'm Leonard, the workman that found the unfortunate young woman today."

"Sit down and tell me everything you heard and saw."

"I went to the Bayne Tower to install a molding on the south wall. When I entered I saw Anna Marie lying on the floor and I thought she was dead. I heard the fire crackling in the other room where the boiler for the bath was located. I left immediately. I saw no one."

"Do you have any idea how long the body was there before you discovered it?"

"Yes. I was in the room first thing this morning to measure the space where the molding was to go. The murder had to have occurred within two hours of the discovery of the body."

"Who else had access to the Bayne Tower?"

"Every workman at the Palace. We have a deadline for completion that is only six weeks away. Carpenters, glaziers, painters, and plumbers are all racing to complete their work, particularly on the first and second floor."

"Did you know this spotless maiden?"

"Yes. She was the Palace librarian. Anna Maria was always friendly, polite, and carefully dressed."

"I don't care about those things. Did you ever see her out late, in the shadows of Hampton Court, or with an unsavory person?"

"No, exceptin' for one rainy, windy night three weeks ago when I saw her slipping out through the Great Gatehouse. She had a long dark cloak pulled over her head, but I could tell it was her by her walk."

"Where was she going?"

"Don' know."

"Who was she going to meet?"

"No idea, sir."

"Did you every see William Suffolk and Anna Maria Wimbledon together?"

"Sir Moulton's staff ate dinner with the Palace staff each evening. Even though I wasn't invited I would guess that it was a group of twelve or thirteen. So I'm sure they talked at least casually."

"You have been most helpful. Do you know who murdered this young woman?"

"No I don't, Sir."

"Thank you for your time. You're thoughtful and observant and I may call you back to answer more questions."

Leonard left the apartment. Sir Weatherby finished arranging his invaluable books and then walked down to the laboratory.

Dredge had a series of beakers and retorts connected by long glass tubes and sealed with black rubber stoppers. Heat was provided by a small charcoal brazier. Clear, blue and gold colored liquids bubbled slowly and were transferred themselves in slender rivulets from beaker to beaker.

"I was just coming to get you, Sir," Dredge said excitedly. "The pieces of the various organs we collected during the William Suffolk autopsy look normal under the microscope. I also finished my analysis of his stomach contents. Most of the contents were food from the fare served at the Palace that night—mutton, carrots and turnips. However, I also found a large quantity of alcohol and laudanum present in the fluid."

"Laudanum, a tincture of opium, is a powerful sedative, as you know," Weatherby observed. "It may be the best agent for dulling the sensorium, making a recipient more acquiescent. So our victim was sedated and then bludgeoned to death. It suggests that the murder was premeditated."

"I will try to find the source of the laudanum either in the Palace or the town." "I think that might advance our case. I fail to see any connection between our two murder victims. They were from different social circles; had no common interests that I have found, and I don't find a common motive or really any motive for their tragic deaths. Even the methods of their demise were totally dissimilar as far as I know."

"Perhaps their deaths were simply a tragic coincidence."

"You could be correct; however Chertsey says unequivocally that the last murder at Hampton Court Palace was in 1338. Now we have two deaths on two consecutive days after nearly 70,000 days, by my calculation, without such an event. That strains one's credulity. I wish Amarantha were here. I could use her advice."

"It's 130 miles from her home in Betws-y-Coed to Hampton Court, Sir," Dredge remarked. "She couldn't possibly be here for another day."

"We need to organize a search of the Palace and grounds for the iron adze or mallet that was used to dispatch William Suffolk."

"I will have Warder Chertsey start the search this afternoon."

Sir Weatherby rose and said, "I will interview Anna Marie Wimbledon's roommate."

Sir Weatherby walked to Wolsey's apartments for the meeting. Anna Maria's roommate was responsible for purchasing and ordering furniture for the Palace. On entering the apartments he found Peggy Ealing sitting on settee, crying loudly.

"Mademoiselle. I am Sir Seamus Weatherby and I am investigating the untimely death of your roommate," Sir Weatherby began, bowing slightly. "How long have you been Anna Maria's roommate?"

"We have lived together on the second floor of the east wing for eight years."

"How did you find her as a chamber mate?"

"She was polite, quiet, considerate, neat and thoughtful."

"Then you mean it was quite impossible that anyone would have a reason to murder such a lovely creature."

"Actually I said she *was* all those things, but in the last six months she changed."

"In what way, pray tell?"

"She was often absent until late in the evening, and then for the past three months sometimes gone all night only to come in disheveled and fatigued shortly after dawn."

"What was she doing?"

"I have no idea. We had always shared every confidence but she spoke not a word about her recent comings and goings."

"Where should I look for the answers?"

"I believe in the town of Hampton."

Sir Weatherby backed toward the door while looking earnestly at Miss Ealing and said, "You have my condolences. Thank you for your time."

Sir Weatherby walked down the stairs to the Base Court where he sat on a bench in the sun. He thought about his work as an investigator. He had solved over fifty murders while in the employ of Henry VIII and usually identified the miscreant in a day or two. First he discovered the motive for the crime, which was almost always greed, jealousy or revenge. The slayer was almost always a family member or friend. He had received praise and gifts of land for his work from the Lord Chancellor and the King. Now Sir Weatherby had two murders, with no known motive or suspects.

# CHAPTER 8

As the sun sank lower behind the walls of the Palace and it quickly lost its already faint spring warmth, Sir Weatherby rose from his bench as the cold descended, and walked out through the Great Gatehouse. He was bored with the Palace food, but even more bored with the company. He was undecided about how he wanted to spend the evening. Almost involuntarily, Sir Weatherby walked toward the Thames, across the worn wooden bridge, and then into the town of Hampton. The main cobblestone street was lined with quaint furnishing stores, haberdashers and grocer's shops, many of which were still open. On one still sunlit corner stood a public house called the Lamb and Flag. It was situated in a two-story, half-timbered building with a thatched roof. The second story of the ancient building leaned two feet out into the street.

Sir Weatherby opened the wooden door that led into the warm noisy interior. He glanced around the room lit by a pleasant golden light, and noticed it was full of working men and gentlemen. He took an empty seat at a table by a large brick fireplace with a roaring fire within. He ordered a tankard of ale from the barmaid and took a small notebook out of his pocket to review notes he had made earlier in the day. When he looked up he saw the social interplay and camaraderie of the local inhabitants. After he finished a second tankard, he noticed his emotions were gentled, his imagination enlivened, and he was feeling more social. He walked into the dining room where he observed most of the cloth-covered tables were occupied. Then he noticed Sir John Moulton sitting alone at a corner table. The plate and several glasses in front of Moulton were untouched, indicating that the Surveyor of the King's Works hadn't eaten yet. Sir Weatherby decided to take a chance and walked over to the table.

"May I join you for dinner, Your Grace?" Sir Weatherby asked.

Sir Moulton gazed at him with a look of consternation that gradually became bland and said, "Please. I meant to look you up, Sir Weatherby and apologize for my abominable behavior yesterday."

Both men ordered from the list of food the waiter recited for them and then sat back to enjoy a bottle of French Bordeaux.

"How long have you worked for the King?" Sir Weatherby asked.

"I studied architecture at Cambridge and then apprenticed myself to John Redman, an extremely talented designer. Sir Redman was mason and architect to the King. I worked with him on Westminster Abbey, York Palace and Cardinal College at Oxford. Then I was given more responsibility for the work he did at Greenwich. When Sir John died in 1528, I was appointed Surveyor of the King's Works. What about you, Your Grace? How did you come to work for the King?"

Before Sir Weatherby could answer, large bowls of steaming vegetable dumpling soup arrived.

"My path was considerably more tortuous than yours," Sir Weatherby began. "I was born in 1490 in Dumphries, Scotland, a small town near the Solway Firth. My father was a greengrocer. I had a normal childhood until one of my teachers, Father John, decided I was very smart. He pushed me to attend better schools until I went to Edinburgh University on a scholarship. I studied philosophy and religion first, but it was too ethereal for me, so I changed to the practical study of medicine."

"That's a long way from your current position, Sir." Sir Moulton replied.

"I would say so," Weatherby replied pensively. "I tried practicing surgery after I received my Bachelor of Medicine but I found it too repetitive. I went back to the University where I studied pathology. Eventually I began illicitly performing all the autopsies on victims of crimes at the university hospital."

"Why illicitly?"

"In those days, the Catholic church felt that the opening of bodies condemned their souls to purgatory forever. In a big city like Edinburgh there were many murders, and therefore a lot of bodies to autopsy. I learned a great deal."

Plates of turnips, beef and squash were brought to the table, and there was no talking for several minutes.

In time, Sir Weatherby continued his tale, "I wanted to apply what I had learned to solve actual cases, so I went to London and was employed by the constables. Eventually Henry VIII heard of my work, and one of his minions offered me a job. I've been in his employ for five years."

"I'm surprised we haven't run into each other before this."

"I'm usually in the provinces investigating a crime, and it doesn't sound like you're usually at Whitehall either."

"True."

When dinner was concluded, the venerable retainers of the King walked leisurely through the town and back over the bridge across the Thames. They bade each other goodnight in the Base Court. Sir Weatherby checked on Dredge and then went to bed.

Early the next morning, Warder Chertsey reported to Sir Weatherby in the latter's office in the Wolsey Apartments.

"I have some preliminary results from the searches you requested," Chertsey began. "We found laudanum in eleven rooms. It seems that many females living here in the Palace have trouble sleeping. However, the bottles of tincture are small, usually only three ounces. Two large bottles were found one in Jason Mitchell's room and one in Humphrey Coke's trunk."

"I know about Coke, but what can you tell me about Jason?"

"He serves as a part-time apothecary so I would expect him to have larger quantities of a variety of drugs. I can think of no good reason for Humphrey to have such a large amount."

"I agree. It looks bad for him," Sir Weatherby replied.

"The search for mallets and adzes with iron heads turned up thirty-five such implements in the Palace. They are all assembled on a table next to Sir John Moulton's construction office."

"Very good. I will have Dredge inspect and test them all."

"Also here a list of the five men at Hampton Court that are five feet eleven inches or taller."

"Thank you, very much. Did any of these men have a reason to kill William Suffolk?"

"I doubt it, sir."

"I will have someone interview them."

Warder Chertsey noted that Sir Weatherby was still disinclined to do any interviews himself. Sir Weatherby walked to his laboratory. Dredge was completing a chemical analysis.

"Tell me about that fiber you found on the first victim," Sir Weatherby said without preamble.

"The victim was wearing a wool, fur-lined, front-opening coat. The fiber I found was linen and Suffolk was wearing nothing made of linen."

"Linen is only a moderately common fabric, so that may help us. Here is a list of five possible suspects who work at the Palace. Please have her interview them when she arrives. Also, there is a pile of mallets and adzes in the Base Court. Please check all of them for blood, hair and tissue."

"Yes, Sir," Dredge said as he got down from his stool and began to collect equipment in a canvas bag.

Sir Weatherby sat down in the laboratory to review the information they had collected on the William Suffolk murder. He had no reason to look outside the Palace for the murderer, thus far. The killer was probably a man almost six feet tall. The type of murder weapon used was known, although the particular iron implement hadn't been found. The real impediment to the progress of the investigation was motive. It could be one of the seven capital vices made popular in the fourteenth century by Dante. Sir Weatherby knew them best by their Latin names: *luxuria, gula, avaritia, acedia, ira, invidia and superbia.* He translated them as lust, gluttony, greed, sloth, wrath, envy and pride. He had already solved murders where all but gluttony were the motives. Most were due to greed. But how could greed have been the motive for this crime?

So far, Sir Weatherby had seen a polite, superficial society at Hampton Court Palace, a façade that was presented to unsuspecting outsiders. What he needed to know about was the unsavory underbelly of the Palace, where thievery, drunkenness, carnality and gambling ruled. He went to his apartment and clothed himself in shabby indistinct clothing and then set out on a new tour of the Palace focusing on the back stairs, hidden corners and out-of-the-way-places.

He worked under the older east side of the Palace first. He found some stairways that ended in blank walls. He discovered old storage rooms and stone foundations, but no workers were seen in any of these areas. When he transferred to the north side, he found older foundations and more warrens. Several unshaven men with dirty clothing lived in this area. Some seemed mentally defective to Sir Weatherby and others appeared just to be poor. He asked each one about William Suffolk, but most didn't know who he was talking about. Them he ran across a younger man who wasn't quite as dirty as the rest.

"Do you know William Suffolk, fifth son of the Duke of Suffolk?"

"Yes, Your Grace."

"Did you have any dealings with him?"

"Yes. He brought me pieces of colored glass which I took to a buyer in Weybridge for him."

"Do you know the name of the person who received the glass?"

"I only know him as Thomas. I always met him near the road to an estate called Oatlands. It was always dark."

"How many times did you make the trip?"

"Fifteen or twenty."

"Did you run any other errands for him?"

"No, Your Grace."

# CHAPTER 9

Sir Weatherby walked up out of the undercroft and into the Base Court. It had grown dusky. As he walked across the middle of the square a small dark horse and rider came through the Great Gatehouse at a full gallop. The rider was low over the neck of the horse, but appeared to be a young man. The horse set his hooves in front of Sir Weatherby, spraying clumps of dirt on his greatcoat. The rider leapt from the saddle and ran to Weatherby engulfing him in a firm, ardent hug, and nuzzled his neck with a cold nose and mouth.

"Thank God, you're here and safe," Sir Weatherby said. "I missed you."

"I missed you, too," Amarantha Thompson said softly while trying to catch her breath.

After she relaxed her hug, Sir Weatherby led Amarantha to his apartment. He sent a manservant to tend to the horse and to bring some food from the kitchen. When they arrived at his apartment he removed her greatcoat and then his. They sat together by the fire.

"I'm sorry to call you back early from your family visit," Sir Weatherby said.

"It's quite fine. I was bored, and Mum and I were beginning to fight."

Amarantha Thompson was a barrister who had joined Seamus Weatherby's investigative enterprise three years ago. Any discipline Seamus was weak in, Amarantha Thompson was strong in, and vice versa. They were both diligent, compulsive and intelligent. They had only one problem: a forceful, knowledgeable, aggressive, young female was not acceptable in any part of society in 1530. To allow freedom of action Amarantha devised a ruse, when working on a case in a public area like a village, she either dressed and acted like Sir Weatherby's older aunt, or as a young man. She hadn't settled on a disguise for her work at Hampton Court Palace and was undecided as to whether she needed one. A knock on the door of Sir Weatherby's apartment stopped her ruminations. A serving girl entered with a tray of warm bread, squash and chunks of roast chicken. Amarantha hadn't eaten since starting her ride fourteen hours earlier in northern Middlesex County, and she was ravenous. Both ate quietly for several minutes. With their plates clean, Amarantha sat back and relaxed.

"I need to go to bed soon," she said in a weary voice.

"Yes, my dear," Sir Weatherby replied. "But let me bring you up to date on our investigation. We think that the killer of William Suffolk must have been five eleven or taller. I will show you how we arrive at that conclusion on the basis of blood splatter tomorrow. Here is the list of tall workers here in the Palace I want you to interview. I also want you to attend the autopsy on Anna Maria Wimbledon early in the morning. She may be our second murder victim."

"My training is as a barrister, Seamus, not a doctor or pathologist as you know."

"Yes. I should have done the autopsy today, but something about it is restraining me. I know it's not rational. It may have to do with her young age or comely visage, but I feel somehow almost embarrassed even though I am a pathologist who has done six or seven hundred necropsies during his career. In any case, I was hoping against hope you would arrive today, and I'm very glad you are here."

Amarantha rose from her seat and gave Sir Weatherby a hug before saying, "Good night."

Sir Weatherby walked her to his door and then down the gallery to her identical two-room apartment where a fire was roaring in the fireplace. Both investigators slept soundly even though a thunderstorm beat on the Palace from two hours and streaks of lightning lit their rooms with eerie silver-white light. While dressing Amarantha found a peculiarly large spider sitting placidly on her bed cover. She captured it.

All three investigators appeared in the Great Kitchen at six a.m. Each had eggs and ham with thick pieces of warm bread covered with fresh butter and strawberry jam. Each had a tankard of ale, the traditional breakfast beverage at Hampton Court. Amarantha disliked alcohol before noon, which sometimes gave her a headache. However, Sir Weatherby had finally convinced her that drinking beer for breakfast was much safer than water or the fresh milk that she preferred. He had shown her drops of water squirming with spiral, round and bean-shaped animalcules which he suspected were the culprits in cholera, typhoid and dysentery. Sir Weatherby had shown her similar creatures in milk. At times very stubborn and strong-willed, Amarantha had not been convinced until Sir Weatherby added drops of beer to the liquids and the animalcules became motionless when viewed through the microscope. He explained that it was the alcohol in the ale that disinfected the beverage.

Amarantha showed the spider to Dredge.

"Ah! The Wolsey spider," Dredge began. "It's half as long as a bodkin, named for the Cardinal and only found at the Palace. He was deathly afraid of them, you know."

Amarantha released it onto the floor at the edge of the room.

After breakfast, all three went to the Laboratory where Dredge had already placed Anna Maria covered by a thin white sheet on the long zinc-covered table. The tools were clean, sharp and laid out in a long precise row. Sir Weatherby flicked the sheet off of the body, revealing none of the nervousness he had expressed to Amarantha the night before. The pale white body of a young, shapely woman lay before them.

External examination showed no bruises or cuts on the front of her body. On her back, multiple small healing cuts ran in a diagonal pattern from her shoulders to her mid spine. Closer examination showed old scars in the same pattern.

"I'm sure these marks are from self-flagellation encouraged by her bizarre religion," Sir Weatherby opined. He and Dredge carefully placed the body supine and Sir Weatherby made a small incision in the neck. He quickly dissected the hyoid bone. When he removed it, he showed it to Amarantha.

"This delicate bone, found in the neck, almost always breaks if the victim has been strangled. You can see that this bone is intact."

With Dredge's help Sir Weatherby examined the victim's perineum. He found multiple severe vaginal lacerations.

"This poor woman was sexually assaulted, perhaps by multiple assailants before her death," Sir Weatherby said sadly.

Dredge set up a small easel so Sir Weatherby could draw what he had found.

Next, Sir Weatherby made his traditional Y-shaped autopsy incision, beginning at the shoulders, meeting in the midline, and then extending down to the pubic bone. Once the skin was retracted, Dredge cut each rib anteriorly with a short saw. He lifted the sternum and attached ribs away, revealing the heart and lungs. Even Amarantha knew something was amiss. The lungs were purple rather than blue, but also exhibited large nodules and sacks throughout. Sir Weatherby cut the bronchi detaching them from the body quickly and submerged them in a pan of water provided by Dredge.

"I suspect contagion," Sir Weatherby said. "We are less likely to contract it if the lungs are under water."

Sir Weatherby used long forceps and sharp, curved scissors to take multiple samples from the lungs. Then turning back to the body, he checked the heart for size and lesions and opened the chambers to look at the valves. Nothing appeared untoward. Sir Weatherby turned his attention to the abdomen and noticed normal pink appearing intestines with fat on the connecting membranes, suggesting good nutrition. The liver was red-orange and smooth and the stomach normal sized. Sir Weatherby cut along the greater curvature as was his custom. He found no food in the stomach—only a large quantity of yellow fluid. Again he noted a bitter rose smell that he had first noticed in the Bayne Tower where the body was found.

"I want you to collect all of this fluid," Sir Weatherby said to Dredge. "I have never smelled this aroma before. It may be a new poison."

"Yes, Sir."

Amarantha detested the sight of blood, disliked dead bodies, even though they were critical to her occupation, and reviled bad smells.

"May I be excused, please?" Amarantha said.

Sir Weatherby felt compassion for her and was just about to excuse her when he reached into the lower abdomen and felt a melon-sized mass.

As Sir Weatherby dissected the mass free, Sir Weatherby said gently, "I think you had better stay."

Once he freed the ligaments and supports, he placed the swollen uterus on the zinc table. He delicately cut through the strong muscular wall revealing a small perfectly formed fetus. As Sir Weatherby gently straightened the flexible spine, Dredge measured the length of the male embryo from head to toe at seven inches. Despite her aversion to things medical, Amarantha felt drawn to this perfectly formed miniature human. She walked toward the autopsy table and then leaned closer.

"How miraculous and very, very sad," Amarantha said softly.

"How old is this fetus, Dredge?" Sir Weatherby asked.

"According to my table of length versus age, it is four months old."

"So something happened last December that may have led to this young woman's demise."

Sir Weatherby handed the tiny fetus to Dredge who quickly wrapped it in a sheet. All three hoped that once the tiny human was out of sight, their somber moods would lift.

Turning to Amarantha, Sir Weatherby said, "Thank you for staying."

"I'll begin conducting my interviews," Amarantha said as she left quickly.

While Dredge finished sewing the body closed, Sir Weatherby assembled all the evidence he had on Anna Maria's murder. He knew that this unfortunate young woman's death had something to do with her pregnancy and rape. Had the same man been responsible for both of these events? It seemed unlikely. How had a beautiful woman, with a circumscribed life as a librarian, been dragged into something so ominous that it took her life? Had she gone in a new more dangerous direction of her own volition or had this change been forced upon her? Finally, what relationship existed between William Suffolk and Anna Maria Wimbledon? As he amassed more evidence, the cases became cloudier not clearer and he didn't like it.

# CHAPTER 10

To clear his head, Weatherby went for a long walk along the south bank of the Thames. First, he cut a stout stick to aid him in his ramble along the bank of the river, which was clogged with vines and bushes. Most plants were just beginning to leaf out, although the violets and marsh marigolds were already in bloom. Chiffchaffs, evening grosbeaks and woodcocks scrambled around in the underbrush. The croaking of leopard frogs and bullfrogs filled the air. Stately pairs of large white mute swans swam placidly on the river. Every swan in the realm belonged to the King, so they could afford to swim calmly.

He needed time to think about his complex cases and a strategy for solving them. He decided to focus on two things. First, as a source of information, he needed someone intelligent who had been at Hampton Court Palace for a considerable time. Such a person would understand the strengths, weaknesses, and vices of the many workers and construction people at the Palace. Secondly, he needed someone with a superb understanding of personalities and societies. A person who had both of these qualities would be rare.

His intelligence connection could be one of the master carpenters or master masons or one of the architects that worked with William Suffolk. It might also be the Privy Councilor of the Palace or the Quartermaster. Warder Chertsey, master of the guards, had vast knowledge of the Palace and decades of experience, but only average intelligence. Sir John Moulton was probably the smartest man in the county. Sir Weatherby decided to curry a relationship with him.

His relationship connection would be harder to come by. His prejudice was that a woman would better understand and explain interaction at Hampton Court Palace. But where was he to find such a person? The librarian would have been a logical choice but she had been raped and murdered. He would interview her two assistants. The Office of the Greencloth was located above the Kitchen Gatehouse. Several young women worked there doing calculations. They were charged with keeping the Palace solvent and ordering supplies. He would enquire about their personalities from Warder Chertsey. A woman was also in charge of the Officers of the Spicery, he knew. She was responsible for all herbs and spices as well as for fruits consumed in the Palace. Certainly one of these women would have the qualities Sir Weatherby sought.

He stopped thinking about his cases and enjoyed the rest of his walk. Swallows dipped and turned over the river catching insects in acrobatic display. A group of goldeneyes swam slowly up river, their glossy black heads and round white spot below their bills readily visible. A pair of great spotted woodpeckers had nested in a tree. He sat on a fallen tree and observed their frantic flights to bring straw and twigs to line their nest.

When Sir Weatherby got back to Hampton Court, he felt refreshed. After a tankard of ale, he sought out his minions. Dredge had spent the morning examining and cataloguing the mallets and adzes that Warder Chertsey accumulated.

"I have examined every implement, and there appear to be two problems," Dredge reported.

"And they are?"

"First Warder Chertsey failed to identify where the tools were recovered and whom they belonged to."

"I'm sure you've discovered a way to overcome that."

"Yes I have, but the second problem is more severe."

"And that is?"

"Almost half the tools had some blood on them, so I examined the hands of the workers. They all had blisters, fissures and healing sores on their palms, explaining the blood that I found on their tools. However, I deduced their blood would be on the ends of the handles of the mallets and adzes where their hands held the tools. That eliminated all but three of the tools that had blood at the end of the wooden handle where the wood met the metal. I thought these three tools might have been involved in the bludgeoning and placed them in the laboratory for you to exam."

"Let us go look."

They walked together to the lab. The two mallets and one adze lay on a table. Dredge pointed out the areas of blood on each one.

"I believe any of these three could have been the murder weapon," Sir Weatherby said thoughtfully. "However, I wonder if a mallet and an adze don't make differently shaped wounds. Perhaps we can test that once you have reconstructed the skull."

"What are you suggesting?" Dredge asked.

"We could actually test our hypothesis," Sir Weatherby said. "I'm going to propose that William Suffolk's fatal wound would be easier to produce with a mallet than with an adze."

"We usually think about which tool could cause that particular injury," Dredge said. "And then proceed from there."

"Yes, we have talked about that," Sir Weatherby replied. "That is the time-proven method of Aristotle called deduction."

"Then unlike you, I deduce that the injury was caused by an adze."

"You remember in March, I told you about a paper written by Galileo Galilei. He proposed a revolutionary method of proof, different than deduction, called *induction*. In his method, observation or experiments are performed to decide if the hypothesis is correct. That's what we are going to do here."

"How would we possibly do this?"

"By actually crushing some skulls. Obviously we can't use people. The most similar skulls are those of monkeys but I suspect we don't have any of those, either, do we? We have dogs, goats and pigs, but their skulls aren't much like human skulls."

"You are correct there are no monkeys, but cats have reasonably similar skulls."

"I agree. Have Warder Chertsey bring us any dead cats found in the Palace for the next few days and make a small mallet and adze one-twentieth normal size."

"Yes, Sir."

"Why are looking at me like that?"

"You have the most unusual and interesting ideas, Your Grace."

Dredge was Sir Weatherby's servant, and for a moment he thought he should be offended by the familiarity of the remark, but then he thought better of it. Without saying another word he marched out of the lab. He sent the first servant he saw to find Amarantha and then went to his office in the Wolsey Apartments. Amarantha arrived a few minutes later.

"How was your ramble?" Amarantha said.

"Excellent. It cleared my head. How were the interviews?"

"All done. I found all five of them with a little effort."

Sir Weatherby noted that Amarantha Thompson had decided on the 'elderly aunt' disguise. Her ample breasts were wrapped tightly, her hair was colored grey, and she wore the dress of an older woman with no makeup.

"Are you sure you need that cumbersome disguise here at the Palace?" Weatherby queried.

"Not entirely. This is a fairly small, closed society and I may just be able to be myself. I'll just feel my way."

"Very good. Any suspicious stories?"

"Three of the five are guileless and simple, and I don't think they could execute a crime or lie about it if they did."

"But, what about the other two?"

"One spent four years in the Redding Gaol before he came here as carpenter. His name is Thomas and he assaulted a minor nobleman—a Baron, I believe."

"When I went to work for King Henry, I thought it prudent to learn the hierarchy of nobles," Sir Weatherby remarked. "I believe it goes, God, Angels, Kings, Archbishops, Dukes, Bishops, Marquises, Earls, Viscounts, Barons, Abbots, Knights, Ladies-in-Waiting, Priests and Squires. So, indeed he was a minor nobleman of the tenth rank."

"The Baron ended up with a broken nose and a sprained arm. Thomas is a burly fellow at least six feet tall. The altercation was about a bull of dubious ownership, and he claims the Baron started it. Obviously, the judge disagreed."

"And the other?"

"Much more interesting, actually," Amarantha began.

"Let me pour you a glass of wine, and tell me all about it."

"The rogue's name is Nathaniel Philbrick, and he is currently the master glazier of Hampton Court," Amarantha said after taking a large sip of wine.

"Glassmaking seems to be involved in this crime at every level."

"He was born in England, the son of a marquis, but went to Venice—actually to the island of Murano in the Venetian Gulf—to learn glassmaking when he was thirteen. He returned to England twelve years ago, and worked for the King first at Whitehall and then at Greenwich. While in Greenwich, he was in a fight in a public house one night over a woman and the other man was knifed and died three days later. Nathaniel was convicted of the crime and spent two years in the Tower of London."

"How did he get rehabilitated from that bad beginning?"

"Apparently he was an inspired glazier who had learned the techniques of the Murano glassblowers and then extended them. His glass was as delicate and graceful as anything created in Italy, so King Henry pardoned him. Cardinal Wolsey sent him to Hampton Court Palace to create the glass for his Chapel."

"Has he fit in here?"

"No. Nathaniel has been at odds with Sir John Moulton and many of the other glaziers since he arrived here. He spent a week in the Hampton Village Gaol after a public disagreement with one of the masons."

"Do you think he is our killer?"

"He has the history and the temperament for it," Amarantha said as Sir Weatherby poured her another glass of wine.

"I will interview this recalcitrant person myself."

# PART 2

# CHAPTER 11

Sir Weatherby walked from the Wolsey Apartments, puzzling over the problem of finding the woman who would explain the occupants of the Palace to him. Perhaps Warder Chertsey had any ideas. Sir Weatherby found him in his office hunched over some papers. Not having forgotten Sir Weatherby's angry midnight visit to his rooms, the Warder looked up warily from his desk.

"Yes, Your Grace," the Warder said timidly.

"You have a complex little community here at Hampton Court Warder, and if I am to catch the murderer or murderers I need to understand how the diverse groups interact with each other. I was hoping you could help me."

"I will try, Your Grace. However, even though I have lived and worked here for a very long time, I'm not sure I appreciate how the various groups intermingle."

"Good insight! I couldn't agree with you more. I don't think you have the faintest idea about such subtleties. I simply want you to make me aware of the various women who are woven into the fabric of the Palace so I can determine who to talk with. Women are much more attuned to the group connections that I need to uncover."

"Very well, Sir. One of the women who was here since childhood and understood the fabric of Hampton Court was Anna Maria Wimbledon."

"Good God, man, she's dead and cold in ground! How could she possibly help me?"

"Yes, I see what you mean. How about her two assistant librarians? One is very quiet and private and would be of little help. However, the other, Margaret Sedgwick has been here seven years and is known and liked by everyone. She formed a sewing circle that is very popular. I will arrange a meeting for you."

"That's precisely the type of person I want to meet. What about the woman who is in charge of the Office of the Spicery?"

"Dame Brandon is a solid member of the Palace staff. She might fit the bill quite nicely."

"And the Office of the Green Cloth?"

"I say! You have been doing your homework, Sir! There are two sisters there, Meg and Mary. It is most unusual in this day and age to have women in such responsible posts. Either of them might be of assistance despite their arithmetic occupations."

"Who am I forgetting?"

"Only the most connected female in the whole Palace, Ellen Iverson, even if she is a gossip and a busybody."

"Where is she employed?"

"Why, she runs the Confectory. The courtiers love their sweetmeats, marzipans and custards. The best sugar comes from the Canary Islands but it is too dear for most households. Even though it is located outside the Palace in the Outer Court nearly everyone in Hampton Court finds a reason to go by there every day."

"I don't believe you showed me the Outer Court," Sir Weatherby said.

"True, because technically, it isn't really part of the Palace. Its two hundred yards to the west of the Base Court right on the banks of the Thames."

"But aren't the Office of the Green Cloth, the Office of the Spicery, the Pastry House, where the pastry coffins are made for meat pies, and the Boiling House located there, also? I imagine twenty or thirty people work in that Court. I need to know everything about the people who work there."

"You've just mentioned a good number of them by name so I suspect you're well on your way to knowing them all."

"Please set an interview with Ellen Iverson for me, and set the other interviews to follow. If you think of any other matrons or maids I need to talk with now, let me know."

Sir Weatherby stood and left Warder Chertsey's rooms. He went to check on his assistant Dredge in the laboratory. He found him hunched over a clay model of the first victim's skull.

"A very nice replica, Dredge," Sir Weatherby began. "So it was the right occipital lobe and adjoining temporal bone that were crushed in the blow."

"Yes, Sir, and I've already received three dead cats for your experiment. The miniature tools were easy to construct with the help of the iron monger. He shaped the heads of the tools out of scraps of metal."

Dredge opened a draw and pulled out an exact replica of a mallet and an adze.

"A nice bit of work," Sir Weatherby said as he ran his fingers over the smoothly crafted miniature tools. Once we have a few more cats we can proceed."

Sir Weatherby left the laboratory in search of Amarantha Thompson and found her in the second floor wing where the women staff had their lodgings.

"How about a spot of lunch," He boomed.

A startled Amarantha looked up and nodded. They walked through the galleries to the Wolsey Apartments.

Once seated, Sir Weatherby spoke, "How was your trip to Wales?"

"It was good to see Mum and Da," Amarantha began. "I hadn't been home in two years. You've never been to Wales but the northern part is hilly with poor, rocky soil. They had a severe drought last year. Da keeps a cow, a few pigs and chickens, but mainly he grazes sheep. He had to cut his herd from seventy ewes and two rams down to thirty. They had a hard winter, but luckily some early spring rains have already caused the grass to green up."

A tray of dishes followed by a tray full of cold meat, bread and pickles arrived. After they had eaten some, Sir Weatherby continued.

"I was sorry to cut your visit short, but I needed your help here at Hampton Court."

"It's quite all right. As I said, Mum and I had begun to disagree just like we used to. It started when I was a mere strip of a lass as you Scots would say. I suppose because we are so much alike. But now she doesn't approve of my life's work. She thinks I should be married with children and have laundry to boil and stir everyday."

"Am I making your life more difficult?"

"Of course not. You are not oppressing me. I love what you allow me to do. Our society tries to subjugate and belittle me as a woman, but I struggle against it. You have always treated me as an equal, Seamus, and never as a woman, unlike every other man in England. I'd throw myself in the river if I was stuck home with some mewling bairns."

"It's not that I don't see you as a woman, Ran. You know that I do."

"Of course I know that. Why are you so insecure today? It isn't like you. You are the most confident person I have ever met, Seamus."

"There is something about these murders that is vexing me, and I can't quite put my finger on it."

Amarantha pushed herself back from the table, put her napkin on the table cloth, rested her hand on top of Seamus's and said, "Let's go solve these crimes."

Sir Weatherby stood and watched her move toward the door in her disguise.

"I'm going to talk with Sir John Moulton," Sir Weatherby said as he headed toward the door.

"With the help of her roommate, I'll search Miss Wimbledon's room," Amarantha said as she walked down the gallery.

Weatherby found Sir Moulton on a scaffold well above the floor of the New Great Hall. Sir Weatherby called up to him and was invited to join him near the roof. Sir Weatherby climbed a series of unsteady ladders separated by rickety planks, and found himself standing next to Sir Moulton thirty-five feet off the ground.

"We are having trouble with the placement of this hammerbeam," Sir Moulton said without preamble. "It's a horizontal beam that extends into the room at the level of the roof plate and is supported by an arch that attaches to the wall post which rests on a corbel."

As he spoke he drew a diagram of the hammerbeam, arch, wall post and corbel in the sawdust. Then he continued, "It was employed in 1395 by Hugh Herland, a brilliant Royal Carpenter. It allows a wider space to be vaulted without center posts. He used it first at Westminster Hall for a magnificent span that was seventy feet across. The problem we have here is that the hammerbeam is twisted."

Sir Moulton began to climb down while yelling directions to Humphrey Coke, "You must plane the two sides before inserting the beam."

When he reached the floor he led Sir Weatherby to his construction office and called for two tankards of ale.

"You have lived here in Hampton Court for almost a year and a half, and I need your help," Sir Weatherby began. "You must understand something about the factions in such a place. You have also lived at

York Palace, Whitehall Palace and Westminster Abbey and there must be similarities from palace to palace."

"I had never thought of it in quite that way, but of course you are right, Sir Weatherby. I have been at Whitehall, York, Greenwich and now Hampton Court," John Moulton said after taking a large swig of ale. "I never thought about it consciously, but there are two segments of Palace life, and this is true of every English Palace I have been to. There is the monarch phase, which is brief like the life of a butterfly of the same name. For, when the monarch is present, Palace life is full of fêtes, balls, plays, and grand dinners. Also, of course, the Ladies in Waiting and the Knights and the Earls are all present and competing for the attention of the King. The courtiers describe the King's presence as like being in the bright sunlight. However, the King and his retinue never stay long. The Princess Mary alone has a staff of three hundred, and she's only fourteen. The King and Queen have many more servants, attendants and hangers on. The total retinue of the King and Queen may total three thousand. By simply eating, drinking and making merry, they ravage the countryside of all the livestock, game, grain, fruit, vegetables, wine and beer within a twenty mile radius. Like a plague of locusts, they *must* move every six weeks or starve."

Sir Moulton suggested continuing their discussion over tankards of ale in Hampton. They adjourned to the Lamb and Flag.

# CHAPTER 12

Once they were seated, Sir Moulton drank deeply from a second large tankard of ale while they waited for his shepherd's pie. He hadn't had any lunch. Then the Surveyor of the King's Work launched back into his discussion of Palace politics.

"If the butterfly phase is that brief colorful period when the monarch is present, then the longer quieter time is the caterpillar phase," Sir Moulton continued. "The metabolism of the Palace is slower but jockeying for position continues. However, I believe the goals change. Since the monarch is geographically remote, the residents compete for favors from the Master of the House. They curry favor to obtain better rooms, better food and privileges. Am I boring you with all this detail?"

The shepherd's pie arrived steaming from the oven and was slid off a long wooden board onto the table.

After eating a mouthful, Sir Weatherby replied, "Not at all. This is just the information that I need. I hadn't even heard of the Master of the House."

"The Master of the House is responsible for Hampton Court when the King isn't in residence. The Master of the Guard, the Royal Chef, the Master of the Wardrobe, and the Officer of the Greencloth all report to him."

"Why have I never met or heard of this person?"

"His name is Richard Weston. He is a very shadowy figure. Technically, I report to him also, but I didn't meet him until I had been at Hampton Court for five months. He has an office near the Royal Chapel but he seldom leaves it. His minions report to him there."

"How do his workers win favors from him?"

"The usual ways. They bring him unsolicited gifts of food, wine, art, precious clothing or sex. He seems reasonably honest, but he is bribable and he's very open about it. I had a deadline that I couldn't meet last summer. Weston put in a good word with the King to extend the time after I gave him two cases of Rhenish wine."

As Moulton finished his shepherd's pie Sir Weatherby said, "Thank you for your insight, Sir Moulton."

The two men walked down the main street of Hampton and back across the bridge to the Palace. Weatherby retired to his apartment for a night of dreamless sleep.

In the morning Sir Weatherby sought out Amarantha. She was in the laboratory cataloguing the dead woman's possessions.

"Good morning, Amarantha. So what did you find?" Sir Weatherby asked.

"Anna Maria Wimbledon had a surprising number of possessions including rich clothing and more jewels than I would have suspected. She may have had more property than she could have acquired given her modest salary. I located her Bible, plus two scourges each with several leather thongs attached to a single handle. Both had dried blood on the thongs and were well worn. She must have self-flagellated regularly. As you know, self-mortification has become quite common amongst devout Catholics. Saint Peter Damian wrote a treatise in praise of it in the eleventh century, and it has gained currency here in England since then. Anna Maria appears to have been a devout Catholic. All of her other books, which were borrowed from the library, were about religious topics. She also had a hair shirt. A friend of mine had one in private school, and I tried it on. It was a vest made of cowhide with the hair left on the leather. I tried to put it on, with the hide toward my body, after I removed my doublet and corselet. She took it from me, turned it hair side in and helped me put it on. The itching was intense and immediate. I only had it on for a few seconds, but I itched for hours. It's just another form of self-mortification, I suppose."

"Did you find anything else?"

"No."

"What's notable to me Amarantha," Sir Weatherby said. "is that there are no personal writings."

"I agree. I turned the room and all its corners and nooks inside out, and I found no journals, diaries or even handwritten poetry."

"It makes me wonder if she had another abode or a secret compartment somewhere."

"I will query her roommate, Peggy, further, and search that part of the Palace again."

"Thank you. Now, let's go see what Dredge has been up to," Sir Weatherby said.

They walked together to the laboratory. Dredge had constructed a small wooden device to help with his work to determine the murder weapon used on William Suffolk. On a small wooden platform he had a dead cat mounted in an upright position. The miniature mallet he had constructed was attached to a wooden arm that, when released, would fall from above the cat's head.

"A nice bit of work, this, Dredge," Sir Weatherby said. "It is a new kind of inductive reasoning based on experimentation as proposed recently by Galileo Galilei. I believe it has considerably more power than the deductive reasoning of Aristotle, but let's compare the two techniques. Which of these two instruments caused the damage to William Suffolk shown here in the reconstruction?"

"I believe the damage was caused by the adze," Amarantha said after examining the victim's skull.

"And you, Dredge?" Sir Weatherby asked.

"As I said before, Sir, I believe the instrument of death was the adze. Therefore, I agree with Amarantha."

"I believe this wound was created by the mallet," Sir Weatherby began. "Let us proceed with the test."

Dredge released the lever and the miniature mallet fell completely missing the dead animal's skull. He adjusted the cat's head and the arm of the lever. This time the mallet struck the skull crushing the right side.

"That does look like the wound," Amarantha said.

"It is too early to tell, Ran," Sir Weatherby cautioned. "We need more information."

All three helped set up the next test. After two more blows from mallet, they carried out three identical tests using the miniature adze that Dredge had crafted. They all helped cut away the fur and skin over the recently fractured cat skulls with sharp scalpels.

Amarantha spoke first, "I think that the adze was the murder weapon."

"Why?" Sir Weatherby and Dredge said together.

"Look how the adze carried away the back and side of the cat skulls," Amarantha said picking up two of the skulls.

"Yes, but you have to compare the adze-disrupted cat skulls to William Suffolk's wound," Dredge said.

"Here," Sir Weatherby said lifting William's skull off the table and handing it to Amarantha.

"You can see there are some differences," Dredge said.

"Now hold these two cat skulls that we fractured using the mallet," Sir Weatherby said. "Move them toward the candles."

"This isn't fair," Amarantha said as she cradled the two skulls near the candles. "I'm trained as a barrister and you, Seamus, have studied the human body in medical school, and then instructed Dredge."

"That is the beauty of Galileo's method, Ran," Sir Weatherby replied. "It does depend on your training, but little. What it truly depends on is the power of observation, which is most acute in you."

"In that case I notice that the adze creates a wound with a smooth edge and the mallet created a rough irregular edge," Amarantha replied. "And the edge of William Suffolk's wound is most irregular. Therefore, I'd like to change my mind and conclude that the skull was fractured by a mallet."

"I agree with Miss Thompson's acute observation," Dredge replied. "I have changed my mind; I now believe the fatal wound was caused by the mallet not the adze."

"Then on the basis of the evidence we are all congruent and each believes the wound was caused by the mallet and not by the adze," Sir Weatherby said. "The method of induction has led us here. Mere deduction would have pointed us in the wrong direction. I am pleased with the result, and I am most impressed with this unique new method that we used. How many mallets are bloody by their heads, Dredge?"

"As I told you, I thought only three tools had blood in a suspicious location and two of them were mallets," Dredge replied.

"How will you determine their owners? Since Warder Chertsey didn't specify ownership when he collected them for you."

"I've decided to use a ruse and a prize. I'm going to call all the workers together and thank them for their cooperation and offer them a prize for their help. I'll invite them to take their tool or tools from the table and write a small number on the end of the handle. Then I'll call the number of the two mallets I'm interested in and reward the owners with a half a crown."

"It's devious," Amarantha replied.

"But it should work," Sir Weatherby said fishing two half crown coins out of his leather purse and handing them to Dredge.

"This was a nice bit of work, Dredge," Amarantha observed.

"Thank you, Mum."

"I heartily agree," Sir Weatherby replied. "The laboratory that you brought here from London seems to be working out well."

"I concur," Amarantha added.

"Have you had a chance to analyze the stomach contents of the unfortunate Miss Wimbledon?"

"Only preliminarily, Sir. Like the first victim, the contents contained a lot of alcohol—a good vehicle for a poison—but the contents were also very strongly acid. I sent a man back to our London library for several tomes on poisons. The first report we got of a bludgeoning death here at Hampton Court pointed me away from poisoning, so I didn't pack them. The books should be here in two days. I will also consult the neighboring apothecary. He will know someone local with knowledge of potions."

"Carry on," Sir Weatherby called over his shoulder. "I'm going to take Miss Thompson on a walk about the Castle before the light fades."

Sir Weatherby led the way across the Base Court and out through the Great Gatehouse and then turned right along the Thames. They circled the Outer Court, disconnected from the Palace itself, where the Spicery, Confectory and Office of the Greencloth were located. Maids and men were kneading bread and moving supplies outside in the warm afternoon sun. Rejoining the Palace itself, they walked along the Gallery and then past the very ancient Great Kitchen, where William Suffolk's body had been laid out on the first night. Beyond the kitchen, were the Cloister and the Great Chapel, taller than any of the adjacent structures. The copper that clad the roof of the Great Chapel hadn't even begun to turn green. The single cupola in the center of the roof reflected the sun's rays.

Beyond the Chapel, they walked by the Knot Garden. Then they turned into the long Gallery that led to Cardinal Wolsey's apartment nearly completing the circle. As they walked down the gallery, they smelled the fragrant aroma of beef and leeks awaiting them in the Wolsey Apartments.

# CHAPTER 13

After eating a large and hearty meal of beef and leeks, Sir Weatherby and Amarantha relaxed in some overstuffed chairs and finished a second bottle of French red wine.

Apropos of nothing in particular Amarantha said, "I believe this is one of your hardest cases, Seamus."

"I would have to agree, Ran," Sir Weatherby replied. "While we are on the track of the first murder weapon, the weapon in the other death is totally incomprehensible. The motive for both murders is obscure and we have no suspects. I think we are at square one in this chess game, and the next move belongs to our opponents."

"That may be wishful thinking. What if the murdering is done now and the culprits have only to cover their tracks?"

"Your intuition about such things is usually dead-on, Ran. However, let me remind you that these two victims were as different in every way as they could possibly be. I don't wish for any more deaths, but a third crime might help us considerably. I've arranged to spend some time with Sir John Moulton tomorrow. Hopefully, he'll help me unravel the parts of the little society here at the Palace."

Amarantha excused herself to retire to her own apartment. Both slept well.

In the morning Sir Weatherby visited Sir Moulton's construction office. He found the King's Surveyor smoking his clay pipe and studying the plan for the roof of the new Gallery. The construction shack was full of blue smoke.

Sir Weatherby spoke as he stepped inside, "Good morning, Sir John."

"You're up and about early this morning," Moulton said.

"I was hoping you had some time to continue our conversation about the society and factions here at the Palace."

"Of course. All the carpenters, stone masons and glaziers have been given their assignments for the day. Things should be quiet this forenoon unless something unexpected occurs. Let's walk out to the Knot Garden and talk."

Both men walked along the Gallery and then outside onto the south side of the Palace until they reached the Knot Garden. A bench was located in the center and they both sat down and faced the rest of the gardens.

"You are aware that I have only been here a year and a half," Sir Moulton demurred, "Warder Chertsey has been here for forty years."

"I am fully aware of that," Sir Weatherby replied. "But I suspect you have learned more about the dynamics of Hampton Court Palace in your brief stay than Chertsey has in all his decades here."

"All right, then. My perception when I first arrived here was that the staff of the Palace was quite homogeneous. It was a strongly knit Catholic community of about two hundred people. I brought slightly over a hundred construction workers who by themselves could cause a lot of unrest. In reality, the staff of the Palace was diverse with an upper class that had attended a university or traveled the world, a large middle class and few lower class peasants for hauling and shoveling."

"And I imagine most of the Palace community was very stable."

"Yes. Many of the residents had been here since the Cardinal obtained the property. Most of my workers were from the lower class except for the three architects, which included William Suffolk, and the occasional artisan who trained abroad like Toto del Nunciata. He was imported from Venice to paint the frescos in the Bayne Tower. The integration of my workers into the Palace staff took several months and there were bumps along the way. I had a handful of meetings with the reluctant Master of the House. Usually the problem was the crude manners of my workers. Often they inadvertently offended members of the Palace staff. Once the differences were explained, the problem usually resolved itself. For example, we had a problem with muddy boots in the dining hall; but once I informed the workers that this was unacceptable, the problem virtually disappeared. Of course, we had more serious problems, too. Often the workers spoke blasphemously or made unwanted sexual advances toward the female staff. That's improved but it isn't completely resolved."

"I'm more anxious to know if there were any natural or unnatural schisms among the employees," Sir Weatherby said. "That might explain the animosities."

"As I said, initially we were quite a homogeneous Catholic community. However, during my time here that heretic Martin Luther and his teachings have led to the development of deep divisions in the community. He posted his 95 theses in Wittenberg in 1517, and his doctrines spread from there. I'm sure this had already happened in London, but his Lutheran ideas spread to the provinces more slowly. Suddenly, we had peasants arguing about the buying of indulgences and the fine points of theology. The trouble here was spurred by a Gregory Townsend, a stableman, who decided he was a lay preacher and an ardent Protestant. Initially, he held secret meetings in the undercroft, but when he got bolder and had some converts he started meeting in the Great Passing Hall. Suddenly, people who had been friends and colleagues for many years shunned each other. Eventually, it began to affect daily life at Hampton Court. For example, two Catholics decided they could no longer work with a Protestant. Richard Weston and I held a series of meetings with the resisters and then with all of the staff. We encouraged them to keep their religious beliefs to themselves and not to proselytize. Overall, it has been fairly successful on the surface but underneath the tensions remain. Do you find this tedious?"

"Quite the contrary." Sir Weatherby replied. "It's the background I need to link the two murders. However, my legs are stiff. Could we walk a bit?"

The two men rose from their bench in the Knot Garden and walked to the orchards to the north. They walked amongst the blooming apple and cherry trees. Large banks of cumulus clouds, pure white and fluffy billowed in the west. While they were walking Sir Moulton resumed his narration.

"We also have Druids."

"Surely you jest. That isn't even possible in the sixteenth century. They were powerful in these islands before Christianity but the last Druids I ever read about were in Ireland in the seventh century."

"They are certainly not as common as they once were but Newland's Corner in our county of Surrey remains a Druidic site and the Palace has several members who are still active in that ancient pagan religion. They keep a very low profile especially since the recent religious strife."

"I will have to read about them, but what I recollect is that they worship certain groves, hills and plants, a form of animism and believe in reincarnation. And they sacrifice animals and sometimes humans."

"You are correct. I believe that local Druids actively practice their religion. They meet regularly in a glade to the east of Hampton Court and dance and carry out pagan rituals with animal skins and painted faces. They also appear likely to sacrifice animals."

"Therefore any of these three groups—the Catholics, the Protestants, or the Druids—could have carried out these murders for religious purposes. Is that what you believe?"

"That is correct."

"Thank you for your insights," Sir Weatherby replied as he walked off toward the Base Court.

After lunch, Sir Weatherby went to the laboratory to see what experiments Dredge was working on. He found his amanuensis hunched over a pile of very old, dusty, books with cracked leather bindings.

"We haven't had a poisoning case in over a year. I had forgotten how many poisons there are," Dredge remarked as Sir Weatherby entered the lab. "I'd like to have a farthing for every poison that was ever invented. I'd be very rich indeed."

"I recall both Egyptians and Indians were quite adept at it," Sir Weatherby replied. "And that was thousands of years ago. It is so much more subtle than an arrow in the chest or a sword blow to the neck. The Egyptians knew about antimony, copper, lead, opium, and crude arsenic as poisons. I believe most of those compounds are still in use today."

"Yes, but I don't think any of those substances were used on Anna Maria. Our best clue is still that bitter rose smell. I found something called the 'stinking rose' but that turns out to be garlic, which is hardly a poison."

"Perhaps we're looking for something used just in this area or county."

"I took some of the stomach contents to the local apothecary, but he had never smelled anything like it before. He gives chemicals and potions to witches and seers on occasion and will ask them about the smell."

"Truth be told, I suppose we don't even know if it is a poison."

"You may be right."

"I suggest another experiment. Find six young rabbits and feed three of them a dram of the stomach contents and three of them a dram of alcohol and report the results to me."

"Is this another of those Galileo induction experiments?"

"Quite so. I was reading Chaucer's *The Canterbury Tales* last night. A man goes to an apothecary for a potion he says is to quell his infestation of rats but in reality he hopes to dispose of a troublesome rival. He's given a, 'confiture no bigger than a grain of wheat that will cause him to forlete his life.' Now that is a powerful poison."

"The rest of our tomes about poisons and potions should arrive tomorrow and I can do a more systematic search."

"Very good. I wish I was could see a link between our two victims and their sad demise, but so far it escapes me. I do continue to think that religion is at the root of these evil deeds."

# CHAPTER 14

Sir Weatherby walked from the laboratory to Amarantha's apartment. He found her arranging clothes in the garderobe. He invited her to accompany him to the Wolsey Apartments for dinner. Neither spoke of the murders during dinner, but as soon as they were done eating both of their minds strayed back to the recent crimes.

"We are working on the poison that might have killed Anna Maria Wimbledon," Sir Weatherby began. "But so far we have made little progress."

"Dredge will figure that out if anybody can. I conducted a more thorough search of the victim's room in the Palace but still found no diary or personal writings. It leads me to agree with your assertion that she had an abode some place outside the Palace. Her roommate, Peggy Ealing, is opaque and of little help."

"Is she actively obstructing you or just very unaware?"

"I'm not sure."

"I planned to interview her earlier, but ran out of time. I will interview her myself. The town of Hampton is the only logical place for an additional domicile. It is close to Hampton Court and offers a variety of lodgings. You may have to canvas some of the landlords there."

"I shall do so tomorrow." Amarantha replied.

Both retired.

Early the next morning, Weatherby went to the glass shop for an interview with Nathaniel Philbrick, the master glazier.

Philbrick, a tall, slender man, was sitting in the first room wearing a leather apron and a cloth cap. Sir Weatherby quickly thought it likely that he had been the perpetrator who swung the mallet killing William Suffolk with one blow.

"You look like a dead man," Sir Weatherby said without preamble.

Nathaniel looked up, surprised and then said, "How's that, Your Grace?"

"It's very rare for a vicious murderer like you to get out of the Tower of London alive."

"The conviction was a mistake."

"Do you take me for a bloody fool? You were drunk. You started a fight over some trollop. You stabbed the man five times and were arrested with a bloody knife in your hand, I suppose because you were too drunk to flee."

"I . . ."

"Shut up. I suppose you were released because you are a talented glassmaker even though you are a miserable excuse for a human being. There hasn't been a murder at Hampton Court for almost two hundred years. Now in the space of a week there have been two and there is a convicted murderer, you, running loose in the Palace."

Philbrick jumped to his feet. "I had nothing to do with either of these murders!"

"I have an order right here remanding you back to the Tower, if I so wish it," Sir Weatherby yelled back grabbing a rolled-up vellum that had nothing whatsoever to do with Nathaniel Philbrick. "Now sit down and start talking."

Nathaniel Philbrick sank back into his chair visibly shaken.

Sir Weatherby loomed over him and queried, "How well did you know William Suffolk?"

"He was an architect here and I was the chief glazier. Over the last year and a half, we worked together on projects for the Bayne Tower and for the Council Chamber off the Cloisters. When we were designing and executing a project we saw each other daily."

"Did you form any opinions about him?"

"He was an inspired designer, as good as anyone I have ever worked with, but given to lapses from work."

"Do you know where he went?"

"I have no idea. The other glaziers thought he went to see a woman in the nearby village of Coombe, but I never heard any particulars. I suspected it was just idle speculation."

"What was he like personally?"

"He was an arrogant, self-important man who shabbily treated those he felt were beneath him, which was everybody."

"You had disagreements?"

"Frequently. I'm sure you've spoken to others who heard that we argued loudly every few days. We argued about the designs of the glass because often he would design something like a ribbon of yellow glass three feet long and only an inch and a quarter wide. To get the color that he wanted, I had to add pitchblende from Germany, but yellow is one of the most brittle glasses. I knew such a piece would only break. We would also argue about the supports for stained glass which he always designed insubstantially to show off the colors. I felt the glass would soon fall under its own weight. We were both passionate and would often yell at each other for an hour. Honestly, if I'd had a razor, I would have cut his throat."

"But, did it ever come to blows?"

"No. He outranked me, so after all my ranting, he would let me cool down, and then he decided how it was to be done, and I did it. I tried to make a ribbon of yellow glass everyday for two weeks, and every one that I made broke, just as I predicted. I saved every piece for him."

"What ended up happening?"

"He changed the color to green and I made it in an hour."

"Did you ever meet him outside of work?"

"No. We ran across each other occasionally at a tavern in town, but rarely spoke."

"You are a murderer, who hated the dead man. He provoked you regularly, but you didn't kill him. Is that what you are asking me to believe?"

"Yes, Your Grace."

"Well I don't believe you. And I've a good mind to lock you up until I get some honest answers."

"I didn't tolerate incarceration well, Sir. It makes me a little wild and crazy."

"Well then come up with a verifiable alibi for Thursday last."

"Um. Let me see. I was at the Lamb and Flag during the evening, drank too much ale and lost some money at dice. Then I went upstairs with a prostitute named Dotty and staggered home about 2 a.m."

"Will she remember you?"

"Yes because I didn't have enough money to pay her."

"I'll check your story in the morning."

Nathaniel got up quickly, put his hat on, and left the glazier's shop. Sir Weatherby had a feeling that Philbrick had learned lying well in the Tower and wasn't telling the truth—at least not the whole truth. Sir Weatherby was fatigued. He spent the afternoon reading in the orchard. Later, he called for dinner in his apartment and asked Amarantha to join him. After they ate they took turns reading aloud from Dante's *Inferno*. Sir Weatherby slept well, then was awoken by his terrifying vivid nightmare. He lit a candle on his nightstand. His mechanical watch showed that it was 3:07 a.m. His nightshirt was dripping wet, but even after changing it, he was unable to sleep. Instead, he spent the rest of the night thinking about his mysterious unsolved cases.

In the morning Amarantha walked across the bridge to the village of Hampton to search for Anna Maria's apartment. Dredge tagged along. He was to talk to the trollop, Dotty, at the Flag and Lamb to confirm Nathaniel Philbrick's alibi. Sir Weatherby had a series of interviews with the ladies of Hampton Court Palace. He hadn't had time to interview Peggy Ealing yesterday. He would talk with Margaret Sedgwick one of the assistant librarians, the two sisters that worked in the Office of the Green Cloth, and Dame Brandon who ran the Office of the Spicery. He ate a hurried breakfast in the Great Kitchen and then went to the Wolsey Apartments. One of the sisters was already there.

"I'm investigating the recent murder of two members of the Palace staff," Sir Weatherby began without preamble. "And you are?"

"I'm Meg Claiborne, Your Grace," the nervous young woman replied. "And I work in the Office of the Green Cloth."

"You are the Comptroller of the Castle, as I understand it."

"Along with my sister, Mary, who also works in the office. Yes Sir."

"Did you know either of the decedents?"

"Yes. I knew both of them. I had a passing acquaintance with William Suffolk as our paths crossed infrequently, but he was always pleasant and well bred around me."

"He has been described as being insufferably arrogant by many. Did you find him so?"

"Not in the least. He was polite and quite courtly when we were together for events such as the Christmastide party."

"Let's turn to Anna Maria Wimbledon. You knew her well?"

"Quite. I am still grieving over her sudden loss. It came as a great surprise to me."

"Were you close?"

"Yes. She and my sister and I often spent evenings together either reading or sewing. Sometimes on Saturdays we went for rambles through the countryside. She was pretty and smart, but most importantly she was kind. We laughed a lot when we were together."

"Her roommate describes her as changed over the past six months or so. Did you find that to be the case?"

"Perhaps she was more thoughtful, but otherwise much the same. It didn't seem a bad thing."

"Who would have wanted her dead?"

"I find that most puzzling. I never heard her say a cross word to anyone. In all the years we spent together I never heard her disparage a living soul."

"Well, thank you for your time," Sir Weatherby said realizing that he had received no useful information from this pleasant young woman. "Send your sister in."

"I wasn't much help was I?"

"No, you weren't," Sir Weatherby said as he turned abruptly to a stack of papers on his desk. Mary came into the office and sat quietly on the edge of a chair, hands folded in her lap. After several minutes Sir Weatherby turned to her.

"I'm sure you are cut from the same piece of cloth as your sister, and if you are only going to spout pleasantries you may leave now," Sir Weatherby said brusquely.

Mary started to rise.

"Sit back down. I don't want to hear all the nice things that are said about a dead acquaintance. I need to know her dark longings and secrets, so I can apprehend the vicious person that murdered her," Sir Weatherby said as he leaned very close to Mary's face.

"I don't know anything secret about her."

"Yes you do. Think back to a time when she was very frustrated or very tired or had had too much to drink."

"I had known her for several years and she was always cheerful and buoyant. However, that truly changed six months ago. She seemed more pensive. I thought it normal at first but then she started brooding."

"I'm sure you asked her about it."

"Yes. Usually she just deflected my comment, but about ten days ago she pulled me aside and broke down crying. I wrapped my arms around her. She said that she had a terrible secret. I asked her what it was, and she said she would tell me everything in a fortnight, but she didn't survive that long," Mary said as she burst into tears.

Sir Weatherby walked over to Mary and put his hand softly on her hunched back. He stood there for several minutes without moving. Finally, the sobs subsided and Mary stood, slowly.

"Thank you for talking with me," Sir Weatherby said as he guided Mary to the door.

# CHAPTER 15

Sitting back at his desk, Sir Weatherby decided that he knew something, but he wasn't sure just what. Before she was murdered, Anna Maria knew she had a secret. By the time of her death, she very likely knew from the changes in her body, such as swollen breasts and a thickening waist, that she was pregnant. She'd a relationship of long or short duration or she wouldn't have been pregnant, and so far it seemed that it was clandestine. But did she have another secret that sprang from her relationship or from somewhere else? Sir Weatherby wasn't sure how to attack the puzzle further at present. He decided to check on Dredge in the laboratory. He walked across the Base Court, appreciating the balmy spring afternoon. On entering the lab, he noticed Dredge was writing in his elegant flowery hand in one of his journals. When Sir Weatherby entered, he looked up.

"Good afternoon, Your Grace. The warder's men brought me six rabbits. I fed three of them a dram of the bitter rose solution and three a dram of alcohol late last night. They are in these two cages. The ones in this cage . . ."

"No. Don't tell me which is which, I should be able to distinguish one from the other. In this first cage I see three sleepy rabbits, but they are easy to arouse and move normally. These could be the ones fed alcohol. In the second cage two of the rabbits aren't moving. In fact, I believe they are dead. So I believe these lagomorphs were given the bitter rose solution and that it is a very potent poison."

"I concur. In fact it is the stronger and quicker poison than any I have ever read about. I just wish I know what it was."

"I'm sure that if we find its source, it will give a clue to the murderer. We may have to interview all the witches and seers in the area."

"I will start a list."

"How did your little contest to identify the owner of the bloody hammers go?"

"Just as I expected. The workers fell all over themselves trying to get the money. The two owners of the bloody hammers are Giorgio Tomas and Will Mellors. I'm not sure either of them is tall enough to have actually delivered the blow. Giorgio has only worked at Hampton Court for five weeks and no one knows much about him. Will is from a nearby town and came here when the new construction started. He is quiet, but I hear he may be a religious zealot."

"I will interview both of them. Anything else?"

"Yes. I interviewed that trollop Dotty that Nathaniel Philbrick was using as an alibi. I found her asleep with three other whores in a filthy bedroom at the local whore house," Dredge said with disgust in his voice. "She was badly hung-over and clothed only in an ill fitting shift with one breast hanging out. I had to bring her some ale before she would talk to me. Eventually, she said that she did remember spending a night with Nathaniel Philbrick but she wasn't sure if it was a Thursday or a Friday. No amount of coaxing improved her recollection."

"So Philbrick doesn't have an alibi."

"I believe you are correct."

"I'm going to check with Amarantha. I believe you can let those three rabbits go. Let me know how your research on the poison goes. You know, in Italy lethal substances for murder have been used for centuries. In Venice poisoning has become so common that there are actual schools to teach the 'art' of poisoning. A guild of alchemists called the Council of Ten was formed. They specialize in poisoning and their existence was public knowledge. These poison-welding assassins administer lethal substances to victims when an enemy pays them a sufficient sum."

"I hope we don't emulate the Italians," Dredge replied.

Sir Weatherby left the laboratory to get an update from Amarantha. He found her in the Wolsey Apartments.

"How did your search in Hampton go?" He asked as he walked through the door.

"I found a bloody lot of rooms for let in such a little village," Amarantha answered. "I took your postmortem sketch of Anna Maria so they would know who I was talking about. I must have interviewed twenty landlords, but none of them recollected her. Unfortunately, there may be forty more in the village. After that I'll start on the surrounding crofts and farms."

"Do you still think Miss Wimbledon had such a place?" Sir Weatherby asked.

"I'm more certain than ever. Her room was simply devoid of anything personal. If she were an accountant or a baker perhaps she would have no personal writings, but she was a librarian. She certainly had a love of books and words, and it only seems logical that she would have written or at least copied passages during her leisure time."

"Perhaps she had another hiding place here in the Palace."

"That's a possibility that probably deserves further pursuit."

"She was the librarian. Maybe she secreted her papers right under our noses in her library. How big is it?"

"All the volumes are kept in two rooms with an archway between them. I'd guess that there are fifteen hundred books and scrolls on the shelves. There is also a workroom attached where books were repaired and rebound. It's a cluttered mess. A lot of material could be hidden in that dusty, dark, disorganized space among the papers and miscellaneous tomes."

"Perhaps a search of that work room would most likely turn up the personal papers you are seeking."

"You could be correct. I'll redirect my search and employ the two assistant librarians to give me a hand."

"What do know of them?"

"The junior assistant, Judith Scotman, is young, demure and a bit of a cipher. I have never gotten her to answer a question with more than three words. I doubt she will be of much use. However, the senior assistant, Margaret Sedgwick, has worked in the library with Anna Maria for over seven years. Anna Maria apparently trusted her and gave her a lot of responsibility."

"Thank you for interviewing them. I think you should question both of them closely about places in the library and work room where they might, in retrospect, have noticed that the librarian tarried. Perhaps that would narrow your search."

"I will do all of that. However, in the meantime may I suggest a ride in the countryside this afternoon? We are all working too hard and I want you to check the gaits of my new black stallion."

"You are a much better atop a horse, Ran, than I am, but I would enjoy the company and the relaxation. So yes, I will accompany you with pleasure."

They agreed to meet at the stables in an hour. When Sir Weatherby arrived, Amarantha was standing next to her small black stallion as he pulled at his reins. A large roan gelding three hands taller than the stallion had been saddled for Sir Weatherby. The stable boy first helped Amarantha, and then Sir Weatherby into their saddles. The two headed off to the northwest through Hampton Parish toward the town of Hanworth. They took a narrow trail through a beech forest not wide enough for a carriage and were soon all alone in the woods. They rode companionably side by side except for the occasional open meadow where Amarantha insisted on galloping. Sir Weatherby, sitting taller and less at ease finished these headlong chases a good three or four lengths behind and more out of breath. The afternoon was cool and breezy with stacks of billowing white cumulus clouds to the west as they left the Palace. As their ride progressed, the wind strengthened and blew steadily from the west. Amarantha's great coat and her horse's mane and tail were blown forward, Sir Weatherby noted from behind. A light rain followed by squalls of cold rain washed over them. They decided to look for shelter, but as they crossed a meadow, hail the size of walnuts began to fall. The swiftly falling balls of ice were large enough to hurt horse and rider. The spheres were particularly painful when striking skin with little padding such as skulls and wrists. They bolted for a fallen stone house at the edge of the clearing and tied their horses under a large beech tree. The meadow was now covered with sparkling crystalline ice three inches thick. The walls of the ancient house were intact, but only half of the timbered roof remained. Sir Weatherby piled dry fallen roof boards near the edge of the fallen roof and struck his flint to catching a small spark. While he was tended the fire Amarantha peeled out of her wet clothing. She had planned to leave her linen shift on but found it soaking wet, cold, and transparent as it clung to her every curve. Putting modesty aside, she quickly removed it and began rubbing her body and her goose bumps with her hands. The only truly warm thing within a mile was Seamus's large body. Sir Weatherby was intent on his fire, bending down to blow on the feeble flames as he shed his clothes in a pile on the floor. He was down to a brief damp loincloth when he felt a gentle hand on his back. He started and then turned and in the firelight saw Amarantha in all of her lovely white skinned nakedness. He wrapped his arms around her and pulled her close running his warm hands over her back, buttocks and thighs.

As the fire grew in light and warmth he spun them both around so her back was to the fire, but he didn't release his grip. He had known for several months that he was in love with his beautiful red-haired assistant. But he had never said a word about it. He had often imagined her body when he caught a glimpse of an inadvertent ankle, thigh or shoulder, but in reality she was much more evocatively beautiful than he had ever imagined. When the fire was blazing he released his grip and placed the dry inside if his great coat on her shoulders. He kept his hands inside rubbing her shoulders, breast, buttocks and lower belly with rapidly moving, but gentle hands. After several minutes she tipped her face up and kissed him very briefly and gently on the lips.

"Thank you," Amarantha said in a husky, soft voice as she moved away and then brought the clothes to the fireside. She placed each item on a timber angled toward the flames.

After an hour, the rain stopped. Their clothes were nearly dry and the two horsemen headed back toward Hampton Court Palace at a walk. They arrived after dark a little saddle sore but elated.

# CHAPTER 16

Sir Weatherby spent the early evening alone by a large fire. He ruminated on his inability to speak while holding the woman he loved. As he drank more wine he realized that women often made him tongue-tied. He saw himself as forceful and in command in almost every situation unless it involved a female. This evening he had been alone with Amarantha; she was vulnerable and open, and he hadn't managed to say a single word!

In his anger with himself he walked into Hampton to The White Swan the larger and tidier of the two whore houses in the village. The parlor was nicely appointed with upholstered furniture, a harpsichord, and several Venetian glass lamps fueled by oil. The madame looked clean, but Sir Weatherby knew from his years in medicine that looks were often deceiving, at a time when bathing was frowned upon, at best. He asked for a girl.

"We have many to choose from, Sir" the Madame intoned. "Most are young and quite new to the profession."

Sir Weatherby knew this to be untrue but at least the madame wasn't claiming she had several virgins in her establishment. She led Sir Weatherby into the next room where several women were sitting on two long sofas. Their clothing was gaudy and they were in dishabille with patches of pink breasts and white upper thighs clearly visible. Sir Weatherby scanned the lot quickly.

"I'll take that one," Sir Weatherby said, picking a tall buxom redhead that didn't resemble Amarantha in any particular.

"Lois, go with the gentleman," the Madame ordered.

Lois rose smiling, took Sir Weatherby's hand and walked him toward a hall of bedrooms. They both undressed. Before proceeding Sir Weatherby took a sheath of oiled sheep's intestine from a pouch and placed it on his member. He tied it in place with a piece of pink ribbon. The device had been invented by the renowned anatomist, Gabriel Fallopius, in Italy to prevent the spread of venereal diseases. Of the many venereal diseases, syphilis was the most dreaded not because of the chancre, the ugly shallow ulcer that developed on the genitals, or the generalized rash that came next. It was the third phase of syphilis, the gradual descent into madness that was feared most. Sir Weatherby had Dredge fabricate two of the devices that were later named after the Earl of Condom.

When he was finished with Lois, his desire was still unslaked. He went back to the sitting room and picked another prostitute. When he was finished with her, he walked unsteadily back across the bridge to the Palace. He was filled with self-loathing as he stumbled into bed with most of his clothes still on.

Sir Weatherby awoke early, with a fierce headache from too much wine. He still felt dirty and unsettled and washed more thoroughly than usual in cold water before going to breakfast. Amarantha would be interviewing the two assistant librarians, Judith Scotman and Margaret Sedgwick today. Dredge would be given last night's condoms for cleaning for without scrupulous cleaning and oiling after each use Dr. Fallopius reported that the sheep's intestine became brittle and then provided less effective protection. Then Dredge would continue the study of the mysterious bitter rose poison. Sir Weatherby decided to query Ellen Iverson, the director of The Confectory. He had been surprised to learn that this house of sugar and sweets was the nexus at the center of the Palace. According to Warder Chertsey all persons and all information traveled through these small sugary smelling rooms thanks to every Englishmen's overwhelming desire to eat sweet things. Despite his headache, Sir Weatherby found himself very hungry after the exertions of last night. He ate ham, eggs, scones and porridge with a large pot of black tea.

When he was finished eating he walked out of the Base Court and turned right and strolled along the Thames to the Outer Court where the Confectory was located. He wanted to talk with Ellen Iverson in her own environment. The river was misty but he enjoyed the short walk to the older frame buildings. The Confectory was pleasantly warm after his brief walk in the mist.

"Come in Sir and have some marzipan," Ellen Iverson said with a large spoon in hand as she wiped the sweat and a lock of hair from her forehead. "I don't know you, and I make it a point to know everyone."

"I'm Sir Seamus Weatherby, special envoy to King Henry VIII," Weatherby said in a self-important voice.

"Are you married?" Ellen Iverson shot back.

"What an impertinent question, madam," Sir Weatherby responded. "I decline to answer."

"You were seen at The White Swan last night. At least it is the more reputable of our two brothels. But a man of your age taking two young strumpets in the space of an hour is a bit unseemly, don't you think?"

"I believe our conversation is over," Sir Weatherby said in a flustered voice.

While he had come to terms with his sexual appetite, he wasn't pleased that someone he barely knew had detailed information about his exploits.

Slowly stirring a large copper pot of custard, Ellen said, "Suit yourself, Your Grace. However, I believe you are the one that requested this interview."

Sir Weatherby stormed toward the worn Dutch door, but just as he put his hand on the handle and looked out through the open upper half, he thought better of it. He walked back to the large marble table and picked up another piece of marzipan. He ate it slowly without saying a word. Once he was back in control of himself he turned toward Ellen Iverson.

"What can you tell me about William Suffolk?" he said in his blandest voice.

"An unhappy young man, Your Grace and not just about his birth. Of course, he felt he was just a few pregnancies from being an Earl. Had he been the first son, he would have been one of the wealthiest men in the realm. He knows he would have had all the servants, land, women and horses that a man could ever want. He would have had a life of complete leisure. Instead, he had little, worked for a pittance, and was shown very little respect. He was handsome enough, smart and educated. Not surprisingly, he spoke well but he didn't smile often and I never saw him laugh. He approached two women during his first year here and both of them turned him down flat."

"Did you notice any changes during his tenure here?"

"By all accounts he was an exceptional architect, and I think that sustained him at first," Ellen Iverson said. "He received a lot of attention and praise for the brilliance of his work and initially it seemed to be enough for him. Then he became less focused. He was absent for several days at a time. During most of those absences I think he made long trips to the south coast of England."

"What was the purpose if these trips?"

"That is something that I don't know. I know everything that happens within the Palace and the village of Hampton. I know a lot about the surrounding villages of Weybridge, Escher, Chertsey, and Kingston, but my knowledge stops there. Here at the Palace, William Suffolk became caught up with the people of the undercroft. Do you know about their subculture?"

"Somewhat. In an effort to solve the first murder I was trying to find the underbelly of Hampton Court where gambling, thievery, harlotry and graft held sway. I stumbled down there one day during my quest," Sir Weatherby replied.

"It's a mix of lowly employees that remove garbage and manure from Hampton Court, the mentally deficient, beggars and thieves. They are often involved in petty crimes. What William got there was a way to dispose of the building materials he was stealing from Sir Moulton's projects."

"I met his shill when I explored the undercroft."

"Yes. His name is Billy and he is the pettiest of crooks. Billy took the valuable supplies to Thomas Croft at Oatlands, received money and returned it to William."

"Why did William Suffolk suddenly need these sums of money and what did he do with them?"

"I believe he took it to the south coast and came back without it, but I don't know that for a fact. Let me contact some people I know in the coastal region," Ellen Iverson said as she began to pour the smooth, hot, vanilla custard into pots.

"I would appreciate that," Sir Weatherby said as he turned toward the door.

It was warmer outside now, and the mist had lifted from the Thames. A pair of mute swans swam slowly upstream in the sparking water. He walked leisurely from the Outer Court back to Base Court to find Amarantha. She had just finished her interview with Judith Scotson, the junior assistant librarian.

"I want to hear about your morning," Amarantha called to him from several yards away.

"I'll have a picnic lunch sent to the orchard and meet you there in thirty minutes," Sir Weatherby called back.

He changed into some lighter clothes, as the air was warming quickly and there was no breeze. Amarantha found she was well accepted by the residents of the Palace, and had gradually come out of her disguise as Weatherby's aunt. On this spring day she was wearing a form fitting light green dress. Then he walked Amarantha around to the north side of the Palace along the impressive brick wall of the Great Kitchen to the orchard. As they sat down at their lunch table covered with linen, they looked out over the Palace fields that were just beginning to green up. To their left was a large tiltyard for one of Henry's favorite sports, jousting, and beyond that the Outer Court where Sir Weatherby had spent the forenoon.

"How was your morning?" Sir Weatherby asked.

"Puzzling, but I want to hear about yours first," Amarantha replied.

Sir Weatherby described Ellen Iverson in all her impertinence and the degree of her knowledge about everyone and everything that happened in and around the Palace, omitting her knowledge of his previous evening's activities. He also recited what he had learned about William Suffolk. His conclusion was that Suffolk had gotten mixed up in something illegal about six months ago, and that suddenly he had needed large sums of money. He also spoke about the victim's probable connection to the south coast of England, at least forty miles away.

"You've learned a lot," Amarantha replied.

They turned their chairs toward the sun and enjoyed a savory lunch while speaking little. Sir Weatherby ordered two bottles of Rhenish wine for their meal. They both had large bowls of cream of leek soup followed by plates of veal and parsnips. When they were finished they pushed their chairs back and enjoyed the rest of the wine. Neither of them spoke about the horseback ride of the previous evening or their intimate embrace.

# CHAPTER 17

Setting his wine glass on the table Sir Weatherby said, "Now I want to hear about your interviews with the other librarians, Ran."

"I'm sure they weren't as entertaining as your visit with Ellen Iverson, the Palace gossip," Amarantha began. "I talked with Judith Scotson first. She had only worked in the library for three years. She had a genuine affection for Anna Maria Wimbledon who was mentoring her work. Judith told her boss everything and often asked her advice about personal matters. In return, Miss Wimbledon seemed open, often telling Judith about her relationships with other Palace staff and when she was approached by young suitors. Judith thought the combination of Miss Wimbledon's beautiful face and pleasant smile garnered lots of attention from the swains of the Palace and the village. Anna Maria seemed bemused."

"Were any of these beaus serious or different in any way?"

"Yes. Judith reports that there was a dark-complexioned young man that she saw last summer. He was from the village but worked frequently at the Palace. He spoke English with an accent that she couldn't characterize. Anna Maria told Judith that she liked him, and often blushed when she talked of him. The three librarians had often go gathered in one of their rooms in the evening to sew or read, but starting in September, Anna Maria was sometimes absent from their group."

"What else do we know about this man?"

"Not very much. She never heard his name or if she did she forgot it, and Judith hasn't seen him in three months. She is certain she would recognize him if she saw him again."

"I think you have stumbled on something important, Ran," Sir Weatherby observed. "Unfortunately, it won't be easy to follow up. What about the other more senior assistant?"

"I had my hopes pinned on Margaret Sedgwick. She seemed older and smarter. I thought I would learn a lot about the victim from talking with her. In reality, she was much harder to interview. She had worked in the library for seven years and had learned most of the tasks. She often did projects on her own with little input from Anna Maria. During their first six years together they were inseparable. They were like twins or sisters. I almost suspect an unnatural attraction of Margaret toward Anna Maria and . . ."

A servant ran into the orchard yelling at the two, "Your Lordship. There has been an explosion and a fire! Come quickly!"

Amarantha and Sir Weatherby jumped up and followed the servant. Weatherby was worried that this was an additional act of the murderers and that another corpse would be the result.

"Where was the explosion, my man?" Sir Weatherby shouted as he ran.

"First floor of the Clock Court west side, Your Grace."

"But that's where our laboratory is located!" Amarantha yelled.

"That's where the fire is, Mum."

Sir Weatherby and Amarantha broke into a full run. They cut through the Serving Place and Privy Cellar and spilled out into the Clock Court. Smoke was still coming from the windows of the laboratory. Dredge, covered with soot, lay in the grass attended by one of the serving girls. Sir Weatherby ran over and knelt down. He found a strong pulse and regular breathing. Dredge had several cuts on his face and arm, but all were superficial.

"Are you in pain?" Sir Weatherby asked.

"No, Your Grace. Just embarrassed, Sir. I was mixing *aqua regia* and it occupied my full attention because it is so corrosive. I simply forgot that I was heating some camphorate wax. It got too hot and exploded."

A small amount of smoke still came from one of the windows as the fire brigade carried leather pails full of sand into the laboratory. England had had fire brigades under the Romans, but they were disbanded when the Romans left in 415 AD. A great fire ravaged London in 1212 with the loss of over three thousand lives. Apparently, Henry VIII had decided that fire brigades were a good idea and he reinstituted them for all his many properties.

"I'm glad your injuries aren't worse," Sir Weatherby replied.

"I need to get back in there, Sir," Dredge said in a weak voice.

"You need to rest," Amarantha replied.

"There are some dangerous chemicals and delicate models that need to be put away first," Dredge retorted.

"With a little direction from you, Amarantha and I can do that," Sir Weatherby said.

After Dredge was back on his feet, the three walked toward the laboratory with the injured party supported between them. Inside the smoke made them all cough and it was hard to see. Following the amanuensis's direction the few delicate and dangerous things were soon stored in cabinets. Sir Weatherby was pleased to see that none of their valuable collection of books had been damaged by the explosion or smoke. Next, Sir Weatherby cleaned and bandaged all of the Dredge's cuts. He and Amarantha helped Dredge to his pallet in the servant's quarters and brought him food and drink. Finally, the two of them went to the Wolsey Apartments and sat on a long settee.

"I need to hear about the rest of your interview, Ran," Sir Weatherby said.

"First I need to get out of these smoky clothes."

She went to her apartment and changed out of her form-fitting light green dress. The dress had a large bow at her back in the French fashion. The front was low cut and showed off the top of her shapely white breasts. Influenced by France, low-cut gowns had recently become the fashion and were favored by Henry VIII who was an admirer of the female bosom. The red color set off her wavy red hair. When she returned, Sir Weatherby took in her new appearance with his eyes, but made no comment. He offered her a seat and a glass of Scotch.

"I told you about Judith Scotson and I had started on my interview with Margaret Sedgwick. I told you I thought she had an unnatural attachment to Anna Maria. I say this because of the wistful, longing way that she talked about the victim. She did notice two places in the library where Anna Maria spent an inordinate amount of time. I will search those two areas thoroughly to see if she hid any writings, letters, or messages there. I also think there is a chance she will open up to me, but unlike Judith, it will take me some time to get close to her. Up until about six months ago the three librarians spent most evenings together. Then Miss Wimbledon withdrew from the group. They even went to the Lamb and Flag together on occasion. I will see if I can reinitiate those evening get togethers."

"It's been two weeks since the first murder, Ran, and I am not close to solving this case. I don't know who murdered William Suffolk. I suspect that the killer was tall and that he used a mallet to kill his victim with a single blow. I know our victim had taken to stealing materials from the Palace, but I don't know why he needed the money. Although William had been acting strange for six months, I am baffled as to why someone would want to kill him. Religion, politics and passion come to mind, but I have no rational reason to pick one over the other right now."

"What can I do to help you solve this case?" Amarantha asked.

"I think I have to make the next step toward its solution."

"Perhaps you need to lean on the two tall mallet-owning construction workers or Nathaniel Philbrick."

"Good idea. I think I need to talk to the dead man's fence also."

"I think your bigger problem is Anna Maria's murderer," Amarantha interjected. "She was pretty, smart, thoughtful, kind and well-liked. I find her murder inexplicable. This murder was premeditated, and I don't understand how anyone could have committed it."

"She wasn't without blemish or she wouldn't have been sixteen weeks pregnant. Anna Maria had a secret life that we haven't uncovered yet."

"If only we had a test that would tell us if the person who raped her was the same person that impregnated her," Amarantha mused.

"Someday they will have such a test," Sir Weatherby replied.

Sir Weatherby and Amarantha ate a light cold supper. Then Amarantha took a plate of food to Dredge in the servant's quarter. She found him much better after resting for a few hours. Sir Weatherby and Amarantha spent the evening reading in the new first floor of the Bayne Tower before a large fire. At midnight Sir Weatherby walked Amarantha to her apartment and then wandered down the hall to his own apartment. He dreamed of another horseback ride with Amarantha, which helped him, sleep well.

# CHAPTER 18

Sir Weatherby had urgent personal business in the city. Whitehall was in an uproar over two murders in such a short time frame at one of their foremost properties. Sir Weatherby would report his progress on solving the deaths to the King's Chancellor, and attend to his private dealings. Before leaving, Seamus had Amarantha and Dredge provide him with a list of things that they needed from the city. While there he would also consult with Dr. Richard Talbot his old chief at the London Gaol about the complexity of his murder cases. The two had worked together successfully to solve many difficult and convoluted crimes in London.

Sir Weatherby awoke at 4 a.m. He ate a quick breakfast and then walked to the Water Gallery, a two story brick building with a crenellated top, to the west of the Palace. The wooden landing stage extending out over the Thames was made of stained oak boards and creaked with every step. King Henry's barge was tied up at the dock. Sir Weatherby boarded the gently rocking craft as he stifled a yawn, and took a seat in the stern. A few more sleepy passengers came aboard before the barge was untied and drifted out into the Thames where the current was swifter. The sleek wooden boat was forty feet long with brightly varnished gunwales and gold and red trim painted on the sideboards. The front two thirds of the craft was occupied by ten oarsmen sitting on open benches with twenty foot long oars painted white. The helmsman stood in the rear of craft with his hand on the tiller. A small shelter with six seats occupied the last third of the barge. The wooden roof was supported by varnished pillars at each corner with red velvet curtains to keep out the weather.

At Hampton, located above the tide, the Thames flowed toward London at three knots per hour. At the next town downriver, the tide from the North Sea, ninety miles away, came into play. The town at that salty river location was called 'tide end town' or Teddington. The voyage was timed for the full tide that peaked at 1 a.m. that morning, following the full moon, to carry the barge swiftly on the falling tide to London. When he first came to Hampton Court he had ridden all night in a hansom on the post road. He had enquired at Whitehall Palace, and found that the road was the fasted way to travel west to the Palace. However, going the opposite way, despite its many twists and turns, if the tide was right, the Thames, flowing downstream, was much faster.

Sir Weatherby sat comfortably in one of the six plush seats as the oars pulled the barge downstream in the dark. Within a half an hour the sky started to lighten in the east. For the first time, Sir Weatherby noticed the only other passenger sitting on the starboard side. He looked vaguely familiar.

"I say. I'm Sir Seamus Weatherby," Weatherby called out. "I don't believe we've met."

"I'm Christopher Dickinson, Master Mason to Henry VIII."

The barge was passing Teddington and surged forward with the outgoing tide. A pair of crested grebes mated noisily along the shoreline.

"You are responsible for designing new venues at Hampton Court Palace," Sir Weatherby replied.

"Yes. Currently, I am laying out the last touches of the Great Hall in my tracing room. It will have an ornate heraldic ceiling with hammerhead beams and decorated with heads, pendants, badges and spandrels. The colors will be gold, blue and green. The floor will be oak with a tile border. Right now I'm designing a stone hearth for the middle of the room. The room will have louvers in the ceiling so the smoke may escape." Christopher Dickinson paused sheepishly, "But I'm sure I'm boring you with things architectural."

"Quite the contrary," Sir Weatherby replied. "Sir John Moulton has educated me a bit, and I find the subject quite fascinating. I even know what a hammerhead beam is, and that it was developed by one of your brilliant predecessors, Hugh Herland. The one term I find I don't understand is spandrel."

"It's the triangular space between the outside curve of an arch and the adjacent wall and ceiling," Dickinson replied smiling, pleased by Weatherby's interest.

"I would love to see your tracings," Sir Weatherby ventured.

"I will be back at Hampton Court in two weeks and we can spend some time pouring over them."

Sir Weatherby decided to seize the moment and declared, "I'm at Hampton Court to investigate the death of William Suffolk. Did you know him?"

"Of course. He was our most brilliant young architect. I used his window and door treatments in most of my designs. His death was a loss to the design team and to me personally."

"Did you have more than a professional relationship with him?"

Both stopped talking to look at the river as the barge accelerated noisily past a small island near Twickenham.

As the boat slowed again by Richmond, Christopher Dickinson answered, "He was more than an acquaintance but less than a friend, I suppose. I was shocked by his murder. We don't have a violent community at the Palace, let alone a murderous one."

"What things did you do together?"

"We spent hours pouring over tracings and drawings for the Palace. Sometimes at the end of the day we had supper together or went to the Flag and Lamb for a pint. He seemed quite satisfied the first year he was at Hampton Court. Then rather abruptly, last fall, suddenly, he changed. He became more introspective, which I thought was a good thing. However, all he wanted to talk about was politics and religion rather than art and architecture."

"Any particular politics?"

"Just the issues all of us are worried about. As you well know, Henry VIII was crowned in 1509. He married Catherine of Aragon two weeks before his coronation. She had been the wife of Henry's older brother, Arthur, before he died suddenly of a fever. Catherine and Arthur were very much in love and a very lusty couple, even though Catherine avowed to Henry that they had never consummated their marriage. Perhaps she sensed that she needed to lie about her sexual past to keep her head. As everyone knows, Queen Catherine had two still born daughters and two short-lived sons by Henry, followed by a daughter who survived. Now, twenty-one years later Henry is thirty-nine and beginning to recognize that he hasn't produced a viable heir for the Tudor line. His daughter Mary, being a woman, can never be the ruler of England. Henry blames Catherine for not producing a robust son. I believe we know that the woman determines the sex of the child, don't we Sir Weatherby?"

"That is what I was taught in medical school," agreed Weatherby.

"Besides, Henry had a healthy boy with his mistress, a married woman named Lady Elizabeth Blount."

Tired of talking, both travelers sat quietly for a while. They looked at the passing river scene alive with birds and river otters. Large marshes lined both sides of the Thames in this area. The trees along the bank were fully green now and came in a variety of shapes particularly as they passed Kew Park. They passed the quaint villages of Chiswick and Putney now traveling at almost five knots. Due to the strong tide, the oars were almost superfluous and used mostly for steering. Sir Weatherby knew that the tide was twenty-one feet high at Southwark just opposite London town. He also knew in the Thames, the flood tide becomes progressively shorter and the ebb tide progressively longer the further upstream you go. In other words, the upper reaches fill quicker than they emptied slowing the course of the barge just a bit.

Suddenly, Christopher Dickinson resumed his oration, "So our liege claims that God is punishing him by not giving him a son because he married his brother's wife. Apparently there is a passage in Leviticus forbidding such a marriage. However, I suspect the real reason is Catherine has reached menopause, and can have no more sons. Now, Henry lusts after Anne Boleyn just as he lusted after and bedded her sister Mary. Anne was twenty-one when Henry began to pursue her."

"What does all of this have to do with William Suffolk?" Sir Weatherby asked somewhat impatiently.

"I do prattle on, but every real Englishman loves to gossip about the royals," Dickinson replied. "William Suffolk took it all very personally. He was a devout Catholic and feared for the future of his religion. Anne Boleyn and her father Thomas are rabid Protestants. William at first hoped that the King would tire of Anne as he had of every other mistress, but Anne was smarter and simply teased the King rather than letting him bed her. Her sister, Mary, had made that mistake and had become known as the King's whore. William told me all of his fears one night at the Lamb and Flag. Shortly after that he began missing working and taking trips to the south coast."

"Do you know exactly where he went or with whom he met?"

"Unfortunately, no. He never told me the details."

"So you think this unlucky young man was murdered because of religious fervor and the acts he was impelled to commit?"

"Yes, I do." Christopher Dickinson replied thoughtfully.

"I'm glad I happened across you this morning," Sir Weatherby replied, shifting his gaze to the river.

The barge was still moving rapidly downstream as it entered the outskirts of London. Houses and wharves were now frequent with little space between them. Sir Weatherby recognized Battersea and then Chelsea as the Thames widened and the curves straightened. The bustling, dirty and smoking town of London with seventy thousand inhabitants was all around him now. Despite its squalor, poverty and susceptibility to fire and disease he found London town an exciting place to be. For the first time during the trip, there were other ships on the river heading either up and down stream. The oarsmen began to pull hard again and to guide the barge to the port shore despite the strong current. The barge stopped at Westminster and all the passengers except Sir Weatherby, disembarked. He wished Dickinson a pleasant visit.

Once the lines were retrieved the barge surged downriver again, rapidly gaining speed. They traversed the area known as King's Reach and then made a sharp turn toward starboard. A long broad stretch of river lay in front of them with London Bridge, a city landmark in place since Roman times five hundred yards away. The King's bargemen stopped just short of the bridge. Once the lines were secure, Sir Weatherby strode across the dock and up a cobbled street where a line of hansoms waited. He hailed the first one giving the driver a nearby address, and settled on the worn, cracked leather seat inside.

It was only 8 a.m. and Weatherby had traveled nine miles as the crow flies. However, the river trip had covered eighteen miles, twice that distance, with most of the journey in the tortuous upper reaches of the Thames.

# CHAPTER 19

The hansom stopped at number 177D Threadneedle Street, a three-tory building, in an old but bustling part of London. Sir Weatherby put a foot through the door after it was opened by the driver and pressed angels into the coachman's palm. Allowed to live in Whitehall Palace because of his station, Sir Weatherby preferred the privacy of his own apartment. Seamus had the whole third floor of this venerable stone building to himself. Since it was the top story, it had tall windows that admitted a lot of light. There was room for all of his books and a laboratory twice as big as the one Dredge had built at Hampton Court. Mrs. Pansy, his housekeeper, kept everything clean and dusted even when Sir Weatherby was away for several weeks. This morning she busied herself fixing some breakfast for her employer.

"Anything exciting happen in the last two weeks, Mrs. Pansy," Sir Weatherby asked as he sat down to a plate of hot sausage and eggs.

"No, Sir. Nice spring weather this. Oh, the family on two tried to put a bay window on the south side of the building but all the other residents objected. Also, I caught two rats while you were gone."

Sir Weatherby gave the housekeeper both Amarantha and Dredge's list of wants from the city. Mrs. Pansy was a good soul, and an excellent housekeeper, Sir Weatherby thought, but her conversation was so trivial that he usually sought solace in a book. After he finished eating he changed to a more formal jerkin and took a hansom to Whitehall Palace. He was early for his meeting with the Chancellor so he visited with a friend who staged plays and musicals for the King. At ten o'clock he was shown into the offices of Thomas Cromwell, the King's new chancellor. Henry had recently stripped Cardinal Thomas Wolsey of the

Chancellorship when the Cardinal was unable to secure a divorce for Henry from Pope Clement VII.

Cromwell was very a capable and efficient administrator, and Sir Weatherby was shown into his office promptly. The Chancellor sat at a large maple desk and signed documents, throughout the interview, with a quill that was placed before him by a clerk.

"Thank you for coming to Whitehall to give me a report, Seamus," Cromwell said as he looked up.

"It's my pleasure, Your Lordship," Sir Weatherby replied. "I just wish the news was better."

"As you know, the King has invested a great deal in Hampton Court since he acquired it from Cardinal Wolsey. Even before his new additions are complete, it is the King's most extensive palace from among the nearly sixty that he owns. Obviously, he is concerned that two murders have occurred there in such a short space of time. Have you apprehended a suspect?"

"I'm afraid not, Your Lordship. But we do have leads that we are pursuing vigorously."

"May I tell his majesty that the crimes will be solved in a fortnight?"

"I fervently hope so, but it may take more time than that to bring these deeds to a resolution. Of the fifty or so murders that I have investigated for the King, so far, these two have proved the most vexing. I will, of course, report frequently on my progress to you, Lord Chancellor."

Sir Weatherby rose and backed out of the chamber, bowing as he went. He felt that he had escaped severe castigation, perhaps because Thomas Cromwell was preoccupied. He knew that he had made very little progress solving either case, and he had expected a vicious tongue-lashing. As he walked out of Whitehall he hailed a hansom and headed to an address on Whitefriars Street near the infamous Newgate Prison, where public hangings were held. Sir Weatherby's personal barrister had a second story office there.

William Bruce was an ancient Scottish attorney that had practiced in London for fifty years. Sir Weatherby had found him through the recommendation of his mentor at the University of Edinburgh. William Bruce had proved ethical, conservative, colorful, and quite humorous over the years, and Sir Weatherby trusted him implicitly.

When Sir Weatherby had practiced surgery, just after graduation, in a small town in southern Scotland, he had put his money in the Bank of

Dumfries. He was frugal and his account grew by several pounds a month. Then in his fourth year of practice, a rumor about a bad loan caused a run on the bank and it failed within seven hours. The bank kept less than ten percent of its funds within its walls, as was the practice then. The rest of the money was loaned out-earning interest. Sir Weatherby was not one of the first few creditors to enter the bank and he lost everything. Since then he had always invested only in land because Weatherby felt that it couldn't vanish into thin air. Earlier that week, he had received an urgent message from William Bruce, which prompted his visit to town. The office was old and dusty with no clerk at the front desk. Sir Weatherby knocked and upon getting no reply walked in.

"Top of the morning to you, Seamus," William Bruce roared pushing a green eye shade off of his forehead. "You don't resemble the prosperous and handsome investigator the gossipy Ladies-in-Waiting at Whitehall speak about."

"I'm not feeling very prosperous these days, Mr. Bruce. I'm afraid I'm not making much progress on my current double murder," Sir Weatherby replied dejectedly.

"A bit like a gluttonous woman who can't squeeze her bum through a doorway even if naked and greased, are you?"

"A very unpleasant, if comical image, but quite apt."

"I'm afraid I only have more bad news. After you hear it you could throw yourself in the Thames, however the tide is out for seven more hours and you'd end up stuck in the mud like a disconsolate clam."

"What, pray tell, is the bad news?"

"There was a drought in southern Scotland last summer, as you know, and unfortunately one of your leaseholds didn't sell his livestock in time. He lived through the winter eating his seed stock and had nothing to plant last month. My overseer reports he, his wife and his six ragamuffin children decamped last week. I dare say, he needed to spend more time furrowing his fields and less time furrowing his wife. You owe the bank a mortgage payment on that farm. The three adjacent properties you own were better managed and the renters will survive unless there is another drought this summer."

"How much do I owe?"

"The bank wants a payment of £ 68 but will settle for half and loan you the rest at the usurious rate of twenty-five percent interest per year. The silver lining, as you know, is that a Scottish pound is only valued at a quarter of an English pound."

"How I hate the smug bankers and their grasping ways. I brought you twelve English pounds that I had been saving for a rainy, or in this case for a dry, parched series of days," Sir Weatherby said as he placed a pouch full of coins noisily on the barrister's desk.

"This will go a long way toward assuaging the problem," William Bruce replied, placing the pouch in his desk. "Let's have lunch."

The two walked out into Whitefriars Street, squinting from the sudden brightness. The bustling sidewalk was crowded with Londoners and quite slimy thanks to their waste thrown out of upstairs windows. It was very noisy from hawkers selling wares and the clatter of iron rimmed carts on the cobbled street. The twisty old road was packed with carriages pulled by one or two horses. Sir Weatherby took his barrister's arm and guided him across the street to Ye Olde Waiting, a pub where the lawyer was well known. They both ordered fried eels and a stout called Old Peculier. They talked of Scotland and of their fair country being trapped under the English yoke. When they were done eating, Sir Weatherby bid his attorney adieu, and took a hansom back to his apartment.

Mrs. Pansy had placed all of his mail neatly on his desk and he spent two hours reading it and cataloguing it for Dredge. Next, he spent some time looking in his books for a poison with the smell of bitter roses, but had no success. He found a hundred year old bottle of French Bordeaux and drank a glass after which he took a nap on his own padded sofa. When he awoke the afternoon sunlight was playing on the back part of his office where the sofa was situated. A play by Molière, *The School for Wives,* was being performed that evening at Whitehall Palace and Sir Weatherby planned to attend, so he forced himself to get up and get dressed.

Sir Weatherby usually dressed well but very conservatively. He favored black, brown and dark blue clothing. He seldom gave in to the fashion of the day and rarely wore the popular necklaces men wore that were made of gold and jewels that rested on the shoulders and came down over the breastbone in the front. However, tonight, Sir Weatherby chose a flashier outfit. He pulled on gold leggings and a bronze colored doublet and jacket. The jacket had slashes, on the arms, in the German fashion, that revealed patches of bright blue satin underneath.

He arrived early for dinner in the great dining room at Whitehall Palace where places had been set for at least one hundred and forty diners, Sir Weatherby estimated. The King and Queen, arriving late as usual, were seated at an elevated table at the head of the room, so all the guests could see them. Anne Boleyn was placed near the head table within the King's gaze in a tight red satin dress that highlighted her small waist and pushed the top of her white breasts defiantly into view. Sir Weatherby noted her small pixie-like face with slightly pointed nose and small pouty mouth. He observed that she was attractive, but certainly not beautiful. In fact, she wasn't as pretty as many of the Ladies-in-Waiting or even her older sister Mary Boleyn. Anne's best feature was her alluring and engaging black eyes. Sir Weatherby realized, with a start, that England might be thrown into revolt or even civil war over the King's lust for this unintelligent but conniving lass.

Dinner consisted of large joints of mutton. Servants in the King's livery cut large pieces of meat off of a trolley onto each guest's plates. Large platters of vegetables were passed around and huge fowl pies four feet in diameter were carried steaming to the center of the room and then opened to rounds of applause. Music was provided by a wooden flute, a viola da gamba, a drum, and a lute. Sir Weatherby visited with courtiers he had become acquainted with over the years.

After their meal and a great deal of drinking, the guests adjourned to the great hall for the play. *The School for Wives* was performed in Italian by a troupe from Venice. Sir Weatherby followed the dialogue easily because his medical training had all been in Latin, which was very similar to modern Italian, but most of the audience seemed perplexed by the words. At the conclusion of the play Sir Weatherby walked part way home, then changing his mind, climbed into a hansom and headed across London Bridge to his favorite pub, the Anchor, in Southwark. Some of his cronies from his former employment at the constable's office were there at a center table. After three tankards of ale, raucous conversation, and several losing games of dice the King's premier detective wobbled home. He slept well in his own bed. He hadn't had his terrifying nightmare in over a week.

# CHAPTER 20

Friday morning, the third day before Ides, in April, Sir Weatherby rose early. Mrs. Pansy had already made a hearty breakfast. While he ate Weatherby mused on the two systems for keeping track of the days. The more modern system simply numbered the days so today was Sunday, April 10th, 1530. However most of the country people and witnesses he interviewed used the medieval system that divided each month into three parts—Nones, Ides and Kalends. By that system the Ides of April was the thirteenth so today was known as three days before the Ides.

Mrs. Pansy broke into his daydreaming. She gave her employer a small package for Amarantha and a larger one for Dredge. After eating, Sir Weatherby walked to a nearby stable. It was time to return to Hampton Court. The barge trip back, while it would be pleasant, would take the better part of two days because of the unfavorable current. He usually traveled by carriage, but he had been stung by his very rusty and clumsy horsemanship during the hailstorm ride with Amarantha. He decided to ride back to the Palace.

When he got to the stable a large roan gelding was saddled and waiting for him. He placed his few possessions and the packages in the saddlebags. The stable owner helped him mount the horse and Sir Weatherby set off at a walk heading west through the crowded streets toward London Bridge. A long line of carts, carriages and riders were waiting in a disorderly queue to cross to the south side of the river. Built by the Romans, it was the only way across the river save a ferry and travelers went miles out of the way to walk or ride across the Thames. He traveled across London Bridge at a very slow walk to Southwark and then headed further south to the Escher Pike, which followed an old

Roman road. Traffic was heavy for the first hour but then began to thin out. Horse and rider started to make good time. As they continued through woodlands and past fields the traffic became very light. The road was straight and mostly cobbled, and when Sir Weatherby stopped for lunch at a tavern he was already more than half way to Hampton Court.

After eating and resting his horse Sir Weatherby took the next three miles at a gallop. The road was wide and flat and ran through a tall beech forest. After his gallop, Sir Weatherby walked his steed the last two miles to Hampton Court Palace. He entered the Great Gatehouse five hours after leaving his apartment. The ride had been enjoyable. He liked being in control of his own passage. He pulled up in the Base Court and gave the reins of his horse to a servant. He had his luggage and packages taken to his apartment. Sir Weatherby sought out Amarantha first and found her working on some papers in the Wolsey Apartments.

"Welcome back, Seamus," Amarantha said in a delighted voice when she caught sight of the tall angular man. "How was your trip?"

"The barge trip downriver was idyllic and quick. I had never seen many stretches of the Thames. What a great river. There are huge marshes along both sides. It changes at every bend and it's full of wildlife. Plus, as a little bonus, I got to talk with Christopher Dickinson, the Master Mason, about Suffolk. He happened to be on the Royal Barge. He does go on and on once he starts talking. The ride back along the Southwark to Escher Pike was a contrast. I had a good, strong mount and the road was in good condition, dry without washouts. I don't think I've ever been atop a horse for such a long period. I'm sore but quite content. I'm amazed at being able to visit a distant city one day and come back the next day before sunset."

"I'll wager that you're famished," Amarantha replied. "Let me order you some food. While we are waiting let me rub your neck, shoulders and back."

Sir Weatherby slipped off his great coat and jerkin and sat willingly on a chaise. Amarantha's hands were small but surprisingly strong. She used a balm he had bought for her in the city to sooth his sore muscles.

"What happened while I was gone?" Sir Weatherby asked.

"Very little. Dredge seems fully recovered from the explosion. His cuts are healing nicely. I spent the day with Judith Scotson searching the library to no avail. I've never seen so many dusty, old books. One of the Office of the Green Cloth ladies disappeared. I'm not sure which one and no one seems to know why."

"I'm sure Ellen Iverson can help with that."

A plate of pickles and cheese with a tankard of ale arrived. Sir Weatherby slipped his jerkin back on.

"Thanks for the massage."

"It's the least I could do after you rubbed me back to life following the hailstorm. I had never been that cold in my life. I played in the snow for hours when I was a child in Wales and refused to come in until I was numb, but I wasn't half as cold as the other day when you held me," Amarantha said as she looked hopefully at Weatherby.

Ignoring her references to holding her, Weatherby replied, "There was something about the rain squalls and wind that went right to my core as well."

"I'm going back to the library to resume my search," Amarantha said in a wistful voice.

"Thank you for the food. Now that I'm refreshed I need to talk with Gregory Townsend the self-styled Protestant preacher. Christopher Dickinson, Sir John Moulton and Ellen Iverson all feel that religion is mixed in this murderous stew, and I need to figure out how."

Amarantha and Sir Weatherby both left the Wolsey Apartment heading in opposite directions. Sir Weatherby walked to the stables where Townsend worked. As he approached the stable yard, he quickly calculated that there was room for over eighty horses. Today several horses and grooms were in the area in front of the stalls. Horses were being shod, brushed and curried. Sir Weatherby asked after Gregory Townsend and was directed through the large opening that led to the stalls. He found the stableman in a small office in a corner of the stable. As he entered the office, Townsend looked up.

"Gregory Townsend, I am Sir Seamus Weatherby and I was sent here by the King to investigate the recent murders at the Palace. What can you tell me about them?" Sir Weatherby intoned.

"Peace be with you brother," Gregory Townsend replied. "I am a man of God and know nothing of what you speak."

"You are an uneducated, self-appointed, and pretentious so-called man of God," Sir Weatherby thundered back. "So cut your pompous acting."

"Forgive him Lord, for he knows not what he says," Gregory Townsend said as he fell to his knees in a prayerful stance.

Sir Weatherby stepped forward in a rage and struck the kneeling man in the face with his fist. Townsend toppled over sideways and lay still.

"I have the full authority and confidence of your employer Richard Weston, the Master of the House. I can put you in a cell until you are old, arthritic, and grey without ever having to charge you with any misdeed. Now get a grip and start answering my questions."

Gregory Townsend worked himself slowly onto his hands and knees and then into a sitting position.

Townsend began to speak in a barely audible voice, "I knew Anna Maria Wimbledon, and may her soul rest in peace. She was a member of my fellowship and believed in the teachings of Martin Luther. As an orphan she was raised, against her will, as a Catholic. She renounced that corrupt, ancient religion and embraced a new cleaner faith."

Sir Weatherby realized he was still being told more about religion than about his victim. He considered delivering another blow, but instead stepped forward threateningly.

"Did you or one of your congregation murder this beautiful young woman?" Sir Weatherby asked menacingly.

"Most certainly not. We read the Bible in English now and in the book of Exodus, chapter twenty, it says, 'thou shalt not kill.'"

"Anna Maria Wimbledon was pregnant when she was murdered," Sir Weatherby shot back. "Did you have knowledge of that?"

"That cannot be true. She was the purest of women and without stain."

"In the new testament, chapter three of Colossians, verse five, Paul's letter forbids intercourse before marriage," Weatherby offered.

"You know the Bible," Townsend replied. "What are your religious beliefs?"

"That isn't your business, but just so you know, although I have studied the Bible carefully, I find all religion a dangerous fiction. Who impregnated Miss Wimbledon?"

"I don't know. I know it wasn't a member of my congregation. I saw her twice, while I was on errands around the Palace with a dark complected young man, but I don't know his name."

"I have given you a lot of information about Anna Maria, Townsend," Sir Weatherby said in a loud voice. "And you have given me very little back. I will clap you in irons for a few weeks and see if that loosens your tongue."

"She was impure!" Townsend said in a rush. "She was raised at Hampton Court as an orphan. All the young girls without families slept in a half finished dormitory under the eves. Their chaperone was a deaf woman who was a heavy sleeper. Young men in their late teens snuck into the dormitory with some regularity to flirt and diddle the girls. Anna Maria started allowing young men into her bed when she was eleven. She liked the treats she received, at first candy and then later kittens and toys. When she got older they brought her clothes, jewelry and sometimes even money."

"She was eight and twenty when she died. Did her promiscuity continue into her twenties?"

"Yes, while she was a Catholic. She had relations almost regularly and confessed her sin on Sunday so she could begin anew on Monday. As you know our months are divided into 'before Nones' for the first days of the month, 'before Ides' leading up to middle of the month and then 'before Kalends' which led to the beginning of the next month. She never had relations before Ides and was quite proud of her restraint. When she joined my prayer group she confessed and then gave up all of that behavior."

"Do you know who she was having relations with just before she joined your congregation?"

"No, but I know who to ask."

"Get back to me with that information, please. What about William Suffolk? Could he have been her lover?"

"I believe the answer is no. However, his is a most bizarre and twisted story," Gregory Townsend said. "But now I must see to Richard Weston's mount. He will be here to ride at six of the clock and I daren't be late."

"Very well. I will stop by early tomorrow to resume our conversation," Sir Weatherby said as he rose and walked out of the stable office.

That evening Weatherby enjoyed a quiet dinner with Amarantha in her apartment and both spent the rest of the evening reading in front of the fire. Sir Weatherby had brought a new copy of Boccaccio's *Decameron* from his apartment and he read some passages to her. Finding the stories inventive, erotic, and enjoyable, he continued reading aloud long after midnight when his voice became hoarse. He stumbled down the hall to his own apartment and collapsed into bed.

At three a.m., deep in his dream of being chased by sinister men on three black steeds Sir Weatherby was suddenly awakened.

"We have found another body, Your Lordship!" Declared a servant standing at his bedside.

# PART 3

# CHAPTER 21

Sir Weatherby slowly awoke from a nightmare only to face another one. He pulled the nearest pair of pants over his nightshirt and rubbed the sleep from his eyes.

"Take me to him there at once," he intoned in a raspy voice. "And send someone to wake my associates."

The servant led the way along the Gallery and through a door into the Base Court. It was a dark, windless night. The lantern the servant carried cast a small circle of weak yellow light just beyond his feet. He looked up involuntarily at the imposing, five stories tall, Great Gate House. A form lay in the graveled courtyard. Warder Chertsey and Tobias, the night watchman stood nearby.

"Thank you for not disturbing the body," Sir Weatherby said. "Who found it?"

"I did, Sir," Tobias said. "I usually don't go this far out into the center of the Base Court, but I heard a muffled scream and went to investigate. That's when I found him."

"When was this?"

"About a half an hour ago, Your Grace."

"So about half past two. Did you touch the body?"

"No, Your Grace."

"Good man. Did you see or hear anything unusual?"

"No, except there was this strange squeaky sound almost like a wheel that needed grease, only more high-pitched."

Amarantha and Dredge arrived somewhat out of breath. Dredge carried a canvas bag full of instruments, which he placed near the body. Sir Weatherby approached the body and pushed the victim's cloak

115

away from his face, which was frozen in a look of contorted agony. He immediately recognized the face of the self-styled lay minister.

"The Gods be damned!" Sir Weatherby roared. "It's Gregory Townsend! I had learned a great deal about Anna Maria from him yesterday and was to talk to him his morning about William Suffolk. I should have forced him to keep talking. Damn Richard Weston and his infernal evening ride."

"But why would he commit suicide, Your Lordship?" Warder Chertsey asked.

"I wouldn't know, Warder. I was just getting to know the man, and know he had a lot of answers for me."

Dredge set up an easel so Sir Weatherby could sketch the position of the body and his facial expression. Townsend's face was drawn up in a look of horror that would be hard to dispel. Once Sir Weatherby was done drawing, Dredge helped him turn the dead man over onto his back. Clutched tight in Gregory Townsend's right hand was a worn brown leather volume that turned out to be his personal Bible.

"I don't understand why he would commit suicide," Warder Chertsey asked.

"Perhaps he couldn't wait any longer to see the pearly gates," Tobias answered.

Sir Weatherby silently checked the body through its clothing for broken bones. A dislocated shoulder. Both femurs, both tibias broken. It suggested to him that Townsend landed on his feet, but the force of falling eighty-three feet broke both legs. An autopsy would reveal if the victim's back was also broken. There were abrasions on eight of the preacher's fingertips. As he continued his examination, Amarantha and Dredge searched the area around the body for clues. They found some fibers, a splinter of wood and a small coin. They hoped these seemingly miscellaneous clues might be related to the crime and not to the horse and carriage traffic that went through the Great Gatehouse. Being naturally suspicious, Weatherby purposely avoided answering Warder Chertsey's repeated questions about suicide.

"Measure the distance from the center of the body to the base of the Great Gatehouse," Sir Weatherby instructed Dredge.

Dredge took a cloth tape out of satchel and with Amarantha's help measured the distance at forty-one feet, six inches. Dredge knew his master would use this information to create a geometry problem, so he suggested the next logical step.

"I will calculate the height of the tower by measuring a step and then multiplying that number by the number of steps, Sir," Dredge replied.

"Don't forget to add the height of the parapet at the top."

"No, sir."

"I'll go up to the parapet to look for clues." But before heading up, he turned to Warder Chertsey. "Please notify all the members of Gregory Townsend's Protestant congregation of a meeting in the Great Waiting Chamber in an hour."

"But, but it will be four of the clock by then, Your Grace."

"I am aware of the time, Warder," Sir Weatherby replied sharply. "Do you take me for an imbecile? I want to speak with them before they have a chance to construct an alibi, not that it is really any of your business."

"But clearly it was a suicide, and they are all fervently religious, Sir. None of them would violate the fourth commandment."

"Have you no knowledge of history? Millions upon millions of innocent men, women and children have been killed in the name of religion. It dwarfs the thousands taken by the sweating sickness and the Black Death. What's more, 'thou shalt not kill' is the sixth commandment, not the fourth."

Dredge and Amarantha had already departed, so Sir Weatherby walked toward the gate to inspect the parapet for clues. He motioned for two serving girls with large candelabras to follow him.

"Have the body taken to the coolest part of the Palace," Sir Weatherby called over his shoulder as he left the scene.

He pushed open the heavy oak door into the tower, and held it for the two young girls who both yawned as they entered the passageway. The anteroom was finished with brick walls; to the left side, a limestone stairway spiraled upward. He bounded up the steps ahead of the weak circle of candle light. Later, Dredge told him there were one hundred and three steps in the Great Gatehouse tower. When he reached the parapet at the top, he leaned against the lintel short of breath. He was pleased to see the young serving girls were more winded than he was.

Once his breathing slowed, Sir Weatherby pulled out his magnifying glass and got down on his hands and knees to examine the wooden floor. He collected some mud, a large drop of sticky material, and a small piece of brown cloth. He also found a streak of dried liquid on the inside of the parapet wall. He would have Dredge sample and analyze the material in the light of day. When he was finished, he ambled down the steps in a more leisurely fashion, checking each riser for anything unusual. He walked across the Base Court, up the steps and angled to the left toward the Great Waiting Chamber. As he approached he heard the murmur of voices.

Warder Chertsey had told Weatherby that the Great Waiting Chamber had a part for royalty and a part for commoners. The royal part had more windows and richer tapestries. The congregation had naturally settled in that more opulent end.

Seated on benches, placed in a large irregular circle were twenty-five to thirty men and women. Most congregants were in their twenties, and a good number were in their night clothes. Amarantha was speaking with each member and writing on a parchment as she went.

Sir Weatherby walked to the center of the circle and without preamble spoke, "The body of Gregory Townsend was found in the Base Court an hour ago. I need information from all of you who were close to him as to what transpired."

Many of the women burst into tears, and the men began speaking to each other in sad voices. Sir Weatherby allowed this cacophony for about a minute.

"Silence!" he boomed. "Who saw your Reverend last evening?"

"We had a midweek Bible study group last evening at seven," a young red headed woman answered meekly.

"Which of you attended?"

Nearly everyone in the circle folded their hands prayerfully in front of themselves and then raised a hand high in the air.

"Did anything untoward happen at that meeting?"

"We were studying the third chapter of the Book of Matthew and we had in a heated discussion, but we parted peaceably after the Reverend led us in a prayer," the red-headed woman replied.

"Did he mention my interview with him?"

"Perhaps indirectly. During his closing prayer he said Beelzebub lurked in the Palace and we must all pray daily for his defeat."

"Did preacher Townsend often speak of the Devil?"

"Yes, of course but this reference had more passion to it," the red-headed woman replied.

"You seem to be the one answering all of my questions, What is your name?"

"Sarah Brandon."

"Were you an officer in the congregation?"

"No. I was betrothed to Gregory Townsend. The banns had already been published and we were to marry in three weeks," Sarah said as she burst into tears.

"Had you quarreled recently?"

"No. We were very much in love and planning our wedding every day."

"This doesn't sound like a man who would leap from a tower. Do any of the rest of you know a reason for Reverend Townsend to kill himself?"

No one spoke. Most slowly shook their heads. Amarantha was finished collecting information from the Protestant congregation and joined Sir Weatherby at the side of the circle.

"Then perhaps he was murdered," Sir Weatherby said. "Who would have benefited from his murder?"

"He was a Christian who preached and practiced Matthew 5:43," Sarah responded.

"So you say that he loved his enemies? Please enumerate them for me."

"As the spokesman for the true religion, he was hated by many in the corrupt Catholic Church. Father Williams of Our Lady of Hampton was his most vicious and dogged critic. We heard he spoke against Protestantism and our spiritual father, Gregory Townsend, from his high pulpit nearly every week. However, the bishop and prelates in surrounding communities were also his sworn enemies."

"Had any of them threatened Gregory Townsend's life?"

"I never heard of such a threat other than Father Williams saying more than once that all Protestants should be declared heretics and burned at the stake."

Sir Weatherby turned to Amarantha and said in a low voice, "Do you have any questions?"

Amarantha shook her head while yawning.

"You are all dismissed," Sir Weatherby said as he looked around the circle. "But don't go far, as I may call you back at anytime."

The congregants slowly rose and shuffled out of the Great Waiting Chamber.

# CHAPTER 22

Amarantha and Sir Weatherby walked slowly out of the Great Waiting Room after the congregants left. They descended the stairs to the first floor wearily.

"Do you really believe one of the people in that room killed Gregory Townsend?" Amarantha asked between yawns.

"I rather doubt it," Sir Weatherby replied. "One of them may have had a quarrel with him but I don't think there was a murderous bone in the room. Besides, perhaps Warder Chertsey is right and it was a suicide."

"You don't believe that for a second, Seamus, and I know it," Amarantha replied.

"You are right, but before I can prove it once and for all, we need to get a little sleep."

Sir Weatherby walked past his apartment to Amarantha's door and opened it for her. He gave her a gentle hug.

"Thank you for helping me, Ran."

Amarantha stumbled through the door without saying a word. Sir Weatherby walked back to his apartment, shed his clothes on the floor, and went to bed. He was asleep in seconds.

He awoke to a flood of light brought on by the curtains being thrown back. A serving girl held an armload of clothes.

"It is eleven of the clock, Your Grace," she said as she pulled back the covers. "Warder Chertsey instructed me to bring you vittles."

Pulling his robe on over his night shirt, Sir Weatherby walked into the anteroom where a large tray of food lay on the table. First he poured some black tea. Then he started eating a thick slice of ham while holding a chunk of bread in his other hand. He was ravenous. Slowly, as his hunger was satiated, the events of last evening intruded on his thoughts. His wish had been granted. He now had another murder victim, but unfortunately he failed to see any clear connection from one to the other. First, a talented young architect is struck down with a terrible blow to the skull with a mallet. Then a comely woman, in a rich dress, is found across the Palace in the King's new bathing room. Apparently poisoned, as there isn't a mark on her body. Now, the reverend dies in a fall from the gatehouse. The murder weapons used in each case differed as much as the venues where the bodies were found.

Hundreds of people lived at Hampton Court, and the three victims barely knew each other! His head ached. He decided to discuss the cases with Amarantha in hopes of gaining clarity. He hastily dressed and walked down the hall. Amarantha was still in bed, although her clothes and her breakfast were nearby.

"Get up. Ran!" Sir Weatherby shouted. "I need your help."

"I can't, Seamus."

"Are you ill? Do I need to call a doctor?"

"No. Not in the usual sense of the word."

"What is it then?"

"I'm dispirited. Suddenly, I don't even have the energy to get out of bed and everything looks black. My da had this all the time. He called it 'the big black dog.' I had it once before when I was in law school. I stayed in bed for five days and then it was gone."

"Dear, Ran, what you have is depression, and staying in bed in the dark is the worst thing for it. I will have Judith Scotson take you to the cottage on the hill to the west of Hampton Court. There is more sun there, and you must exercise there four hours each day."

"But I would rather stay here in my bed."

"Yes, I know. But trust me on this, Ran, I know whereof I speak."

He called for the assistant librarian, and told her what he wanted her to do. Next he looked up Dredge, and explained to him what he wanted him to accomplish.

"We need to do another experiment, Dredge."

"I suspected that, Your Grace."

"Yes, but this experiment is large and can't be done in the privacy of our laboratory. Howerver, if our testing is seen we will be castigated. We must proceed in secret. We need to determine if Gregory Townsend jumped off the tower or was thrown off."

"How will we do that, Your Grace?"

"You may already have the answer, Dredge. How many feet did the body fall?"

"Seventy-four feet, three inches."

"And how far from the base of the tower was the body found?"

"Forty-one feet, six inches."

"How much did the victim weigh?"

"Ten stones."

"I need two dead animals that weight ten stones, and four strong men that can carry them and then keep their mouths shut."

Dredge thought for several minutes about the various animals in and around the Palace that weighed one hundred and forty pounds. It was too heavy for a deer or a sheep but too light for a cow.

"I think two pigs would fill the bill," Dredge finally answered. "And I know some men who are in my debt, and will keep their mouths shut."

"Arrange it for tonight at eleven of the clock when the Palace is asleep."

Sir Weatherby left the lab and went in search of Ellen Iverson, the gossipy head of the Confectory. When he found her, she was making sheets of gingerbread husbands using a small wooden mold shaped like a man.

"Good day, Your Grace," Ellen called across the kitchen. "You're staying out of the bawdy houses, I see."

Sir Weatherby couldn't help but smile before saying, "I'm reassured and comforted that you are watching over me."

"The next time you go to the White Swan, ask for Theresa. She is quite beautiful and from southern France. She speaks delightfully."

"Thank you. What can you tell me about the unfortunate Gregory Townsend?"

"He was poseur and a phony."

"Why did you dislike him so much?"

"He was a stableman that supposed he had a vision from God and then put on airs. He expected all of the simple people in his congregation to do things for him. Apparently, he was too busy talking with God to wash his own clothes or polish his own boots. He dressed lavishly and carried himself like a prince of the realm."

"He must have had some redeeming qualities, Miss Iverson."

"He was kind to the poor, and he took up for the members of his congregation if they were put upon," she conceded grudgingly.

"Was he a liar or a thief?"

"He lied about the collections from his congregation. It's the reason I left his flock. Since he used the money that was given to Christ for his own aggrandizement, I would say he was a thief."

"Was he capable of murder?"

"I think not."

"Could he have killed himself?"

"Absolutely not. He had too many pleasures here on earth to want to go to heaven just yet."

She handed Weatherby a warm, soft, fragrant gingerbread husband.

"Thank you for the information," Sir Weatherby said as he went out the Dutch door.

Judith Scotson had departed early that morning with Amarantha. They should both be at Leith Hill by now, Sir Weatherby thought. He had sent Amarantha to the highest point in the county so she would be exposed to more sunlight. He also had asked the apothecary in Hampton to concoct a mixture of St. John's wort, damiana, valerian root and ginseng. The decoction had just arrived at the Palace and Sir Weatherby sent it to Leith Hill carried by a fast rider with a note for Amarantha.

Sir Weatherby ate a hurried lunch in the Great Kitchen. The cook had made roast duck with orange sauce, and Seamus quickly ate two helpings. He had finally been granted an interview with Richard Weston, Master of the House. His office was off the stairs to the Privy Garden in an isolated part of the Palace that Sir Weatherby hadn't even visited, so he allowed extra time to find it. He cut across the Base Court and Little Court, then walked along the King's Long Gallery before finding the stairs to the Privy Garden. He found a large oak door with a brass plate on the top floor and knocked. A voice beckoned him to come in.

"Sir Seamus Weatherby for the Master of the House," Weatherby said in an authoritative tone.

"Have a seat, Your Grace," Weston's male secretary said with a look of disdain mixed with curiosity.

After waiting an interminable length of time, Sir Weatherby was finally shown into the Master's office. It was heavily paneled in oak that had been stained almost black. A limestone fireplace occupied one wall. The drapes were closed on the south windows and the room was knee-banging dark. The clerk guided Weatherby to a plush chair across from Weston's large desk.

How may I help you?" Richard Weston said in a deep voice.

Sir Weatherby peered across the large black desk but could barely make out the speaker.

"I am Sir Seamus Weatherby, and I was sent here by the King to investigate a murder in Hampton Court Palace," Weatherby said in a formal voice.

"My minions told me you were here." Weston offered neither welcome nor greeting.

After a long pause, Weston replied, "Will you be staying long?"

"Only until the cases are solved, Your Grace. That time period could be considerably shorter if you provide me with the support of your office."

"I'm afraid all my staff is fully employed with Palace duties and no one will have the time to assist you, Mr. Weatherby."

"Did you know either of the victims, Sir?"

"I have other appointments this afternoon, and I don't have the luxury of answering your questions now. Perhaps you could make another appointment with me in a fortnight or so?"

Sir Weatherby rose without saying another word, and strode out of Weston's office, slamming the large oak door behind him. We'll see if I have to wait two weeks before I talk to you again, he thought. He went directly to the laboratory and had his amanuensis, Dredge, write a note of complaint to the Chancellor, Thomas Cromwell, about the Master of the House. He had his horse saddled and rode the long way round to the Lamb and Flag. He drank for a couple of hours, perhaps more than he should have, and then ate a large formal supper of roast chicken and Brussels Sprouts.

# CHAPTER 23

Sir Weatherby had brought paper with him to the Lamb and Flag, and once settled at his table he called for a quill and ink. Between courses, he wrote a long letter to Amarantha. He had read a newly published poem by Richard Lovelace that he laboriously printed on a separate page, because his cursive was cramped and illegible. It began:

*To Amarantha, that she would dishevel her Hair*
*By Richard Lovelace*

*Amarantha sweet and fair*
*Ah, braid no more that shining hair!*
*As my curious hand or eye*
*Hovering round thee, let it fly!*

*Let it fly as unconfined*
*As its calm ravish the wind,*
*Who hath left his darling, th' East*
*To wanton o'er that spicy nest*

*Every tress must be confest,*
*But neatly tangled at the best;*
*Like a clew of golden thread*
*Most excellently ravellèd.*

*Do not wind up that light*
*In ribbands, and o'ercloud in night,*
*Like the Sun in 's early ray;*
*But shake your head, and scatter day!*

He rode home in the dark under a bank of lowering clouds that threatened rain but held off until he was back at Hampton Court. Once home, he chose Chaucer's *Canterbury Tales* to read in front of the fire as he waited. At eleven p.m. he exited his apartment and met Dredge and two burly workmen. Lying on the ground before them were two dead pigs that weighed about one hundred and forty pounds or ten stones each. Even though the light was low, Sir Weatherby quickly took in the scene.

Turning to Dredge, Weatherby said, "Take these two pigs to the top of the tower. Have these men throw one of the pigs from the wall and then have them roll the second one off the parapet. I don't want to know which they do first. Give me the measuring rod so I can compute the distance from the base of the wall to the 'body.'"

Dredge and the two men departed with the boars. Sir Weatherby waited an interminable time before he heard a shout from the top of the tower followed by an object falling through the gloom at a high rate of speed. The pig's carcass hit the driveway with a loud 'plop'! It bounced once and then was still. Sir Weatherby walked over to the pig and measured the distance from base of the Great Gatehouse to the middle of the pig's body. Then he measured it again. He was just writing down his measurement of thirteen feet, when he heard another shout, followed by the falling remains of another pig. This one landed thirty-seven feet from the tower. In a few minutes the two workmen appeared at the door. Dredge waited at the top, as his disability made going down stairs difficult.

"Take the animals back to the top and follow Dredge's instructions," Sir Weatherby said to the two burly men.

Each hoisted a carcass onto their shoulders without a word and disappeared through the dark portal. Soon, two more carcasses came hurtling off of the tower. The first measured forty-two feet, and the second one eleven feet.

Sir Weatherby cupped his hands around his mouth and called up the tower, "Come down, Dredge, I have what I need."

In a few minutes three figures emerged from the portal, and Dredge sent the two men away with the carcasses.

"I deduce that in the first and fourth trials the animals were slipped over the wall like a man committing suicide, and in the second and third the pigs were hurled off the tower. The body of Gregory Townsend was found forty-one feet six inches from the tower, so he was thrown from the Gatehouse probably by at least two men."

"That is what the experiment shows," Dredge replied. "But one thing doesn't fit with your scheme."

"What would that be?"

"When you turned over his body he was clutching his Bible. A holy man committing suicide would want to meet his maker with the good book in his hand. A murderer wouldn't think of that."

"Good point, but for now I stand by the evidence we collected here tonight."

Exhausted, Sir Weatherby stumbled into bed, pleased with the experiment. It had been carried out away from the prying eyes of the residents of Hampton Court, who would have found the falling carcasses bizarre at best. The results had been unequivocal: Gregory Townsend was definitely thrown from the parapet of the Great Gatehouse. The lay preacher had certainly been murdered. Sir Weatherby worried about Amarantha and then fell sound asleep.

In the morning, Weatherby sent a letter by courier to Thomas Cromwell inquiring about Richard Weston and his previous postings, and any foibles or idiosyncrasies he might have exhibited.

Weatherby didn't feel like working, so he took a ramble along the Thames, going upriver this time. He was lucky to find an old overgrown trail, and used his walking stick to amble along the south side of the river. It was the Ides of April, and in the last two weeks the vegetation had grown thicker. The woodlands were alive with calls from wood thrushes and chaffinches. Hedgehogs scurried shyly through the duff on the forest floor. After walking for an hour, Sir Weatherby found a large rock at the river bank, and sat down. A pair of swans swam by followed by a line of four small grey-brown hatchlings. A rowboat with two fishermen hugged the opposite bank, their willow poles curving gently toward the surface of the water.

Sir Weatherby made a conscious decision not to think about his vexatious triplet of murders. Instead, he let his mind wander freely as he walked back to Hampton Court. Weatherby had taken up the study of botany for relaxation while he was in medical school. So he focused on the wild flowers that were in full bloom, including large bunches of buttercups and drifts of pink ragged robin. He also found the pure white star-shaped flowers of the loggon lily near a fallen tree. Just before getting back to Hampton Court the King's detective spotted the flashy snake's-head fritillary with bunches of mauve flowers.

Weatherby returned from his walk refreshed, and ate a light lunch in the orchard. He decided to relentlessly interrogate some members of Gregory Townsend's congregation in hopes of finding his killer. But first he would turn to Ellen Iverson first for background information. He strolled out of the orchard, cut across the jousting yard to the Outer Court, and then opened the Dutch door into the Confectory. Ellen was making daryole, a kind of cheesecake made from cream, cheese and sugar, which Sir Weatherby didn't care for. He found it far too sticky.

"Ahh. The great investigator returns," Ellen chided as he walked through the door. "You've got quite a pile of bodies, Your Grace, but no wrongdoer."

"Quite correct, Miss Iverson. I hoped you might be of help."

"I thought about your problem as I stirred this daryole, and I may have some ideas for you."

"Capital. I'll take a chair and you can tell me what you think."

"I know more gossip about Gregory Townsend than about your other two victims combined," she began. "He claimed God spoke to him one stormy fall night, but I think he made it up. I believe he saw the Protestant movement coming, and he was tired of being just a stable boy. Gregory realized that he would spend the rest of his life grooming and saddling horses. He got an English Bible and started loudly preaching and praying around Hampton Court. The weak and the lonely and some of the forlorn women at the Palace responded. You never heard him give a sermon, but he had a wonderful, deep speaking voice."

"So you believe he exploited the weak?"

"Did you notice that three quarters of his congregation were women?"

He had them tithe clothes and money and jewelry, and I think he also had some of the women lift their skirts. One, Amanda Stevens, would pray with him often. Both would kneel on the ground and face each other and then after praying in a soft and husky voice Gregory would place his hands on her head and then slide them down her body, lingering at certain places. Amanda told me all about it."

"Why would she tell you about that, Miss Iverson?"

"She always liked and trusted me but, honestly, mostly because she never could stop talking. She has a large, ill-tempered brother, Clarence. I suspect you should be talking with him."

"Is he over six feet tall?" Weatherby said, thinking of William Suffolk's murder.

"Easily, and he weighs twenty stone."

"Where can I find Clarence Stevens?"

"He works as a farm hand, but he moves around a lot. The last I heard, he was on a farm two miles west of Hampton."

"Thanks for the tip, Miss Iverson."

"Take some daryole."

"No, but thank you."

"Then there is a box of gingerbread husbands by the window."

Sir Weatherby took two of the soft, aromatic brown cookies as he went out the door. He walked back from the Outer Court to the Palace proper along the Thames. Just after he passed through the Great Gatehouse, a carriage came by and Weatherby saw Judith Scotson inside. Realizing that Amarantha would also be in the carriage, he walked around to the other door as the horses came to a stop. He jerked the door open impatiently and stuck his head inside.

"Amarantha! Are you better?" he said in a booming voice.

"I'm much better, thank you, Seamus," Amarantha said as she held out a hand for him to take.

She stepped down gingerly and gave Weatherby a long, firm hug. He thanked Judith Scotson for her help.

"I started feeling bright as soon as I took the decoction," Amarantha said. "Thank you for it."

"I'm sure it helped, but I suspect that the sunlight on Leith Hill and the exercise, did the most good," Weatherby said. "Either way, I'm just glad you're back, Ran. I missed you, and we have lot of work to do."

# CHAPTER 24

In the morning, Weatherby had a large breakfast laid in the Wolsey Apartment for Amarantha, Dredge, and himself. He was in very good spirits as he brought Amarantha up to date on the interview with Richard Weston and the pig drop. Weatherby explained in detail how the experiment showed that Gregory Townsend had been hurled to his death from the parapet, probably by two large men.

After swallowing a large bite of scone with currant jelly, Amarantha asked, "But how do you relate these murderers to each other?"

"I had a long ramble along the Thames and thought about that very question earlier today," Weatherby replied. "What if they aren't related? What if tension has been growing here at Hampton Court as Sir Moulton said and now it has just spilled over? Perhaps once the first murder occurred, it gave the idea to two others and they just followed suit."

"That would explain the three very different causes of the victim's demise," Dredge agreed.

"What you two are saying is very true," Weatherby said thoughtfully. "Because we cannot seem to link these three together."

"How can I help now that I'm back?" Amarantha asked.

"I need two things from you if you are up to it. Please enlist Judith Scotson and Margaret Sedgwick to look into every volume in the library. I'm certain that Anna Maria Wimbledon left a diary or some personal notes somewhere."

"It will take several days, but I can do that," Amarantha replied.

"I also want you to interview Amanda Stevens, a member of the Protestant congregation. I think that Gregory Townsend may have been molested her."

"I'll do that first."

"In the meantime, Dredge and I will do the autopsy on the unfortunate stableman turned lay preacher."

Weatherby arose from the breakfast table and walked to the laboratory with Dredge following him. Gregory Townsend's body was laid out on his back with his clothing on. When Weatherby straightened the victim's arms and tried to remove the Bible, it didn't come away easily. In doing so he noticed a spot of material on the book and on the victim's coat. Dredge leaned in close and scraped a sample into an envelope.

"I suspect it is fish glue, Sir," Dredge said.

"So much for your theory of the suicidal minister clutching the good book as he jumped to his death on his way to heaven," Weatherby replied.

"I stand corrected," Dredge replied. "It appears to be a premeditated killing. It takes at least fifty minutes for a glue like that to dry."

An external exam revealed both femurs and tibias were broken—two pieces of shattered bone poked raggedly through the flesh. Weatherby presumed the victim landed feet first. The pads of all eight fingers were abraded and each wrist bore bruises. Rolling the body over, Weatherby made an incision that revealed that Gregory's lower back was also fractured. Examination of Townsend's internal organs showed no abnormalities for a relatively young man. Examination of his stomach contents revealed undigested food and the smell of alcohol, but no bitter rose aroma. Sir Weatherby usually loved doing necropsies because suddenly the cause of death became real and obvious to him. However, this morning his mind was elsewhere, and he knew he was just going through the motions. Fortunately, Dredge was paying attention and noticed a small, barely discernible lump over the victim's left shoulder. Weatherby deftly cut it out and removed the fibrous tissue that adhered to it. A flat, shiny, smooth black stone one quarter inch in diameter remained.

"Let's look at it under the microscope," Dredge suggested, picking up the item and carrying into the next room.

Dredge arranged the microscope to collect strong sunlight through the window and placed the object on the stage. Then he stepped back so Weatherby could look through the eyepiece.

Weatherby studied the black stone for several minutes. Finally he reported, "There are two incisions on the stone. On one side is a capital 'P' followed by a capital 'C'. On the other is a complex linear design with a vertical line and several straight and angled lines radiating from it. Take a look. I've never seen anything like it before."

Weatherby stepped back so Dredge could look through the eyepiece.

"It looks very deliberate and stylized, but I don't know what it is supposed to represent. You are the master of languages, Your Grace."

"I can read several and recognize others. It's not Latin or any other language that uses the Latin alphabet. I've seen Hebrew and Arabic, and it isn't either of those, nor is it Chinese or Japanese. Sir Moulton says there are still Druids in Surrey County, but I don't believe they ever had a written language, or at least one that has ever been found. Make several large copies on parchment, and I will mail them to some of the professors at the University of Edinburgh."

As Weatherby turned, Amarantha entered. "I walked to the village to interview Amanda Stevens," she said.

"How did you do?"

"Miss Iverson is correct, Amanda talks too much. I gather she had a very routine little life until Gregory had his vision, then she got swept up in his religion. She reports they often knelt facing each other and prayed. After an hour or so, she seemed to go into an ecstasy or trance. She remembers little that happened during these periods except that she was warm in various parts of her body and when she awoke her clothes were in dishabille. Her brother visited two weeks ago and she told him about these ecstasies. She says he got enraged and left."

"Perhaps he killed Gregory Townsend. Apparently, Clarence weighs twenty stones."

"It's possible, but Amanda says that despite his size he has never hurt anyone or anything," Amarantha replied.

"But is this his only sister and also younger?"

"Yes and yes."

"He may feel that she is special. I will interrogate him on the farm where he works. Iverson says that is currently near Village Coombe. I believe I will take one of Dredge's louts with me."

"I've never known you to be physically afraid, Seamus."

"I'm not. I don't believe Stevens is smart enough to elude me, but the presence of two of us should intimidate him so that he is more compliant. I will visit him in the morning. In the meantime let's go and have lunch together at the Lamb and Flag."

"All right. Then this afternoon I have to start on the search of the library with the two assistant librarians," Amarantha said in a resigned tone.

The three of them walked out through the Great Gatehouse at a steady clip. It was a beautiful English spring day. Insects and birds filled the warm, soft air, which was cooler on the bridge thanks to the sparkling water rushing below. The village was full of farmers and tradesmen buying and selling. Amarantha stopped to admire a bonnet in front of a haberdasher. Weatherby and Dredge were still solicitous of their associate because of her recent infirmity. The Lamb and Flag was crowded with noisy patrons, but the three found a table in the back. Weatherby and Dredge had pigeon pie, and Amarantha had wild mushrooms in a puff pastry. They agreed before hand that they wouldn't discuss the murderous mess at Hampton Court. Instead Amarantha described her struggle to get a law degree in a humorous way that had all three laughing.

"Sister Agnes decided I was smart enough to go to university even though girls don't do that," she began. "She came over to the farm to discuss it with Mum and Da. Once Sister was seated, Mum served berries and cream on her only silver tray. However, she was so nervous she spilled the tray. The bright red berries and globs of cream flew through the air and landed on Sister Agnes's pristine white habit. My Mum was so upset she left the room crying, and she was my only support. My Da thought I should stay on the farm or become a nun. I was repelled by the sexless, pinch-faced mincing life of a nun, but I saw my university career disappearing before my eyes as those berries fell."

"How did you ever get an education after that?" Dredge asked incredulously.

"Mum and I cooked up a plot. I pretended to be forgetful and then behaved strangely, dressed badly and looked crazy. Mum said she couldn't handle me any more and sent me to the nunnery. Once I was there, Sister Agnes sent applications to universities all over Europe. Some didn't even reply. All the others rejected me. The University of Padua said that educating a woman was a sin and an abomination, and that they would report Sister Agnes to the Pope. She screeched and stamped her feet like a large white owl when she got that letter."

"So who got you into the university?" Weatherby asked.

"Sister Agnes did not give up," Amarantha said. "She just got more determined. She changed my name to Anthmar Thompson, and I reapplied as a lad. I got accepted to the University of Utrecht, in north Holland, and the Sorbonne in Paris. I went to Utrecht."

"So, you had to masquerade as a male for three years?" Weatherby asked.

"Yes, and I was only fifteen my first year. I was too vain to cut my hair and it constantly fell out of my cap. I wrapped by breasts flat with a long strip of linen, but they often slipped out. I had a male roommate in Utrecht each year. I tried to be discreet around them, but it was daunting as there was no privacy in those small rooms. It was especially hard when I had the curse. After a few months each roommate got suspicious, so I changed suite mates every year."

Weatherby called for three tankards of ale as their dirty plates were cleared.

Weatherby lifted his tankard and said, "To Amarantha Thompson, the only known female lawyer in Christendom."

After finishing their ale, the three associates walked back to Hampton Court

# CHAPTER 25

Once back at the Palace, Amarantha reluctantly headed to the musty library. Dredge returned to the laboratory to finish the autopsy samples on Gregory Townsend. Weatherby also requested that Dredge make a large chart listing everything that was known about the three victims. Questions about Druids had been troubling Weatherby for the past three days. He had thought that they had practiced human sacrifice and that they were long extinct, and was surprised when Sir John Moulton mentioned they might still exist in Surrey County. He decided to seek out Sir John to get some more information. He checked in the construction shack and found that Moulton was working in the Great Hall. Sir Weatherby walked along the Long Gallery and through the Great Watching Chamber past the Chapel Royal to the Great Hall. As usual, Sir Moulton was up on a scaffold instructing an architect.

"Sir John. I need to ask you some questions," Weatherby yelled.

"Great. Climb on up if you don't mind," Sir Moulton yelled back.

Weatherby started up the series of rickety ladders and worn planks. It took him five minutes to get up above the hammer beam where Sir Moulton studied an unrolled parchment.

"I see you have another victim," Sir Moulton said by way of greeting.

"I hope your roof is going better than my murder investigation," Weatherby replied. "In fact, that's why I'm here. I need more information about the Druids in the county."

"I don't know as much about them as I would like," Sir Moulton replied. "But I'll tell you what I know. I was quaffing ale one night at the Lamb and Flag, and the couple next to me had had too much to drink. They started talking about a ceremony the next night. I realized that the next night was December 21$^{st}$, the winter solstice. They were gathering at a stone circle in Wycombe just before midnight, for a ritual. The man said he had to buy a goat so they could sacrifice it during the ritual. The woman volunteered that if it wasn't a male goat the chief Druid would be murderously angry."

"Did they mention the name of the chief Druid?" Weatherby asked.

"No."

"Did you recognize either of the two who were talking about the Druids?"

"Unfortunately not, but I'm sure neither of them are from the Palace or the village of Hampton."

"How can you be so sure?"

"Well, I've lived here for a year and a half, and I spend a lot of time in the town—especially at the Lamb and Flag. If they lived nearby, I would recognize them."

"Thanks for your help." Weatherby headed for the first ladder. "I'll start looking in Wycombe. I hope I don't have to wait until the summer solstice for another gathering that's seven weeks away."

Weatherby knew that Amarantha wasn't looking forward to spending days in the dark, dusty library, especially after her recent bout of depression. He decided to stop by. He cut across the Clock Court, entered the South Gallery, and headed up the Great Staircase to the library. As he entered the library, he was struck by its overwhelming gloom. Judith Scotson, Margaret Sedgwick and Amarantha were all taking volumes off the shelf one at a time, and looking through each before dusting it and replacing it on the shelf.

"Thank you all for doing this tedious, dirty work," Weatherby called out. "I asked that a plate of gingerbread husbands be sent over from the Confectory for you."

"We will need more than that for this job," Amarantha replied.

"I truly believe it's the best place to look for something that I'm positive exists," Sir Weatherby said in placating tone. "In the morning, Dredge and I are off to Wycombe to look for Druids. If things go badly, we may spend the night."

"I thought the Druids died out in the seventh century," Amarantha said. "Are there still people who practice such paganism?"

"According to Sir John Moulton there are. And according to the stories about them, they practice ritual killings."

Weatherby left the library just as the gingerbread cookies arrived. He spent the evening reading alone in his apartment. When he was in medical school he learned that he viewed life with equanimity when he read every day.

Early the next morning, he met Dredge in the stable yard, where two horses were saddled for the five-mile journey. Dredge was actually much more comfortable in a coach, but he hated to be coddled. A small horse like the ones that worked in the mines, a Shetland, had been saddled for him. Both men mounted and headed off. Weatherby's horse was sixteen hands high to accommodate his large frame. Dredge barely came up to the taller rider's saddle, even when mounted. They made an odd-looking pair as they rode off to the east. The road was wide and flat for the first three miles, and they made good time. The last two miles were over a narrow, hilly trail full of branches across their path. Weatherby had to stop twice to ask directions. The two travelers arrived in the very small village of Wycombe a little before eleven of the clock.

Sir Weatherby had pondered his strategy along the way. He had ultimately decided against visiting the village farm houses one by one and asking if there were any Druids in the home. He felt such an approach would make everyone suspicious and disinclined to talk. The only thing he knew for certain was that a stone circle located near the town was used for religious ceremonies. Weatherby tied his horse outside the only store in the village, and walked inside.

"Good day, Sir," Weatherby called out as he walked into the store. "I'm from Oxford University and I'm making a map of primeval religious sites. I have been told an ancient stone circle may exist near here. Do you know anything about it?"

"I have never heard of that," the shopkeeper, Martin Stoddard, said after a pause. "Even though we are small village, we do have a very old Catholic church that was built in the year of our Lord 825."

"Thank you but I'm only mapping pre-Christian sites," Weatherby replied. "Might I ask someone else?"

"My father is resting in the back," the shopkeeper replied. "He is almost ninety, but he has a sharp mind. Perhaps he has a recollection."

"My assistant and I would be most grateful if you would ask him."

Stoddard went to the back of the store, and didn't return for fifteen minutes. When he walked back through the curtain that separated the store from the living quarters, the shopkeeper was carrying a piece of parchment.

"My father saw such a circle when he was a young man, and he has drawn you a map of where he thinks it may be located," the shopkeeper replied as he set the parchment on the counter.

Weatherby scrutinized the map and then asked, "Can you orient me?"

"Yes. This black box represents the store, and this direction is north," the shopkeeper replied, drawing an arrow on the parchment.

Dredge and Weatherby walked out of the store and mounted their horses. Weatherby directed them south through the small village. Weatherby held the parchment on the horn of saddle as he rode out of town. The road quickly narrowed and looked less and less like a trail. Weatherby followed the map, branching off from the trail by noting where the diagram indicated streams. Both men dismounted when they arrived in the area indicated by a circle on the parchment, and walked independently through the woods looking for stones. When no stone circle was found, they widened their search area, returning to their horses after an hour. Dredge and Weatherby conferred and decided to split up and ride east and west three minutes before resuming their search. First Weatherby marked the center of their search area with a cairn. Weatherby rode east, and Dredge west. Two hours later as the light in the woods faded, and the shadows got long both men, met back at the cairn.

"Perhaps the old man's recollection is wrong," Weatherby said. "In any case we are done for now. Let's go back to the village for the night."

Weatherby led the way back along the trail without referring to the map and was sent to a house near the store that had an extra room. Before retiring, Weatherby asked the woman of the house about the stone circle. She studied the parchment map by candle light for a long time.

"This is a very accurate map," the housekeeper began. "However, old man Stoddard made one error on the third turn. You needed to go east, not south at this point," she said as she pointed to a spot on the map.

In the morning, Dredge and Weatherby rode out at early light following the revised map. In forty-five minutes they were at the stone circle. The circle was set in a clearing of beech trees and consisted of sixty or seventy granite blocks eighteen inches tall and three feet long. The center was clear of all vegetation, suggesting it was used often. A thorough search of all the stones revealed no writings or markings.

"This circle suggests that there are Druids in this area, Dredge," Weatherby said. "I will ride back to Hampton Court, but I want you to stay for a few days and see if you can discover the names of any of the Druids."

"Very good, Sir," Dredge replied.

Sir Weatherby turned his horse onto the trail and rode toward Wycombe. Several stags were startled from the underbrush but easily jumped the trail in front of Sir Weatherby's horse. He rode more slowly along the road back to Hampton Court. When he first arrived at the Palace, he went directly to the library. Amarantha and the two assistant librarians were still looking through the volumes one by one.

"Has anything turned up?" Weatherby asked in a cheery voice.

"Nothing has turned up except a lot of dust, spiders, and silverfish," Amarantha replied forlornly. "But we are not even through one third of the books."

"If you can spare the time, meet me in two hours in the Orchard for some lunch."

"May I bring Judith and Margaret?"

"That would be perfect," Weatherby replied, while silently wishing he could be alone with Amarantha.

# CHAPTER 26

The lunch went well. The first course was a cold cucumber soup and the main course was salmon, fresh from the Thames with boiled parsnips. Judith Scotson and Margaret Sedgwick were knowledgeable and charming, and the three women laughed a lot. Weatherby enjoyed seeing Amarantha so relaxed and animated. They all had too much white wine, and after lunch no one felt like working. However, the women returned to the gloomy library, and Weatherby went to the laboratory to look at Dredge's chart. He was surprised at how little information was available on the three murder victims. He sat down to ponder what his next move should be. He made a list of issues that needed to be investigated:

1) The blue glass Suffolk had stolen
2) The owners of the bloody mallets
3) The source of Wimbledon's money
4) The dark stranger Anna Maria was seen with
5) Weston, the bizarre Master of the House
6) Gregory's relationship with Amanda Stevens

Weatherby had written the list on a small piece of parchment with a pencil and tucked it in his pocket. It didn't seem daunting. He would simply work on the items one by one and move closer to the solution of all three murders. He decided to work on Gregory's relationship with Amanda first. Weatherby walked into the village to continue the interview with Amanda Stevens that Amarantha had started. He enjoyed the walk across the bridge and through the bustling village. Miss Stevens was in her backyard hanging out laundry.

"I'm here to ask you some more questions about Gregory Townsend's murder, Miss Stevens," Weatherby began.

"I believe I told your assistant everything, Your Grace, perhaps too much," Amanda replied with a clothespin in her mouth.

"I don't believe you have, young lady. Have you ever lain with a man?"

"No. What do you take me for? I am a young Christian woman."

"All of us, Amanda, had tumbles as we were growing up at picnics and hayings that involved touches, caresses and kisses. Please don't tell me this never happened to you."

"Well, a few times, but that was before I was saved."

"How far did it go?"

"Well the kissing and touching might go on for quite a while, but then we were almost always discovered. I never shed my clothes like happened with Reverend Townsend."

"So during your prayer sessions with Gregory you removed all your clothing?"

"I didn't remove anything!" Amanda said forcefully. "I was never awake during those prayer sessions, and once when I did awake, I had nothing on. I was quite cold and Reverend Townsend was struggling to pull my chemise over my shoulders."

"Did he say anything?"

"He mumbled that during the ecstasy I ripped my clothes off, but they weren't torn at all."

"Did he remove his clothing also?"

"No he was always neatly and completely dressed. Although lots of times, my things were all higgledy-piggledy when I awoke."

"How often did you two have these prayer sessions?"

"At first they were rare but right before he died we were praying together about three times per week."

"Thank you for your time, Miss Stevens." Weatherby picked up his notes and departed.

As he walked back across the bridge, Weatherby wondered if Amanda's brother had heard about the "prayer sessions" and murdered Townsend in a fit of anger. He planned to find out in the morning. Weatherby ate supper alone in the Great Kitchen and spent the evening quietly reading Thomas More's *Utopia*.

Early the next morning, he had his horse saddled for the ride west to talk with Clarence Stevens, Amanda's hulking brother. Originally he had planned to take one of Dredge's louts along to insure cooperation, but on rethinking the matter, he decided to travel light and alone. He knew the roads toward Walton were few and poorly maintained, perhaps because the land was much hillier toward the west. He mounted and headed out from the Palace. Since the hailstorm, he had purposely ridden more, and now felt quite at ease in the saddle.

Some of his comfort derived from a new saddle he'd had made to his own specifications. After reading that the Tartars often rode all day with a piece of steak under their saddle to tenderize it, he decided some extra padding might also make the ride smoother. He had a layer of felt sewn to the bottom of the saddle and also raised the cantle, the curved piece behind the rider. The morning was cool and misty as the road to the west narrowed. The forest was alive with squirrels and stoats. Even a large lazy badger ambled across the road. Weatherby pondered adding another member to his team of three investigators. However, for most of their cases which were easily solved in a week, the team of three sufficed. He knew that if he met another woman as knowledgeable and smart as Amarantha he would hire her, but that was unlikely. Each one of them had far too much to do investigating the current triple murder, but Weatherby doubted he would ever have such a case again.

After passing the village of Walton, Weatherby asked after Clarence Stevens and was directed to a farm near Oatlands. Unlike those that sent Dredge and Weatherby scrambling to find the stone circle, these directions proved accurate. As he approached the farm, he saw a large man working at the forge near the barn. The ringing sound of his hammer on the anvil as he shaped the hot iron could be heard from far away.

As he approached the blacksmith, Weatherby called out, "Where might I find Clarence Stevens?"

"That word be me," Clarence said putting down his hammer and wiping his hands on his leather apron. "Her wants to know?"

"I'm Sir Seamus Weatherby, I am in the employ of his Majesty King Henry VIII," Weatherby replied. "I'm investigating the heinous murder of the right reverend Gregory Townsend."

"I'm full pleased that, that ther' fake man of God is dead and cold. May he rot in hell for molestin my sister," Clarence Stevens replied.

Clarence untied his apron and placed in on a table in the forge.

"As a Christian, then, you are happy that he is dead?"

"I'm not a believer and I donna' care a fig about him."

"Where were you six nights ago?"

"Let's see. I believe I was in Hampton."

"Can anyone vouch for that?"

"I donna' believe I saw anyone. I was there on a personal matter."

"Is that how you describe the murder of the Reverend Gregory Townsend?"

"I didna' murder that underhanded bastard."

"I believe you did, and I arrest you in the name of the King."

Before Weatherby could finish his sentence, Clarence dodged out of the blacksmith's shed and sprinted for the nearby woods. For a big man, he was surprisingly quick. Blocked by the shed and also taken by surprise, Weatherby knew his chances of catching the farm hand were slim. Now he wished he had brought one of Dredge's strapping friends. Weatherby walked back to his horse feeling that he had one of the murders solved. He would have the Sheriff of Surrey track down and apprehend Clarence Stevens. He ambled back to Hampton Court enjoying the warm, late spring morning. On his way, he led his horse off the track to another stone circle he had been told about. It was on a hilltop and smaller than the one they had found at Wycombe.

When he got back to the Palace he found Amarantha in the library and took her outside for a leisurely lunch. He made his meeting with Clarence Stevens into a long story. He described how he was outwitted as he watched the broad backside of his suspect bouncing through the weeds. Then Clarence disappeared into the dense forest huffing and puffing as his arms flailed.

After she stopped laughing, Amarantha said, "I thought you were taking one of Dredge's oafs with you."

"I was, and then my male bravado took over and I decided I could do it all by myself," Weatherby said sheepishly. "I was clearly mistaken. I'm cynical about human behavior, but I thought I had Clarence intimidated, and it never occurred to me that he would try to escape. How are things in the library?"

"No better. We have looked at well over half the books and nothing has turned up," Amarantha replied. "I now believe her stash of document is hidden elsewhere."

"Would you like to stop working in the library and go back to canvassing the village for spare rooms for rent?" Weatherby asked.

"No. I have developed a good bond with the librarians and I want to keep it," Amarantha replied. "Plus spending time in the library has taught me a lot about Cardinal Wolsey. He loved and admired tapestries, and nearly every room of the Palace has elegant and colorful hangings. It's rumored he spent 20,000 angels on one piece that hangs near the chapel. On the other hand, Wolsey didn't care much about books. His library is large, but the quality of the books is low. He seems to have gone more for fancy red bindings with gold letters rather than for content. Once we have looked through every volume, I will resume my searches in Hampton."

"You are very determined, Ran," Weatherby replied. "I suggest we have some fun tonight."

"There is a dance in Hampton and I would like to take you."

"I'm not much of a dancer."

"Let's try. It could be fun."

Weatherby and Amarantha agreed to meet at 7 p.m. She wore a form-fitting green dress that Weatherby had seen before. He wore a red velvet doublet with gold hose. A hansom took them to the Inns of Court where a crowd was already gathering. The first dances were old-fashioned rounds and squares. Weatherby was reluctant at first, but once he had danced a while and was short of breath, he became less inhibited. After the players took a break, a series of eight dances called the 'Old Measures' was offered. It consisted of pavanes and almans which both Amarantha and Weatherby knew but also galliards, which neither of them was familiar with. The galliard started with a line of men and women facing each other across the floor. Amarantha grasped the side of her skirt delicately with her left hand and danced toward the middle with the line of women. Then she gracefully raised her right hand high over her head to meet Seamus's hand. When they finished dancing they were tired and a little tipsy, but excited. They caught a ride home around 2 a.m. and Weatherby walked Amarantha to her apartment. After she passed through the door, she turned back toward him, and he leaned slowly toward her. For a moment, he thought she might invite him in, but instead she said good night softly and closed the door.

# CHAPTER 27

In the morning Weatherby was awakened by a courier knocking on his outer door. He was in his loose linen night rail as he stumbled across the cold floor in the dark and opened the door. He often wondered why his sleeping shirt should be called a night rail. The courier handed him a slender leather pouch through the narrow opening.

"For Your Grace from the Chancellor," the courier said in a loud self-important voice.

Weatherby took the pouch and turned back, closing the door behind him. He lit a candle. He decided to read the missive in the Wolsey Apartments, so he pulled on some clothes and ordered some breakfast to be sent there. Once settled, he took a sip of tea and then held the wax seal on the parchment in a flame to soften it. Then he used a sharp knife to cut under the seal. Most of the letter, written in the clear and flowery hand of a clerk, was about Richard Weston's early career. He had been educated at the St. Paul's and then at Oxford University. He worked first as a stapler, a buyer and seller of raw wool, and then became steward of an earl's estate near Penzance. The King sent him to France as an envoy where he negotiated a treaty with Francis I. He never married, but during all those years he was reliable, hard working, and diligent. The letter continued:

"He was made Master of the House at Hampton Court as a reward for his many years of good service, but the moment he took the post, he changed dramatically. He shunned people, where previously dealing with people had been one of his fortes. He shunned the light, also. He insulated himself from others with obsequious lackeys. Some suspected these changes were due to strong drink, but no person had ever seen him take a sip. He once had written poetry in his spare time, but that has stopped. More recently he had shown violent tendencies. Shortly after his arrival at Hampton Court, he was attending a state dinner and quarreled with the Earl of Norfolk. Weston got so angry he pulled a small stiletto and lunged at the Earl. One courtier thought he saw Weston in a hood at an archaic animistic religious ceremony."

"He will soon be removed from his post by order of the King. In the meantime he should be handled gingerly.

> Thus indebted to you for your
> Efforts, I bid you farewell.
> Thomas Cromwell.
> From Whitehall Palace the 29d of April 1530."

Weatherby realized that Richard Weston could have committed one or more of the murders, but that because of his suspicious nature and the way he shunned people, it would be hard to investigate. Recognizing that the letter could be dangerous if found by the wrong person, Weatherby hid the document in a book. Weatherby had been told that Dredge and his Shetland pony had returned late last night from his investigation of the possible Druids in Wycombe. Weatherby walked to the servant's quarters, where he found Dredge getting dressed.

"What did you find?" Weatherby asked without preamble.

"Those country people are very close-mouthed and suspicious," Dredge replied as he stifled a yawn. "They ran me around in circles, no pun intended, from farm to farm and told me very little."

"Did you get any names?"

"I believe I did. Eventually I found a Christian farmer who had no patience for pagan religion, but was tied into the community. He talked. He suspects that a wealthy farmer named Conrad Wellford is the Grand Vizier of the Druids. I went to the Wellford farm, but the farmer was in Putney selling sheep and wasn't expected to return for four days."

"Did your farmer think the Druids practiced sacrifice as part of their rituals?"

"He said the rumor was that they frequently sacrificed goats and sheep, that they stole from local farms. Occasionally they sacrificed a bullock."

"Did he suggest they might have slit the throats of innocent young women to ensure a good crop for the year?" Weatherby asked.

Just as Weatherby finished, Judith Scotson ran in from the library. The servants' quarters were located on the ground floor off of the Clock Court, and the Library was under the eves in the north wing. Scotson was out of breath from her long walk.

"Amarantha sent me to fetch you," Judith Scotson said breathlessly. "We were only ten volumes from finishing our survey of the library. Margaret was already planning a celebration of completion for us at the Lamb and Flag. The three of us had worked nonstop in that dark, dusty room for the past four days, and we were dreaming of a glass of cool ale. I pulled down a large folio titled *Harris's Voyages* and out fell stacks of foolscap covered with writing, or lines of symbols, written in an elegant hand."

"Were these pages written by Anna Maria Wimbledon?" Weatherby asked in an excited voice.

"Amarantha thinks that is a strong possibility," Judith replied now that her breathing had returned to normal.

Weatherby rose from his desk and walked quickly back to the library with Judith Scotson. As he walked through the door he noticed Amarantha and Margaret Sedgwick poring over papers spread on a large table.

"Did you finally strike gold, Ran?" Sir Weatherby asked as he walked across the room.

"I'm not sure, Seamus," Amarantha replied. "But whatever it is, it's fascinating. Take a look."

Amarantha slowly turned several of the large yellow pages while Weatherby looked over her shoulder. He saw rows and rows of lines going all the way across the page. Attached to these lines were shorter lines that ran at various angles toward the top of the page.

"You are the master of languages, Seamus," Amarantha said. "Do you recognize this writing?"

"It's none of the European languages based on the Roman alphabet, and it's not Hebrew or Arabic," Weatherby answered. "With those continuous lines running across the page, I don't see how it can be a language from the orient."

"Perhaps it isn't a language," Amarantha queried. "Could it be a code?"

"Of course, but if it is why not use standard letters and just substitute say a 'b' for every 'e'?" Weatherby asked. "If this was written by Anna Maria Wimbledon, why would she invent a whole new writing system?"

"What shall we do next?" Amarantha asked.

"I want each of you to make two copies of the first ten lines of this document," Weatherby said without hesitation. "I will mail one copy to linguists at three universities and each of us will study a copy for clues. Also make a copy for Dredge, please. I've found he is very adept at puzzles. But first I want to take all three of you for a fancy lunch at the Lamb and Flag."

It was a warm spring day, so the four walked across the Thames and into the village. After a quick pint of ale, all three women began talking at once. Amarantha raised her voice over the others.

"What were the chances of finding those writings with only ten volumes left for us to survey?" Amarantha asked.

"You can do the mathematics as well as I can, Ran," Weatherby replied. "But since you three did the physical work, I will do the calculation. How many volumes were in the library?"

"Before we started we had guessed fifteen hundred, but we actually looked at over seventeen hundred," Judith replied.

"I think the way to solve this problem is to divide the books into groups," Weatherby replied. "For example, the chance of finding the right volume in the first half or in the first eight hundred volumes is fifty percent, right? If we divide the books into groups of ten, the chance of finding one book in any one group is one in a hundred and seventy. So the chance of you three being that unfortunate was slightly more than one in two hundred. You were extraordinarily unlucky!"

A large platter of roast pork and turnips arrived at the table, and all four diners ate quietly for a while. Margaret Sedgwick broke the silence.

"I wish we were sure it was dear Anna Maria's writing," she said wistfully. "If it had been in the Roman alphabet, both Judith and I would recognize her hand."

"It is unfortunate, and you make a good point," Sir Weatherby mused. "Another person such as Richard Weston or even Cardinal Wolsey could have written it. I'll have Dredge analyze the ink and the parchment; perhaps he can give us some information about their origin from that. In the meantime, I want to reward you for your diligence. I'd like the three of you to spend the afternoon shopping in the village at my expense."

Weatherby reached into his pouch and gave Amarantha a stack of thirty gold angels.

"That's fifteen pounds, Seamus. That is a lot of money," Amarantha replied.

"I have no doubt you three can spend it on ribbons, hats, chemises," Weatherby said as he stood up from his chair. "I'm going back to Hampton Court to work on some papers."

He walked back across the river, stopping only briefly to admire the water with the sunlight shimmering on its surface. When he got to his desk he drew an element from memory of the strange writing on a fresh piece of parchment:

Weatherby recalled a horizontal line that was uninterrupted from one side of the page to the other, and on some of the pages the top line continued down along the left edge of the paper before stopping. All along the horizontal line, little branches attached to the top or the bottom or to both as in the element he had drawn. These vertical branches numbered from one to four. The spaces between the branches suggested the beginning or end of words or phrases. The side branches were perpendicular or slanted with respect to the horizontal base line. After much study, Weatherby decided it must be a simple alphabet. He counted twenty-six possible symbols or 'letters' in the manuscript.

Weatherby laid the parchment aside and reread the letter from Thomas Cromwell about The Master of the House. He needed someone to shadow Richard Weston for a few days to learn about his activities. Dredge was smart enough to do it, but he was too easy to spot and too slow because of his physical deformity. Weatherby determined that the assistant librarian, Judith Scotson was smart enough to carry out the task, so he wrote her a note asking her to visit him.

# CHAPTER 28

Weatherby spent the evening reviewing his three cases in front of a fire in the Great Watching Chamber. He decided that of the three, he was making the best progress on the last one. He was convinced that Gregory Townsend was probably killed by Clarence Stevens in a fit of rage because the Reverend had made inappropriate advances toward his sister. If the secret writing was done by Anna Maria Wimbledon, which seemed likely, and if the code could be cracked, then all Anna Maria's secrets would be revealed, which would certainly aid in the resolution of her murder. Weatherby decided the case that had really stalled was the murder of William Suffolk. He lacked a strong suspect in the bludgeoning death of the Earl's son. Weatherby wanted to send Amarantha to interview the Earl of Suffolk, but he wasn't sure such a traditional and powerful man would be open with what the Earl would regard as a mere woman. Even though it was evening, Weatherby called for a courier, and wrote a brief note asking if the Earl was at home and if he would receive him. Then he put on his night rail and crawled into bed.

At three of the clock, Weatherby was awakened by his recurring nightmare. As he changed out of a sweaty night shirt, he realized he hadn't had the dream in a fortnight. As long as he was wide awake, he decided to analyze the dream as he had been taught in medical school. He tried to focus first on the setting of the dream. It was a fen that he didn't recognize from his extensive travels in England and Scotland, but from the vegetation he knew it was wetter and hillier than the area around Hampton Court. He would talk with Sir Moulton about areas in England that were moister, and then he fell back asleep.

In the morning Weatherby felt rested despite the interruption of his sleep. He realized he had spent little time recently with Dredge and even less time in the lab so he decided to spend the day there. After breakfast he had Dredge pull out all the evidence, including the autopsy report on each of the three victims. They spent an hour on each case.

In the William Suffolk case there was a mysterious fiber that hadn't been matched. Dredge made a list of the things it might be. In the Anna Maria Wimbledon case the poison that smelled like bitter roses was still unidentified. Dredge had spent days studying their many old volumes on potions and poisons, and had turned up nothing. He had even had a fruitless conversation with the village apothecary. Now he was compiling a list of witches, seers, and necromancers in the area that he could interview.

As for the last victim, Gregory Townsend, Dredge had analyzed the glue used to hold the Bible in the victim's arms during the seventy-foot fall. It matched fish glue found in a pot in the Outer Court. Unfortunately, it was kept in an area near the Office of the Greencloth where supplies were stored. Dredge thought anyone from the Palace could easily have used the glue pot. After pondering the evidence for many minutes, Weatherby suddenly headed off in a new direction.

"I would like to write a technical paper for presentation to the Royal Society in London," he began. "It is the most prestigious scientific forum in the world, and a paper read there would gain wide currency. When I spent those six months in the Netherlands with Anton von Leeuwenhoek learning about the microscope, I was immediately struck by its possible utility in solving crimes. Leeuwenhoek has gone off in another direction and is using the instrument to discover and classify animalcules."

"I have analyzed and classified sixty different kinds of hair, Sir. We could include a section on hair types," Dredge suggested.

"Yes, and you have also collected fibers from different kinds of fabrics that we could include. How many of those do you have?"

"Dozens. We could count how many in a few minutes," Dredge replied.

"The microscope was also invaluable in documenting that Miss Wimbledon had been sexually assaulted. We can write a section about that application, and you could do a drawing showing the shape and coloration of spermatozoa."

"I'll make a note to do that."

"Just to round it out so the paper will be about twenty written pages long, let's analyze soil type. We often find mud on the boots of victims and suspects, and it would be valuable to know where it came from. Let's collect ten different samples from different locations around the palace and look at them under the microscope. If we can tell them apart, you can show me an unknown sample, and I will tell you where it came from."

"Very good, Sir."

"Before you start, let's have quick lunch in the Great Kitchen," Weatherby said as he headed out the door.

After eating, Dredge went back to the laboratory to collect a satchel full of bottles, labels and scrapers. They agreed to meet at the Great Gatehouse in thirty minutes. Dredge arrived on time carrying a large satchel. Weatherby was often torn about what to do at such times. Dredge was a servant and therefore expected to stoop and carry. However, because of rickets and his resulting saber shins, he was over two feel shorter than Weatherby. Carrying large, heavy objects was onerous for him. On this occasion, Weatherby compromised and took one of the straps on the canvas satchel and they carried the load together.

They walked around the Palace collecting dirt samples from carriageways, gardens, stables and fields. While they were obtaining their clumps of dirt a courier arrived with a message for Weatherby. The rolled parchment said that the Earl of Suffolk was at home and that he would be happy to receive Sir Weatherby. Once back in the laboratory, Dredge dissolved a small amount of each sample in water so that the soils could be seen under the microscope. Both felt that color, grain size and mix of particle types would make telling one sample from the other easy. Dredge presented Weatherby with the first unknown sample. After studying the specimen under the microscope for several minutes, Weatherby spoke.

"This sample contains tan particles which are nearly all the same size, with an occasional dark brown larger particle," Weatherby began. "I think it is sand and it is quite distinctive-looking. I believe this sample came from the Clock Tower Court."

"You are correct. We should put a section about soil analysis in the paper," Dredge said.

"Yes. I think it could be very useful if a body has been moved and we needed to locate the precise scene of the crime," Weatherby replied. "With the fibers, hairs, soil analysis and sperm I believe we have enough material for our paper."

Weatherby found Amarantha in the library copying the symbols the three librarians had found. He invited her for an early dinner in his apartment.

After they had eaten, Weatherby said, "I've received permission to interview the Earl of Suffolk about his fifth son."

"I could do that for you, Seamus," Amarantha answered.

"I thought about that, Ran. But I'm afraid he will turn out to be too much of a stodgy old aristocrat to give a woman the information we need about his son."

"I suspect you are correct."

"The village is forty-three miles from here, and my only decision is whether to go by horse or by carriage."

"I think you should ride that beautiful roan."

"As you know, I have been riding more since you showed me up the day of the hail storm, but I've never ridden anything like forty miles."

"You'll be riding through rolling country toward the northeast and I know the roads, and they are good."

"Then I think I should give it a try," Weatherby answered thoughtfully.

"Would you mind if I came along?"

"What a capital idea!" Weatherby replied gleefully. "I think we should get an early start. I'll notify the stable."

"I don't think we or the horses will be able see before six."

"I'll arrange some food for a picnic and have some blankets packed in case the weather turns bad."

"So you don't have to surround my naked form with your warm flesh like you did during the hailstorm?"

"I will always treasure that memory, Ran. You have a truly beautiful figure, and it is sad that you must disguise it so often to perform your work. Perhaps we could agree that if we get soaked by the rain again, we will remove our clothes and then wrap the warm blankets around the outside."

"I agree to that," Amarantha responded thoughtfully. "Now let us get some rest so we will be fresh in the morning."

They met at the stable just before six and started on their journey. The first part of the trip was through the open woods that surrounded the Thames. Once they were out of sight of Hampton Court, Amarantha picked up the pace. They headed mostly east for the first few miles and then turned more toward the north along a road built in Roman times. The Roman roads were straight and wide and had speeded transport and travel in England for the past thirteen hundred years. Usually the route was wide enough that they could ride side by side. As they rode, Weatherby told Amarantha the legend of King Arthur and Guinevere. He embellished the tale with details about the round table, Lancelot's horse and the how the lover's first kiss felt. At mid day, judged by the height of the sun, Amarantha determined that they had gone about twenty miles. They stopped in a glade. Weatherby spread one of the blankets on the ground and arranged the food on it. They had a loaf of rye bread, chunks of ham and bottle of malmsey, a dark fortified wine from Madeira. Fresh radishes and pickles formed an accompaniment. After they were finished eating, Weatherby pushed some of the duff on the forest floor into a mound like a pillow beneath their blanket and they rested for half an hour.

During the afternoon ride the road was narrower and wound through hillier country so they rode single file. They still made good time and by four of the clock were in the village of Suffolk below the manor house. The village looked run down and impoverished. The inhabitants were shabbily dressed, and the lanes in the village were ill kept. They continued to the east on the lane toward the manor. Here everything was well kept and tidy. To their right was a vast perfectly manicured lawn several hectares in size. Near the bottom was a 'ha ha.' Weatherby was never sure whether it was the idea of the 'ha ha' or the name he liked the best. The 'ha ha' built by the landscape architect was there so that the Earl could look out on a lawn unencumbered with animals or a fence. To achieve this, the architect needed a structure that would keep the animals out and also create an unseen fence. So he created a steep-sided trench dug across the lawn, which was too wide for any animal to jump across and then placed it so that the trench couldn't be seen from the manor house.

# CHAPTER 29

Weatherby and Amarantha rode slowly up the lane toward the mansion across the long sloping lawn. A pool a half mile long went from the lawn to the house. Reflected in the pool was a four-story Romanesque mansion with twenty double windows across the first floor. The mansion was made of a light yellow stone that was ornamented with stone tracery and small columns on every surface. Amarantha thought the manor house resembled a very large rectangular wedding cake with an intricate butter frosting.

They brought their horses to a halt in front of a broad flight of eight steps topped by two large wooden doors. They dismounted and tied both animals to a black iron ring atop a post. They walked stiffly up the steps. Weatherby lifted the huge brass knocker and let it fall with a clunk. A butler in dark red livery opened the huge door with some difficulty, and Weatherby handed him his card.

"Good afternoon, Your Lordship and Madame," the butler said with a slight bow. "You are expected. Welcome to Suffolk Hall. Let me show you to your rooms and then we will set high tea for you in the library."

The butler led the way up the broad staircases to the second floor where the guests had adjacent rooms looking out over the reflecting pool. Both riders took off their dusty riding clothes and poured a big bowl of water from a ewer. Amarantha used a damp cloth to wash her arms, legs, and face. Weatherby was content to splash some water on his face and to wash his hands. When he had changed, he tapped on Amarantha's door and the two went down the broad stairs arm in arm. A large platter covered with scones, biscuits, jams, and fresh butter had been set out. Two young serving girls in ruffled aprons poured cups of hot tea with sugar and milk in it. After they had munched and conversed for a few minutes, the butler returned.

"The Earl is hunting on a farm to the west and sends his apologies," the butler began. "However, he will return for supper about eight. He suggests in the meantime that one of his secretaries take you on a tour of the manor house, outbuildings, and grounds."

"Thank you for your consideration," Sir Weatherby replied. "We would love to see the manor. My aunt wonders how formal dinner will be, so that she might dress appropriately."

"The Earl and especially his wife, Esther, are quite formal," the butler replied. "Two of their sons are also at home and while they care less about dress, their daughter Emily, who is also here, is very conscious of the French fashion."

"Thank you for your information," Amarantha replied.

The Earl's young secretary Jack arrived and introduced himself to the guests.

"I will start my tour by showing you the oldest part of the manor which was built in the twelfth century," Jack began. "And then we will work up to more modern times. If there is anything you particularly want to know about just mention it."

"I'm interested in Italian painting and I understand that you have two Bellini's," Amarantha volunteered.

"They are quite wonderful, and I can show you both," Jack replied.

"I've heard that the manor house is an excellent example of Romanesque architecture," Weatherby said as he swept his arm around the room they were in. "I would like to know about the elements of the design."

They followed Jack to the two large central, curving staircases.

"This was the first room that was built. It was started in 1108. Each staircase curves up in a gentle arch to the first floor. The floor is alternating black and white tiles. You will observe that the black tile is harder. The tiles were level when installed, and now the white marble tiles are a quarter inch lower from wear over the centuries. The blown glass central chandelier was made in Murano and holds three hundred and twenty candles."

Jack walked slowly into the next room, a hall sixty feet long, thirty feet wide, and twenty some feet high.

"This great hall is the largest room in the manor. There are sixty-two paintings in the room hung one above the other, but the place of honor is held by the Bellini located over the large, marble fireplace. It is the *Naked Young Woman in front of the Mirror* painted by Giovanni Bellini in 1515. It is the most valuable painting in the county."

"Look how placid the young woman in the foreground is, and how ominous and gray the clouds in the background are," Amarantha said. "The folds in the small red cloth she holds are beautifully draped."

All three of them stood gazing at the impressive work of art. Next, Jack led them down a long hallway to a series of sitting rooms each decorated in a different color. Up the broad stairway to the first floor were a number of large bedrooms occupied by the family.

As they walked, Weatherby asked, "Did you know William Suffolk?"

"He and I are the same age," Jack replied. "But I only met him twice."

"What was he like?"

"He was good-looking and always pleasant. The servants who knew him better than I found him very studious, and thought him the smartest of the seven children."

"Did he ever cause any trouble?"

"Nothing serious. The usual problems when he was an adolescent—taking a horse without asking, staying out all night and trouble with one of the serving girls. They hushed it up by sending her away. The servants found him very likable."

"Thank you for your candor," Weatherby replied as they reached the top of the stairs.

The second floor consisted of twelve smaller guest bedrooms. Because of their elevation, these rooms had an excellent view of the grounds. The top floor was occupied by a large billiards room, a library and a smaller sitting room. The second Bellini, *Madonna of the Meadow,* hung in this room. Amarantha thought it was an excellent portrait, but not as accomplished as the painting on the ground floor. Jack pointed out that it had been painted ten years before the Bellini that hung over the fireplace.

Jack led the way back down the stairs and out the front door. He walked them a hundred yards from the yellow façade, so the whole front of the manor house could be taken in without a turn of the head.

"This is a strong example of Romanesque architecture because of the mansion's thick walls, rounded arches and sturdy piers," Jack began. "Suffolk House is made lighter-looking by the large multipane windows. It has groin vaults and decorative arcading. As you know, Sir

Weatherby, another mark of Romanesque architecture, most popular between the tenth and twelfth century, is a very strict symmetry. Look at the façade of Suffolk House, and you will note the whole pile is perfectly balanced."

Jack guided the two of them on a more cursory tour of the out buildings including the kitchen, the bakery, and an aviary, and then Amarantha and Weatherby retired to their rooms to dress for dinner. Amarantha wore a sapphire-blue gown, and Weatherby an elegant gold doublet. The Earl of Suffolk, a portly man in his sixties, greeted his guests as they entered the dining room just as the butler had predicted. In addition to the Earl's wife, two sons and a daughter were present with their spouses and several guests from a nearby manor. A total of sixteen guests were seated at a mahogany table. An elegant meal with many courses occupied the guests for the next three hours. Weatherby lost track after chicken soup followed by turtle soup and a salad of fresh greens. There were at least five main dishes of meat or fowl. The Marquis of Stafford sat on Weatherby's right, and his interest in optics and astronomy helped pass the time.

After dinner the guests adjourned to a nearby room for cards. They played gleek, a new game favored by Queen Catherine of Aragon. Neither Weatherby nor Amarantha had heard of it. It was played in groups of three with twelve cards dealt and eight left in a pile face down. Each player tries to improve his hand by drawing so that he has a gleek (three of a kind) or a mourvinal (four of a kind), followed by trick play. Betting occurred at three different times with each hand. Soon Weatherby had lost four sovereigns, but judging by her laughter and little shrieks Amarantha was winning at another table. Both wandered up to bed at 2 a.m., according to a large wooden clock in the front hall.

In the morning after a large breakfast, Sir Weatherby sat down with the Earl of Suffolk.

"Thank you for talking with me, Your Grace," Weatherby began. "I have been investigating the death of your son William for a month, and I'm sorry to tell you that I don't have a motive or a strong suspect. I'm hoping you can help me."

"William was one of my seven children," the Earl of Suffolk began. "I believe I knew less about him than about any of the others, as he was very quiet and also a loner. William was a nice young man, and I was most surprised that he was murdered."

"So you don't know of anyone that would want to harm him?"

"I hadn't seen him in over a year, but he wasn't fanatical about politics or religion. William was twenty-eight and had never had so much as a romantic entanglement."

Weatherby was very disappointed with the interview. He had gained no new information that would help him solve the murder.

"Thank you for your time, Your Grace," Weatherby said as he rose and walked toward the door.

Weatherby ordered their horses saddled, and then found Amarantha studying the Bellini again.

"I believe if we leave now, Ran, we could be back at Hampton court this evening," Weatherby said.

"I'm packed," Amarantha replied. "Let's try it."

Both walked quickly up stairs to collect their belongings and then met their horses at the front door. They rode in silence for the first few miles. Then Weatherby began to express his frustrations.

"We rode all this way for nothing, Ran," Weatherby opined. "I got no useful information from the Earl. I got the feeling that he barely knew William and cared little about him."

"I ran into the Countess before breakfast this morning, and we talked over a cup of tea. She is much more involved with the children than the Earl is," Amarantha replied. "And she was very fond of William. Although he visited Suffolk House seldom, I suspect because he didn't get along with his father, he wrote a letter to his mother every week. She found him happy in his work and life until about six months ago. Then he got involved in some sort of cabal that consumed him."

"Was it political or religious?" Weatherby asked.

"He never said specifically in his letters who was in it or what their goals were," Amarantha replied. "However, six weeks ago he wrote his mother an ominous letter saying that he feared for his life and that if anything happened to him she should contact King Urien of Gore."

"And who could that possibly be?"

"I have no earthly idea. You are the well read one. I was hoping you would know."

The road narrowed and became hilly for the next several miles and both attended to their riding. When it flattened out, Amarantha spoke again.

"I couldn't decide how to address the Earl's wife at first. I thought of a Duke and Duchess and a Marquess and a Marquise, but I knew there wasn't an Earless."

"I had to learn all the ranks and titles of the peerage when I started working for Henry VIII," Weatherby replied. "I was told that an Earl was the equivalent of a Count on the continent. Since there was no female equivalent of Earl, they borrowed the continental equivalent Countess."

"I suppose that makes sense," Amarantha replied. "Fortunately, one of the other card players called her Countess and saved me the embarrassment."

"I'm glad I brought you on this trip, Ran," Weatherby mused. "I enjoyed the company, and you stumbled on some potentially valuable information even though we don't have any idea what it means."

"It was a good ride, Seamus," Amarantha replied.

They arrived back at Hampton Court at 9 p.m. in near total darkness. They were tired but somehow pleased with the mysterious information they had gleaned. Weatherby knew he was too tired to have the nightmare that night, despite the fact that on their ride to Suffolk he had seen some ground that looked suspiciously like the setting of his night terror.

# CHAPTER 30

Weatherby slept beyond his usual hour in the morning, but by the time he had his clothes on his mind was at work on his three troubling cases. The reason that William Suffolk stole colored glass from the Hampton Court glazier's shop and pawned it at Oatlands was still unclear. Weatherby decided to talk with Nathaniel Philbrick, the felon who was master glazier once more. Sir John Moulton had said that Philbrick had done excellent work at Whitehall and then Greenwich before he killed a man in a bar brawl.

After breakfast, Weatherby walked over to the glazier's shop. Philbrick was making a piece of glass that was a royal red. First he blew a sphere of red glass and added some gold powder. While it was still hot swung it around to make a long cylinder. As the glass cooled, Nathaniel cut the cylinder along the side and laid the glass out flat on a clean iron table. Nathaniel and two assistants quickly cut the glass in to a series of shapes following a pattern hung on the wall. Weatherby watched with fascination at the smooth and orderly way the glaziers performed their work before the bright red glass hardened.

Placing his tools on the table Philbrick turned toward Weatherby and said, "Sorry to see Your Worship again."

"Not near as sorry as I am to see you, Nathaniel," Weatherby quipped. "Your alibi didn't hold water—or perhaps I should say ale. Dotty, the drab you spent the night with couldn't remember which night it was that you took advantage of her and then didn't pay her. So you are still my prime suspect for the murder of William Suffolk."

"I told you I had murderous thoughts about him all the time," Philbrick replied. "But I never laid a bloody finger on him!"

"You lured him to a dark part of the Palace and then struck him down with another workman's hammer."

"There is only one reason that I am no longer a violent and impulsive man."

"And what, pray tell, is that?" Weatherby replied in a sarcastic voice.

"I have been in the bloody Tower of London and I don't ever want to go back, not even for a second. It is the most dark, depraved and bone-chilling place in Christendom."

"I fail to be impressed by your protestations of innocence."

He was again, however, impressed by Philbrick's slender build, and from his experiments felt Nathaniel Philbrick could be a murderer. In any case, he had really come to talk with the master glazier about another topic and he segued into that subject.

"Why was William Suffolk stealing glass from you?"

"I always thought it was to supplement his meager salary so he could buy fine things for a woman."

"What woman?"

"It is true I never saw one or even heard anyone speak of one."

"What other reason could he have for taking random pieces of glass from your shop?"

"Oh. It wasn't random at all. He only took only one kind of glass, and that was Chartres blue."

"Why only that glass?"

"Well it was the most expensive glass we ever got, but also it was an amazing light blue like no other glass. A color like it didn't even exist on the island of Murano, where I learned glass-blowing. For hundreds of years, Murano has been the most advanced and innovative center for glass techniques, however they still don't have a color that is anything like Chartres blue."

"You think he stole it because it was the most valuable, and therefore he could pawn it for the most money?"

"For some reason I don't believe that is true. I think it was something else."

"Where does your glass come from?"

"We make some here, but our needs are too great for us to blow all of it," Philbrick began. "We get crates of special glass packed in straw from Murano and from the German States."

"And the Chartres blue glass?"

"It comes from a small glass shop south of the city of Chartres and is in high demand. We usually have to wait several weeks for a delivery."

"Could the glass have been used for something else? Such as transmitting a message?"

"Yes, but I doubt it," Philbrick replied. "I've looked very closely at dozens of pieces of Chartres glass, and never seen anything that looked like writing or code."

"Do you have any of that glass that we could look at?"

"I have a couple of large sheets and a lot of scraps."

Philbrick enlisted one of his associates to help him look through the midden of glass outside the glazier's shop. They found several scraps of blue glass and two larger sheets. Weatherby examined the sheets very carefully with his magnifying glass. He saw no letters or symbols hidden in the beautiful blue transparency. In spite of that, Weatherby had Dredge collect the scraps of glass so he could inspect them under the microscope. When the glass was collected, Weatherby turned back to Philbrick.

"You are still my prime suspect in the death of William Suffolk, Nathaniel," Weatherby said. "I will be watching you, and I don't want you leaving the Palace without my permission."

Weatherby walked out of the glazier's shop slamming the door behind him.

Weatherby wrote a brief message to be sent by courier to the sheriff of Surrey enquiring after the sheriff's efforts to capture Clarence Stevens. He was actually surprised that Clarence hadn't already been captured. Weatherby felt Clarence was not very smart, and as a farmhand had few resources and would quickly fall into the hands of the sheriff's men.

Weatherby found Amarantha and together they enjoyed a leisurely lunch in the orchard. Weatherby told Amarantha about his interview with Nathaniel Philbrick.

"William Suffolk became very focused on stealing the glass from Chartres when he 'changed' about six or seven months ago. I think the blue glass may be an important clue, Ran," Weatherby said. For some reason I think it may have been a way of transferring secret messages."

"Is there evidence of that, Seamus?" Amarantha said.

"No, but I have Dredge analyzing some of the shards of glass now. I may take a trip to Chartres to explore the glass's connection to our crime."

"We seem to be making progress on the Suffolk murder. I wish we were doing as well on Anna Maria's demise. I still see her as the most innocent of our three victims."

"At least you found the clandestine writing that holds her secrets."

"If it really is her writing. And if we can crack the code."

"Once the copies are made I will send them off to the universities."

"We finished the ten copies you asked for this morning and put them in the Wolsey Apartments for you."

"I'll send them out by courier today."

A large dessert of pears soaked in port and topped with fluffy mounds of whipped cream arrived. All conversation stopped for several minutes. Amarantha found the full sweet taste of the pears complemented the rich tart taste of the aged wine. When the plates were clean, Weatherby continued thinking about the murders out loud.

"We both think that Anna Maria had far too many clothes and fine jewelry for her modest librarian's salary. I need to discover the source of Miss Wimbledon's extra funds. Did the assistant librarians ever comment about her rich taste while you were trapped with those dusty books?"

"Not really. But Judith Scotson made one unusual remark when she was nurturing me back to health at Leith Hill. She was talking about a beautiful and expensive garnet necklace set in gold that Anna Maria had recently been given and that Judith coveted. She mentioned that every two weeks or so, Anna Maria would slip away for a couple of hours in the morning. Judith said that when the head librarian returned her clothes were impeccable, but she would notice small beads of perspiration on Anna Maria's upper lip and a distracted look in her eyes. I was too ill to think much of it at the time, and I wrote it off as women spending too much time together."

"Would you ask Judith about that?"

"Yes."

"You made such a quick recovery from your depression, Ran. Is it fully resolved?"

"Not completely. Every so often, the big black dog bounds up to me and licks me on the face, but if I go outside or take a quick walk, he retreats into the shadows just as quickly."

"I am so pleased you are better."

"Not near as delighted as I am," Amarantha said, resting her hand gently on top of Weatherby's.

"I have one more assignment for you, and this one will take all of your wiles," Weatherby said. "I showed you the frank but disturbing letter that Thomas Cromwell wrote about Richard Weston. I think he is just bizarre enough to be capable of a violent crime, but neither Dredge nor I can shadow him: it would be too obvious. I'm hoping you can think of a reason to meet with him and then strike up a 'friendship.'"

"If I'm to have any hope of success at that, Seamus, I will have to shed all of my Aunt Amarantha costume for more colorful attire that shows off my figure. If I know men, an occasional glimpse of ankle or shoulder would help my cause. I'll start on that project today."

"I'm so glad I know you, Ran," Weatherby said with an emotional tone. "How would I ever get along without you?"

"You wouldn't, Seamus." Amarantha loosened her dark red hair and let it fall onto her shoulders. "You would try to kill yourself by throwing yourself into the Thames and be hopelessly stuck in the smelly mud along the bank and forlornly washed out to the North Sea on the next high tide."

# PART 4

# CHAPTER 31

Weatherby began to plan his trip to the Chartres. First he went to the Hampton Court library and had Judith Scotson pull out maps of the area. The village of Chartres was thirty miles southwest of Paris, but all the main roads ran through the enormous capital, the largest city in the world. Weatherby would be obliged to go to the French capital and take a coach from there to his final destination. Using calipers and a ruler, he calculated the distance from London to Paris at 213 miles. The harder question was to determine if it was faster to go to LeHavre, on the French coast, by coach and ship or take a ship from London directly to Calais. Weatherby thought that Dredge would be able to complete such a calculation accurately and advise him.

The King's premier detective went to the laboratory in search of his amanuensis. He threw all the charts and calipers and rulers on a clean, marble-topped table in the spotlessly clean laboratory.

"I need to make a trip to Chartres, Dredge," Weatherby began. "And I need to know the fastest way to get there. Cost is no object. Can you help me?"

"Yes, Your Grace," Dredge responded. "I quite enjoy puzzles that require a knowledge of rates of speed, frequency of trips and prevailing winds and tides in the spring. I can have it for you this evening."

"Excellent. I'm going to interrogate Anna Maria's roommate again and see if I can glean some more information about Miss Wimbledon's secret habits," Weatherby said as he left the laboratory.

Peggy Ealing purchased furniture and other staples for the Palace, and Weatherby knew her office was in the Outer Court near the Office of the Green Cloth. He walked out through the Great Gatehouse and headed downriver to the Outer Court. It was warm, but a light mist was falling, so he ducked inside as soon as he could. Weatherby recalled his first sarcastic interview with the dead woman's roommate. He walked into Miss Ealing's office after knocking lightly on the outer door. She was sitting at a desk and crouched over a large leather-bound ledger.

"Good evening, Miss Ealing," Weatherby began in a pleasant voice. "I need some information about the private life and personal habits of Miss Wimbledon. We have a killer loose at Hampton Court and I don't know who his next victim will be. It could very well be a comely young person such as yourself."

"I have had that very thought, Sir Weatherby, and to be honest, I haven't slept well since Anna Maria's body was found," Peggy Ealing replied.

"In that case, I need the intimate details only you may know about your roommate."

"I believe I told you everything I know when we first met. How she changed about six months ago suddenly became less reliable and was absent more often. I didn't think much about it at first. But then it became more apparent, and she wasn't willing to talk about it. I also noticed that she began dressing more carefully and suddenly had much finer clothing. The last week before she died she awoke early, and ran from our room. At least once I heard her retching outside. That's really all I know."

"No. Peggy I think there is more. If you had been found dead I would want your roommate to tell me about the man you were seeing and perhaps were enmeshed with," Weatherby replied in an insistent voice based on nothing but a wild hunch.

Peggy looked down and became silent.

"It's not very easy to keep secrets at Hampton Court, Miss Ealing, because people are always. Busybodies are everywhere."

"I'm very embarrassed that you know about my assignation with Richard Weston," Peggy Ealing replied in a soft, shaky voice. "It is really quite innocent. Usually it just involves talking over tea with some hand-holding."

"You have a right to your private life, Peggy, but I need to know more about your roommate's circumstances."

"One night about six weeks ago, Anna Maria asked me to spend the night elsewhere. When I came back in the morning there were muddy boot prints in our room. It looked to me as though perhaps three men had been in our chamber."

"You know more than you are telling me, Peggy. I'm tired of playing this cat and mouse game with you!" Weatherby pounded his fist on the desk.

Peggy jumped.

When she recovered, she spoke in a soft, hurried voice, "I snuck back that night to see what was transpiring in our room, and hid in the shadows down the hall. I saw three men in great coats go into our room at about eleven thirty. They were all bundled up, and I didn't recognize any of them. However the last man turned my way as he went through the door and I glimpsed his face. He was young, slight and very dark-skinned. I had never seen him before. Then I slunk off to bed."

Weatherby remembered that Gregory Townsend had mentioned seeing Anna Maria Wimbledon twice with a dark-complexioned stranger just before he was thrown from the Great Gatehouse.

"Was this man Moorish or African?" Weatherby asked.

"I'm not sure. The light was very bad."

"Thank you for your candor, Peggy," Weatherby said as he pushed his chair back. "I only have one bit of advice for you. Don't see Richard Weston again."

"Thank you, Your grace. I won't," Ealing replied as she lowered her head slightly.

Weatherby sent a note to Amarantha telling her about Peggy Ealing's relationship with Richard Weston and saying that he didn't believe she was being completely honest. With Ealing warned off, Weatherby hoped his assistant could get close to the Master of the House.

Weatherby went to his apartment where a fire had been laid. He ate a cold supper and read by the light of candelabra before drifting off to sleep.

In the morning, he went to his laboratory. Dredge was bent over a table covered with charts, maps and instruments.

"What is your advice on getting from Hampton Court to Calais?" Weatherby asked as he came into the room.

"It involves more assumptions, which may be right or wrong, than most such calculations," Dredge replied. "I'm assuming a coach can go seven miles per hour on a good road and that a ship that crosses the English Channel goes between zero and ten knots, depending on the wind. Therefore, the average is five knots per hour. If you go down the Thames to Ramsgate in the east and then sail south to Calais it will take you forty-nine hours to reach your destination. However, if you take the coach to Portsmouth and sail to Le Havre it will only take thirty-nine hours. Therefore, I recommend a coach to the south. It will save you ten hours. I recommend you plan on the trip to Chartres taking five days."

"Thanks for your help, Dredge," Weatherby replied thinking that if he pushed he could be there in three days. "Please, set it up for me a departure tomorrow morning. While I'm gone, work on the cipher we found in the library. I also want you to scour the county for anyone—seers, witches, or chemists who can tell us about the poison used to kill Anna Maria."

Weatherby went in search of Amarantha to tell her he would be gone for the better part of a fortnight. She was sewing in her room.

"I had no idea you did handiwork, Ran," Weatherby began. "It is very domestic."

"What you mean is, 'it's so feminine' and you don't find me feminine at all, do you?" Amarantha answered in an accusing tone.

Weatherby, after pondering what he had wandered into, walked over and put a hand gently on Amarantha's shoulder.

"Despite your intelligence and drive, my dear Ran, I find you to be the epitome of femininity," Weatherby replied. "And I would be deeply hurt if you felt otherwise. I also find you to be very beautiful."

"What a wonderful response, Seamus," Amarantha replied as she was warmed by the compliment. "I need to fish for compliments more often. That one was wonderful."

"I meant every word of it, Ran. I hope you know that."

"I appreciate your openness and sincerity."

Here was another opportunity to tell the alluring Miss Thompson of his undying love for her, but again something held Weatherby back.

"I arranged a meeting with Richard Weston," Amarantha went on. "He is a strange duck. We met in an almost totally dark room. I hadn't realized how much flirting relies on a downcast look, a raised shoulder, or a jut of the hips—they all require visibility. However, I did my best to give him some signals with my hands and lips."

"Please spare me the details, Ran," Weatherby said suddenly feeling a wave of jealousy. "I discovered Peggy Ealing had been moving toward a relationship with him. I warned her off so you would have a better chance."

"Thanks for the boost," Amarantha replied. "I will keep you posted on my progress."

"I came to tell you I'll be taking a trip to Chartres," Weatherby replied. "I plan to learn more about the glass that Suffolk was stealing.

I suspect it is an important clue to the unraveling of the mystery. I leave in the morning and I will be gone less than a fortnight."

"I wish I could go with you, Seamus. You know it makes me sad when you are away, but while you are gone I will carry out the assignments you gave me."

"Please don't think I want you to have sexual congress with the Master of the House to get the information we need." Weatherby clarified in an alarmed voice.

"You needn't tell me that, Seamus," Amarantha said. "I am a modest and chaste Christian woman. I can be quite seductive without delivering the ultimate prize."

"I didn't know you were a devout Christian, Ran."

"I am modest and chaste, Seamus, but I admit that I may have exaggerated the Christian part a bit," Amarantha replied. "I did attend a whole service religious service at the Cathedral of Utrecht in 1519."

"In an age consumed by religious fervor and persecution your honesty is most refreshing, Ran. If the big black dog visits while I am gone, talk with Judith Scotson and restart your medicine."

"I will Seamus," Amarantha replied. "But don't worry about me, I am doing fine."

# CHAPTER 32

Weatherby arose at four a.m. to catch the coach from the village of Hampton to the port of Southampton. He had packed a small brocaded bag for the trip. It was half full of clothes, and half full of instruments for measuring and collecting that Dredge had picked for him. A servant loaded the satchel in a hansom and drove Sir Weatherby to the coach stop in the village of Hampton. He waited outside in the cold morning air until the carriage, pulled by four black horses, arrived some thirty minutes late. He had pulled his collar up to keep the chill off his neck while he waited impatiently. Once the carriage was at a full stop the driver jumped down from his seat in a long leather coat, carrying some letters and small packages into the store. He returned quickly. The driver was already late and hoped to make up the time on the flat stretch of countryside just south of Hampton. The trip from Hampton to Southampton was sixty-six miles long and even if the weather held, and there were no major mishaps, it would be a long day on the highways.

The carriage was a large wooden model with seats for six. Fortunately, only two travelers occupied the coach when it stopped. A tiny woman dressed in black was curled up in one corner. A rotund young man in a priest's cassock sat across from her. Weatherby mumbled a greeting and sat on the opposite end of the seat occupied by the old woman. The carriage lurched out of town. Weatherby had brought a book to read but found it too dark inside the coach to see the words. He folded his coat against the wall of the carriage and rested his head on it, but found he couldn't sleep. He was surprised. During medical school he occasionally had fifteen or thirty minutes to himself. If it was fifteen minutes he ate hurriedly, and if he had the luxury of thirty minutes he trained himself

174

to sleep. He could be fast asleep in under a minute. However, for some reason sleep eluded him this morning. He decided to talk with the priest.

"Where are you going, Father?" Weatherby asked.

"I am Father Croceus Lawrence and I have been assigned to the Church of St. Germain des Pres in Paris for further instruction in the creation of manuscripts," the priest replied in a superior tone. "Our priory makes illuminated religious texts that we purvey to religious orders and wealthy patrons. And what do you do, pray tell?"

"My name is Seamus Scott Weatherby and I am a special envoy to King Henry VIII," Weatherby replied.

"Very good," Father Lawrence replied. "But what has the King charged you with?"

"I'm responsible for sleuthing out the scoundrels that attack His Majesty's property and minions," Weatherby replied in an attempt to be as abstruse as possible.

Father Lawrence appeared puzzled, so after a minute's contemplation he replied, "What specific dilemma tests your powers at present?"

"A vexatious triple homicide at Hampton Court Palace."

"Even in an increasingly violent and careless age, that is a collection of misfortune. God rest their souls," Father Lawrence said as he crossed himself.

"'Tis true. In my travels for Henry over the past five years to all parts of England as well as Scotland, Wales and Ireland, I have never seen anything like it."

"Perhaps it is just a coincidence, like the rare alignment of the earth, moon and sun, which causes an eclipse and a gradually change in the moon's color from radiant white to a bloody red color."

"May chance. However that is not what you really think," Weatherby replied.

"You are correct. My first thought is that it is the work of Beelzebub, the Devil incarnate. I believe since the rise of the heretic, Martin Luther, the Devil has been bolder and more active in the world."

In an effort to make up time, the coachman had driven his four steeds at a fast pace since leaving the village of Hampton. The occupants of the carriage had suffered from the bumping and lurching of their vehicle. Suddenly the driver stopped at the village of Woking to rest and water his horses. Weatherby and the priest were happy to alight from the carriage for a few minutes. However, soon they were headed toward Guilford but now at a slower pace as the road was hillier and narrower. Weatherby resumed his analysis of the triple homicide.

"Each victim was dispatched in a unique way," Weatherby remarked. "One bludgeoned, one poisoned and one suffered a long fall. The young woman, who was poisoned, left an extensive diary in secret writing which we haven't been able to decipher. You must have a familiarity with many written languages as part of your work."

Sir Weatherby took a piece of parchment out of his pocket, steadied it on a hat box in the carriage, and then drew a sample of the writing with a lead pencil, a new invention, that drew attention everywhere he went. He passed the parchment to Father Lawrence along with the pencil as the priest had also requested to see it. The good Father was much more fascinated by the writing implement than the secret code.

"Where did you get this convenient portable writing implement?" Father Lawrence asked.

"They come from Borrowdale in the northern county of Cumbria," said Weatherby. "Huge blocks of the material are mined and then cut into square rods which are inserted in those hand-carved wooden holders. They are called lead pencils as the material is thought to be black lead, but my amanuensis assures me that it is another substance altogether."

"The word 'pencil' comes from the Latin 'penicillus' which means 'little tail,'" Father Lawrence replied.

"You may keep that one, Father. What do you make of the writing?"

"Most of our illuminated manuscripts are in Latin, but a few are in Greek," Father Lawrence began. "But this is certainly neither. The puzzling element to me is the continuous horizontal line that runs through the text, and seems to support the individual letters. I have seen dozens of other languages, and none have anything like it."

Father Lawrence rotated the parchment very slowly while he studied the markings. He tried folding the parchment along the long line, to see if the hatch marks formed some familiar letters. They didn't.

"In the third century BC, the Greeks invaded and conquered Egypt," Father Lawrence began. "A written language called Coptic resulted that combined the Greek and the Egyptian alphabets. I mention it because each of the numerals has a long straight line over the top. If these lines were simply extended, a numeric Coptic code would be the result. Give me that hat box, and I'll write some common words in a Coptic numeric code."

Father Lawrence was lost in thought, distracted by the parchment and his new writing implement right up until the carriage stopped in Guilford. Sir Weatherby spent the time constructing an elegant equilateral triangle on a large piece of parchment. William, Anna Maria and Gregory each occupied a point. Then he built a tracery of elegant lines from one to the other based on personal habits, likes and dislikes, politics, philosophy and religion. The horses slowed through the wooden gates of an old country inn, the Stag and Swan. Both Father Lawrence and Sir Weatherby helped the frail elderly woman down from her perch, as she had finally awoken.

The next morning at 8:30 a.m. a large breakfast of eggs and ham was quickly laid in the main dining room. Warm, round loaves of coarse bread, with the bran in it and tankards of ale completed the meal. Sir Weatherby was ravenous. After they ate Father Lawrence spoke of his home church, St. Mary's in the Lace Market in Nottingham and the Cloisters where they educated young priests. Once back in their carriage, with fresh horses, the three travelers found that another traveler; a young gentlewoman, Emma Wedgewood, had joined them. Introductions were made all around. Weatherby and Father Lawrence were soon lost in a deep discussion of codes and murders. Weatherby obtained another lead pencil from his grip and began drawing his triangular imaginings on a large piece of parchment. Father Lawrence tried various iterations of his Coptic numeric code on his piece of parchment. After two hours, both sides of the parchment were covered with Coptic symbols and phrases. Finally, Father Lawrence rolled the parchment tightly.

"I need a large work surface to study the code that I believe your young victim used," Father Lawrence said. "I will work out the details once I'm settled in Paris and I will write you a letter about my findings."

"Thank you for your interest, Father Croceus," Weatherby replied. "I've also reached a dead end on my triangular murder blueprint. Let's talk about a lighter subject. Can you tell me who is the most famous resident, past or present, of your abode in Nottinghamshire?"

"Several notable artists, writers and clergymen came from our county," Father Lawrence began. "But far and away our most famous resident is the notorious Robyn Hude. His name is mentioned first in the records of several English justices in 1227."

"He is frequently mentioned in ballads and in gossip now, and I had hoped to read a book about him."

"There are no books, nor does he deserve one, just a lot of gossip and hearsay," Father Lawrence replied. "He was nothing but a brigand, a thief, and a criminal."

"Many would agree with you, but some think him to be a hero because, he robbed from the rich, gave to the poor, and fought against injustice and tyranny."

"I believe him to be vengeful, self-interested, and guilty of barbaric punishments."

"But, is it not true, that the Sheriff of Nottingham, his arch enemy, was venal, grasping and dishonest?"

"Some say so. However our bishop at the time investigated the Sheriff, and found him a God-fearing and honest man."

"I have visited your church, and the largest chapel is named for the Sheriff which means he gave the Bishop a lot of money," Weatherby replied. "Perhaps the bishop's opinion was influenced by all those sovereigns."

"That is an insult to the Holy Catholic Church!" Father Lawrence said turning his reddening face toward the window.

"Father Lawrence, you and I are both worldly enough to know that the engine of the church, and therefore its salvation, is lucre. Obtaining that money involves compromises and cutting corners. We have both seen it."

"You seem one of the most rational men I have ever met. Why are you so taken in by Robyn Hude and his merry men?"

"You misunderstand, Father Lawrence, I was only seeking information about his moral character. Now that I have your perspective, may we move on to another topic?"

# CHAPTER 33

Before the Father could reply to Weatherby's request, the carriage pulled into Winchester. The last leg of the trip from Guilford to Winchester was the longest at twenty-nine miles; however the land was open and rolling with a wide fast highway. The carriage stopped at an inn on the edge of town. After four and a half hours in the carriage all the riders were stiff. The stop here would be for two hours, so Father Lawrence and Sir Weatherby headed to the tavern. It was warm inside and the tables were quickly filling with local patrons. Both men ordered tankards of ale. They talked companionably about their families and friends. After an hour, they were summoned to the dining room for a large dinner of roast beef, beets and broad beans. Later, much revived, they climbed back into the carriage for a late afternoon ride to Southampton. The last eighteen miles went quickly, and Sir Weatherby was dropped at a portside hotel at nine p.m. Father Lawrence had been deposited at the Cathedral first. In an age when a good day's travel was thirty or thirty-five miles, thanks to good roads and a relentless driver, Weatherby had managed to go sixty-six miles.

As he stepped down onto the wet cobblestones, Weatherby looked south toward the sea. Dozens of slender masts pointed skyward. Above the masts, a silvery full moon lit a tinseled sky full of small fluffy clouds. Horse and mule-drawn charts hurried along the broad cobbled street loaded with goods for departing ships. Slender street lamps lit the sidewalks with a pleasant yellow glow. It was a very different scene from the pacific vistas of Hampton Court Palace in the evening.

Weatherby checked into the Goddard Arms Hotel and followed the porter to his room on the third floor. An elegant house of ill repute stood across the cobbled street from the hotel, and Weatherby considered a visit before deciding on the tavern of the hotel. The city of Southampton's name is abbreviated as, "So'ton." A resident is then called a Sotonian, and the tavern at the Goddard Arms was jammed with them. Sir Weatherby couldn't find a seat in any of the rooms and ended up standing at the bar three rows back. He spent the evening talking with the captain of a man-of-war whose ship would be sailing for the Canary Islands in the morning. After finishing a couple of pints, Weatherby retired.

Early the next morning, after breakfast at the hotel, a hansom took him to the docks of the Normandy Shipping Company. He boarded the *Eye of the Wind,* a hermaphrodite brig, which was still loading crates of cargo. A crew member showed him to a lounge below deck, but he wandered back up to the deck to watch the preparations for sailing. As the last few crates were loaded, men climbed the rigging to unfurl the sails. A series of square sails were attached to the fore mast and a fore-and-aft sail was attached to the mainmast. Weatherby walked to the poop deck and spoke with the first mate named, Blucher who smoked a pipe while he oversaw the loading of cargo.

"This ship makes the run to Le Havre every other day?" Weatherby asked as they had been introduced below decks earlier.

After a long drag on his pipe Blucher replied, "Aye. We sail every bloody day of the year even Christ's burtday. The only thing that throws *Eye* off is the weather. The prevailing wind in the Channel is from the west-north-west and it blows a steady eleven to thirteen knots an hour, except when it doesn't. When we're becalmed the trip across can take two and a half days of wallowing."

"Any chance of that happening today?" Weatherby asked.

"It ain't very likely in the spring. We might see a wind of fifteen or sixteen knots this time o'year. Once we wear out of the harbor it'll be plain."

"As a physician I know the term hermaphrodite means having both male and female parts. How does that apply to a sleek ship like *The Eye of the Wind?*"

"It's not like that. It's not about her sex. Ships is always she. It's 'cause almost every ship is rigged like a schooner with the front of the sail attached to the mast and the bottom attached to a boom, or square-rigged where the sail crosses the mast. But *Eye of the Wind* is one in the front and t'other in the back."

Weatherby grabbed the taff rail as the first mate yelled, "Cast off!!"

Three seamen lifted the hawsers holding the ship off the stanchions and slowly, very slowly, the hermaphrodite brig eased away from the dock and headed south among man-of-wars, merchantmen and East Indies traders.

Weatherby found a seat on a wooden, louvered ventilation house that stuck up through the deck and he watched the scene go by. As one of the best and deepest harbors in England, where three rivers flowed into the sea, Southampton had been a bustling port for hundreds of years. As *Eye of the Wind* cleared the headlands, the wind picked up and the sails both fore and aft snapped full. The wind was a steady fifteen knots from the west. The ship gradually accelerated. The swell was four feet with twenty feet between peaks, Weatherby noted. The brig pitched fore and aft and leaned to port.

Weatherby was impervious to seasickness, and as land faded off the stern he went below to read. After several hours of travel a lunch of beef stew and bread was served in the dining room amidships. The wooden tables had inch tall wooden lips around the edges to keep the crockery from crashing to the floor if the vessel heeled. Many of the guests were too seasick to eat. They clustered along the port side near the stern with their heads out over the gray-green water. Weatherby brought some parchment to the deserted dining room and worked on his triangular design for the three murders. He loved symmetry which is why he enjoyed the architecture of the Romanesque Suffolk House when he and Amarantha had visited. He wanted to find an equilibrium in his murders. He also wrote letters to several professors about King Urien of Gore, the person Suffolk had mentioned in his last letter. He noticed that the wind held. Weatherby decided to go back on deck to stretch his legs. The first mate was at the helm.

"We're a makin' good headway, Your Grace!" Blucher yelled over the wind and the snapping of the sails.

"How far yet to go?" Weatherby cupped his hands to his mouth and shouted back.

"I reckon we are well over half way. If the wind holds it'll be a fast crossing or a record!"

Weatherby knew that Blucher was only guessing. He could determine his latitude or distance from the North Pole easily by the position of a star or the sun. However, he had no reliable way of determining his longitude or distance from the prime meridian that ran through London. Without a measure of longitude, he was literally lost at sea. Monthly, the newspapers reported ships that had gone on the rocks and sunk, often with terrible loss of life because a captain could not know where his ship was on the vast sea. Some of England's greatest scientists were working on the longitude problem using sophisticated clocks and complex moon tables.

"How will you know when we are close?" Weatherby asked.

"We'll see the headland of *Cap d' Antifer* above 'er," Blucher replied. "She's not much of a town, wadn't founded until thirteen years ago. Nothing like So'ton, but she's a sweet harbor."

Weatherby walked to the prow of the ship and looked out at the ocean lost in thought.

The ship arrived in Le Havre at 7:15 p.m., missing the record by twenty minutes. Weatherby walked to a nearby hotel and asked about the coach to Paris. He found it left at 6 a.m. and that the trip took two days. He washed up in his room, and felt better once the salt spray was banished from his face and hair. He went downstairs to an excellent meal of *Coq a Vin*, with a rich red wine, and a chocolate soufflé for dessert served in the hotel dining room.

While he ate, he mused on the French. Most Englishmen had a visceral dislike of their neighbors, and burst out swearing when France or its people were mentioned. His reaction was less forceful, but in much the same direction. Since William the Conqueror subdued England in 1066, there had been nine wars between England and France. In Weatherby's clear memory was the War of the Holy League in 1513 and then Henry VIII's failed invasion of French territory in 1522. Henry knew that much of his own father, Henry VII's, popularity stemmed from his successful war with France. He had tried to emulate it but couldn't secure a victory.

In truth, Weatherby admired French food, architecture, their stylish dress, and their *joie de vivre* but overall he found them woefully deficient as a people. He thought they had little industry or determination. Actually, Weatherby was really talking about French *men*, whom he found loutish. He felt French women were beautiful, stylish, charming conversationalists, and very accomplished in bed. He admired the *demimonde*, literally the half world, between polite society and common prostitution occupied by a group of very intelligent and beautiful courtesans. There was nothing as elegant in England. He had learned French third after English and Latin, and found it beautiful and powerful. Someday, he hoped to make love to Amarantha while they spoke French tenderly to each other. With thoughts about the strengths and weakness of the Normans filling his head, he wandered upstairs to bed.

Weatherby awoke at three a.m. shivering in a sopping wet night shirt. He had had his awful nightmare once again: galloping black horses chasing him, and then a small baby in the path blocking his escape. He was fully awake and knew he wouldn't sleep again before it was time to catch the carriage to Paris.

After breakfast he boarded a very large wooden carriage pulled by six horses. The velvet-covered seats could accommodate eight passengers. Unfortunately, every seat was taken. Weatherby ended up sitting between a young girl and a nun. He began to read *The Canterbury Tales*. The total distance from Le Havre to Paris was one hundred and twenty-seven miles, twice as far as from Hampton to Southampton. The trip would take two days.

# CHAPTER 34

The coach ride seemed longer than Weatherby had expected. A light rain slowed travel the first day, and the carriage stopped in Rouen for the night. Weatherby got up at dawn the next morning, before the carriage headed on, to tour the gothic Cathedral, Notre Dame of Rouen. In the nave of the Cathedral, he knelt by the tomb of one of his heroes, Richard the Lionhearted. Finally, after travelling all day, the carriage pulled into a station on Ile de la Cité in the middle of the Seine. Weatherby stepped out into a cool clear evening invigorated to be in the largest city in the world. Although he knew London well and liked it, Weatherby found Paris more exhilarating. He checked into the Hotel Crillon, an elegant hotel located on the right bank of the Seine, near the Palace de Louvre, where he had stayed many times before. He took a late night walk along the Seine and stopped at a sidewalk café for a glass of wine. He bundled up and sat on the street so he could watch the carriage traffic. He vowed to spend more time here on the way back from Chartres.

In the morning he took the local carriage to Chartres twenty miles southwest of Paris. The tiny village sat in a vast, flat area of farmland. The fields had just turned a bright yellow-green as the wheat began to grow. The famous Cathedral was so much taller than its environs that it came into view eight miles out of town. At first it was a small bump on the horizon but with each mile it grew taller. The edifice rose heavenward from the flat, fertile earth to an improbable height. The carriage stopped at an inn south of the Cathedral of Our Lady of Chartres. Weatherby walked to the glazier's shed near the apse of the Cathedral.

It was midmorning, and several workers were heating glass in the furnaces, and cutting pieces of the shimmering red vitreous. Some of the most famous glass in the world was made right here, Weatherby thought. He had been given a name by Nathaniel Philbrick, the master glazier at Hampton Court.

"Good day, is Henri de Lèves about?" Weatherby asked in French.

"I'm afraid he's no longer here," An older man with wrinkled brown skin said suspiciously as he set his iron tongs on the table. "May I ask who's inquiring?"

"I'm Sir Seamus Scott Weatherby, special envoy to King Henry VIII of England," Weatherby replied as he made a slight bow of his head. "I sent a letter to Monsieur de Lèves a few days ago."

"I am Jean Favier, assistant master glazier," the man said, extending his hand. "I remember the day he got a letter from England. He seemed very agitated. Let me take you on a tour of our beautiful Cathedral while we talk."

As they walked along the south portal, Weatherby looked up and saw a statue of a naked, leering devil carrying off a nun. It gave him a chill. Favier led the way along the nave and into the dark interior of the Cathedral itself.

"A fire destroyed much of the Cathedral and the town in 1194. Due to the faith and industry of surrounding worshippers the body of the Cathedral was rebuilt in only twenty-six years," Favier said as he walked toward the altar.

Weatherby stopped frequently to admire the famous stained glass windows. The blue was particularly intense and deep. He also gazed along the aisles and was surprised at the size of the Cathedral which he estimated to be over four hundred feet long.

"What is the nature of your visit, if I may ask?" Favier asked in a hesitant voice.

"I am not a very trusting person, Mr. Favier," Weatherby began as he moved closer to the glazier. "And I am here on a somewhat delicate matter. The only person I know to contact, Monsieur Henri de Lèves, is incognito. Therefore I must put my faith in you. I am investigating a series of murders and the famous blue glass from Chartres is involved. Therefore I am asking for your help."

"I don't care for the English, as a rule, but I am touched by your plight," Favier said after a minute's contemplation. "It would be safer to talk in the crypt," the Frenchman continued as he gestured across the nave with his hand.

The two walked across the midsection of the church, past several kneeling worshippers. Favier led Weatherby to a locked iron gate which he opened with a key from his belt. A spiral stone stairway led down into the dark. The assistant glazier lit a nearby lantern and held it in front of himself. A heavy smell of damp and mildew struck Weatherby's nose. The crypt consisted of several small rooms with vaulted limestone ceilings. Favier set his lantern on one of the sarcophagi.

My good friend and colleague, Henri de Lèves was taken away by the authorities five days ago," Favier said in an anguished voice, "and we have had no word from him since."

"Who took him?"

"Three men in an official-looking carriage assisted by four men on horseback came to the glazier's shop and seized him one morning," Favier said. "Henri was always polite and soft-spoken, but they grabbed him and half dragged him to the carriage. He protested but to no avail. They said they were from the Préfecture de Police."

"Chartres doesn't seem big enough for a prefecture," Weatherby mused.

"It isn't, and we have no crime here to speak of. I'm sure these officials were from Paris."

"What possible reason would the authorities have to pinch your supervisor?"

"I have wracked my brain for the answer to that question," Favier said with some anguish in his voice. "And I have come up with nothing."

"Perhaps his incarceration has to do with the glass," Weatherby mused. "After all, it's the reason I came to this petite place from England. Let's search the glazier's shed."

Favier led the way out of the crypt and across the nave to the glass shop. He sent the other workers off to lunch. Weatherby took out his magnifying glass and began to study the large pieces of glass of every color that were stacked against every wall, in the storeroom and even against the sides of the bench.

"We are installing stained-glass windows on the west front, so we have five times the normal amount of glass in our shop. Our Cathedral has two very dissimilar spires. The Romanesque south tower survived the devastating fire in 1194. The north tower, which is Gothic, was just completed a few years ago, and the glass windows we are building now are adjacent to that tower."

"I want to look at the blue glass first," Weatherby said. "because my victim only stole pieces of Chartres blue, but then I think we should look at every piece of glass in the shop."

"What, exactly, are we looking for?"

"I don't know. Anything that looks out of the ordinary, I suppose."

Favier and Weatherby donned gloves to prevent cuts and began looking at the glass, one piece at a time. Over the next several hours they inspected hundreds of sheets of glass. Favier found a chain of bubbles in the shape of a 'c' in one piece of yellow glass, but no other meaningful bubble patterns. Weatherby found a series of lines on one piece of green glass that resembled a six-pointed star, but no other linear designs. They worked into the evening, and when both were exhausted Favier invited Weatherby to his home for the night. It was a modest cottage with a thatched roof. A rich lamb stew was warming in the fireplace. Both men wolfed down the food with large chunks of dark bread. Weatherby slept soundly.

In the morning he was ruminating over his breakfast when Jean Favier came in from feeding his animals.

"Monsieur de Lèves was involved in something so sinister," Weatherby began, "that the police felt they had to act quickly and decisively. The object that connects his nefarious activity to my murder victim is Chartres blue glass. We are missing something. Perhaps the message is hidden from the naked eye and only reveals itself when a chemical or special light is applied to it. Did you ever see Henri applying solutions to the glass?"

"No, but he often worked alone in the evening after the lot of us went home," Favier replied. "He had his own little corner of the shop."

"Let's inspect that area carefully," Weatherby replied as he arose from the table.

When they arrived at the glazier's hut the furnaces were hot and the assistants were making sheets of red glass. Henri de Lève's work area was littered with pieces of glass and notes written on random pieces of parchment. Favier read through the writing, while Weatherby searched all the cubby holes. Several solutions stood along the top of master glazier's workbench in glass bottles. Weatherby smelled each one. He wished he had brought Dredge, who would know most of the chemicals simply by smell. Lacking that, he placed a piece of blue glass on the workbench and applied some of each solution to the vitreous. Even after several minutes, most did nothing. However, one that smelled like acid to Weatherby caused a green haze to form on the surface of the glass. When he inspected it he realized that the chemical allowed him to look below the surface of the blue glass.

Favier had found nothing noteworthy on the parchment, so Weatherby sent him to bring pieces of blue glass to de Lèves's bench so he could apply a thin layer of the acid. Once the green haze formed, Weatherby studied each piece with his magnifying glass in the bright sunlight. The two worked for several hours with no results. They walked across the street from the Cathedral to an inn for lunch.

"What are we missing?" Weatherby asked in a discouraging tone over a tankard of ale.

"Perhaps we are using the wrong solution or the wrong colored glass," Favier volunteered.

"The only glass my victim was interested in was the blue glass from this shop," Weatherby said thoughtfully. "But you may be right about the solution even though it is the only one that has that amazing effect on the glass. How many more sheets of glass do we have to test?"

"I believe we have looked at fifty some and only a couple dozen remain," Favier replied.

"Let's go test the rest."

After testing a few more sheets of glass, Weatherby realized he was running out of the acid solution and he wanted to save a small sample for Dredge to analyze. Favier brought him another sheet of the beautiful glass that was the color of the autumn sky. After the solution dried, Weatherby began his inspection with the magnifying glass. In the lower right corner the sunlight caught a complex series of lines.

"I believe we have found something," Weatherby said in an excited tone.

# CHAPTER 35

Weatherby had found a wavy line that branched like a tree with little twiglets coming off the main branch. He could only see it with his magnifying glass and even then the lines were faint. He showed Favier what he was seeing.

"Have you ever seen anything like this?" Weatherby asked.

"No, but Henri kept a tool here at his bench that would make marks like that," Jean replied. "I had never seen such a tool in my training."

Favier reached into a drawer and pulled out a brass tool in the shape of a pen with a clear stone embedded in its end. He picked up a scrap of glass and ran the incisor across it making a readily visible mark.

"It must be a very hard stone," Weatherby mused.

"It's a diamond, which is many times harder than glass," Favier replied.

"I need to make a rubbing of the branching design on this piece of glass," Weatherby said placing a piece of paper on the bench and taking out a pencil.

For the next two hours, Weatherby labored over a duplicate of the symbols hidden on the glass. He asked Favier to arrange a carriage back to Paris that evening, and thanked him for all his help. The French countryside was bathed in the golden tones of evening while Weatherby enjoyed his trip back to the Hotel Crillon. He dined on veal at a restaurant on the Rue de Rivoli. Then he met Geneviéve, a *demimonde* he was acquainted with from his last visit to Paris two years before. They spent the night in her apartment where under her guidance they pleased each other in every way possible. They only slept for an hour. Weatherby wondered where the French courtesans learned such tricks.

In the morning Weatherby went to the Palace of Justice to enquire after the master glazier. For the first hour, he was shunted from clerk to clerk with no satisfaction. Frustrated he sent a message to the nearby English consulate and an attaché arrived within half an hour. This time the clerks were bypassed immediately and the Under Secretary of Prisons agreed to see Weatherby and his influential friend.

"I am an envoy of the English King and I seek an interview with one of your prisoners, Monsieur Henri de Lèves," Sir Weatherby began. He has information material to the murder of a nobleman in England."

The Under Secretary whispered to his assistant who left before replying. Then he offered his guest a cup of tea. When his assistant returned, with a full pot of tea, more whispering ensued.

"The person you speak about is in the Bastille and is allowed no visitors," the Under Secretary replied in a haughty voice. "He is a prisoner of the Crown and is being held on charges that are yet to be specified."

"We are at an impasse," the attaché whispered in Weatherby's ear. "There is nothing more to be done at this time," he continued as they walked down the steps of the Palace of Justice.

Weatherby thanked him for his time, and spent the remainder of the day with Genevieve seeing the sights of Paris. She wore a large pink hoop dress with lots of ribbons and lace. Her hat consisted of a large bunch of flowers and a bird's nest. She thought herself quite stylish. They visited the Notre Dame Cathedral, the Concierge, the Bois de Boulogne, and the old Roman baths at Cluny before Weatherby spent another night in Genevieve's pale white, shapely arms.

Early the next morning, Weatherby took the carriage back to Rouen and then to Le Havre. Unfortunately, this time the Channel was becalmed and the crossing from Le Havre to Southampton in the *Eye of the Wind* took two days. Weatherby finished reading both of his books and continued to work on the three murderers.

The minute he discovered the symbols on the blue Chartres glass, Weatherby realized he had a possible link between two of his victims. The cipher on the glass was different from, but clearly related to, the secret writings that were presumably done by Anna Maria Wimbledon in her diary. William Suffolk must have stolen the blue glass so that he could read the secret message and then pawned it so that prying eyes at Hampton Court couldn't find the same cryptogram. Wouldn't it have been simpler just to break the glass into a million pieces? Yes, but Weatherby thought there were two reasons Suffolk didn't do so. First, William admired beauty and the Chartres glass was the most strikingly handsome glass in the world, and secondly pawning the precious glass financed his nefarious activities.

The *Eye of the Wind* finally docked in Southampton early one Sunday morning and Weatherby caught the morning carriage back to Hampton before it departed. He arrived that evening, tired from his long trip but excited about what he had found. He was surprised to see workmen laboring in the Bayne Tower and on the grounds. He made a mental note to ask Sir John Moulton about it. Weatherby ordered a meal for his apartment and then quickly walked down the hall and knocked on Amarantha's door. She had been reading by the fireplace.

"Welcome back, traveler, I missed you," Amarantha said as she gave him a warm, long hug. "Were you successful?"

"Yes. I found a cryptogram, but I will tell you and Dredge all about it in the morning. What happened while I was gone?"

"It was quiet," Amarantha replied. "Dredge has been researching ancient languages and working on the bitter rose poison."

"I missed you, Ran," Weatherby replied. "I forgot how lustrous and full your hair is. The trip from Southampton today was long and I'm tired. Let's meet in the laboratory at seven a.m. I'll order some food for *le petit déjeuner*."

"Good night, then," Amarantha replied. "I'm glad you are back and safe. I worried."

Weatherby walked to his apartment, removed his traveling clothes, and fell into bed.

In the morning, when Weatherby arrived in the lab, Dredge and Amarantha were already there. They ate a hearty breakfast of strong black tea, ham and eggs. While they were eating, Weatherby talked about his trip to Paris and Chartres. Of course, he carefully neglected mention of Genevieve. Once they finished eating each talked about their efforts during the past two weeks. Amarantha went first.

"I'm seeing Richard Weston, the Master of the House, every two or three days now," she began. "I often go to his office for tea and sometimes we have lunch in the garden, but it's quite an effort to lure him outside. It's much easier to flirt in the light. He seems to be responding and now touches my arm and calls me by endearments. I'm ready to start pumping him for information."

"Be careful around him, Ran," Weatherby interjected, "the Chancellor thinks he may be unstable, he has changed so much."

"I'll be careful."

"What did you discover, Dredge?"

"I've interviewed all the pharmacists and apothecaries in the surrounding countryside about our bitter rose poison," Dredge began. "It took me four days to ride to all the little villages, and to no avail. Next I tried the seers and fortune tellers and midwives with no more luck. That took three days with a lot of backtracking. By the last day I was cursing myself for not doing both groups at once. Then as a last desperate measure, I decided to try the witches and sorcerers. There are more of them in the county than you can imagine. Unfortunately, I still came up with nothing until I found one old toothless crone, in Oatlands, who recalled a very potent poison that smelled like roses she had heard about years ago."

"Could she tell you where she heard about it?"

"After some prodding and cajoling she said admitted hearing about it from a younger witch named Hepsibah."

"Can you track her down?"

"She's from Kew. I sent a courier to fetch her, but she had left for Stonehenge the week before and she isn't expected back for a month."

"Good work, both of you!" Weatherby exclaimed.

"Now tell us what you discovered in Chartres," Amarantha said excitedly. "I'm dying to know."

"As you both know, I wondered if William Suffolk was receiving messages in the blue glass from France," Weatherby began. "However, when I got there, my contact, Henri de Lèves, had been imprisoned in the Bastille and wasn't allowed visitors. I worked with Jean Favier, Henri's assistant, and after much searching we found a solution that brought out symbols in the blue glass. I brought a sample, Dredge, so you can tell me what it is."

Weatherby took a small vial of the solution out of his pocket and handed it to Dredge. Next he unfolded a parchment with copies of the symbols printed on it. The three investigators huddled over it for several minutes. No one spoke. Dredge displayed samples of the ciphers Amarantha had found in the library for comparison.

She spoke first, "These two codes aren't the same but they seem like siblings."

"What makes you say so?" Weatherby asked.

"Unlike any language I have ever seen, both of these 'languages' are based on a continuous uninterrupted line. The difference is that in the code I found in the library there is one continuous line, and in the sample from Chartres the line is branched."

"I agree," Dredge said as he pointed to similar figures on the two parchments. "These codes are twins. While you were gone, I went to the library at Oxford University and researched as many arcane languages as I could find, and none of them are similar to our ciphers. I even checked inscriptions from the New World and none of the Indian languages resemble our samples."

"I thought about this problem while I was becalmed in the English Channel," Weatherby interrupted. "Perhaps our efforts are misdirected. I don't think we need to know what the language is; we just need to crack it. It might be something as simple as a substitution code for example each 'e' in the message could be written as 'l' and 'x' could mean 't' and then 'h' could be 'c'. Therefore, if the encoder wanted to convey 'the' he would be write 'xcl'. I want you to try various substitutions and see if you can crack this code.

# CHAPTER 36

The trio of investigators broke up. Amarantha had a date for tea with Richard Weston. Dredge laid out material to begin cracking the code and Weatherby went to the Wolsey Apartment to check his mail. On his way Weatherby stopped in the Clock Court to enjoy the warm spring morning and admired the astronomical clock that had just been installed for the King. The gold hands and numerals shone in the bright sunlight and the background was a rich blue color with stars and comets also in gold. Above the time was a window that showed that the moon was full on this day. Weatherby wandered into the South Tower and climbed up to the Wolsey Apartments.

A stack of mail sat neatly on the corner of his desk. Most of the letters and messages were old news or of little value. He was surprised to see a letter so quickly from Father Croceus Lawrence. Weatherby tore it open and read:

Sir Seamus Scott Weatherby,

Just a quick note to tell you what I discovered about your cryptogram. Once I had a large table, I could spread out your parchment and my Coptic alphabet. I told you that Coptic numerals all have a long dash over each figure and could easily be made into a straight line. All of the twiglets that were attached to your baseline were straight so I analyzed segments of the Coptic numbers for shape. I found that eleven segments were straight but another nine were curved. I can't see how the curved segments would fit into your code.

My conclusion is that the Coptic alphabet wasn't the basis of your code. I hope you are well.

Go with the Lord,
Fr. Croceus Lawrence
9 day of May, Kaldens, 1530.

Weatherby was mildly disappointed but not surprised. The only other important message was from the Sheriff of Surrey County, who stated he had captured Clarence Stevens. The county seat was in Teddington and Weatherby quickly discovered that the jail was there as well. The royal barge had left for the day, so Weatherby had his horse saddled. He rode east along a well-kept road. When he arrived in Teddington he asked for directions to the jail, which was located in a dilapidated older part of town near the river. On introducing himself he was shown into the sheriff's office.

"He war' siteated in a pig sty on the edge of ther' forest," the Sheriff replied from behind a filthy desk. "He war' in the las' cell below."

Weatherby walked down the rickety steps and took a lantern with him. He found Clarence lying on the dirt floor with bruises on his arms and torso. There was severe swelling and bruising on his face and neck. Both eyes were swollen shut and his lips were split open and bloody. Clarence didn't respond to the simple questions he was asked. Weatherby bounded back up the stairs and slammed his fist down on the desk of the sheriff.

"Who the hell beat this man?" Weatherby roared.

"He fell down a lot," the sheriff answered sarcastically.

Weatherby reached across the sheriff's desk and grabbed a handful of the sheriff's filthy doublet and pulled him upright. The other jailers edged toward Weatherby.

"I am the King's envoy, and his guards will be here within the hour to take this man to the hospital. You will have a week you don't deserve until the new sheriff arrives, you swine," Weatherby spat at the sheriff as he released his grip. "If any of the rest of you derelicts wants new employment either step over here or give me some lip right now."

Weatherby stomped out of the sheriff's office. Clarence Stevens was his prime suspect in the death of Gregory Townsend, and Weatherby realized Clarence might never speak again. As his fury surfaced again, he wrote a note to the guards asking them to take the sheriff to the Tower.

His anger didn't abate until he was halfway back to Hampton Court. When he arrived he invited Amarantha to a dinner set in the orchard. They enjoyed a joint of lamb and a bottle of Rhenish wine.

"I took me four and a half days to travel to Chartres," Weatherby ruminated. "And it is only 217 miles away as the crow flies."

"But you said that your coach went quickly over good roads," Amarantha replied. "And that strangely named hermaphrodite brig was a trim little ship. How fast did you want to go?"

"I wanted to be there in two hours."

"That's preposterous!"

"I don't think so."

"Nothing goes that fast."

"Sometime in the future, people will go that fast. Mark my words. Think of a bolt of lightning, Ran. It crosses the sky in less than a second. I just want to go half that fast."

"That will never happen, Seamus."

"I wouldn't be so sure," Weatherby replied, lifting his glass of wine. "What if you could capture a bolt of lightning in a glass tank, and then attach it to a capsule made of brass and glass. Then open a valve and release the power of the strike and drive the capsule across a field."

"It sounds quite preposterous, Seamus. I'm sure you and Dredge will soon be rocketing mice across a meadow."

The two continued conversing, but Weatherby was distracted by thinking of ways he might capture the power of lightning. When they finished eating, Weatherby went back to the Wolsey Apartment and wrote a long letter to his superior, Thomas Cromwell. He wanted to write about his successes in capturing the three murderers and sending the criminals to the tower. Instead he wrote about the industry of the three investigators. He recounted his trip to Chartres, Dredge's efforts to identify the poison, and Amarantha's efforts to get close to Richard Weston. He sent along a sample of the mysterious writing from the library in the hopes that someone from Whitehall could identify it. When he finished the letter he realized how much more work would be involved in solving the crimes. He felt temporarily stymied, and he retired with the same frustrated feeling.

In the morning Weatherby decided to tap some of his local sources for information. He ate a hurried breakfast in the Great Kitchen before heading out. He hadn't visited Ellen Iverson in the Confectory for several weeks and she often had good information to share. He walked down the stairs, across the Clock Tower, admiring the colors of the astronomical clock, again, and then through the archway into the Base Court. He began to whistle. From The Base Court he walked through the Great Gatehouse. As the warm spring sun struck his face, he turned upstream along the river to the Outer Court. Weatherby pushed open the Dutch door of the Confectory, where Ellen was filling a large tray of fruit tarts. The room smelled of warm strawberries.

"Well look what the cat drug in!" Ellen called out. "I haven't seen you in the Outer Court for quite a while, Your Grace. I understand you were in France. How did you find the frogs?"

"Actually, they were quite charming and helpful, thank you." Weatherby replied as he worried that the nosy confector would begin talking about his courtesan Geneviève. "I was investigating the murder of William Suffolk and it was a productive trip."

"I never liked the French," Ellen retorted. "I heard that you dethroned the Sheriff of Surrey. Nice work. He was a petty tyrant that had abused the poor and underprivileged with beatings and trickery for decades."

"Thank you," Weatherby said as he grabbed a fruit tart and sat down. "He nearly beat Clarence Stevens to death and it made me see red."

"Clarence is a simple, but good man," Ellen said thoughtfully. "I know you think he murdered the preacher, but my intuition tells me he didn't."

"I hope he regains consciousness so that I can at least question him," Weatherby said as he grabbed another warm tart. "I'm stuck in the mud on all three investigations and can't get free. Do you have any other information for me?"

"I understand you are looking for a tall dark-skinned man that was seen with Anna Maria Wimbledon."

"True."

"There is an itinerant Muslim jewel dealer that started coming to Hampton Court about eight months ago. His name is Ishmael. I always thought that he was up to something else and that the jewelry was just a cover."

"Where might I find him?"

"That, I don't know, but I will put out some feelers."

"Thanks, Ellen." Weatherby said as he grabbed a third fruit tart and turned toward the door.

"You must be very worried about your literary secretary, Dredge," Ellen said as Weatherby put his hand on the door to leave.

"Not in the least bit. He's quite smart and does excellent work."

"No. I mean about the gaming."

"What gaming?"

"Dredge has been seen going into the village very late, two or even three nights a week. He goes to a tumbled down house on the edge of town where there are all night card games and dicing. My sources tell me he is losing more than he can afford."

"I had no earthly idea," Weatherby said in a worried tone as he left.

As he walked back to the Palace he reflected on the fact that he took Dredge for granted. His amanuensis had always delivered high-quality work, no matter what the obstacles, without complaint. In some ways, Dredge was treated like a complex and reliable apparatus rather than as a human being. Weatherby rushed into the laboratory and found Dredge doing a complex distillation involving a small forest of glass tubes, beakers and bubbling liquids. Weatherby sat down patiently and waited until Dredge was finished.

"I'm trying to recreate that bloody poison without much success," Dredge said as he sat down. "What can I do for you this afternoon, Your Grace?"

"I'm here about the gambling, Dredge," Weatherby blurted out. "I've seen it ruin men's lives and I'm worried about you."

"Thank you, Sir," Dredge replied as he slumped onto a stool. "I've always done it a bit, but I'm afraid it has gotten out of hand. I'm so far in debt that I have to play and bet big stakes to get it back. But instead of pulling even I sink down further every night."

"I have known you for years and something must have started this," Weatherby mused out loud.

"We've never been away from London, Sir, for this long on a case. I have a circle of friends there and I miss their company. They are dwarves, rachitics, like me and some were maimed in accidents, but they are a jolly group and I miss them. I've never frequented the bawdy houses, the trollops were fine but a lot of the other customers poke fun at me. And the only gambling I've done before was just for fun. The gamblers in Hampton are stern professionals."

"I've been insensitive. And your work has been exceptional. Let's go settle your debts tonight, and then send you on a holiday to London. I simply need a promise that you won't let this happen again."

"You have my word on it, Your Grace. And thank you."

# CHAPTER 37

Weatherby spent the rest of the afternoon in the library looking at books in various languages. He hoped to find some writing that resembled the mysterious codes he had found, so that he could translate the victim's intentions and actions. While there he enjoyed the company of Margaret Sedgwick and Judith Scotson, the assistant librarians. Judith had become one of his favorites at the Palace after she so readily cared for Amarantha during her depression. She was pleasant to look at with brown wavy hair and soft brown eyes, but Weatherby especially liked her intelligent answers and quick wit.

The ladies organized an impromptu high tea during the early evening. In addition to tea, they found cucumber sandwiches, strawberries, and some apple tarts from the Confectory. All three talked easily about the events at the Palace over the last few weeks and about tomorrow's visit. King Henry VIII and his intended, Anne Boleyn, were coming to Hampton Court to inspect the new construction. Weatherby had seen both of them many times at Whitehall, but the assistant librarians had never seen either. They talked about it excitedly.

"Is the King as handsome as they say?" Margaret asked Weatherby.

"He was very handsome as a young man with red-blond hair and beard and lively dark blue eyes," Weatherby began. "But more than that, he is commanding. He towers over his subjects at six feet six inches tall. He is very vain about his calves, which is why the men's fashion now is to wear tight hose. He likes gambling with cards and dice, but enjoys hunting more. He loves tennis. I've watched him joust twice and he is excellent and fearless at that dangerous sport. He also writes treatises,

199

poetry and music. When he is here, I'm sure the musicians will play his composition 'Pastime with Good Company.' I find it his best tune. He's also interested in architecture. Like Michelangelo and Leonardo da Vinci, Henry is a Renaissance man. I'm sure both of you will get to meet him personally during his visit."

"What about Anne Boleyn?" Judith asked.

"The King is thirty-nine years old now, and Anne is only twenty-three," Weatherby replied, half thinking out loud. "He has been pursuing her for five years. I think he realizes that Catherine of Aragon, his present wife of many years, would at her age, never give him a son. Without a male heir, the Tudor legacy and Henry himself are unsafe. He has had healthy male children with Lady Blount and his other mistresses. He feels the problem of succession is Catherine's fault, and he would be rid of her by any possible means."

"But what is Anne like as a person?" Margaret asked impatiently.

"I should have picked up that you weren't interested in the things I was telling you," Weatherby said with embarrassment in his voice. "She has thick black hair and piercing blue eyes. She has a good figure but can't be over five feet four inches tall. She looks very petite when she stands next to Henry. She has peerless white skin but her nose, and especially her chin, is too pointed for her to be beautiful. She was raised at the family home in Hever, but educated about fashion and manners in France. Anne is more crafty than smart. She plots her career like a chess game with her brother George, her father, and the treacherous Duke of Norfolk. She is a good dancer and rides well enough to hunt with the King."

"Will she be Queen?" Judith asked.

"The Boleyns fervently hope so. Her father was made Earl of Wiltshire and then Viscount Rochford by the King in a failed attempt to get Anne to loosen her girdle."

"Are you saying that after five years, Anne still doesn't sleep with the King?" Margaret asked incredulously.

"My sources say that is correct," Weatherby replied. "That isn't to say they don't fondle each other frequently and publicly. You see, Henry took up with Anne's older sister Mary when Mary was only fourteen. He declared his undying love, but after he had his way with her, he discarded her, and she became known as the King's whore. Anne and her father had that lesson burned into their memories. Anne won't make the same mistake."

"How pleasurable it is to talk with you, Sir Weatherby," Judith replied merrily. "I had forgotten how much time you spent at Whitehall and how observant you are."

Just then, Amarantha pushed in the heavy wooden doors to the library.

"Here you are," she said. "The meeting concerning the King's visit is about to begin."

The four acquaintances headed off to the Great Hall. The three women walked hand in hand down a broad stairway and into the hall. The walls of the Great Hall were of carved oak hung on the lower level with large tapestries. Above were mounted the heads of stags with large racks of antlers. Next, in the upper story, large clear glass windows in a diaper or diamond pattern let light into the Hall. Above that was the hammer beam that Weatherby had learned about from Sir John Moulton and a dark wooden barrel-shaped roof.

Benches filled the entire stone floor of the Hall and two or three hundred people milled about. The noise of their conversation filled the space with a pleasant buzz like a giant beehive. Judith, Margaret, and Amarantha sat toward the back. Weatherby found a seat next to the Surveyor of the King's Works. A broad dais had been erected on the east wall of the Hall.

After a half hour of waiting as the natural light of the Hall began to fade, Warder Chertsey climbed on the platform and pounded a gavel on the podium. The sharp sound resounded through the Hall and echoed off of the ceiling.

"Here ye! Here ye!" the Warder boomed. "The assembly is about to commence. Take a seat!"

As the Warder backed away, the form of Richard Weston appeared from the gloom. How appropriate, Weatherby thought. The man who fears the light holds a meeting at deepening dusk.

"I wanted to tell you in person about the visit of His Royal Highness. You have all been preparing for this visit over the past weeks, and now the waiting is over. Tomorrow Henry and Miss Anne Boleyn will arrive sometime in the afternoon. The Royal Barge will be accompanied by a barge of musicians to fill the river with music. Then will come eight barges carrying ladies-in-waiting, earls, viscounts and the King's friends. Less important nobles, cooks, servants, grooms and fowlers will come by horseback and wagon. The King will be bringing eight hundred servants. For the duration of the King's visit, the population of the Hampton Court will be nearly three thousand souls. We don't know how long the royals will stay, but we shall treat them with every consideration."

While Weston spoke, Weatherby reflected on the fact that it would be impossible to work on the three murders while Henry VIII was in residence. Since as many as three murderers might be loose in the Palace, he hoped a bloody torso didn't drop in front of Anne Boleyn while she was walking to a masque.

"I imagine the main reason for the King's visit is to view the construction at the Palace that is currently sucking his treasury dry," Weatherby said quietly to Moulton.

"Zounds. I have spent a God-awful bunch of his money," Moulton replied. "But the buildings are quite beautiful, if I do say so myself. You should come with us on the inspection tour the day after tomorrow."

"I shall."

The Master of the House droned on until the meeting was adjourned. Amarantha invited Weatherby to her room for a cup of tea and their usual amicable conversation. He told her about Dredge's gambling problem.

"I need to meet him now in the Base Court so we can settle up his gambling debts," Weatherby said as a he rose from his seat.

When he arrived there, Dredge was already in the hansom, and as soon as Weatherby climbed aboard they headed toward the town. Dredge directed them to a tumbled-down house with old thatch and crooked windows on the edge of the village. It was a dark night with no moon. Dredge limped to the door and knocked, Weatherby stood to the side out of view as a small slit was opened. The door was unbolted and Dredge went in with Sir Weatherby behind him. Weatherby saw four tables in the dim, smoky light; three were set up for dice and one for cards. Several men clustered around each table. Dredge led the way to a large man sitting apart with a tumbler full of liquor.

"I'm here to pay my debt, Manchester," Dredge said.

"You owes seven sovereigns, but if you ain't going to gamble again then it will be eleven to make us square," Manchester replied.

"I don't have that much money, and I only owe you seven," Dredge said plaintively.

"Then I'll thrash the rest out of youse," Manchester said as he picked up a small cudgel from the table.

Weatherby had been standing back in the shadows to see how this would play out, but now in a motion so quick that Dredge couldn't follow it; Weatherby pulled a long knife from inside his coat. He rested the sharp point of the blade menacingly at the base of Manchester's throat.

"This man is employed by the King," Weatherby said in a menacing tone. "He will pay you seven sovereigns, and you will never bother him again. If you make a false move or even a twitch I will drive this dagger through your bloody neck and into your spine. I haven't killed in over a month and you look like a suitable victim. Make your move so I can dispatch you."

Manchester laid both of his hands open and palm up on the table, and Dredge counted out the seven gold sovereigns before backing toward the door. Weatherby followed, watching every roué and drunk in the house. They sped back to Hampton Court in the hansom.

"I can't thank you enough, Your Grace," Dredge blubbered.

"You are a good and loyal servant, Dredge," Weatherby replied as he patted his amanuensis's shoulder. "You just made a mistake."

# CHAPTER 38

In the morning Weatherby arose late and ate breakfast with Amarantha. He told her about the trip to the gambling den. When he got to the part about pulling the knife on the proprietor, she could contain herself no longer.

"I hate it when you take chances like that, Seamus," Amarantha said. "If you had been hurt, I would never forgive you. Why didn't you take one of those large oafs from the undercroft with you?"

"I know I made a mistake when I went for Clarence Stevens," Weatherby said. "You were right. I should have taken someone from the Palace with me and he wouldn't have escaped. It was pure bravado. However, I didn't take anyone else last night because I thought the proprietor would think something was up and not let us in."

"You were probably right, but I don't like it."

"Let's go over and bid adieu to Dredge. He leaves this morning for London."

Amarantha took Weatherby's arm and they walked across the Base Court, through the Clock Court and into the laboratory. Dredge had a large vellum book bound in leather out on the desk and was busily writing in it.

"I took your advice, Your Grace," Dredge said as he looked up. "About breaking the code. I read a treatise by a German monk name Thrithemius. He points out that a substitution code like you mentioned is the most common. To crack such code I needed a frequency table for the English language. It turns out that the most frequently used letter in standard English text is 'e', followed by 't', then 'a', and then 'i', 's' and 'o.' So I substituted the commonest symbol for 'e' and the second commonest for 't' and the code still looked like gibberish. For the next several days I made a series of substitutions, but none then made any sense. I've concluded that the cryptogram wasn't a substitution code. Thrithemius has some other types of encryption, and when I get back from London I will try them.

"Enjoy your time off, Dredge," Weatherby said, as he and Amarantha rose to leave the laboratory.

"What do you have to do during the King's visit?" Weatherby asked Amarantha.

"I have to attend Miss Boleyn along with her Ladies-in-Waiting for at least three days and attend all the plays, masques, and dances. I've been having dresses made for three weeks. The only part that I'm looking forward to is the dancing. Did you know there are four separate groups of Ladies-in-Waiting?"

"I didn't know that and I don't care. I have to go stag hunting, on horse back with the King and Lady Anne," Weatherby said. "And you know I'm not that good a horseman."

"That's no longer true," Amarantha replied. "You did well on that eighty-mile ride to Suffolk."

"It's not the same as hunting!" Weatherby retorted. "And the King likes such carnage. He won't be happy unless fifty stags are slaughtered."

"I never hear you talk like this," Amarantha retorted. "You are such an optimist. Perhaps these murders are getting you down. I hope you just throw yourself into the hunting and don't give these vexatious cases a thought."

Amarantha and Weatherby agreed to meet at the dock at 1 p.m. to welcome the King. In the meantime, Weatherby decided to take his roan for a ride. He was still feeling insecure about the hunting. When he arrived at the stable it was transformed. The large brick stable had stalls for eighty horses with a central area for grooming, washing, and shoeing. However, usually only fifty horses and a few mules were kept at the Palace. As he walked into the central area, proud, animated horses were tied everywhere. Weatherby found Gregory Townsend's replacement, Tom Walker, carrying two saddles.

"What happened?" Weatherby asked as he walked alongside Tom.

"Horses started arriving Tuesday week, but most arrived yesterday and the day before," Tom said in a strained voice. "We have two hundred and forty animals now. We worked all last night feeding and grooming them. The joisting horses are magnificent half Belgians that weigh one hundred stones, and Miss Boleyn has a pretty little black Arabian that is only ten hands high."

"Is there any chance I could get my roan saddled?" Weatherby asked in a deferential voice.

"Of course, Your Grace. I'm not going to master this anytime soon," Tom said as he swept his arm around the congested central part of the stables.

In fifteen minutes, Weatherby was riding out of the stable, and headed into the fields to the west. He had done more riding recently, but most of it was on highways. On this day, he took narrow forest trails with small jumps over fallen trees and creeks. He did well, mostly he thought because his large roan was well trained. After riding about ten miles he stopped at a tavern in Oatlands for a tankard of ale. On the way back he found some even narrower trails. He arrived back in time for the landing of the Royal Barge at the Water Gate. A crowd had gathered at the landing, but he found Amarantha with ease. They watched as the craft rowed around the last curve of the Thames. The twenty-six rows men moved their oars with coordinated sweeps. The blades of the oars were painted white to stand out. The barge itself was a rich brown with red velvet curtains and gold trim. Two people waved from the back of the barge. Weatherby presumed they were King Henry and Anne even he couldn't make out their faces due to the distance.

Weatherby had spent the last week organizing a force of men to protect the King and his mistress while they were at Hampton Court. He used Warder Chertsey's men as the main force and added fellows from the constabulary in Hampton Court. The ranks would be swelled when the King's men arrived, but he planned to have three trusted men around Anne Boleyn and Henry the VIII at all times.

Behind the Royal Barge was another barge filled with forty musicians. The drums could be heard the most easily, but the horns and even the strings could be heard wafting over the water. They were playing a sinfonietta by Boccherini that Weatherby recognized. As the Royal Barge pulled up to the landing, Anne Boleyn was first to alight, followed by King Henry. A loud huzzah went up from his subjects who lined the riverbank four deep.

The first event on the Royal's schedule was a small luncheon hosted by the Master of the House. It was to be a intimate event which Weatherby and Amarantha weren't invited to. So the two of them spent a quiet afternoon in the laboratory reviewing all of the autopsy and other pertinent information they had collected. Weatherby was again struck by how different the mode of death was in each of the three victims. Both of them studied Dredge's now voluminous notes about the poison that smelled like bitter roses. Neither of them had any new insights.

Amarantha wondered what similarities existed between these cases and the others Weatherby had solved for the King. After some searching, she found a book of previous cases in Dredge's library. They both sat down at a laboratory bench with a candelabra and the large volume between them. They leafed through the pages slowly. The first case Weatherby solved for the King involved the death of a Lady-in-Waiting to Queen Catherine. The unfortunate young woman was found one morning hanging from a railing over a circular staircase. She was from Aberdeen, Scotland and she was found in her nightgown with her hair carefully braided.

The warder of Whitehall declared it a suicide. Chancellor Wolsey knew the lady and found her very intelligent and cheerful and not given to depression. Wolsey had recently hired Sir Weatherby to investigate crimes against persons on the King's property, so Weatherby was dispatched. He found a chaste wife who had a very jealous older husband. The husband claimed to be home in Aberdeen, but Weatherby found he had signed the register at an inn near the Palace on the night of the murder. When confronted with this lie the husband broke down and confessed. Weatherby sent him to the Tower.

They reviewed some other cases, but none matched the Hampton Court murders for their brazen ferocity.

"I've come to the conclusion, Ran," Weatherby said. "that we have a single killer who is very smart, utterly ruthless, and who is hiding a very dark secret."

"He also holds you in low regard, Seamus," Amarantha replied. "He committed two of the murders while you were right here in the Palace. He did it under your nose if you will."

Amarantha closed the journal. A large banquet was planned for the King's first evening at Hampton Court and both Amarantha and Weatherby were expected to attend. Amarantha needed time to get ready. They strolled leisurely to their apartments where both found they had roommates. Weatherby had a courtier from Kent to share his apartment. Amarantha had a Lady-in-Waiting from near her home in Wales. That night not a single sleeping space in Hampton Court would go unoccupied.

Weatherby and Amarantha put on their finery and left early for the dinner in the Great Hall. They arrived early so they went to the Knot Garden and sat for a while. It was a pleasant spring evening with warm sunlight flooding the garden. Off to the west, mounds of fluffy white cumulus clouds like whipped cream piled up in the sky. Neither Weatherby nor Amarantha cared for formal events and royal events were not only formal but long. Finally, they reluctantly wandered into the Great Hall and were escorted to their assigned places. Nearly all the guests were present. The trumpets sounded as the King entered, dressed in a doublet of red with a long coat of gold and maroon. He wore a very large gold necklace that was as wide as his shoulders and descended nearly to his navel. Each element of the necklace had a ruby nearly an inch in diameter set in a clasp of gold. Amarantha thought the necklace alone must be worth five thousand pounds. The diminutive Anne was on his arm in a blue velvet dress which fit her slender figure perfectly. The dress was of the richest blue and had a bodice that exposed the upper half of her breasts. The revealing style may have come from France, but Anne Boleyn made the fashion popular in England, at least at court. She wore a necklace of blue sapphires set in gold. Rumor had it that the necklace had been given to Catherine of Aragon by the King, and had been taken back when she fell out of favor.

Everyone stood while the two walked to their seats on a raised platform that spanned one end of the Hall. The guests were all drinking mead. Large trays of small stuffed and roasted birds were brought in, followed by two kinds of fish, and then three varieties of meat and then after a pause, fruit tarts from Ellen's Confectory. Conversation echoed off the high ceiling between speeches praising the King, and performances by dancers and musicians. The evening closed with the performance of a short play in French.

As the guests wandered out, neither Weatherby nor Amarantha were eager to confront their roommates in their apartments, so they walked into Hampton for some ale at the Lamb and Flag. They wandered back two hours later, pleasantly tipsy.

# CHAPTER 39

Weatherby rose at five the next morning for the dreaded hunt. He walked to the stables where dozens of horses, including his, were already saddled. A large table outside the stable area was loaded with ham, bacon, eggs and scones. Hot tea and small glasses of whiskey were available. Large packs of beagles on leashes were held outside the stables by their owners; however their baying and barking made conversation impossible. Courtiers, hunters and the King's friends arrived sporadically over the next forty-five minutes.

Weatherby was intolerant of the Royals whose Keeper of the Seal set the time for events. All mortals were expected to arrive on time, but the King always arrived one or often two hours late. Weatherby hated standing around. He always had enquiries that he wanted to pursue, and he thought two hours was a precious block of time. This morning, he ruminated about a problem while the clock ran, and then surreptitiously wrote shorthand notes with his pencil to remind himself of his conclusions. Just when Weatherby was ready to go inside and escape the cold, the King and Anne Boleyn arrived.

They were already mounted. The King rode a shiny black hunter, which was bigger and more elegant looking than any horse in the stable. Anne rode a small dappled Arabian sidesaddle. Weatherby heard that sidesaddle was necessary to maintain a woman's modesty, but he found the concept flawed. Both of Anne's feet were on the left side of the horse, one in a conventional stirrup and her right leg circled a strange wooden post. In that way, the woman didn't have to spread her legs apart in an unladylike fashion. However, she was dangerously unbalanced especially when hunting which involved a lot of jumping. He thanked God that Amarantha rode astride her horse like a man.

Once the King arrived, the Hunt Master had a horn blown and the troupe set out at a walk with the hounds in front, followed by the King and his mistress. The other forty hunters, including Weatherby brought up the rear. The sky was just lightening as they rode into the woods east of Hampton Court. The hounds quickly raised a hind and were called back. Then they roused a stag and the entire company galloped after him. When the stag was exhausted the King got off his horse and shot the animal with an ivory-inlaid flintlock.

"Not much sport in that," the rider next to Weatherby murmured.

"Roger that," Weatherby replied. "Are you from around here?"

"No I'm from London," the rider replied. "I'm the Duke of Northampton and one of King's childhood friends. We had the same tutors when we were growing up at Whitehall. We play dice together several nights a week." The troupe of horses took off again. The duke caught up with Weatherby. "As you know, you always have to lose to the King, and besides he cheats at dice. I'm one of the few men in the realm rich enough to sustain those kind of losses night after night."

"It doesn't sound like a great friendship."

"Actually, we have a lot of fun, joking and telling stories and he shares his mistresses once he is tired of them, which sometimes takes only a fortnight. They are some of the most beautiful and supple young women in the realm. Besides, what else would I do? My huge castle in the foggy north is very dull."

"Do you hunt with him frequently?"

"Yes. He's a good shot and a better rider. Absolutely fearless. But he kills too many animals. The kitchens can handle ten or twelve stags, but he prefers to kill fifty. There are no large stags on any of his lands near Whitehall. One reason for the visit to Hampton Court is because of the fresh game."

"I thought the King was coming here to examine his expensive new construction on the Palace."

"I believe that was the excuse for the visit," the Duke of Northampton replied.

The next trail the horsemen took was hillier and narrower. Two horsemen failed to jump a large pile of brush and fell—luckily, without their horses landing on top of them. They were shaken up and bruised, and began walking back to Hampton Court leading their mounts. The next stag leapt from the brush beside the trail, startling all the horsemen at the front of the pack. However, soon the dogs and horses gave chase. Low-hanging branches slapped all the horses and riders. Once the stag was collapsed with fatigue, the King climbed down and shot the magnificent animal at close range. Weatherby noted the look of fear in the deer's large brown eyes.

The next three stags were smaller, but efficiently dispatched. On the following chase, Anne slid off her saddle on a steep downhill. She landed in a large bramble, and was extracted by three courtiers before the King could turn around and dismount. Anne was dressed in a brown tweed hunting jacket and skirt with a small brown feathered hat. She got up laughing, brushed herself off and straightened her hat.

A half a mile further on, the party dismounted in a large field where tables had been set out. They were laden with food and drink that had been brought by wagon from Hampton Court for dinner.

The only two chairs were for the King and his mistress, so everyone else stood. They pulled their chairs together and fed each other pieces of fruit kissing between bites with open mouths and probing tongues. The King's friends and courtiers from Whitehall had seen this behavior so long that they were either bored or disgusted with it. However, the members of the party from Hampton Court watched avidly as they had never seen such a display of public affection. In Tudor times, public hand-holding even by a betrothed couple was frowned upon.

The afternoon went much like the morning, only it was hotter. Everyone sweated in their heavy wool clothing. More animals were killed. Finally in the waning afternoon the troupe headed back to Hampton Court. Weatherby felt like he had acquitted himself well. His only goals were to not fall off or call attention to himself, and he felt he had accomplished both objectives. A large gathering was planned for the hunters in the Base Court, but Weatherby took his horse to the stable and then retired to his apartment. Fortunately, his roommate wasn't there. He tried to find Amarantha and the Ladies-in-Waiting but had no success. He settled back and read Chaucer's *Canterbury Tales* until he fell asleep on his sofa. Instead, he was awakened an hour later by a gentle hand on his cheek. It was Amarantha, back from her duties with Anne's Ladies-in-Waiting.

"How was the hunting?" Amarantha asked with some concern in her voice.

"Two falls, neither very bad," Weatherby replied sleepily, "And Anne slid off of her silly sidesaddle. Also we slaughtered at least twenty magnificent stags. That should please our bloodthirsty King."

"But I gather you acquitted your self well?" Amarantha queried. "Just as I thought you would."

"Yes. No major gaffes. The King took me aside and asked about our investigation and Anne's safety."

"Considering that we have no suspects how did that go?"

"He was dismissive, but surprisingly temperate."

"I wish we could skip the banquet to night."

"I do too, but our absence would be commented upon. Let's get ready."

Weatherby and Amarantha reluctantly dressed for another banquet. They were seated together and the crowded hall was noisy enough that they could carry on a private conversation through the many courses. The rest of the evening was taken up by a dance. The Great Hall had been decorated with pine boughs and hundreds of candles. A group of the King's musicians were on a platform to one side. The twenty musicians played viola de gambas, flutes, trumpets, many lutes and a harpsichord. Their playing filled the entire hall with sonorous tunes.

The men were dressed in rich doublets with slashes in the material that revealed patches of brightly colored silk. The women wore elegant taffeta and satin gowns adorned in lace and pearls. The skirts were getting more and more voluminous and were now several feet in diameter. An observer standing on a balcony would have seen a colorful sight as the dancers twirled and bowed.

Weatherby had two left feet on the dance floor. Amarantha had been giving him brief lessons for the past three weeks. He acquitted himself well during the first gavotte. He liked the dances where four couples circled and intertwined. However, soon the dancers changed to a long line of men facing a line of women that approached and retreated in time to the music. The dancing went on for hours with occasional breaks for wine and ale when the dancers got overheated. Many of the dances followed the form of the English country dance which had its origin at court. The dances were characterized by dozens of moves that bewildered Weatherby. When the dance master called for 'three mad robbins', Amarantha would whisper to Seamus—back to back with your neighbor, maintain eye contact with your partner, and he would know to take one step forward then slide to the right passing in front of his neighbor, before taking a step back. That step might be followed by two circular heys or a three-hands star.

Weatherby danced with Anne Boleyn several times and was amazed at how diminutive she was when he held her in his arms. She felt like a tiny, delicately boned bird. She turned her gaze on him several times, and he was startled by the force behind her bright blue eyes.

"Will you protect me from the murderer, Sir?" Anne asked toward the end of the night.

"I will, to the best of my ability, My Lady," Weatherby replied.

After hours of dancing the guests adjourned to the east lawn for champagne and a brilliant fireworks display. Weatherby enjoyed the controlled violence of pyrotechnics and had built some rockets as a young man. He reveled in the bright greens and blues but the startling, vibrating reds were his favorite. He just wished they all lasted longer.

# CHAPTER 40

Weatherby shambled to his apartment around two, only to find his roommate already in bed and snoring loudly. At a time in history when everyone in England but the King and Queen shared a bed, Weatherby had a marked aversion to sleeping with others. He hung his fine clothes in the garderobe and pulled on his night rail. He took a quilt and settled on the sofa in the front room. It was well padded but far too short for his long legs. He slept fitfully for a few hours, and then got up and pulled on some clothes.

He walked out through the Great Gatehouse and along the foggy, still banks of the Thames. Carts of grain, apples, potatoes, and vegetables were already arriving at Hampton Court from the countryside. Small herds of bleating sheep, and lowing cattle were intermixed with the carts. Wagons carried hogsheads of beer, and hundreds of wine bottles packed in straw. Weatherby remembered a conversation he had with Sir John Moulton shortly after his arrival at Hampton Court. Moulton had said that the King and his entourage ravaged the countryside of every green and edible thing like a million locusts, and needed to move every six weeks or faster if they were to avoid starving to death.

Weatherby ducked through the dense gorse and headed toward the river bed. Suddenly it was very quiet except for bird calls and hedgehogs scurrying amongst the underbrush. He sat on a stump and looked out at the river. To satisfy the King's blood lust, another hunt was planned for the day. Weatherby decided not to push his luck. Perhaps, only he knew how lucky he had been the previous day. He would skip the hunt and ride to Teddington and talk to Clarence Stevens in the hospital.

Miss Anne Boleyn had taken a liking to Amarantha, Weatherby thought, because his assistant was smart and independent. Perhaps Anne saw some parallels in their lives during a time when women were expected to be respectful, subservient and docile. Regardless, Anne would tour the new construction including the Bayne Tower and Amarantha would be her close companion.

Weatherby set out mid-morning for Teddington. He could get there quickly by barge, but the return trip, upriver, would take hours. He decided to ride. It would be good to stretch his muscles which were still sore from hunting the day before. The ride was only two miles but over narrow and confusing country roads. Weatherby had Warder Chertsey draw a map. He had ridden so much since the trek that was cut short by the hailstorm that he was beginning to enjoy it. He had a well trained horse, and he liked the solitude of it. Even with one wrong turn it took less than an hour to get to Teddington a corruption of 'tides end'. The town marked the point at which the tidal bore from the North Sea ended and therefore where the salt water in the Thames ended. He got directions to the hospital on High Street and found Clarence Stevens wearing a robe and sitting under a tree. He recognized Sir Weatherby immediately.

"They tells me I owes my life to you," Clarence began. "That I was more than half dead when you found me."

"Yes," Weatherby replied. "You had been beaten very badly. I was afraid you wouldn't survive."

"I s'pect, I made a mistake running from you in the first place."

"Perhaps, but at least you recovered, and now we can talk. You were very angry at Gregory Townsend for the way he treated your sister."

"He hid behind his fakey churchy stuff and used it to take advantage of my sister for his own kernel desires."

"The word is 'carnal.' So you came to the Palace to kill him?"

"Yes, I did. I was bigga and stronga than he was. I bringed a rope. I asked one of his believers where I could find him and I sneaked to his room after dark."

"Why did you change your mind about how to kill him?"

"I didn'. When I gots there he was already gone."

"My dear man. You came all the way to Hampton Court with a rope in your hand and murder in your heart, and then you didn't kill the cad?"

"Ye Gods. When I left his room, I saw people scurryin' and I follered. Gregory Townsend were dead, facedown in the gravel in below the Great Gatehouse."

"After you threw him off the parapet!" Weatherby yelled.

"I wish'd to slaughter him, but I dina' do it."

"And how shall you prove that?"

"I dina' need to prove it. You may rebook' me for it, now that my sister is dishonored, I dina' care."

Weatherby stopped and for the first time hunched down in the grass. He had to entertain the idea that Clarence Stevens hadn't killed Gregory Townsend. The idea of Clarence being clever enough to deny the crime but still be willing to take the punishment was incredible to him. But, if not him, then whom?

"I will send for you when you are recovered, Clarence. In the meantime, don't leave Teddington," Weatherby said sternly as he moved toward his horse.

The ride home was uneventful except for the confusion Weatherby felt.

Amarantha had breakfasted early with Anne Boleyn and her Ladies-in-Waiting. She reported they were led on a tour of the new construction by Sir John Moulton. A long hallway of store rooms and additional kitchens were constructed parallel to the gallery where Weatherby had his apartment.

"These new kitchens double the cooking capacity of the Palace," Moulton had said as he led the ladies into the new buildings that smelled of curing mortar. "One of the major problems before was inadequate space for the serving men to collect dishes."

The range of new offices was over three hundred feet long and extended eighty feet past the Great Gatehouse. A small open corridor separated the two rows of offices and cooking areas. It became known as the Fish Court.

Moulton had led the group of twenty ladies along the east edge of Hampton Court. Each was dressed in a fine but simple gown, and they prattled pleasantly while they walked. Near the Great Hall Moulton's men had constructed a Council Chamber. It was the least completed part of the construction and still had rough walls with no woodwork.

"When it is completed, the King's Privy Council will meet here," Moulton said as he ushered the ladies through a door on the outside of the Palace. "As you know, the council consists of the King, the Chancellor, the Lord Privy Seal, and several religious and secular leaders that advise the King. The council consists of twelve to fourteen members, so the chamber need not be overly large."

Outside the Council Chamber a table of refreshments had been set for the tour members. Fruit drinks, tea and pitchers of milk and ale were supplemented by gingerbread husbands, daryole, and fruit tarts in a variety of inventive shapes. The Ladies-in-Waiting stood in small groups and held their food on linen napkins. Anne was talking with Amarantha and a lady named Clarissa.

"After you were admitted to law school, you traveled alone to the Low Countries?" Anne asked Amarantha.

"No, my mother accompanied me to Utrecht and helped me get settled," Amarantha replied.

"How many women were in your class?"

"There were sixty-two people in my class and one hundred and fifty some in the law school, and I was the only woman. Sometimes Cardinal Wolsey or men of title make fun of me because of my simple background in Hever or because I am a young woman," Anne said dejectedly.

"Did the students and professors make fun of you?"

"I never gave them a chance. I posed as a young boy who hadn't yet developed a beard or a low voice."

"But these were clever university students, certainly some got suspicious."

"Yes. But, if the questions got too pointed, I stopped socializing with that person, and I changed roommates every year."

"I wish I could do that," Anne said wistfully. "Instead I am caught up in a daily struggle with Catherine for the King. She is not only a Queen, but a Princess of Spain in her own right."

"Will it ever be over?" Clarissa asked.

"It has been over eighteen hundred days so far and I suppose it may go on another eighteen hundred," Anne replied with determination in her voice. "I will be Queen Consort."

Sir John Moulton moved his tour group along the Knot Garden and to the Bayne Tower, the last and most lavish stop on his tour. The outside of the three-story structure was made of rich red bricks used throughout Hampton Court, but the corners were quoined with limestone blocks.

"This is the most elegant sleeping and governing building ever created," Sir Moulton said with pride in his voice. "On the ground floor is an office for Sir Brian Tuke, Treasurer of the Chamber. He pays the members of the Privy Chamber. Next door is the Wardrobe of the Robes where the King's clothes are stored, repaired and cleaned."

Amarantha wasn't interested in any of this and she found her mind wandering. She looked around and noticed the ladies-in-waiting were also fidgeting. Moulton lead the way up a broad staircase.

"On the first floor is the King's new bedchamber with an in-suite bathroom."

The bathroom was served by a small furnace in the room behind. Sir Moulton had the fires lit early that morning, so the circular wooden tub was filled with steaming hot water. Each lady in turned dipped her fingers in the hot water and then sighed.

"Also on this floor is the King's Privy Closet or study," Moulton remarked. "The King took a keen personal interest is this room down to the murals painted below the ceiling by the Italian, Toto del Nunciata."

Moulton walked his group out to the landing by the stairs to the second floor and then paused.

"Up these stairs is the King's new library and jewel house which we will not see today because work is ongoing. Please feel free to stay as long as you wish."

Sir John Moulton bounded down the stair toward his construction shack as if happy to be getting back to work where he wouldn't need to be charming. Anne Boleyn whispered in Amarantha and Clarissa's ear and then led the way to the large wooden bathtub. The three stripped quickly to their shifts and then sank into the hot steamy water. After an hour of giggling and talking they emerged clean and relaxed.

# PART 5

# CHAPTER 41

Weatherby arrived back at Hampton Court during the afternoon. He left his horse in the stable and walked to Amarantha's apartment. She had just returned from bathing with Anne Boleyn. The Palace was still overwhelmingly crowded with royals and hangers on. Weatherby and Amarantha went to the Great Kitchen and requested a basket of biscuits, honey, ham and cold pickled vegetables. They added a table cloth and two bottles of malmsey wine. A serving girl carried the food. They walked to the north through the Privy Orchard and into the farm land beyond. Most of the fields were planted with barley and oats. For ease of walking, they stayed on the wagon paths between the fields. A gentle breeze blew through the fields of grain creating a complex pattern of dark and light as the stalks of grain were pressed and released by the wind. The sun was hot, so they found a spot beneath a beech tree on the edge of the fields. Weatherby helped spread the tablecloth on the ground while the serving girl laid out the food. Then, they told her to take a walk and return in an hour or so.

"How was your visit with Clarence?" Amarantha asked.

"First off, he is much recovered," Weatherby began. "And he readily admits to wanting to kill Gregory Townsend for what he did to his sister. He was planning to hang him and came to the Palace the night of the murder with a rope."

"At last a break, Seamus! You have one of the murderers!"

"Not so fast, Ran. He says that when he got to Townsend's room, he wasn't there. Then he saw people scurrying to the Great Gatehouse, and when he followed them he saw Townsend's body lying in the gravel."

"He just made up an alibi, Seamus, and not a very good one at that."

"Then he asked me to punish him for the crime, even though he didn't do it."

"I suppose that is either very clever or very foolish. I'm just not sure which."

"It took me aback." Weatherby shook his head.

Amarantha poured both of them another glass of wine as they lounged on the grass.

"You don't think he did it," she mused. "Because you don't think he's smart enough to lie."

"I suppose you are right, he seems a simple man. I will have to see if any witnesses saw him the night of the murder, and can confirm his story."

"I can help with that. When does Dredge get back?"

"Two more days. I certainly could use his help. How did the tour go?"

"Swimmingly, I'd say," Amarantha said impishly. "Sir John had the boiler fired up in the King's private bath in the Bayne Tower just to tantalize us with its spacious warmth. So, Anne, one of her Ladies-in-Waiting and I locked ourselves in, stripped to our shifts, and took a bath in the steaming hot water. We soaked and splashed for the better part of an hour. The tub would have held three more people without any crowding."

"Miss Boleyn seems to have taken a liking to you."

"And I to her. I admire her perseverance and the way she controls one of the most powerful men in the world. She told us about the first time she disobeyed him three years ago. He wanted her to attend a special dinner for the King of France but she had a family engagement in London. As she walked away after telling him no, he bellowed, 'I'm the King of England!'"

"Certainly, he hasn't lost all powers of judgment, I hope."

"She has a profound influence on his religious beliefs, controls his politics to some degree, and makes him jump through hoops for her, just by means of her sex."

"His advisors must be warning him that she has too much power."

"I'm sure they are, but he is besotted with her."

"Rumor has it that three years ago, he offered to make her his one true and only mistress. Anne said something like, 'What have I done that you would abuse me like this?' She spun on her heels and fled. She didn't stop until she got to her family home at Hever where she pouted for several weeks."

"I believe she will be Queen."

"Not if the Cardinals and Pope Clement VII have anything to say about it," Weatherby replied.

"Henry is adamant."

"Yes, but he's up against a rich and powerful religion that has been extending its roots throughout the world for fifteen hundred years. Those stout subterranean branches now extend under every one of Henry's properties, peoples and lands. It will take a tremendous uprooting to change the Catholic Church's mind. In any case, the Pope believes Henry has already bedded Anne and simply wishes to legitimize his adultery."

"How would you know that?" Amarantha replied in surprise.

"The Pope's legates have been paying large sums of money for letters between the two of them, hoping to confirm their suspicions. The Chancellor had me investigate why the letters were being purloined two years ago, and that is what turned up. The stale letters seemed like useless pieces of paper to me, but buyers in the city were paying a hundred angels for them. That's fifty pounds, which is a lot of money. Eventually I traced the buyers back to the Pope's emissaries."

Amarantha and Weatherby left their picnic things and walked leisurely back to Hampton Court. Another large public feast was planned for the evening, and it was to be followed by a play. Amarantha needed time to get ready so Weatherby decided to putter in the lab. He had been thinking again about how long his trip to France took, about how fast lightning traveled, and how fireworks traveled at a speed intermediate between the two. He thought that the speed of fireworks was closer to lightning than to a coach pulled by six horses. He thought he might design an experiment. He sketched some preliminary drawings on a parchment and left them with a note for Dredge. Back in his quarters, Weatherby donned his gold and red doublet and the hose that he had worn at Whitehall. He knocked softly on Amarantha's door anxious to escort her to dinner.

"You look as beautiful tonight as I have ever seen you, my dear," Weatherby said as Amarantha took his arm.

She wore a dark green satin floor-length gown that set off her auburn hair and showed off her tiny waist. A necklace of gold, set with emeralds made her green eyes sparkle. They strolled to the Great Hall, and were shown to their seats by a liveried servant of the king. They were only six places from the King.

"I imagine these enviable seats are due to your bathing, nearly naked, with the King's favorite," Weatherby whispered sarcastically.

"Well it certainly isn't because of your hunting prowess."

"Touché." Weatherby laughed.

The platters and trays of food began arriving regularly, each more spectacular than the last. Weatherby watched the King eat, and could easily see why his waist had thickened noticeably over the past five years. The Monarch often took fistfuls of food with both hands and ate without even breathing between mouthfuls. Anne, on the other hand, took small portions of the lightest fare and pushed it around on her plate. Weatherby noted that she chewed the small morsels that she put in her mouth for at least three minutes before swallowing.

The ranks of the musicians had swelled to at least forty, perhaps because of the play that would be performed later. When the King had entered from the hallway, suitably late, the musicians had struck up 'Pastime with Good Company', one of Henry's own compositions. Several other compositions were performed that weren't familiar to Weatherby, although he recognized John Dowland's 'Pavan: Lachrimae Antiquae.' When he practiced surgery in rural Scotland, Weatherby had traveled to Edinburgh as often as he could to relieve his boredom, and he had attended concerts there frequently and became fluent with modern music. Later in the evening, he recognized the gentle harmony of 'The Silver Swan' by Orlando Gibbon, and the gay and sprightly, 'Galliard-Heigh Ho Holiday' by Anthon Holborne, one of his favorite composers. Fully enjoying the evening, Weatherby and Amarantha both drank too much mead. They found that the addition of the honey to the beer somehow made them more light-headed.

Dancing followed the banquet and Weatherby and Amarantha found themselves in the set with Anne Boleyn and the King. Weatherby was surprised at how light Henry was on his feet. Perhaps it was brought out by his partner, sixteen years his junior. Even Amarantha's partner danced well after the practice of the other night.

After two hours of dancing, the royal troupe adjourned to an outdoor stage set up in The Clock Court. A visiting company from Verona would perform Moliere's *Tartuffe*. Rumor had it that Henry was eager to perform it because it had been banned by his enemy, Francis I, the King of France. The play showed how the hypocrisy of the upper class, can result in outrage and demonstrations by the peasant class.

The actors, all men, were gaily costumed and gestured flamboyantly. Amarantha had learned Dutch and French in law school, but not Italian, so Sir Weatherby translated for her. In the first act, Orgon, a rich man, is persuaded by Tartuffe that he is a religious zealot, when in fact Tartuffe is a scheming hypocrite. Tartuffe gains control of the household and orders everyone about. In the next act Tartuffe attempts to seduce Orgon's wife, Elmire, and their son catches him. However, the son is denounced unfairly.

"Orgon is hiding under the table," Weatherby whispered to Amarantha. "And he will hear Tartuffe seducing his wife."

Finally outraged, Orgon throws Tartuffe out of the house, but unfortunately the rich man has already signed all his possessions over to the rogue. In the last scene, the schemer comes back with the police to evict the family.

"Instead of evicting the owners," Weatherby whispered. "The officer says, 'you are under arrest' to Tartuffe."

At the conclusion of the play, the inebriated audience applauded loudly, stamped their feet and shouted their approval. A fireworks display followed. Weatherby found himself timing the rockets and trying to estimate how far they went into the sky before exploding. More dancing was announced, and Amarantha dragged Weatherby in for two more hours of English country dances and gavottes. When the musicians finally collapsed the sky outside was beginning to get light. Weatherby thought to himself, thank God, as the dancing master announced the last 'mad robin.'

Weatherby escorted Amarantha to her apartment. As he passed the Astronomical Clock it read five-fifteen. At her door, Weatherby gave her a firm, heartfelt hug.

"I may be too old for this."

"Nonsense! You did beautifully!" Amarantha replied. "More than half the younger men fell by the wayside."

"The average man in Britain only lives to be thirty-five and I'm forty!"

"My prescription, Doctor, is more dancing, and more time with younger women," Amarantha said as she slid behind her door, blowing her partner a kiss.

# CHAPTER 42

When he went in the bedroom, the courtier, who had been assigned to Weatherby's apartment during the King's visit, was asleep in the bed, and snoring loudly. Weatherby shook him awake roughly.

"Get out of my bed!" Weatherby shouted. "Find someplace else to sleep!"

The disoriented aristocrat rubbed his eyes and stood up slowly. As he staggered toward the door, the King's Detective threw his doublet at him. Weatherby fell into the warm bed and was instantly asleep. He regained consciousness hours later as a chambermaid set a tea service next to the bed.

"What time is it?" Weatherby said in a groggy voice.

"Almost two of the clock, Your Grace," the chambermaid answered as she curtsied.

Weatherby sat up and took the proffered cup of hot tea. He recalled the merriment of the previous night. In his mind he summarized it as too much dancing and too much drinking. The sides of his head ached. He reached for some ground-up willow bark from his medical bag to ease the throbbing. He reflected on the fact that willow had been prescribed by physicians for pain for over two thousand years. As he slipped on a dressing gown and poured another cup of tea, he was grateful that he had such an effective remedy for his headache. As the headache began to ease, he realized how hungry he was. He knocked on Amarantha's door, and finding no answer wandered through the Base Court and into the Great Kitchen.

It was between meals, too late for dinner and too early for supper, so he asked for a ham sandwich. The scullery maid fixed him a thick sandwich on fresh, warm white bread with mustard on it. She also gave him a tankard of ale which he frowned on at first, but when his mouth got dry from the sandwich he took a swallow. On the second longer swallow he recited a quote attributed to Aristophanes, "If this dog do you bite, soon as out of your bed, take a hair of the tail in the morning." As the food coursed through his system Weatherby began to feel better, but more alert. He inquired after Amarantha and was not surprised to learn that she had gone on a ride with Anne Boleyn at eleven of the clock, and was expected back at any moment. He decided to go to the Wolsey Apartment to work on his correspondence. Two young courtiers were playing dice on the Cardinal's desk. Sir Weatherby chased them out with a stern look and a sweep of his hand.

A couple letters were from universities where professors had looked at the code first discovered in Anna Maria Wimbledon's presumed diary. Both academics failed to identify the code, but suggested other linguists that might be queried. A long wordy letter in French from Father Croceus Lawrence was next. He wrote about his advanced studies of illuminated manuscripts at the church of Saint Germain des Pres in Paris, but he offered no new ideas about the encoded messages.

Another large blue letter bore a French postmark. Weatherby tore the thin envelope open. It was a letter from Jean Favier, the assistant glazier at Chartres Cathedral. It was written in French with curlicues and serifs, which gave Weatherby pause. He struggled through the missive. After reading it three times, he deduced that Jean's boss, Henri de Lèves, was tried and then executed at the Bastille. Jean's letter said they had only heard the news by hearsay, nothing official, but that de Lèves had been accused of apostasy, tried, and beheaded. Weatherby wondered if the renunciation had been of political or religious allegiance. He suspected it was the latter, and wrote a quick letter to the Chancellor asking him to enquire about any particulars since it might relate to the Hampton Court cases.

Weatherby went to Amarantha's apartment. She had returned from her ride with Anne Boleyn and had just finished changing her clothes. They decided on a quiet dinner in Hampton, as the King and his consort were dining alone. They ate a savory mushroom dish made from fungi found in the local woods and spit roasted beef. Weatherby was pleased to see Amarantha with her cheeks windburned from her ride and asked about her day.

"How was your ride with Anne and her ladies?" he inquired.

"Anne sent Lady Miranda back right away," Amarantha began.

"Why, pray tell?"

"She isn't much of a horsewoman, and Anne wanted to try some big jumps without worrying after her. The two of us headed off into those rough, hilly, woods to the west. We rode hard for three hours with just a short rest on the bank of the Mole River. It was windy and I can feel my cheeks are burned."

"How did you acquit yourself?"

"Tolerably. I like high jumps. I just don't like long ones. I worry about my horse's forefeet catching on a limb, and pitching me forward into a rock or a stump."

"I wish you were a little more cautious."

"I know, but it was fun to ride with abandon as I once did with my cousins in Wales when I was growing up. We always picked the steepest trails and rode bareback."

"I hope Anne didn't ride sidesaddle."

"No. She only does that with the King. Clearly, she needed a better platform today. Anne is a good horsewoman, I suppose from growing up way out in the country."

"What did the two of you talk about?"

As usual, I tell her all about the murders. She likes the gory parts the best, so I often tell her about the smashed-in heads and describe the blood in detail. She talked about her struggle over the past five years to be queen and about her efforts to attract and tease the King without delivery of her supposed virginity."

"Why do you say 'supposed'?"

"If there is one thing I know about country girls, it's that they are bedded almost as soon as they learn to ride. I very much doubt she is a virgin."

"When the time comes she will have to use all her wiles to convince the King that she is."

"I'm sure her Ladies are schooled in many tricks."

"No doubt."

"What did you do while I was gone?"

"I went through my damned correspondence. I learned that no one has managed to solve our code and that the glazier from Chartres was put to death for apostasy."

"Do you think his crimes are related to our murders?"

"I'm sure I don't know, but it does give me pause."

Amarantha and Weatherby finished the wine they had been drinking and headed back through the darkened village of Hampton. Amarantha took her escort's arm and stopped several times to admire a hat or a handbag through the multipaned glass window of a shop. Both were feeling quite content after a dinner of good food and the nice wine that accompanied it.

"It's rather like a holiday for us to have the King and his entourage at Hampton Court," Weatherby mused. "We have made little progress on our investigation and we aren't expected to."

"For some reason we have always assumed that the perpetrator or perpetrators are still here in the Palace. But why do we believe that to be so?"

"I suppose because the corpses were laid out so publicly after their tragic deaths."

"You're correct. There was almost a theatrical quality to the display of the bodies, particularly the last two."

"If I murdered someone and wanted to get away, I would hide the corpse in the woods, throw it in the river, or bury it in the undercroft; not leave it posed in the King's new bathroom."

"It is as if the murderer is trying to leave a message for someone who is still alive and present in the Palace."

"But who is it and why?"

As they wandered arm in arm back through the Great Gatehouse, neither Weatherby nor Amarantha was tired.

"Let us go see what the courtiers are up to," Amarantha suggested playfully taking Weatherby's hand and pulling him forward.

In the Great Kitchen it was quite dark, and several of the kitchen boys were asleep on the floor in front of the hearth. They checked the Great Hall which was dark and filled with almost ominous shadows. The Clock Court was also deserted, but then as they walked by the New Council Chambers they heard the faint sound of music. Expecting it to be coming from the Privy Orchard they cut to the east through a passageway. However, it was also dark, and the music was pouring out of the open door of the King's sumptuous new indoor Tennis Court.

As they walked through the doorway, they saw the musicians on a small dais in the corner. With the net removed, the entire length of the court was filled with dancing couples. The ceiling was hung with colorful paper lanterns each with a candle in it. At a break in the music, Amarantha and Weatherby were invited into the long line of dancers by several beckoning hands. For the next two hours the couple curtsied, bowed and turned to the figures of the English country dances. The dancing had started around nine and by one in the morning the hogshead of wine had been drained. A puncheon of ale was still supplying drinks to the thirsty dancers. Once the pair was sweating and out of breath they stopped for a tankard of ale. It was too noisy to talk. The sound from the musicians bounced off the flat wooden roof of the court and then ricocheted off the wall like one of the King's leather-covered tennis balls.

Amarantha and Weatherby took their drinks out into the cool dark garden.

"I believe I've had enough fun for one evening," Amarantha said.

"As the senior member of this pair, I wasn't going to claim fatigue first," Weatherby replied. "But, I concur."

The two walked arm in arm toward their apartments under a canopy of stars as bright as diamonds scattered like flecks of mica across the blackness of the sky.

# CHAPTER 43

Once in his apartment, Weatherby changed rapidly and climbed into bed. Fortunately, his temporary roommate was not in the room. Once he emptied his mind of the murders, he fell asleep quickly. A couple of hours later, he heard a loud noise. He suspected it was his courtier bedmate from the previous night, and was preparing to lambaste him before throwing him out of the room. Then a light shown upon him.

"Anne Boleyn is missing!" Warder Chertsey said in a loud voice.

Weatherby sat up hurriedly and tried to collect his thoughts. He crawled out of bed and began asking questions

"When was she seen last? Who was she with? Did any of her ladies report that she was troubled?" Weatherby said in rapid succession as his mind began to work.

"I—I don't know the answer to any of those questions," Warder Chertsey stammered. Come to the Great Kitchen so someone can address your queries."

Weatherby quickly pulled on a doublet and a pair of pants, and followed Chertsey out of the apartment. The Warder rushed down the gallery on his short legs. When they burst into the Great Kitchen, forty men in heavy outdoor clothes carrying torches were already there. Everyone was talking at once. Weatherby grabbed a walking stick from one of the men and brought it down on the trestle table three times in rapid succession. The loud thud echoed off the high ceiling of the room. Startled, everyone in the room grew silent.

"Before we begin our search," Weatherby shouted in a loud stern voice. "I need to hear what facts we know without rumor or embellishment. How do we know that Anne Boleyn is missing?"

"The King told me himself," Tobias said.

Weatherby recognized the man as the night watchman who had discovered the body of William Suffolk.

"Please elaborate. Tobias, isn't it?" Weatherby replied.

"Yes, Your Grace. We met after the first murder," Tobias replied. "The King's Groom of the Stool approached me about thirty minutes ago. He reports that the King spent the evening dining alone with his intended, and then they played cards for money. They drank three bottles of wine, and retired about one a.m. He reports that the King awoke from a noise in the courtyard at approximately 2:30, and noticed that Anne was not there. He checked the Privy Chamber, the Withdrawing Chamber and other chambers around him without finding a trace of her."

"Did she have a disagreement with the King?" Weatherby asked.

"No. He reports that she won at cards, which she seldom does," the Groom of the Stool replied.

Weatherby worried that perhaps Anne's pretty little neck had already been rung by the murderer. In that case his life was, for all intents and purposes, also over. He needed to organize a search, which he had done many times before, in Scotland. The biggest problem he had observed was communication between the searchers once the hunt began. He called the men available in the Great Kitchen over and quickly counted them. There were forty.

"Divide yourselves into groups of ten," Weatherby instructed. "Appoint two men from each group as messengers. Each group will depart in a cardinal direction and begin searching for Miss Boleyn. Weatherby pointed to each group in turn, telling which direction he wished them to go. "Search the Palace carefully. I want a messenger sent to me every hour or sooner with a report. Now go find her."

The men hurried out through the three doors of the Great Kitchen. Weatherby had Judith Scotson and Margaret Sedgwick, the assistant librarians, awakened and instructed to bring all the maps of Surrey County to the kitchen for his perusal. He also sent for Amarantha. When she arrived, still rubbing sleep from her eyes, he asked her to interview the Ladies-in-Waiting.

"I need to know if any of them sensed a change in Anne or overheard anything," Weatherby said.

"I tried to tell you about the four groups of Ladies-in-Waiting previously," Amarantha began as she sat down. "And you told me that you weren't interested."

"Well I am now."

"There are Great Ladies, Ladies of the Privy Chamber, Maids of Honour and Chamberers," Amarantha replied. "The Ladies of the Privy Chamber are the closest to the Consort, so I will begin by interviewing the four of them."

"Thank you for your help," Weatherby said as he turned his attention to the stack of maps before him.

He noticed the villages of Walton, Escher, Weybridge, Kingston, Wimbledon, Richmond and Hounslow were all nearby, and to be searched. Each was a small village, one much like the other, and he couldn't find a reason for Anne to be attracted to any particular one. Unfortunately, in the two hours since she had been missing, Anne Boleyn could easily have traveled from four to eight miles away on a fast horse whether she had been abducted or she was traveling on her own. She was an excellent rider and could travel quickly even at night.

Amarantha returned quickly with one of the Ladies of the Privy Chamber, Clarissa Dormer. Weatherby showed both ladies a seat and had hot tea brought.

"I am Sir Seamus Scott Weatherby, an envoy of the King," Weatherby began in an officious voice. "And I hope you can help me find Miss Anne Boleyn."

"I have met you at the dances, Sir. Anne is my second cousin, Your Grace," Clarissa replied. "And I have been in her service at court for four years."

"How did you find her today?"

"She was quite ebullient this afternoon."

"Was there a reason for that?"

"Not that I am aware of. We had a very ordinary day."

"Is there anyone here at Hampton Court that Miss Boleyn dislikes?"

"No. However, if there were, the King would have the person sent away. She has enjoyed her time here at Hampton Court immensely. I think the change of scene has been good for her."

"How is the relationship between Anne and the King?"

"I have been instructed not to talk about that, Your Grace."

"I understand that general rule, and feel it is wise. However, the Princess may be lying somewhere injured or in pain, and I want you to tell me about the relationship between the King and Anne Boleyn, right now."

"Yes, sir. My cousin Anne Boleyn found King Henry to old for her taste at first, but now she doesn't see their sixteen-year age difference as an obstacle. She loves him very much. The King is besotted with Anne. He finds her more appealing than any other woman he has ever met."

"So they are the perfect couple and all is pleasantries, soft kisses, and affection between them?"

"Absolutely not. They fight like cats and dogs. They hurl imprecations at each other, throw objects, and slam doors constantly."

"Why is that?"

"Put candidly, Anne Boleyn has been with the King for five years and still isn't Queen. Becoming Queen of England is her only goal in life. The King, for his part, desires her daily and often thinks of nothing else, but she will not yield fully to him until she is crowned."

The first messengers were arriving in the Great Kitchen and were sitting down to catch their breath.

"Thank you for your time Miss Dormer," Weatherby concluded. "I may call you back if I think of other questions."

The messengers reported no sign of the Consort in the Palace or surrounding grounds. Each group was moving farther afield. Weatherby studied his maps more closely. None of the nearby towns offered much glitter except for Richmond. The Sheen Palace, begun in 1299, was located there near a bend in the Thames. It was most famous for its elaborate Christmas pageants that lasted until twelfth night; however the Royals often went there on other occasions. The area to the south of the Hampton Court had few roads and even fewer villages, he noted. Weatherby redirected the south group directly toward Richmond with all haste.

The last messenger arrived from the west. They had heard reports near the Palace of a woman riding a black horse alone toward Escher. Weatherby instructed his search party to head to the village immediately and check out the sighting.

The few remaining hours of the night dragged on with infrequent reports every couple of hours from the messengers. Fortunately, the night was clear, calm, and mild. The negative reports from all directions began to pile up. Warder Chertsey had set up a parchment, and was writing down the location of the four groups, each hour with a quill pen. Weatherby sent word for all of his search parties to eat and then rest for four hours before proceeding. With no positive signs, Weatherby felt he might be on the wrong track and called for Amarantha.

"How can Anne Boleyn have vanished into thin air?" Weatherby asked dejectedly. "Is she a wraith or spirit rather than a real human being?"

"You have held her in your arms when you danced," Amarantha replied. "And you know she isn't. She is a real mortal and while wily, not overly clever."

"Then where has she gone, Ran?"

"She is a young woman and may be as tired as he is of waiting for consummation. Perhaps she has a lover."

"Why wouldn't she simply meet him in the vast areas of new construction, throw down a coverlet and couple quickly with him?"

"You know the answer as well as I. There are three thousand people in the Palace now, and there is no privacy."

"If you are right, where would they go?"

"If I were them, I would rent a cottage in a nearby village and have Anne travel there in a disguise."

"I'll redirect some of the searchers to look for such places in Walton, Kingston and Wimbledon."

"Now, Seamus. I think you need some rest."

# CHAPTER 44

Seamus walked sleepily to his apartment and fell into bed. He planned on sleeping for four hours, but awoke after only two worrying still about Anne Boleyn. He wandered back to the Great Kitchen and called for breakfast. Two messengers were eating at a trestle table when Weatherby came in. One was from the west search party, and he came over to report on the lone horsewoman that had been seen the night before. The search group caught up with the woman near Oatlands. She was frightened at first. However, once they explained what they were about, she dismounted and talked with them. She was the wife of a farmer in Hampton who beat her and she was running away from home. She hadn't seen anyone resembling Anne Boleyn during her escape.

The second messenger was from the east. The search party had progressed to Coombe, which was on the busy pike to London. Traffic was heavy both directions, and the search group had spoken with inn keepers and owners of roadside taverns. Wagons hauling animals and grain were the most common vehicle on the road, next came riders and finally carriages and coaches. The search group compiled a list of vehicles and riders and what observers had noticed about them. The messenger handed the list-fifty items long to Weatherby. Sir Weatherby had failed to recognize how busy travel was toward the huge capital city. He realized he should have sent more of his searchers in that direction.

"There are fifty-some travelers on this list," Weatherby commented. "And the information on many of them is sparse."

"We were relying on sketchy reports from the inn keepers," the messenger replied.

"Thank you. I will study it," Weatherby said as he sat down with a fresh cup of tea.

A small disturbance occurred on the other side of the Great Kitchen and Weatherby saw a short man limping toward him.

"May I help you?" the limping man said.

"I should hope so, Dredge," Weatherby replied. "Welcome back. I'm sure you have already heard that Anne Boleyn is missing and may have fallen victim to our murderer."

"Where would you like me to start?" Dredge said as a buxom serving girl set a cup of tea with milk in it, in front of him.

"Analyze this list of travelers on the Escher-Southward highway," Weatherby began. "And highlight the ones that look suspicious to you. I'm glad you are back," Weatherby said as he handed Dredge a pencil from his inside pocket.

The messenger from the north opened the door to the Great Kitchen just then and pulled off his riding gloves. He approached Sir Weatherby.

"We found nothing to the north, Your Grace," the messenger reported. "As you know aside from the village of Hanworth most of the land to the north is sparsely inhabited woods with few roads. We searched the village thoroughly and found nothing."

"I doubt we will find Miss Boleyn in that uninhabited wood," Weatherby replied. "I wish to redeploy your group to the northeast in the direction of Chiswick along the Staines-London pike. Please redirect your group immediately."

Weatherby had barely taken a sip of tea when the Groom of the Stool arrived in the kitchen.

"Sir Weatherby, the King requests a word in private with you," the Groom said in an officious tone that was just a little too loud.

"Very well, then," Weatherby replied as he rose and followed the King's man.

Weatherby had been expecting to get called on the carpet a long time before this. Anne had now been missing for thirteen hours, and the King must be beside himself, he thought. Following the Groom, he was surprised to see the King with several of his cronies in his new library in the Bayne Tower. They were clustered around a table drinking, playing dice and laughing.

"Your, Highness," Weatherby said as he bowed low before the King.

"Get up, man and approach. I want to know how your investigation goes," the King said as he took the cup with the dice in it, and after shaking them splashed them across the table.

"We have had search parties out in all directions since early this morning, Your Worship," Weatherby began. "A search of the Palace and grounds was unrewarding. I hope to have encouraging news by night fall."

"I don't think the murderer is involved in this," the King said assertively.

"What, pray tell, makes you feel that way?"

"Firstly, it goes against his *modus operandi* and secondly, from what I've heard, the murderer is smart and abducting Anne Boleyn isn't."

"I concur, Your Worship."

"Besides, in the five years I've known my consort, she has disappeared several times like this without a word of warning."

"May I be so bold as to ask where she turned up?" Weatherby said incredulous.

The King spilled some gold angels on the table which were raked in by the gambler sitting across from him and then replied nonchalantly, "Once she was with her sister, Mary, and three or four times with her favorite, her brother, George. On one occasion she didn't come back for five days."

"I'll take my leave to get back to my duties, Your Worship," Weatherby said as he bowed while backing out of the room.

So that's why I hadn't been contacted by the King earlier. He wasn't worried, Weatherby thought as he walked back toward the kitchen. It must be nice to be all knowing. Dredge met him outside the Bayne Tower and suggested moving their operations to the laboratory for better efficiency.

When they arrived, Dredge explained that he had already catalogued all the reports from the messengers and reviewed the sighting from the east group.

"Most of these sightings are too sketchy or don't fit the description of the Princess," Dredge said. "However, look at the ninth entry. An elegant coach passed through Putney just before first light. Two people were in the coach and at least one was a woman. The coach was covered in mud, but the observer saw one wheel spoke was painted purple. As you know that is the color of royalty and to be used only by the King. However, since their recent successes, the Boleyn family has been using the color. Anne even wears purple gowns in front of Queen Catherine. I think it might have been Anne in that coach."

"Good deduction, Dredge," Weatherby replied with admiration in his voice. "I hope you had a magnificent time in London because I'm not sending you off like again for a long time."

"I did, Sir. Thank you very much. Let's look at a map of the area and we can get an idea of where that coach was going."

Dredge spread two large parchment maps out on the table.

"The next village on the road east is Wycombe where, you remember, we hunted for the Druid circle," Weatherby commented. "I'm tired of being idle here, and waiting for reports from the messengers. I will ride out Wycombe way, and see if I can find some more clues about that coach."

"Let me pack supplies and maps for your trip," Dredge suggested. "And I will monitor the messengers."

"Feel free to move them, Dredge, wherever you think your chance is the greatest of finding Anne Boleyn," Weatherby said as he walked out of the laboratory.

Weatherby walked to the stables and called for his horse. In fifteen minutes he was on the pike riding toward Putney. It was early afternoon, so the light was strong. The woods along the road were in full bloom as the spring advanced. The scarlet pimpernel was too short to provide a showy display, but tall flowers of purple rosebay, willow herb and the large white flower of bindweed covered the road side. Weatherby rode quickly between the lines of wagons and coaches going in both directions on the road. One mile from Putney, Weatherby's roan came up lame. Weatherby dismounted and checked his horse's left forefoot. A sliver of wood was jammed under the horseshoe. Weatherby pried it out with his knife. He walked his horse around a circle and initially he thought the horse seemed better. But, when Weatherby remounted the limp had not improved. He dismounted again and walked his stead into town. Putney had a large livery stable and after putting his horse in a stall, Weatherby rented a young gelding to continue his journey.

Before leaving town, he sought the innkeeper that had reported sighting the carriage. He found him in the bar of his inn washing tankards.

"Can you tell me about the carriage you saw early morning?" Weatherby asked.

"Yes, Your Grace," the innkeeper replied. "I was in front of the inn sweeping the walk when the coach went by. It was a new coach pulled by four horses. It was covered in mud, but I was surprised to see that one of the less muddy wheels had purple spokes. I knew the King was at Hampton Court and that purple is a royal color, so I thought I might catch a glimpse of the monarch. The carriage slowed as it went through town and I peered inside. It was occupied by a woman and man, but the man was much smaller that the King."

"So you deduced that the occupants were Royals, but not the King," Weatherby replied. "Did you see which way the carriage went?"

"Yes, they took the branch that goes to Wycombe."

"Thanks for your help," Weatherby said hurried for the door.

# CHAPTER 45

Weatherby was much less comfortable on his rented horse, and soon his legs ached from signaling his desired course to his new mount. However, he had only two miles to go before he came to the village of Wycombe. When he arrived, he dismounted at the village store where he and Dredge had stopped before. Martin Stoddard, the shopkeeper, remembered him.

"I'm looking for a fancy carriage that may have come by here early this morning," Weatherby said after greeting the shopkeeper. "Did you see it?"

"Yes, it is parked at the boarding house in the middle of town," Stoddard replied.

"Thank you," Weatherby said over his shoulder as he walked toward the door.

He walked along the main street leading his horse. The carriage was standing beside the house, and the horses were grazing in a small paddock nearby. The landlady was sweeping the porch.

"Pardon, ma'am, but where are the people that arrived in this elegant coach?" Weatherby asked.

"A pretty brunette and a slender male walked off into the woods holding hands and laughing," the landlady replied pointing to a trail leading out of the village.

So Anne does have a lover, Weatherby thought. He remounted his gelding and started along the trail as the daylight faded. First, he decided to visit the Druid circle that he and Dredge had discovered. He rode along the twisting trails that led toward the circle. As he came over the last hill, he saw that a large fire was ablaze in the center of the circle with flames jumping several feet into the air. A group of people were danced around the circle to the beat of a drum. He dismounted from his horse and tied it to a branch.

Weatherby crept closer to the circle. All of the dancers were dressed in green and brown and some wore masks. So far, he couldn't spot Anne Boleyn. He crouched down and got even closer. But faces were hard to recognize in the flickering firelight as the clearing darkened. Still he saw no sign of the consort, so he worked his way around the circle staying hidden in the underbrush. Finally, when he was only twenty feet from the dancers, he saw Anne wearing strips of green cloth with her legs, midriff and one shoulder bare. She had feathers in her hair and was dancing with abandon.

Weatherby was just about to walk out of the brush and confront Anne Boleyn when his eyes were drawn to a man dancing six feet to the left of her. It was George Boleyn, Anne's younger brother. So, Anne and George had come to this pagan celebration together, Weatherby realized, and he decided not to reveal himself. Instead he made his way back to his horse, with some difficulty in the dark, and headed back toward Wycombe. From there he rode to Putney. Normally, he would have spent the night there because of the late hour, but forty searchers were still in the field, and the King did not know the whereabouts of his consort so he rode on. The last part of the ride was darker and therefore slower. Weatherby left his rented mount at the stables and then went immediately to the laboratory. Two messengers were in the gathering area, and Weatherby told them that the consort has been found. Dredge was instructed to inform the other searchers as they came in to give their reports.

Weatherby raced to the Bayne tower where the King was still playing dice, and on entering bowed low.

"The consort is found unharmed," Weatherby said. "She is in Wycombe with her brother George."

"Zounds! Prithee, I was correct," the King replied as he turned back to his dice game.

"By your leave, Your Highness," Weatherby said with relief in his voice, as he backed out bowing.

Ready to celebrate, Weatherby tracked down Amarantha and Dredge and took them to the Lamb and Flag for a pint of ale. He was pleased that Anne Boleyn was found in nineteen hours. He felt simply lucky that of the forty men and three women looking for her, he had found her.

"Everyone says that the Druids are a long-extinct religion," Weatherby said. "Except in County Surrey."

"The more interesting question is what were Lord Rochford and his older sister doing participating in a pagan ritual?" Amarantha asked.

"They are thought by many to be exceedingly attached to one another," Dredge suggested. "Certainly, George Boleyn is much closer to Anne than to his shrewish wife, Jane Parker."

"You hardly ever gossip, Dredge. And it is so delicious when you do! Pray go on."

"George and Anne have been seen cavorting together in Anne's private rooms at Whitehall, dressed in fanciful and much abbreviated costumes. One of Anne's costumes was described as two small patches of red velvet and dozens of pheasant feathers. They also fondle and kiss each other prolongedly in public."

"I'm certain 'prolongedly' isn't a word Dredge," Weatherby interjected, spoiling the gossipy mood.

Amarantha called for three more tankards of ale.

"I'm sure you catch my meaning, Sir," Dredge replied, before reigniting the tittle-tattle. "I've heard it said that George Boleyn prefers a young slip of a boy to a buxom lass with loose morals and a looser corset."

"I'm sure that can't be true," Amarantha trilled. "I saw him flirting outrageously with Elizabeth, one of the Ladies-in-Waiting at Whitehall not two months ago."

"Henry accuses the French King Francis of having a licentious court," Dredge broke in. "But I wonder if Henry VIII isn't just as wanton."

"I suspect all courts are like that," Weatherby said thoughtfully. "Too many selfish and self-indulgent petty nobles with too little to do."

"I shall write a penny novel about all of their escapades and become rich," Dredge retorted in a slurry voice.

The drinking and gossiping continued for two more hours until all three were unsteady on their feet. Weatherby called for a hansom to take them back to Hampton Court. Weatherby's roommate had decamped permanently, so the King's detective had a whole bed. Unfortunately, he had had too much to drink so he thrashed all night. In the morning, he had tea brought to his apartment and used it to wash down willow bark extract for his headache. He was tired of being at the beck and call of the King and not having time to work on his murders. It was his fervent hope that the Royals would depart soon.

To distract himself, Weatherby decided to work on his ideas about rapid travel. While nearly everyone seemed impressed by the speed with which carriages and ships travel, he thought a four day trip to get to Chartres was far too slow. He dressed and walked to the laboratory. Dredge was decocting a new poison. Weatherby showed him a design for a travel device he had thought up.

"I was watching fireworks the other night, Dredge," Weatherby began. "They seem to travel at a high rate of speed. I tried to time the travel of the mortars into the sky before the colored particles lit up. Here's a diagram showing how high I calculated the shells went. I used the height of the Palace, which I know, to construct a triangle that gives me the loftiness of the projectiles. The height of the Palace is forty-three feet here, and the distance from my location to the mortars that fired the display is two hundred feet. You can see on the diagram that the missiles went up one hundred and seventy-five feet in approximately two seconds. The speed of the projectiles is, therefore, sixty miles per hour, or four times the speed of a sloop sailing in a strong wind."

"So you want to be strapped on the nose of a giant firework and shot to France next time?" Dredge replied sardonically.

"Not exactly. However, I thought we might do some tests on a smaller scale," Weatherby replied as he unrolled another parchment. "We could build a long tube of glued paper and fill it with gunpowder and shoot it off in a horizontal direction and see how far it goes. I even drew a small compartment near the nose where a creature could be confined for a ride."

"From Leonardo da Vinci's work on cannons, we know that aiming your missile at forty-five degrees will make it go the farthest."

"Can you make such a device?"

"Yes, Your Grace," Dredge replied as he started looking around the lab. "If you get several pounds of gunpowder out of the magazine, we might try it."

Weatherby headed to the armory located in the undercroft of the old part of the Palace built by Sir Giles Daubeney in the fourteen hundreds. Hampton Court was never meant to be defended as a fortress, so the armory was one small room ten by sixteen feet. Wheel locks, maces and shields were stored there along with lead Wheelock balls and gunpowder. Weatherby placed ten pounds of gunpowder in a leather pouch and then relocked the door. When he got back to the laboratory, Dredge had already created a heavy, reinforced paper cylinder two feet long and five inches in diameter.

"I put a cone on the tip of the missile," Dredge said. "The Chinese used them on the tops of their fireworks, and I attached a dowel so we can stick it in the ground for launch."

"Let's fill it with powder."

Dredge placed the rocket upside down and poured gunpowder through the copper cone he had attached to the cylinder. He placed a fuse inside the tube when it was three quarters full. Once it was full, Dredge tamped the powder down and sealed the opening with a small piece of paper. The two carried their rocket out into the fields east of the Palace. Once the dowel was stuck in the ground the missile was adjusted to a forty-five degree angle, Dredge lit the fuse. The two stepped back. The powder ignited and then rapidly burned through the paper base of the cylinder igniting the rest of the powder all at once, a ball of fire followed, and then a large bang. Bits of charred paper drifted down onto the two experimenters.

# CHAPTER 46

Weatherby sought out Amarantha for supper. Anne was back but no Royal banquets or fêtes were planned so they ate in the Wolsey Apartment. Both had roasted pheasant with potatoes, onions and carrots. The upper classes ate large quantities of meat and avoided vegetables. Sir Weatherby told everyone who would listen that that eating fruits and vegetables was healthful for them. Both had had too much to drink the night before and therefore had perry, a pear cider, with their meal.

Anne Boleyn arrived back at Palace about three hours ago," Amarantha said. "She looked bedraggled."

"I wish I knew what she was about in Wycombe," Weatherby replied. "Is she having a spiritual reversion or just cavorting with her brother?"

"I think the latter. She is a devout Protestant and her brother could be court jester. He has unusual ideas and likes to act out whimsical things. He finds his older sister a perfect foil."

"I hope you are right. Could you subtly suggest that she tell me if she decides to go off again? There is at least one murderer loose in the immediate neighborhood, and I would promise her that I wouldn't tell a living soul her whereabouts."

"I'll see what I can do."

"How is your relationship with Richard Weston progressing?"

"We see each other more and more, and he is prone to touch and kiss me. So far he has opened up much more physically than mentally. I suspect I won't really learn anything about his inner thoughts until I'm intimate with him."

"I hope that won't be necessary, Ran."

"I'm afraid it may be. I'm still intact as they say, but it isn't something I put much store by. I may be able to trade it for some valuable information."

The whole discussion made Weatherby upset and anxious.

"I don't think you should do that," Weatherby interrupted in an alarmed voice. "It is too much of a price to pay for some facts that we can probably get in some other way."

"As I've come to know him, I think that physical intimacy is at the core of his being," Ran began. "I've also come to think he is a central player in our mystery."

"I forbid you to have congress with this man!" Weatherby said in a loud voice.

"Seamus, I am your loyal employee and devoted assistant, but you are overstepping your authority. This isn't your decision!" Amarantha replied in an irate voice as she stomped out of the Wolsey Apartment.

The minute she was gone, Weatherby began to chastise himself for his inability to tell this beautiful woman his true feelings. He could speak easily to Chancellors and Kings but in front of this woman he was completely tongue-tied. He went to his apartment to read, but even after several hours was unable to sleep.

In the morning, he went to breakfast blurry-eyed and yawning. He had recognized several of the dancers around the Druid circle in Wycombe and he decided to question them about the ceremony. After breakfast he had his horse saddled. His large roan had been brought back from Putney, where he had pulled up lame, and with the application of poultices was back to normal. Weatherby patted his muzzle affectionately.

"Are you ready for a ride?" Weatherby said to the animal before mounting.

They rode out through the Great Gatehouse and through the village of Hampton before taking the pike east. It was a fresh spring morning and Weatherby rode at a leisurely pace. He knew this trip was more about clearing his head after the disagreement last night with Amarantha, than about gleaning information. He stopped along the way in Putney for a cup of tea and then rode on to Wycombe. As he always did, he began at the only store in the village.

"There was a ceremony evening before last at the Druid circle southeast of town," Weatherby said to Martin Stoddard, the shopkeeper. "Were you there?"

"No, but my daughter, Mary, went," Stoddard replied.

"Might I speak with her?"

"Of course. She's out back feeding the chickens and ducks. Come this way."

Stoddard led the way through the store and to the pen behind the building. A young woman with an apron full of grain was being mobbed by several dozen chickens, ducks and geese. Martin Stoddard called Mary over and explained what Weatherby wanted.

"What was the purpose of the dancing?" Weatherby asked the young woman as she emptied her apron.

"It was just a celebration of spring," Mary replied. "And a rare chance to dance and socialize in this boring little village."

"So it wasn't a pagan religious ceremony?"

"Not that I am aware of. I'm a good Catholic," Mary said as she involuntarily crossed herself.

"Could you make a list of the villagers that were there?"

"Of course," Mary said as she walked toward the store.

She took a piece of parchment and wrote out several names in a neat and flowery hand. After thanking the young lady, Weatherby began seeking out the participants. The first three people listed were Mary's friends. They each said that they had attended for the costumes and dancing.

"I thought it would be entertaining," her friend Geoffrey said. "And it was. The costumes were attention-grabbing and some of the revelers were good dancers."

"Did it seem religious to you?"

"Not at all, and I was there from beginning to end."

Other people on the list were not so eager to talk, and seemed to give evasive answers, especially about how often they danced there by the light of the fire. Most visitants seemed quite vague or to have poor memories for such a recent event. Two refused to talk to him altogether. Weatherby concluded that the town's people came to the circle for a variety of reasons, but that for at least some, it had a religious connotation.

Weatherby enjoyed the ride back to Hampton Court. On the way, he decided to talk to both George Boleyn and then Anne about their visit to Wycombe. Near the Palace he stopped along the Thames and gathered a large arm load of wild flowers in blues, whites, pinks and yellows. He left his horse in the stables and sought out Amarantha. She was with

Judith and Margaret, her friends from the library. He handed her the large bunch of blossoms.

"I was mistaken yesterday, Ran, when I tried to tell you what to do, and I apologize," Weatherby said in a contrite voice as he handed her the blossoms.

"Thank you, Seamus," Amarantha replied in a cheerful voice. "How was your trip to Wycombe?"

"Only moderately successful. Do you know where I can find George Boleyn?"

"He is usually near Anne's chambers in the apartments off the Long Gallery."

Weatherby headed in that direction. He found George playing cards with three Ladies-in-Waiting. His countrymen, the Scots, loved gambling, Weatherby thought, but not half so much as the English. They bet on cards, dice, skittles, horse racing and dozens of other things. George was giggling with the women as Weatherby came in.

When George looked up Weatherby said, "A word, Your Grace."

George finished his hand and then stood up. He took two large silver goblets full of wine and handed one to Weatherby. George motioned to a nearby bay window.

"I'm pleased you and your sister are returned safely from Wycombe. The King was worried about his intended," Weatherby said with a bit of exaggeration.

"He needn't have," Boleyn said. "She was perfectly safe with me."

"So it seems. It is just that the King didn't know where she was."

"I suspect she whispered something in his ear, but he was too drunk or too involved in his gambling to hear."

"So the jaunt was your idea?"

"Indeed. You have a dreadfully boring Palace here, and I've been at wits' end to find some entertainment," George replied in a foppish tone while bending both wrists.

Weatherby recalled the droll comments Dredge made about the young man's proclivities toward buggery.

"I thought the pagan dancing would be pleasurable and it was," George continued. "I quite enjoyed all the naked flesh both male and female by the fire light."

"Forty men and several women spent the night looking for you and your sister," Weatherby retorted with an edge to his voice.

"That isn't my problem, my good sir. It's yours," George responded as he turned back to the card table.

Weatherby was fuming. George Boleyn had no real status with the King or at Hampton Court. He was just another hanger on, living off the King's largesse. Weatherby realized he would gain nothing by confronting the young fop.

Weatherby found Amarantha and invited her and the assistant librarians to lunch in the Privy Orchard. He relaxed over the cold meats and bread and enjoyed listening to the three women prattle. After lunch, he asked Amarantha to accompany him on his visit to Anne Boleyn. They found Anne outside in the sunshine doing needlework with three Ladies-in-Waiting. She rose as Amarantha approached and gave her a warm hug.

"How nice to see you both," Anne began. "I understand that you were at that gaily wanton dance in Wycombe, Your Lordship."

"Yes, I was."

"You should have joined in the festivities."

"I lacked the proper attire, Your Grace, and I only appeared in that glade to ensure that you were safe, not to spy on you. As you yourself reminded me, a murderer is on the loose."

"It was thoughtless of me to wander off so without saying a word to a living soul," Anne replied as she took Weatherby's hand. "Can you forgive me?"

"With pleasure, Your Highness," Weatherby responded as he bowed low.

# CHAPTER 47

After their visit with Anne Boleyn, the two decided on a leisurely walk through the Palace gardens. The warm spring days and milder nights resulted in a riotous growth of plants and flowers. Weatherby took Amarantha's arm as they strolled around the gardens. The irises and peonies were heavy with blossoms and their aroma filled the air. Honey bees and improbably large bumble bees visited the flowers in frantic abundance. The two found a bench to sit on under a willow tree.

"When will we be able to get back to work, Ran?" Weatherby asked.

"Not until the King leaves us, I'm afraid," Amarantha replied. "I don't have the sense that our murderer fled County Surrey, and by now is on a ship to the New World. I think he is still amongst us and therefore may strike again."

"That's a very unpleasant thought," Weatherby mused. "If, on the other hand, he has fled across the sea, we won't have to worry about him, Ran."

"Landing in the New World might be its own worst punishment," Amarantha replied.

"What makes you say that?"

"The plants and animals seem quite fantastical in the stories I have read."

"It's the savages covered in writing and wielding spears and arrows that sound the most daunting to me."

"Do you suppose the land there is as extensive as it is here?"

"I don't think we know. So far the explorers have only landed on the shore and explored but a few miles inland. Once I've perfected my rapid travel device, I plan to go there," Weatherby mused. "We have already gotten maize, tobacco, potatoes, and turkeys from there. Think what else I might find."

"I'll go with you."

"I'm afraid there will only be room for one in my missile."

"Then I will follow in another ship."

"I haven't worked out how to steer the contraption. I might end up in China rather than in the New World."

"If so, we could both explore our surroundings and write each other letters."

The two walked back to the Palace musing aloud about fantastic adventures. As they approached the red brick walls of Hampton Court, their conversation shifted back to more mundane topics. Weatherby noticed a lot of carriage traffic out of the Great Gatehouse. Once inside, he asked one of the serving girls what was happening.

"The King and Anne Boleyn are leaving, Your Grace," she said with a curtsey and a smile.

Thank God, Weatherby thought, but he wondered why he hadn't heard about the departure. He went to seek out Warder Chertsey.

"Why the precipitous departure?" Weatherby asked to warder.

"The King heard a rumor, Your Grace, that an epidemic of the sweating sickness has broken out in Bristol," Chertsey replied. "Fifty are dead so far and the disease may be spreading to the east toward us. The King heard the news two hours ago, and he left an hour ago on horseback with Anne Boleyn. He is deathly afraid of disease, you know. Even when there is no sickness about, which isn't often, the Groom of the Stool says that the King has nightmares about the plague."

"Thank you for the information," Weatherby left to find Amarantha and Dredge.

All three gathered in the laboratory. Dredge poured a tankard of ale for each.

"There is an epidemic of sweating sickness in Bristol, one hundred and ten miles to the west of us," Weatherby began. "It has even spread to Bath which is closer."

"Will it be coming here?" Dredge asked.

"If past epidemics are any indication, it is likely," Weatherby said solemnly.

"Can it be treated?" Amarantha wondered.

"It is treated by bloodletting and purging," Weatherby replied. "But, that is our current treatment for almost every malady. I know of no evidence that such therapy shortens the illness or reduces the mortality. The first epidemic occurred in 1485 during the reign of Henry the VII. It spread to London and killed several thousands. It didn't recur until 1507, when I was in medical school and the outbreak was much milder."

"How do doctors know the sweating sickness isn't just smallpox or some other known malady?" Amarantha asked.

"Physicians are not very good at treatment, but we are quite good at diagnosis," Weatherby replied as he sat down in a chair. "Even a lawyer could recognize smallpox, Amarantha. It starts with fever and malaise followed by a raised rash, called papules, followed by vesicles or blisters on top. It is a characteristic picture that I could teach you to recognize. The other epidemic disease that is highly fatal is plague. It starts with nonspecific symptoms, but then the patient develops buboes or large swellings in the groin and armpit, or bloody pneumonia with bleeding into the skin which quickly turns dark. When this form ravaged Europe, it was called the Black Death. The sweating sickness has no skin lesions whatsoever."

"I'm always amazed at how much you remember from medical school, Seamus," Amarantha said in an astonished voice. "You went twenty-three years ago."

"It's a rigorous curriculum so it sticks with you."

"So what are the symptoms of the sweating sickness?" Dredge said, growing tired of the discussion of other diseases.

"The first is a most unusual symptom: apprehension. It is followed by violent cold shivers, giddiness and great exhaustion," Weatherby said. "Then the characteristic sweat breaks out, followed by delirium, rapid pulse and intense thirst."

"It sounds like a very rapid illness unlike smallpox and plague," Amarantha observed.

"Good comment!" Weatherby exclaimed. "It is often fatal in twenty-four hours."

"How delightful," Dredge said sarcastically. "Will it come here?"

"As I already said, most likely, yes," Weatherby replied in a resigned voice.

"What should we do until it arrives?" Amarantha queried.

"Enjoy each other, enjoy life and be thankful for what we have been given in this world," Weatherby replied after a moment's reflection. "First, I propose a nice dinner at the Lamb and Flag."

The three walked across the bridge into the village. On leaving Hampton Court, Weatherby noted the disorder in the Palace. The precipitous departure of the King and his entourage had resulted in clothing, discarded trunks and broken plates being scattered everywhere. An old wagon with a broken wheel partially blocked the Great Gatehouse.

A large dinner of roast lamb and root vegetables improved everyone's mood. Dredge had developed a taste for a new vegetable called potato and he ordered a plate of them to share.

"Can you imagine a funnier name for a food than potato?" Dredge asked. They had two bottles of Rhenish wine with their food. After dining they were a lot more hopeful. Weatherby had already begun making lists in his head of things that needed to be done before the epidemic struck or passed over the Palace without afflicting it, as it sometimes did. The Palace was much quieter without the throngs that accompanied the King, but all three slept fitfully.

In the morning, Weatherby visited the Palace's doctor in residence who had an apartment in the Outer Court. Daniel Wickham, MB was an elderly physician somewhat crippled by rheumatism. They had made each other's acquaintance shortly after Weatherby arrived. They had few interests in common, so a friendship between them had never blossomed. Dr. Wickham dressed in the traditional black gown and black skullcap of a doctor. He had a small office in front of his private chamber where he saw patients, and Weatherby found him at this desk there.

On taking a seat Weatherby began, "I thought we should talk about the epidemic that seems about to descend on us. What are your plans?"

"I have already ordered extra supplies of leeches and purgatives and I suppose we can make the Great Hall into an infirmary," Dr. Wickham replied.

Weatherby suspected the old Doctor didn't know much about the disease he would be fighting.

"Have you seen this disease before?" Weatherby asked.

"Only once in 1517. I was practicing in Cambridge when it struck during the summer with a fury," Dr. Wickham recollected. "The previous epidemic had been milder and we were all hopeful. However, this one was the worst of the lot. I cared for ninety-two patients and over fifty died. I thought the bloodletting was more helpful that the purgatives, but neither worked well."

"I saw some cases during the 1507 outbreak and none of the therapies seemed to make much difference," Weatherby said reflectively. "In any case, isolation seems to help prevent the spread of the disease and we have control of the Palace. I will offer my services when the time comes."

"Thank you," Dr. Wickham replied. "I will need all the help I can get."

Weatherby rose and left the Doctor's office. He repaired to the laboratory and found a recent book by Amboise Paré, an army surgeon in France. He discovered that often a gunshot wound didn't kill but the inflammation that followed did. Paré treated the wound with wine, then sealed it with egg white, and noticed a decrease in the rate of secondary inflammation. Weatherby wondered if wine might be used to prevent the spread of an epidemic by frequent application to hands. The final stages of sweating sickness were rapid heart action, collapse and intense thirst. All seemed to him like signs of decreased fluid volume. Perhaps bloodletting and purgative actually made the patient more vulnerable by removing desperately needed fluid. He struggled to think of an experiment he could do on animals that would resolve the question.

The King and his physicians had the right idea, Weatherby thought. They would flee to an isolated spot and thereby reduce contact with people who were contagious, thus increasing their chance for survival. It wasn't practical to disperse the many residents of Hampton Court in a similar way; however, he could order the doors to the Palace locked and guarded for the duration of the epidemic, reducing contact in another way.

# CHAPTER 48

Weatherby decided that an approaching epidemic wasn't analogous to an advancing enemy army. In the latter case battlements had to be built, soldiers trained and supplies of gunpowder and cannon balls manufactured before the soldiers arrived. With an epidemic the only real preparation an individual could make was to be well nourished, fit and right with their God. Therefore, Weatherby thought staying around worrying about death, disability and the arrival of the sweating sickness was like flogging a dead horse. He decided to take his little band on a holiday before they faced the pestilence. Fortunately, the gayest and most interesting place in England, London town, was the opposite way from the looming epidemic. He called his small band together.

"If it comes here, the epidemic may not arrive for a fortnight," Weatherby began. "There is little we can do to prepare for it. Therefore, I suggest a holiday before the sickness descends. We could also depart from England and go to my family home in Dumphries, in Scotland until the epidemic abates; however, as one of only two doctors at Hampton Court, I feel my duty is here. Neither of you are under such an obligation."

Dredge replied first, "If you are returning, Sir, then I will also. I flatter myself into thinking I may be of assistance."

"You will be of inestimable aid, Dredge. Thank you," Weatherby replied, turning toward Amarantha.

"I am but a barrister," Amarantha began. "However, I may also be of use during the epidemic. Besides, you helped me recently when the 'black dog' visited me, and you are both closer to me than my own family."

"In that case, we will leave early tomorrow morning on the Royal barge. For a few days of revelry," Sir Weatherby intoned.

The next morning they arrived at the Water Gate at five a.m. A servant carried a small suitcase for each placing them on the barge. The barge was crowded with Palace dweller fleeing the epidemic. It left promptly at 5:15 to catch the ebbing tide, which was higher than usual because of a full moon. The trip down river was uneventful and swift. Amarantha, Dredge and Weatherby took a deck of cards and played gleek, a card game for three. Normally, Amarantha and Weatherby would have played for money, however in deference to Dredge, they didn't. With the high tide the trip only took five and a half hours. They disembarked at the London Bridge dock and took a hansom to 177D Threadneedle Street. Mrs. Pansy and the porter dragged their suitcases up to the top floor. Weatherby had planned for them to attend a play at the Duke of Norfolk's house that night. In the meantime they agreed to split up and meet for dinner.

Weatherby went to a saddlery shop near Westminster Abbey to order new tack for his horse. He was riding more, so he ordered some fine Italian black leather reins and halters with silver hardware and a new black leather saddle made to his specifications. He had the new tack sent to Hampton Court.

Amarantha spent her day at the dressmakers and haberdashers getting two new gowns and several new hats.

Dredge visited his uncle in the city and then crossed the river to spend the afternoon drinking with his cronies in Southwark. The three gathered at Rules an old restaurant in the Covent Garden area. Weatherby ordered for everyone. They started with large platters of raw oysters washed down with Rule's own brand of ale. Next, they had partridge in a cream sauce and juniper berries followed by a roast saddle of elk. Finally, a whole baked Scottish salmon was brought in. They enjoyed several bottles of wine from the Canary Islands. They had made a pact before the dinner started, not to talk about the murders at Hampton Court unless one of them could solve it in one sentence. The dessert was fresh strawberries in heavy cream.

They stumbled out of Rules laughing and took a hansom to the Duke of Norfolk's house. Butlers stood on the front stairs to welcome the guests. On the first landing musicians played a lively gavotte. On the next landing they found large silver trays of sweets and glasses of wine. Then they wandered into the theatre on the third floor. The performance was a Flemish morality play by Peter van Diest, *Everyman*. Fortunately, it was being performed in English and not Dutch, so Amarantha wouldn't have to translate. The theatre was already nearly full.

The story was performed by ten English actors in elaborate costume. In the story Everyman, the leading character, is forced to go on a trip to see God and explain his life. Everyman needs a companion for his trip who can speak on his behalf, but the actors, playing Fellowship, Kindred, Cousin, Knowledge, Confession, Discretion, Strength and Five-Wit each forsake him and refuses to go on the journey. Only Good-Deeds whom Everyman has previously neglected eventually goes along. Finally, God is appeased and the morality play ends to riotous applause.

Weatherby was astonished at the enthusiasm of the audience. After all, the story was one of lecturing morality with not a single line of humor in it. Perhaps its success was purely because it was in English when most plays and masques were in Italian or French. Or perhaps, Weatherby wondered, the audience was now focused on seeing God, as the rapidly fatal sweating sickness approached. After the play, Dredge retired and Amarantha and Weatherby joined the dancing. They spent two hours bowing, curtsying and sashaying.

The dancers returned to Weatherby's apartment at 3 a.m. Mrs. Pansy let all three sleep until 10:30, and then fixed them a large breakfast of scones, eggs, and ham. Weatherby's plan for the day was to visit the gardens at Kew. They took a rowboat up river to the bend in the Thames by the gardens. The landing stage was surrounded by weeping willows. A small gazebo up the hill was surrounded by thick beds of purple and blue irises. Dredge walked ahead and Amarantha took Weatherby's arm. The sky was full of billowy clouds and a gentle breeze blew toward the river. Ahead was a sundial surrounded by circular beds of roses. Every bush was covered in exuberant red blossoms, their fragrance filling the humid air. Amarantha and Weatherby walked slower and slower on the gravel path. Dredge had stopped on a lawn up ahead and spread a blanket, and Amarantha and Weatherby sat down on the blanket. Mrs. Pansy had packed a wicker basket filled with wine, cheese and bread. Dredge passed the comestibles around.

"This is delightful," Amarantha said.

"It is, but I haven't worked in so long, I'm not sure I'll ever be able to function again," Weatherby sighed.

After eating, all three stretched out and napped. When they awoke they walked through the rest of the garden by gingko trees and red-leafed

Japanese maples. They strolled back to the dock on the river and boarded their craft for the ride downstream.

When they returned to Threadneedle Street a message awaited on Weatherby's desk. The epidemic of sweating sickness had spread from Bath to Salisbury and cases in that city were light. Dredge and Weatherby pulled down some maps and realized that the epidemic was still seventy-two miles from Hampton Court and perhaps waning.

"The population is very sparse between Salisbury and Hampton Court," Weatherby mused.

"The soil is poor in Wiltshire, Hampshire, and Berkshire Counties so there are fewer towns and villages," Dredge replied.

"Perhaps the epidemic will slow or even die out because there are too few victims. The epidemic of 1517 was worst in Oxfordshire and Cambridgeshire where the fatality rate was very high, but less so in between."

Mrs. Pansy fixed a large meal of corned beef and cabbage which she mated with potatoes. All three ate heartily after their visit to Kew Gardens. Dredge had planned a pub crawl across the Thames in Southwark, so they took a hansom across London Bridge and first went to the Boar's Head where Weatherby often hung out when he worked in London. He had worked with the London constabulary for several years doing autopsies on suspicious deaths and murder victims. After work, the constables usually gathered at the Boar's Head. Even though it was early, the public house was crowded, but Weatherby quickly found a table of his old cronies.

"Seamus, where have you been?" one of the sergeants asked.

"I'm investigating crimes for the King," Weatherby replied in a loud voice so he could be heard. "Right now I'm working on a triple murder inquiry at Hampton Court Palace."

"Is that in County Surrey? Sounds fancy compared to what we do."

"The best part is that I have two able assistants, Amarantha Thompson and my amanuensis, Dredge," Weatherby said as he motioned toward the two.

All three crowded onto a bench along an old scarred trestle table and tall tankards of ale were placed in front of each. The constables took turns telling humorous and unflattering stories about Weatherby. He took the gentle ribbing good-naturedly. After a couple of hours of drinking, the three companions walked along the river to one of Dredge's hangouts called the Dog and Duck. Dredge was avoided by better society on the street because of his severe disability, and the lower classes yelled imprecations whenever he ventured out. He pretended not to hear the shouts of, cur, devil spawn, and God's blight.

The Dog and Duck welcomed the crippled and maimed, probably because the owner was missing an arm. Dredge's cronies consisted of three dwarves, two other rachitics and four men maimed in wagon accidents. They greeted Amarantha and Weatherby warmly. They drank more ale and declined to play dice. When they had drunk their fill, they waited outside laughing and taking for thirty minutes before a hansom came by. Once in the hansom, they went back across the river to the Jamaica Wine Bar where Amarantha spent time with a group of young barristers. None of Amarantha's acquaintances were at the bar, so after more drinks the three headed home. It was only a short walk to Threadneedle Street from the wine bar, but Weatherby knew his neighborhood was dangerous at this hour. He hailed, a ride and the three tired revelers climbed into the coach.

# CHAPTER 49

Weatherby was awakened at eight the next morning by an urgent message delivered by courier. The epidemic of sweating sickness had rekindled itself with forty new cases yesterday and it had progressed to Winchester, only fifty-one miles from Hampton Court. Unable to count on the linear and orderly spread of the disease, Weatherby decided to return to Hampton Court at once. He had planned to take Amarantha and Dredge to the Tower of London that day. Dredge had never seen the grim building or its vast armory, which actually had over thirty towers. An inquiry revealed that the Southwark-Escher Pike was clogged with refugees fleeing the epidemic from the west.

Weatherby decided to take the Royal Barge upstream, even though the trip took longer that direction. The incoming tide was at Greenwich and Weatherby's party would have to be ready to sail in fifty minutes. They packed quickly and hurried by hansom to the dock at London Bridge. When they arrived at the dock the Barge was already there. They hurried aboard with their suitcases. After they cast off, the rowers took the craft to midstream and the incoming tide carried them upstream. The river within the city was alive with boat traffic. Small and large craft with sails and oars floated upstream, downstream and across the large river. The ships were loaded with grain, hay, sheep, beer barrels and people.

As the city passed astern, the traffic lightened and the speed of the barge also slowed. Gardens and manor houses lined the river. The barge stopped at Richmond to let off three passengers and then headed back upstream. A fidgety woman from Teddington in a hideous yellow dress with a bustle and a large feathered hat sat down next to Weatherby. She held a small white dog that growled at Weatherby and bared its teeth.

"I'm Mrs. Eunice Fartingdown," the lady said in a trilling high-pitched voice that grated on Weatherby's ears.

A strong wave of perfume enveloped Weatherby. It had the overpowering fragrance of peonies—one of his least favorite scents. He stifled a sneeze.

"You dress foppishly, like a Frenchman. Are you, perchance?" Mrs. Fartingdown inquired.

Knowing how Englishmen felt about the French, Weatherby gave her a stony look and didn't reply.

"Are you married to that unfortunate young woman over there? She looks less than half your age. Robbed the cradle, did you?" Mrs. Fartingdown continued in a wavering voice.

"No, she is my able assistant and quite capable, unlike many English women of so-called noble birth," Weatherby replied in a frosty voice as he glared at his pink-cheeked questioner.

"My husband, Sir Afton Fartingdown thinks that women of a certain station should be pure ornament," the Lady replied huffily.

Weatherby wondered, "Did 'Ofton' help you pick out that lacy, yellow, confection of a dress, or did you do that all by herself?"

"Often Afton affords assistance as to my attire," Lady Fartingdown replied proudly. "However, he was away during this visit to my ver-r-ry expensive haberdasher. Perhaps I could give the name of my seamstress to your rather drably dressed companion. It might overcome her plain features."

Both Amarantha and Dredge knew how much Weatherby disliked small talk with frivolous people, but they continued to watch him squirm. They chuckled to themselves. There was no escape on the small barge.

Weatherby turned bright red after the last remark and said, "Your unkind and unsolicited remarks about me and my worthy companions are unjustified, Madam. The deuce to you, and your sniveling miniature dog."

These words had no effect on the pompous lady, but before another inane question could escape the ladies lips, Amarantha and Dredge rescued him from the busybody. Amarantha, Weatherby and Dredge happily ate the cold chicken with bread which Mrs. Pansy had packed after moving to the bow of the barge. Between bites they all looked at the shoreline of the river as they were rowed upstream. Herons prowled the shoreline and ducks and swans swam in the deeper water. At Teddington, the tide stopped and the barge slowed again. Several more passengers got off. By then the three travelers had the barge all to themselves. It took seven more hours to navigate the twisty, narrow upper part of the Thames to reach the Water Gate. Back at Hampton Court, the three fell into bed at midnight, knowing they had a full day of preparation ahead of them.

Weatherby got them up at six a.m. and had breakfast brought to the Wolsey Apartment.

"I thought a lot about the sweating sickness on the barge yesterday," Weatherby began after everyone had a sip of tea. "And I think I know how I want to attack it. I have tried the traditional therapy of purging and bloodletting, and I don't believe they help. There will be two doctors at Hampton Court and Dr. Wickham is a traditional old-school practitioner who will use the standard treatment. However, I believe the signs before death rapid; weak pulse, extreme thirst and a collapse of blood pressure suggest a lack of bodily fluid made only worse by purging and leeches. I propose that the two doctors at Hampton Court try different therapies to treat the sweating sickness. I would like to try a therapy of fruit juices, large amounts of water, cool soaks and wrapping the nurses in muslin to reduce the spread of disease."

"You have experimented on cats and rabbits, but you can't do the same with humans," Dredge replied.

"I beg to differ," Weatherby responded vehemently. "If the disease has high mortality, and there is not a shred of evidence that the current therapy works, then Galileo would say an experiment is in order. I know it is heresy, but perhaps doing nothing is better than the current therapy. You and I both know that purging and bloodletting are the recommended therapy for the gout, plague, dropsy, and headache. It seems irrational to think that these diverse diseases would all benefit from the same therapy."

"What are you suggesting, Seamus?" Amarantha asked.

"I think we should pick two areas in the Palace to house the sick," Weatherby replied. "Let one of the two physicians apply the traditional therapy and the other the new therapy. Then when the epidemic passes, we can compare the mortality of the two groups and for the first time see if one therapy is better than another."

"It seems so cold, inhumane, and unfeeling," Dredge mused.

"It isn't cold at all, Dredge; it is just a scientific experiment in a situation where no one knows the right answer. I will tell Dr. Wickham some of what I propose, but I want the two of you to start collecting supplies. We may need lots of clean water, Dredge so I want you to set up a distillery."

Weatherby rose and went to find Dr. Wickham. The doctor was in his house robe, drinking tea in his apartment in the Outer Court. They agreed to close the Palace that afternoon. No one would be allowed to enter Hampton Court for any reason. Anyone wishing to leave the Palace might do so, but they could not return.

"I suggest we divide the sick, doctor," Weatherby began as he accepted a cup of tea. I will care for half of the sick in the Great Hall and you can care for the rest in the Royal Chapel. Those are the two largest rooms we have and hopefully we won't fill them."

"I laid in a large supply of purgatives and leeches," Wickham said as he stretched his arthritic hands. "You are welcome to half."

"I probably won't need them, Sir. My current plan is to use an alternate therapy in hopes of reducing the dreadful mortality rate."

Dr. Wickham continued to massage his swollen joints showing no interest in what the new therapy might entail.

As he rose to leave, Weatherby said, "I will give Warder Chertsey the order to close Hampton Court at four p.m."

Weatherby found the warder and gave him his orders. The population of the Palace had swollen to several thousand during the King's visit. The Palace was now back to its normal population of about three hundred plus two hundred workmen. Chertsey reported that about fifty of the household staff had departed to ride out the epidemic in more isolated places. He knew most of the workers were impressed and couldn't leave. If previous epidemics of sweating sickness held true here, Weatherby thought, three quarters of the people in the Palace, or three hundred and forty-some souls, might contract the disease. He could have as many as one hundred and seventy patients, but hopefully not all at the same time. One good aspect of the dreaded illness was that it was brief, often lasting only thirty-six hours. The plague often took seven to nine days to kill, placing a heavy burden on nurses, food supplies, medicine, and other care givers.

Weatherby shared his projections on the possible number of patients they might expect with Dredge and asked him to calculate the amount of supplies they would need. Dredge enjoyed projections of any kind and set to work on his estimates. Weatherby asked Amarantha to assemble a staff of nurses to care for the sick. Weatherby ate lunch in the Wolsey

Apartment while he went through the mail that had accumulated while he was in London. Two more letters from universities had no good suggestions about Anna Maria's linear writing, as Weatherby had taken to calling it. Most of the rest of the mail was inconsequential, but there was a letter from the Chancellor on the bottom of the stack. Weatherby unsealed the wax and read:

> *Sir Seamus Scott Weatherby,*
>
> *I am writing after a long delay about your inquiry into the death of Messieur Henri De Lèves, the master glassmaker at Chartres Cathedral.*
>
> *He was beheaded at the Bastille Prison in Paris on May the seventh in the year of our Lord 1530, after a brief trial in front of three judges.*
>
> *The charge was apostasy against the Pope and not against the King.*
>
> *Therefore, I can conclude that he committed a major irreligious act. Further inquiry has not yielded any further information. As you know our relations with France and their King are strained at best.*
>
> *Thomas Cromwell, Chancellor*
> *From Whitehall this xxviij*
> *Day of May, 1530*

On the first reading, the letter seemed to Weatherby to contain little helpful information. However, on a second perusal, he concluded that the master glassmaker had lost his life because of a religious crime of such great import the authorities had reached out from the French capital to ensnare and murder him.

While he was discarding his unwanted mail, a messenger arrived sweaty and out of breath. He handed Weatherby a wrinkled, wax-sealed message. The badly written note said that seven cases of 'sweatyng sicknesse' had developed suddenly last night in Escher, which was only a short distance from the gates of Hampton Court. Before he left the Wolsey Apartment, the messenger turned toward Weatherby.

"I'm feelin' a might dizzy, Your Lordship," the messenger said. "May I sit, Sir?"

"No, but come with me," Weatherby said getting up quickly.

Damnation, Weatherby thought, I may have just let the first case of sweating sickness into the Palace! Weatherby led him to the Great Hall.

"Take all of your clothes off and lie down," Weatherby ordered.

He noted some perspiration on the messenger's upper lip, perhaps from his attempt to get to Hampton Court quickly or perhaps from the initial stages of the sweating sickness.

# CHAPTER 50

Weatherby ordered the gates to the Palace closed immediately, and assembled his nascent team of nurses. Amarantha had picked three women from the kitchen that had experience nursing, both assistant librarians, Peggy Ealing, Anna Maria's old roommate, Jason Mitchell, the apothecary, and Meg Claiborne from the Office of the Green Cloth. These eight would form the core of her nursing staff. If the population of patients grew, Amarantha had selected five serving girls that she could quickly add to her workforce. Weatherby wanted them to always work with muslin over their noses and mouths and to rinse their hands in a ewer of wine before leaving the Great Hall.

"Tell me if the messenger has the sweating sickness," Weatherby said to Jason Mitchell. "And if he has it, have him drink a quart of water and then set another quart by his bed."

Jason left and Amarantha set about organizing the remainder of her personnel. Warder Chertsey burst into the room to report that one of the chambermaids had developed the sweat. She was sent to the Great Hall for treatment. The apothecary returned from visiting the messenger.

"The messenger had a sense of apprehension followed by violent cold shivers, pain in the neck and an overwhelming feeling of fatigue," Jason reported. "I believe he has the early sweating sickness, and I watched him drink a quart of water and set a second by his bedside."

"He is young and appears strong," Weatherby replied. "He should have a good chance of survival. We will have a chance to see if our new therapy is efficacious. I want you to talk with the messenger and make a list of every person he came in contact with after his arrival at the Palace. Please isolate them for forty-eight hours. Amarantha, send one of your nurses to check on the chambermaid that has the sweating sickness."

Weatherby went to check on Dredge's progress. He found his amanuensis working on his distillery. He had connected his largest copper kettle to glass tubing that carried the steam into a series of tight loops overhead and then into a second copper vessel. A small wood fire burned under the copper kettle.

"I employed two of the workmen who are idled by the epidemic to run the distillery. As long as we have a good supply of wood, we can distill twelve quarts of clean water an hour. We are storing the water in these carboys and then taking them to the Great Hall when it is cool," explained Dredge.

"I want you to run the distillery around the clock until we get a few hundred gallons ahead," Weatherby instructed. "Once the epidemic peaks, we can cut back on production. How are our supplies of muslin, fruit, juice and food?"

"I planned for ninety patients, Sir," Dredge replied. "I think our supplies will be ample."

Weatherby wandered back to the Wolsey Apartments where Amarantha was compiling a schedule for her nurses.

"What have you heard about the King?" Amarantha asked.

"He fled all the way to Leeds Castle in the east," Weatherby replied. "It is one of his favorite places. The original castle built in 1119 is two grey limestone buildings constructed on two islands in a lake in County Kent. The portcullis is across the lake so all access is controlled. It is the perfect place to hide from the sweating sickness."

"I know the King is deathly afraid of disease and sickness," Amarantha replied. "But what if he were to catch the sweating sickness and die. What would become of England?"

"I agree with you. It is a frightening thought," Weatherby replied in a worried voice. "There is no clear heir apparent. The English would never accept a foreign princess like Catherine as Queen. Henry's daughter, Mary, would hardly be more acceptable. The people want a King. By his mistress, Elizabeth Blount, he has a healthy bastard son, Henry Fitzroy, who just turned eleven. Fitzroy is the second richest person in England, and the King made him Earl of Nottingham, Duke of Richmond and then Admiral of England, Ireland and Normandy."

"Would he be accepted as King?"

"Perhaps. The Earl of Buckingham would also have been a logical choice. He was wealthy, handsome and from a good family. However, he was indiscreet about his wish to be King, and Henry had him beheaded at the Tower on trumped-up charges of treason."

"With luck, the King will escape and live a long life and have many male heirs," Amarantha replied.

"His physicians aren't taking any chances. They have him taking rasis pills twice a day. He also drinks an infusion of marigold, malis Christy, sorrel, linseed vinegar, ivory scrapings, and sugar. There is no evidence that this concoction is efficacious, but it is very expensive, which probably makes the King feel better."

"Let's go examine our two patients," Weatherby said as he walked toward the door.

When they arrived at the entrance to the Great Hall, both wrapped their mouths and noses with muslin. The messenger appeared very ill and was sweating profusely. He was wrapped in wet sheets and being encouraged to drink apple juice. The chambermaid seemed much less ill. She had shivers, headache and neck and shoulder pain. She was being encouraged to drink a quart of distilled water. While he was examining the patients, a message was slipped under the door. It was from one of the King's secretaries and stated that Anne Boleyn had developed the sweating sickness three days ago and wasn't expected to live. Weatherby passed the note to Amarantha wordlessly.

Dredge started a log of all the patients treated in the two areas and dutifully wrote down the name of the messenger and the chambermaid. He reported that three patients were being treated in the Great Chapel with purgatives and leeches. The next patient arrived at the Great Hall. It turned out to be one of Weatherby's favorite Palace residents, Ellen Iverson, from the Confectory. Weatherby spoke with her and had her start drinking a quart of water. He was worried about her chances because she was in her forties and also very corpulent. During the evening two workmen and another chambermaid developed symptoms. They had six patients that night and Weatherby realized it could be four or five times that many the next night.

Weatherby walked over to the Great Chapel. He found Dr. Wickham applying leeches to the back of a serving girl. Wickham now had five patients. Weatherby could see the sweat streaming off of her back. She was so drenched that the leeches had trouble holding on until their suckers were attached.

"How is it going so far?" Weatherby asked Dr. Wickham.

"Everything is just as I remember from the last epidemic in 1517," Wickham replied as he pulled another leech out of a jar. "The real question is how bad will it get in the next few days?"

"It is impossible to tell," Weatherby said thoughtfully. "The epidemic of 1485 was severe with a high mortality. It was sufficiently large to teach us that this sickness attacked the rich more than the poor, and that little children were immune. The epidemic of 1507 was much milder. Then the epidemic you alluded to in 1517 was the most severe of all, and half the population of Oxford and Cambridge and many other towns perished."

"Perhaps it is the wrath of God punishing us for our sins, or even the comet that occurred earlier this year. I'm sure the soothsayers, fortune tellers and witches have already made their predictions as to how severe the epidemic will be," Wickham replied.

"We live in a superstitious age," Weatherby replied as he walked toward the door.

Weatherby ate a cold supper and then went back to check on his six patients, who were all drinking water and juice. Ellen Iverson appeared to be holding her own. The messenger still looked the sickest; he was delirious now and had a rapid pulse. The teachings of the day said that toward the end the victim had an irresistible urge to sleep, and if the patient gave way to it the outcome would be fatal. Weatherby checked on his nursing staff for signs of illness. They seemed almost jovial. He suspected they didn't know what was about to descend on them. Finally, he curled up on the sofa in his apartment with Chaucer's *Canterbury Tales*.

In the morning Weatherby was awoken at five a.m. by a knock on his door. Amarantha said that despite their best efforts, the messenger had just died. Weatherby threw on clothes and after wrapping himself in muslin, examined the body. An autopsy would be too dangerous. However, he could feel no enlargement of the abdominal organs, there was no rash, and the membranes and skin didn't look dehydrated. The body was taken to a common grave that had already been dug to the south of the Palace and covered with lime. Dredge came by with his book of figures.

"One patient has already died on the new therapy," Dredge began in a somewhat accusatory tone. "All of Dr. Wickham's patients are alive this morning. I don't believe the new therapy works and we should begin treating everyone with purgatives and leeches before we lose any more poor souls."

Weatherby felt like berating his servant for his insolence and lack of understanding. However, he was the one that, taking a clue from Galileo Galilei, encouraged open discussion. He decided to construct an example.

"Let us say that red cards are life and black cards are death. There are forty-four cards in a deck of cards, correct? Dr. Wickham and I each hold twenty-two cards or half the deck. We each alternately lay down cards, face up, and Dr. Wickham lays down five red cards and I lay down four red cards and one black card. If the cards were well shuffled, and we lay down the rest of the cards, can you say from the ten cards that you have seen who, by the law of chance, would have the most black cards?"

"No. I cannot," Dredge replied after a few minutes thought.

"I concur. Therefore, I think it is too early in this experiment to reach any conclusion. The sample is too small and I plan to continue," Weatherby said forcefully.

# PART 6

# CHAPTER 51

As Weatherby finished talking with Dredge, six new patients arrived in the Great Hall. The epidemic was growing just as Weatherby had feared. The nurses quickly settled the new arrivals into beds, and began having them drink water, apple, and pear juice. Weatherby examined each of the six to confirm that they had the sweating sickness. Unfortunately, all did.

He walked to the Wolsey Apartment where a stack of messages awaited him. The epidemic had struck the village of Hampton savagely. Seventy-eight cases had been reported, with twenty-six deaths already recorded. The disease had already spread to Teddington and Richmond, and would strike London soon. In the capital city, extra church services were held in hopes of appeasing God's wrath. Supposed heretics had been dragged from their beds and burned at the stake. Religious fanatics walked the streets covered in sack cloth and ashes while chanting loudly in outlandish tongues. Forty residents had been trampled to death in the streets as citizens attacked warehouses for flour and sugar. They planned to ride out the epidemic boarded up in their own cottages and homes away from all human contact. To their credit, few physicians had left London for the country in hopes of escaping death from the sweating sickness. However, Weatherby knew that an epidemic of several thousand cases in London would totally overwhelm the doctors and nurses, and most patients would be cared for by their families at home. Weatherby hoped that home care would actually lower mortality, because he continued to believe that the approved therapy of bloodletting and purgatives actually decreased a victim's chance of survival.

Word was received that Anne Boleyn, at Leeds Castle, had fallen deeply asleep in the last stages of the disease with a rapid pulse, exhaustion and collapse. The town's Protestant minister was called to pray for her after all hope seemed lost. Anne remained in a coma for several hours while her father, Thomas Boleyn, and her brother, George Boleyn, began making funeral arrangements. Then suddenly Anne awoke and sat up in bed. She was still confused but clearly was recovering quickly, the message stated. Her resurrection was widely regarded as a miracle in the County of Kent.

When all hope for Anne had seemed, the King rode his steed over the bridge at Leeds Castle and headed to Wales with four totally healthy hand-picked courtiers. Apparently, he had lost faith in his rasis pills and marigold infusion, Weatherby thought. The latest rumor was that vigorous exercise, to the point of intense sweating, prevented the sickness. The King had been observed in his apartments doing pushups and running in place to the point of exhaustion.

Weatherby walked to the laboratory to check on the distillery. Dredge's workers were busy stoking the fire under the copper kettle and adding water through a tube in the top.

"How is the distillation going, Dredge?" Weatherby asked.

"We have collected a hundred and fifty quarts of distilled water so far," Dredge replied. "I've checked every batch under the microscope, and there aren't any animalcules in the fluid."

"You have enough water for our eleven patients, Dredge. However, if our population of patients goes to four or eight times its current size, we will run out of pure water in eight hours. You should set up another still."

"I have the raw materials to do that, and I can get more workers from the construction crew. I will start on it immediately, Your Grace."

Weatherby walked back to the Great Hall. Amarantha was just coming off her shift. As she unwrapped the muslin from her mouth and nose she discarded the cloth and dipped her hands in wine, Weatherby asked, "How are the patients doing?"

"Quite well, Seamus. They are improved or stable except for one of the older chambermaids."

"How is Ellen Iverson doing?" Weatherby asked in a worried voice.

"Fortunately, I think she has a mild case."

"Would you like to get some lunch?"

"Thank you, but I'm not very hungry and I am very tired," Amarantha replied in a soft voice.

"Are you well?" Weatherby asked in a concerned voice as he reached for her wrist to feel her pulse.

"I think so. I feel a little apprehensive, but I think that's normal with a potentially fatal disease all around me."

Her face was flushed and she had a fine perspiration on her upper lip and forehead. He needed to exam her to decide if she had the sweating sickness, but he didn't want her exposed to others with confirmed illness. He escorted her to her apartment.

"I want you to rest. You have been working too hard," he said. Once she had reclined on her bed he said, "I want to examine you briefly."

Weatherby pulled out two long, wooden ebony tubes that screwed together with a hole drilled through the center. He used it to listen to the abdomen, the heart and the lungs. He called it *le cylindre* after the French, but later it was known as a stethoscope derived from the words from stethos—chest, and scope—to view. Amarantha's lungs sounded clear, but he thought her heart sounds were slightly rapid and weak. Her skin felt velvety and slightly moist.

"I think you have the early stages of the sickness, my darling Ran," Weatherby said in a calm voice despite the underlying fear that he felt.

As a physician he had always hated making a serious diagnosis for a friend or family member. It gave him a deep, sinking feeling of dread and sadness. He likened it to sadly looking at a rose window from outside a cathedral when the glass was grey-black surrounded by grey stone, rather than from inside the cathedral when the rose window was blue, green, yellow and especially red. He wanted to keep Amarantha isolated from the rest of the victims, but he realized he didn't have the resources to manager her separately. He had just received a message that fourteen new patients with the sweating sickness had been admitted for treatment in the past hour, and four of them were already very ill.

He encouraged Amarantha to rise to her feet and walked beside her to the Great Hall. He wanted to wrap her in his arms and tell her she would be all right and that he loved her, but he was disciplined enough not to touch her for he realized that if he were to contract the illness also, her chance of survival would be diminished.

Things were in turmoil when they arrived at the Great Hall. Eleven patients were already receiving care. Fourteen patients had just arrived, not counting Amarantha. After wrapping his nose and mouth in muslin,

Weatherby helped Amarantha into a gown and put her in the best bed to the front, right side of the hall. He brought her a quart of water and a quart of apple juice.

"Please drink both of these, Ran and then rest. I will personally discharge you the day after tomorrow when you have recovered, and we can look back on this and laugh."

"I'm not near as hopeful about this damnable disease as you are," Amarantha replied softly. "You told Dredge and me that the mortality of the sweating sickness is often fifty percent, so I could also be dead tomorrow. If I were more religious right now it would probably be better, but I just don't want to go to heaven yet. I've got too much I still want to do."

"I will do everything in my power to make sure you don't succumb to this awful disease," Weatherby replied.

Weatherby sent for Dredge.

"Amarantha has the sweating sickness and I need your help in caring for her," Weatherby said as soon as Dredge arrived.

"Yes, Your Grace. I will spend the night at her bedside."

Weatherby checked the fourteen new patients and gave orders for the care of each. Weatherby stepped out of the Great Hall unwrapped his muslin and dipped his hands in wine. He had a cold supper delivered to the area outside the large oak doors to the Great Hall. While he hurriedly ate his cold beef and bread he had his first doubts about his treatment plan. What if the traditional therapy for sweating sickness gave the patient the best chance? After all, hundreds of physicians in England had used purging and bloodletting in the three previous epidemics and one of them, the epidemic of 1507, had had a low mortality rate. He strained to remember all that he could of that scourge.

He had been a medical student in Edinburgh in 1507, and he and all his classmates had been pressed into service in the Royal Hospital. He had helped apply leeches to the backs of sufferers. He remembered treating one of the aldermen of the city who was only moderately ill, but after ten leeches became profoundly sick and then succumbed. He began to have doubts about bloodletting then, and never saw evidence that such therapy was efficacious except in dropsy where there was swelling of the legs and congestion.

He went back into the Great Hall and rushed to Amarantha's bedside. She was much worse and complained of severe pain in her neck and shoulders. She had a pounding headache and was sweating profusely.

Weatherby changed her drenched gown, and held her for a few minutes before encouraging her to drink a cup of pear juice. At times she seemed lucid, but much of the time she was delirious and mumbled about childhood things or people he didn't know.

His group of patients numbered twenty-seven. The first patient, the messenger had died, and an older chambermaid would be dead within the hour. Except for Amarantha the other twenty-five were doing tolerably well. He needed information on Dr. Wickham's progress and sent Dredge to the Chapel with his ledger. He returned in half an hour with Wickham's figures.

Dr. Wickham was treating thirty-six patients. His higher numbers, Dredge reported, were due to patients requesting bloodletting because they believed in the traditional therapy. A rumor had spread that Dr. Weatherby was using a new experimental approach.

"Yes, but how many patients of Wickham's have died?" Weatherby asked urgently.

"He has lost three to our two," Dredge replied. "But the nurses think he will lose three more in the next few hours."

"Then, if my math is correct, in two hours he will have fourteen percent mortality and compared to our seven percent," Weatherby said in a voice filled with relief. "It is early but perhaps the new therapy is efficacious."

# CHAPTER 52

A group of Protestant worshippers came to the door of the Great Hall and asked to be admitted. They had just come from the Chapel where they had sung madrigals to the sick and dying. They wished to do the same in the Great Hall. The nurses blocked them at the door and called for Weatherby.

"This vicious disease is highly contagious," Weatherby said when he arrived at the doorway. "I cannot allow you to enter. It might endanger every one of you."

"But we just sang for the sick in the Chapel and it visibly lifted their spirits," the leader of the group replied.

"Then unfortunately you have all been exposed and some of you will no doubt contract the disease," Weatherby said in a stern voice. "Now be gone with you."

Weatherby turned and hurried in to Amarantha's bedside. Her breathing was rapid, and she seemed weaker. She was now too delirious to drink. Weatherby felt he was losing both his valuable young assistant and the love of his life.

When he was younger, Weatherby felt he had too much to do to spend time on a relationship. Of course he had natural urges, so he visited houses of prostitution, which society found quite acceptable. London had hundreds of establishments, and Edinburgh had dozens. There were lower-class stews but also more genteel whorehouses for the upper class. Large numbers of young women who could find no other work were employed there. Officials looked on the houses as ways to protect chaste women from rape and defilement. When Weatherby discovered his *demimonde* in France, his sex without a relationship, was taken to an entirely new level. He replayed in his mind the last night he spent with Geneviève in Paris.

Weatherby knew he was just distracting himself from thinking about Amarantha and her desperate state. He walked quickly to the laboratory and began pouring over his medical books for ideas he might use in treating his beautiful assistant. It was eleven p.m. and the laboratory was dark and gloomy. Weatherby lit every candle in the room. Then he began pulling down volume after volume from Hippocrates to Vesalius, thumbing through each. If the fatal event in the sweating sickness was a progressive loss of fluids, then Weatherby was convinced that a technique must exist to prevent that. It was one-thirty according to the heavy windup clock around his neck and the table was covered with a disorderly pile of volumes. Weatherby was about to give up his search when he came across a new book by a Spanish physician, Michael Servetus. In it he found a description of how blood circulated through the lungs. If the blood actually circulated in the body, Weatherby had an idea that might help Amarantha through her crisis. He picked up the book and walked back to the Great Hall. When he arrived, he found Dredge sitting at Amarantha's side.

"How is our dear colleague?" Weatherby asked in apprehensive voice.

"Worse I'm afraid. She continues to sweat profusely. She cannot be aroused and her pulse is rapid and weak. I believe she will die," Dredge said in a voice full of sadness.

"I brought a book for you to read that might help us save her," Weatherby said as he handed his amanuensis *Christianismi Restitutio* by Michael Servetus.

"But this is a religious book," Dredge replied as he looked at the tome.

"He is a theologian and a physician as well. Read the section I marked with a ribbon."

"I fail to see how the circulation of blood, if it even exists, will help save our partner," Dredge replied in a forlorn tone.

"Here is my idea. If the amount of blood is limited and most needed by her heart and brain, then why not divert what little fluid she has to those organs?"

"That sounds preposterous. How exactly do you propose to do that?"

"What if we wrapped her arms and legs tightly with strips of linen, pushing all of the blood out of her limbs? Wouldn't that conserve her blood for her brain and her heart?"

"Perhaps, but I have never heard of such a thing."

"I think we should try it. We have little to lose."

While Weatherby sat at the bedside and held Amarantha's sweaty hand, Dredge ran off for a supply of linen. When he returned, they tore the cloth into long pieces three inches wide, and began wrapping her limbs with tight, overlapping strips. They were clumsy at first, but as they progressed both grew more adept. When they were finished, both were sweating from the exertion.

"She looks like an Egyptian mummy without the headdress," Dredge observed.

"Let's give her a half an hour and then reevaluate. How are our other patients?" He asked Dredge as he looked across a sea of beds.

"Most are doing quite well. We admitted twenty-one more patients tonight and our supplies of distilled water are low, but we are keeping up. We have treated a total of forty-two patients so far with only three deaths," Dredge replied.

"How is Dr. Wickham doing?"

"I haven't been over since Amarantha got so sick, but at last count he had fifty-nine."

"How many of his patients have died?"

"He's lost nine to our three, but he'll have six more deaths before morning if my information is correct. Everyone in the Palace knows that more corpses are being carried out of the Chapel than from the Great Hall. I suspect you will get nearly all of the new patients until the epidemic is over. If that happens, we will run out of distilled water."

"I suspect you can mix ten percent wine with well water and kill all the animalcules," Weatherby replied. "Perhaps you could try it."

When they returned to Amarantha's bedside, Weatherby noted that her color was somewhat pinker. He had taken her pulse with the watch around his neck, prior to wrapping her limbs and had noted 160 beats per minute. Now her pulse was 142. She seemed slightly more responsive as well. Her hands and feet, however, were cold and blue.

"I hesitate to say it, but I think your therapy is working," Dredge remarked. "I need to check your idea of killing the creatures in water with wine. Please excuse me."

"Yes, do. I will stay with Amarantha."

Weatherby pulled up a chair and sat at Ran's bedside, mopping her brow with a cool, moist cloth. After another thirty minutes she was pinker, mumbling incoherently, and her pulse had fallen to 131 beats per minute. However, her hands and feet were even colder. Weatherby wondered if he might get much the same good circulatory effect by binding only three limbs and unwrapping the fourth one. Weatherby unwrapped Amarantha's left arm, and her hand quickly warmed up. He found that her pink color remained and that her pulse was now 126. She could even swallow small amounts of apple juice. Weatherby asked the nurses to wrap three limbs on the ten sickest patients. He instructed them to change which three limbs were wrapped every two hours to relieve the cold, blue extremities.

As the night went on, Amarantha continued to improve slightly each hour. Weatherby was sure it wasn't just his wishful thinking because her pulse was down three or four beats every hour. Dredge returned to report on his experiments with the water and the wine.

"You were right, sir," Dredge began, still out of breath from his walk. "It takes about twenty minutes, but wine and water mixed at a ratio of one to nine kills all the creatures in the water in twenty minutes."

"In that case we can handle any onslaught," Weatherby replied as he sank down in a chair. He was exhausted.

By dawn, Amarantha was coherent and restless. Her first question was about Anne Boleyn's fate. She had forgotten hearing about it before her own near-fatal battle with the sweating sickness.

"She has miraculously recovered, Ran, as have you. And the King has escaped the illness, but London has not. Seven hundred cases were reported there just yesterday. I'm moving you posthaste to your apartment with Judith Scotson as your private nurse."

Weatherby knew from study of previous epidemics that in addition to a predilection for the rich and an aversion to children, that the sweating sickness could be caught again, and he wished to take no chance of reexposure with his beloved assistant. As the morning wore on, thirty-seven new cases appeared at the door of the Great Hall for treatment. Dr. Wickham had only three new cases. Weatherby asked to borrow some of Dr. Wickham's nurses as his patient load had swelled now to over seventy. He asked Dredge to instruct the new personnel in his new therapy of massive fluid therapy and binding limbs. Then Weatherby left to take before leaving to take a short nap.

When he awoke, Weatherby returned to the Great Hall. He had spent so much time attending to Amarantha that he needed to catch up on his multitude of other patients. Dredge reported that constricting the limbs with linen seemed to reduce mortality and shorten the illness. He opened

Dredge's large book and realized that they had cared for seventy-nine patients while Dr. Wickham had cared for forty-five. It was too early to determine mortality because many patients were still receiving therapy but Wickham had lost twenty-one patients to Weatherby's seven.

Weatherby set to work with his overly busy nurses caring for the hall full of patients. He also watched for breaches in contagion control reminding his workers to keep the muslin completely over their noses and mouths and to always rinse their hands in wine when they left the hall. Many thought that Weatherby's measures were pure superstition, but few could deny that something was reducing mortality in his patients.

# CHAPTER 53

Weatherby only left the Great Hall in order to write hurried notes to several physicians he knew in Scotland and in Kent, where the epidemic had not yet struck. He told them of the method he had used. He didn't frame it as an experiment for fear of raising ire, but instead reported a greatly reduced mortality rate. He suspected that in spite of his report, most would treat the deadly disease with leeches and bleeding.

Twenty-one patients presented for treatment the next day and fourteen the day after that, but dozens of sufferers were also being sent home every day to complete their convalescence there. Dr. Wickham was admitting no new patients. Both Dredge and Weatherby felt the epidemic was waning. It was a good thing, because Hampton Court was running out of food, firewood and cloth. After consulting with Dr. Wickham, Weatherby ordered the gates opened.

Initially, people swarmed in and out of the Palace. Many of those leaving went to the village of Hampton for things that they needed. They were saddened to see the devastation in the village. It was one of the hardest-hit towns, so far, in all of England. Three-quarters of the population had contracted the sweating sickness and almost four hundred had died. The streets were deserted, and many of the shops were boarded up. Most visitors scurried back to the Palace quickly.

Weatherby went to Amarantha's apartment to check on her progress. It had been four days since she was stricken. Judith Scotson reported that her patient was nearly back to normal. Amarantha walked in from the bedroom in a dark blue dress with her hair curled and piled artfully on the top of her head.

"Greetings, Seamus. I'm ready to return to work," Amarantha said in a cheery voice.

"Are you really fully recovered?" Weatherby was incredulously.

"I have a slight headache, but otherwise I feel perfectly normal."

"I will bring you some correspondence and you can work on that today."

"I am eager to solve these cases. We have been diverted for so long."

"Yes. I believe it has been fifteen days since the Nones of May," Weatherby observed. "Before we work though, I propose a lunch in the orchard for the three of us, and then a carriage ride to get you a breath of fresh air, Amarantha."

Weatherby walked slowly through the Base Court and through the Clock Court before ducking through a doorway into the orchard. A table for three with a linen tablecloth and silverware had already been placed. They ate asparagus and leeks with roast coney, a close relative of the rabbit. Weatherby and Judith drank a sweet white wine, but Amarantha drank water treated with wine. When they had finished, an open coach drawn by four white horses pulled up on the nearby path. Weatherby helped the ladies to their seats. For the next two hours they traveled the roads of the Palace and the farmland to the south. The two ladies talked easily, laughing the whole time from under their parasols.

When they returned, Weatherby received a message that Clarence Stevens had been brought to Hampton Court so the King's envoy could confront him about Gregory Townsend's murder. The young man seemed fully recovered from the beating the sheriff had given him. Weatherby had him brought to the laboratory.

"What did you do after you threw Gregory Townsend off the parapet?" Weatherby said accusingly, his face inches from Stevens.

"I din'a kill him!" Clarence replied.

Weatherby wanted to see if he got the same answer as last time, so he continued.

"Why should I believe you? You admitted that you wanted to kill him because of what he had done to your sister."

"Because I tol' you that I went there to kill him but he was gone."

Weatherby had asked Amarantha to interview Palace residents that might have seen Clarence Stevens the night of the murder. Surprisingly, she found Warder Chertsey remembered seeing the young man that night as he was coming back from discovering the body. Weatherby was sure

Clarence hadn't committed the crime but thought he might have seen something useful that night.

"Did you see anything unusual that night at the Palace?"

"It was dark and late and not many were aboot," Clarence replied slowly. "But I did see two large fellows who were sweating and shor' a breath."

"Did you recognize them?"

After a long pause Clarence said, "No I dina'."

"Thank you for your time. I'm glad you recovered from the beating."

"Fur that, thanks be to ya', Your Lordship."

Weatherby was walking to the lab to check with Dredge when he saw Sir John Moulton walking across the Clock Court, a pipe in one hand and another rolled parchment in the other. Weatherby crossed over to talk.

"I haven't seen you in weeks," Weatherby began. "You seem to have weathered the epidemic well."

"I can stand on a four-inch board eighty feet in the air, but I'm not very brave about sickness," Moulton replied. "I went to my farm in Wales."

"How about supper tonight?"

Moulton answered, "Lamb and Flag, seven," around the stem of his pipe.

In the laboratory, Weatherby found Dredge working on Anna Maria Wimbledon's coded diary.

"Any luck deciphering the writing?" Weatherby asked.

"I have filled two journals with attempts to break this code, Your Grace," Dredge said as he handed Weatherby the two volumes.

Weatherby thumbed through the volumes, the leaves of which were covered with dense lines of letters.

"I see you tried all the encryption methods tried by that German monk, Thrithemius?" Weatherby replied.

"Yes, and none of them worked," Dredge said resignedly. "I have found some other arcane texts on codes, but I haven't applied them all yet."

"Keep it up," Weatherby said over his shoulder as he headed out of the lab.

Weatherby walked out of the Great Gatehouse and along the lane that led to the bridge to the village of Hampton. As he often did, he stopped on the bridge over the Thames. Usually he looked downstream, but this evening he looked upstream at the rippling water to the west. Barn swallows dipped around the bridge catching insects, and a pair of the ubiquitous black swans swam smoothly by with three half-grown, fluffy grey cygnets trailing along behind. He walked into the village and up High Street to the Lamb and Flag. Sir John Moulton was in the public room and already in his cups. Weatherby had a quick pint of ale to catch up, and then they moved into the dining room. They were seated by a large bay window.

"I heard some rumors about your selfless and clever behavior, Seamus, during the dreadful epidemic," Moulton said in a slightly slurry voice.

"It worked out well, Sir John, but I think I was lucky."

"You invented a whole new treatment that slashed mortality. I would call that revolutionary."

"I just received the final figures from my amanuensis," Weatherby replied taking a parchment out of his inside pocket. "Let's see. Dr. Wickham treated forty-eight patients and lost twenty-one. My team treated one-hundred and thirty-four and we lost nine."

"So you are telling me he lost forty-three percent of his cases and you lost nine percent?"

"Actually I only lost seven percent," Weatherby corrected him proudly.

"Zounds. How did you have the balls to use a totally radical and untested therapy on one hundred and thirty-four souls?" Moulton asked in amazement. "If you had had a higher mortality than Wickham, for whatever reason, let's say your patients were older or poorly nourished, you would have been finished as a physician."

"True, but my new method was based on my experience with the sweating sickness in 1507, and it was based on a clear deduction. I was confident. My assistant, on the other hand, felt I was experimenting with people's lives."

"Indeed you were," Moulton replied as their pike and broadbeans arrived. He ordered more wine.

"But the mortality of the sweating sickness is almost fifty percent," Weatherby replied thoughtfully. "I didn't have to be very good."

"Besides that a lot of people think that Dr. Wickham is as crazy as Sir Rodney Shrewsbury," Wickham replied.

"Wickham isn't crazy. He is just an old-fashioned physician. But who is Sir Rodney Shrewsbury?"

"He a vicious, disturbed, old hermit who lives in the Palace," Moulton said. "Shrewsbury has resided in Hampton Court for years. Yet the Master of the House, Richard Weston, doesn't even know he exists."

"How can that be?"

"The old man keeps a low profile. He has a series of dirty old rooms with a laboratory and a library of the occult off the North Cloister. I only found him because I couldn't find what was there on the medieval plans from Lord Giles Daubeney. I went exploring and found a large door hidden behind an oak panel."

"What makes him vicious?"

"Supposedly, when he was younger, he was a professor at Oxford. He had a disagreement with one of his students and bashed the student's head in with an andiron."

"I can't believe no one told me about him before this," Weatherby said in an astonished voice. "A murderer living right in Hampton Court, and despite dozens of interviews I had no idea of his existence."

"I'm sure his name was on the tip of my tongue," Moulton said lamely.

Irritated, Weatherby finished his ale and excused himself. He walked back to Hampton Court and fell into bed. He was tired and frustrated but quickly went to sleep. A thunderstorm hit the Palace at three a.m. with bright frequent forked lightning and glass-rattling thunder. Weatherby awoke in a cold sweat, but not from the noise of the thunder. His long absent, disturbing nightmare had recurred. It had begun with three large black, snorting, steeds galloping through a wood. Each was mounted by a tall, skeletal wraith. One carried a sword, one a scythe, and one a long trident. Weatherby rode a white horse into a strong headwind. As he came over a small rise, a toddler in a long white nightgown crawled into his path. He had meant to analyze this night terror for two months, and he knew he wouldn't be able to go back to sleep. Instead he jumped out of bed, pulled on some clothes and walked through a steady rain to the laboratory. Once there, he set up his easel and using charcoal rods he sketched the scene he had just seen in his nightmare.

# CHAPTER 54

By the time Weatherby finished his drawing the rain had stopped and dawn was breaking. He was ravenously hungry and so he headed to the Great Kitchen for eggs and bacon. It was still very early and he had trouble waiting until a decent hour to wake his assistants and tell them about the murderous Sir Rodney Shrewsbury. To fill the time, the King's envoy went to the Knot Garden for an hour and watched and listened to the song birds beginning their day. There he heard constant trilling and melodious swoops that left every second filled with two or more voices. Robins, larks and an occasional nightingale busied themselves as they flitted about the rows of hedges. A golden oriole, with a flashy bright yellow body and black wings, landed on a prominent branch and sang its high, reedy song.

When he could wait no longer, he walked to Amarantha's apartment and knocked gently on her door. Next he found Dredge and suggested they all meet in the Wolsey Apartments for privacy. When they were assembled with a large pot of tea, Weatherby told his crew what he had learned from Sir John Moulton the night before. Both Amarantha and Dredge listened closely.

"I'm surprised that Richard has never mentioned this person to me," Amarantha replied.

"Moulton says he doesn't know of Shrewsbury's existence even though he occupies several rooms in the castle," Weatherby said incredulously. "Let's assemble some tools and meet outside The North Cloister in thirty minutes."

Once the three were assembled with their tools, Weatherby pulled out a rough sketch of Shrewsbury's rooms Moulton had made. Dredge ran his hands slowly along the paneling trying to sense a whiff of air from a void behind the paneling. Along the south wall he found what he was looking for. He gripped the molding, and a large oak panel swung out into the hallway. A stout wooden door only five feet tall stood in the center of the space. It was locked, but Dredge took a ring of keys from his canvas satchel and quickly picked the lock. The door creaked open. Inside it was dusty and dark. Amarantha lit some candles, placing them on any flat surface she could find.

The first room seemed to be an entryway with three closed doors pointing east, south and west. One doorway opened into a closet full of robes and ornate costumes. Many were ladies dresses and gowns. The second doorway opened into a small eating area with a table in the center. The third doorway opened into a large laboratory complete with glassware and supplies of many colorful chemicals in large bottles. Beyond the laboratory was a large, dank, library full of books on astrology, alchemy, the occult and torture. The last group of books was filled with lurid woodcuts that almost screamed with the agony of the victims when the volumes were opened.

Amarantha sat down at a table to sketch the rooms. Dredge couldn't wait to get back to their laboratory in an attempt to figure out what experiments Shrewsbury had performed. In contrast, Weatherby grabbed more candles and then set about cataloguing the tomes in the library. After looking at only a few volumes, he concluded that he was looking into the mind of a violent and disturbed man. Each of three colleagues worked for a couple of hours before breaking for lunch. They were careful to lock the door and close the fake oak panel so the lair appeared undisturbed.

Weatherby had their lunch sent to the rose garden where the roses and columbines were in full bloom. They had a hearty meal of sautéed plaice and oysters served with tomatoes, asparagus and two bottles of Rhenish wine. After lunch they returned to the hidden rooms, and Weatherby took a nap. When he awoke he returned to the room full of books. Many of the books were very old, in poor shape and in Latin with a smattering of books in Italian, French and German. The dust was overwhelming, so Weatherby wrapped muslin around his nose and mouth as he had done during the epidemic of sweating sickness. The cloth quickly turned grey-brown and had to be changed every forty-five minutes. He took a blank volume from a corner of one of the shelves to use in recording the names of the books. He spent the afternoon trying to find a classification system for the books such as geography in one area, biography in a second, and necromancy in a third. In spite of his best efforts he discerned no pattern. He counted over six hundred volumes and thought if the tomes were filed willy-nilly that the library would be nearly useless, unless the owner knew each book and memorized where it was located.

Perhaps most disturbing was that one out of every five or so books was filled with prints made from detailed wood cuts of beheadings, eviscerations, burnings, piercing of multiple victims and torture of babies. All the unfortunate victims' mouths were open, presumably in blood-curdling screams. Many of the rest of the volumes were about necromancy, the practice of communicating with the dead to predict the future. While such black magic was still widely practiced, the authorities continued trying unsuccessfully to stamp it out.

The library also contained many volumes concerning astrology. The position of the planets and constellations was used by commoners to predict business success, luck in love and even to find lost pets. Weatherby knew that the King of England had an astrologer, William Parron, and that before raising taxes, making important political decisions or starting a battle, Parron was consulted. Weatherby regarded such attempts at clairvoyance as foolishness. The light was fading in the hidden rooms, so Weatherby unwrapped the muslin from his nose and mouth and called a halt to their work.

The trio headed into town for a relaxing dinner, with Dredge leading the way. Weatherby and Amarantha walked behind, arm in arm. When the King had been at Hampton Court, his eight best chefs, several from France, had come with him. The banquets had been colorful, perfectly cooked, and savory. Now that they had departed with their employer, the quality of the cooking had suffered. Despite that, the three companions had an excellent meal at the Lamb and Flag and excitedly discussed their finding of the day.

"The library has some wonderfully old volumes that I would enjoy owning," Weatherby began. "But, overall, the subject matter emphasizes human brutality and the occult. So far I have not found any personal writing."

"Perhaps when you do, it will be in Anna Maria's code," Amarantha interjected.

"While it would tie Sir Shrewsbury to the other three, it would also leave us with more unreadable material. What did you find in the laboratory, Dredge?"

"Despite all the dirt, the professor has a very sophisticated set up for chemical analysis and synthesis. Unfortunately, it isn't like looking at a library and knowing the author's intentions from the volumes present. I will need to analyze some residues and make a precise inventory of his raw materials to know what he was about. I will take samples back to my lab, but it could take days."

"What about you, Amarantha?" Weatherby asked.

"The map of the rooms is nearly complete," Amarantha said, unfolding a parchment. "There is an anomaly along the east wall. I'll have Dredge help me resolve that tomorrow. I'm amazed that such a large suite of rooms could exist at Hampton Court and be unknown by nearly everyone."

Weatherby thought a moment and then said, "The Palace is a huge maze that has grown by accretion. Some sections are medieval; others were built by Lord Daubeney, then by Cardinal Wolsey, and some by Henry the VIII. They fit together like a giant, complicated, irregular puzzle. I suspect a full mapping of Hampton Court would reveal other hidden warrens."

The conversation turned lighter as Weatherby ordered three more tankards of ale. The companions stayed until the Lamb and Flag closed, and then walked unsteadily across the bridge over the Thames.

Weatherby spent the next day continuing to catalogue the books and looking for a subtle system that would explain how the books were shelved. He actually read part of a volume in Italian about necromancy on Malta because it was recent and well written. Also, Shrewsbury had made notes in the margins in Latin which Weatherby translated.

Dredge took samples from the beakers and retorts in Sir Rodney's lab to his own lab for analysis. Amarantha took her measurements and notes and drew a large floor plan of the hidden area on a parchment.

The workers took a brief lunch break and then worked into the evening. When they were done for the day, Weatherby tried to assess what each of them thought about Sir Rodney's possible role in the murders.

"I think he is the best suspect we have," Dredge asserted.

"He certainly seems smart enough and twisted enough to have committed these crimes," Amarantha responded.

"He is quite a student of death and murder in its many forms," Weatherby said.

Amarantha and Weatherby spent the evening in Amarantha's apartment playing gleek. Weatherby lost three sovereigns. After Amarantha's fourth yawn, her companion took the hint and went to bed.

The next morning, Weatherby was cataloguing books when Amarantha and Dredge burst in, talking excitedly.

"Dredge helped me check all my dimensions with his measuring rod," Amarantha began, rolling out a large parchment on a dusty table. "An area six by six feet is missing from the floor plan on the east wall," Amarantha said pointing to an area on the parchment.

"Show me where that area is located," Weatherby replied.

# CHAPTER 55

The three walked to the area Amarantha had described. One wall was covered with cooking implements and the other with books. Dredge and Weatherby tapped both walls looking for a hollow sound, but found none. They removed all the pans and spoons and books and ran their hands over the walls feeling for anomalies. Dredge brought a candelabrum from the library and let the light shine tangentially across the two walls. Only then did Weatherby notice an irregularity in the oak molding across the top which he pulled. Suddenly, one of the walls opened a few inches. Dredge and Weatherby pulled the panel open. Inside, they found shelves with stacks of human bones from both adults and children. Some of the other shelves held astrological instruments, and on the top shelves were rows of journals. Weatherby pulled one down and dusted it off. He opened it, fearful that he would find the Linear A code found in Anna Maria's library or the Linear B code found in Chartres that had stumped them so far. Instead, the volume was printed neatly in the Roman alphabet; however, many of the letters were backward. The letters that looked like they weren't backward were the ones that were symmetrical along the vertical axis, like the letter 'H'.

Weatherby recognized it instantly as the secret code that Leonardo da Vinci used. All the words were simply written backward and could be read in a mirror. Weatherby sent Dredge to find a small hand mirror. In the meantime Weatherby pulled all the volumes down and counted them. There were a total of fifty-seven volumes that only he could read, as they were either in Italian or Latin—he wasn't sure which yet.

"What if Sir Shrewsbury returns while we are mucking around in his things?" Amarantha asked. "Even if he isn't our murderer, he certainly seems to be a killer."

"From the look of the place, I don't think it's been occupied in over a month, which was about the time the epidemic hit," Weatherby mused. "Of course he could return at any moment. No one in the Palace seems to know anything about him, but at one he was on the faculty of Oxford University. Go to the library and see if there is any information about him there. I'll have Dredge purloin these journals, and then put this hovel back exactly as we found it."

Weatherby walked Amarantha to the library and then went to the Wolsey Apartments. There a letter from a colleague in Northumberland told about the sweating sickness. The epidemic had spread to the far eastern end of England, but it had gotten a little milder as it spread. Then it began to spread to the north but had mysteriously petered out sparing Wales and Scotland. Weatherby also received a long, chatty letter from Father Croceus Lawrence, who was still copying illuminated manuscripts at St. Germain des Pres in Paris.

At the bottom of his stack of mail was an almost illegible handwritten note from one of the chamber maids at the Palace. Written in a shaky hand with many words crossed out it said, "Theenk youse for savins my lifes. Mays God's blest youse. Sinceresly, Josie Thomas."

Weatherby sat back and read it twice. He reflected again on how lucky he had been during the epidemic. First, he hadn't caught the sweating sickness, which would have prevented him from helping the other victims. He had nearly lost Amarantha, but ultimately she had rallied and lived. He had cared for one hundred and thirty-four patients, and nearly all of them had survived. If he believed in God, he thought, he would thank him for his many blessings. This pandemic was turning out to be the worst episode of sweating sickness yet. In London the mortality was nearly sixty percent but at Hampton Court, his death rate had been less than ten percent! Weatherby decided that he would write a paper about his treatment method and present it to the medical society in London. For now, Weatherby curled up on a sofa in the apartment and took a nap.

He dreamed about being buried alive in a waterfall of old books. The dream was a clear reference to the fifty-seven large journals he needed to read. The writing had turned out to be all in code and in Latin, not Italian, which would make the translation even slower. Nearly all of his medical school classes at the University of Edinburgh had been in Latin, but he hadn't practiced it regularly since, like he did with Italian, French and German. He knew he would become facile again quickly, but he needed a system so that he could skim excerpts. He decided to use the two assistant librarians, Judith Scotson and Margaret Sedgwick to aid him. He had Dredge take the journals to the Palace Library and locate two small mirrors. Both librarians greeted him joyfully as he pushed open the heavy glass doors of the library. Judith had endured a bad case of the sweating sickness, but her pink cheeks and sparkling eyes, which Weatherby had always enjoyed, suggested she was fully recovered.

Placing the two mirrors on the large central table, he said, "I need your help in deciphering these extensive journals. It is likely that they extend back over forty or fifty years. They are written in Latin backwards, à la Leonardo da Vinci. You can help me by dating each volume. There should be approximately one per year. I plan to read the most recent one, focusing particularly on the dates of the murders, and then shall work backwards if time allows. Let me show you how to do this."

Weatherby opened one of the dusty volumes and leafed through the first few pages until he found some numbers. He held the book tight against his chest and picked up a mirror with one hand. After some manipulation, the numbers appeared in the mirror and he could read, *Ceres, Aprilis, 1516 A.D.* He wrote it out on a parchment for them.

Then he explained, "*Aprilis* is the month. *Ceres* refers to a festival for the goddess of grain on the tenth day of that month, and *1516* is the year. This tells us that this journal is fourteen years old and therefore not of much interest. I noticed that sometimes Shrewsbury wrote out the date. That will be more difficult for you to find, but I can help you date such books. Any questions?"

"Is this the man that killed Anna Maria Wimbledon?" Margaret asked.

"Perhaps," Weatherby replied. "He is certainly a killer and deviously smart. In fact, I hope that he is our man because he seems to have decamped from the Palace, making it unlikely he will kill here again. Was Amarantha here earlier?"

"Yes. She looked in some volumes and then left."

Weatherby headed out the door in search of his assistant. He went to the laboratory where he found her poring over three heavy tomes.

"What have you found on Sir Rodney?" Weatherby asked.

"It appears that he's a brilliant but erratic character," Amarantha replied. "Shrewsbury was born in Dublin, Ireland in 1467. He was the illegitimate son of Lord Shrewsbury. However, Lady Shrewsbury died without an heir, so Rodney inherited all the lands, houses and serfs. He didn't care a fig about that and sailed to England when he was thirteen. Once there, he graduated from Balliol College, Oxford University, *summa cum laude*. After graduation he spent two years in Naples, Italy, apparently wallowing in drink, gambling, wenches and petty thievery. He didn't need money but apparently enjoyed stealing for the excitement of it. He returned to Oxford University as instructor and professor of astronomy and astrology. There he was afflicted with syphilis, drank 'til he passed out every night, was surly with students, and worse yet with the officials of the University."

"It sounds like a made-up penny novel to me," Weatherby replied.

"Oh, it gets even better," Amarantha replied in an excited voice. "In his fourth year teaching at the University he got into an altercation with one of his students. It was over a pint of ale. In front of everyone, in fact in a public house, he grabbed an andiron out of the cooling ashes of a fireplace and bashed his skull in. The student, from a rich family in Kent, expired, not surprisingly, on the spot. The boy's father wanted Old Testament revenge and rode in haste to Oxford with a sword and a dagger. He confronted Rodney one night as he walked home. Always a fast talker, particularly since his days as a thief in Naples, Shrewsbury talked the distraught father out of killing him and instead suggested a duel at dawn the next morning. The duelers and seconds, a physician and an audience, gathered at dawn in a field east of Oxford."

"Let me tell you what happened," Weatherby chimed in. "The father's pistol misfired so Sir Rodney moved closer and shot the despondent father in the chest, killing him on the spot. Of course, the pistols were Rodney's."

"How did you know that?" Amarantha exclaimed in surprise.

"I have already taken the measure of this man's character and found it wanting."

"After his time at Oxford, he traveled by land to greater India and spent four years there living in the fleshpots of the east. He consorted with cut purses, harlots and opium dealers."

"How can you possibly know all this detailed information about Sir Rodney Shrewsbury?" Weatherby asked incredulously.

"He wrote a book about his life called, *Confessions of an Irish Opium-Eater,* and we had a copy in our library", she replied puckishly.

"Aren't you the clever one."

"You are the one who asked me to go to the library and discover what this Irish wastrel was all about. I believe I have carried out your instructions to the letter. Apparently one day, he simply gave up opium and sailed back to England, writing his memoir as he went."

"Where do you think Sir Rodney is now?"

"He is the sort of iconoclast who really could be anywhere," Amarantha answered promptly, suggesting that she had been thinking about that very problem. "I can detect no evidence of disease, other than syphilis, or wounds in his early years. However, he is now sixty-three years old and probably not as spry or adventurous as he once was."

"Perhaps when he left Hampton Court, he went back to the family estates in County Kildare just north of Dublin."

"I have already sent a messenger to enquire surreptitiously if Sir Rodney was in residence at the family seat. I should have an answer late tonight."

"Good work," Weatherby replied. "You are one step ahead as usual, Ran."

"You need to be working on the journals, Seamus. You are the only one who can read them."

# CHAPTER 56

Weatherby went back to the library and picked up the journals the librarians had identified—so far there were journals for 1526, 1528, and 1529. The volume for 1530 hadn't turned up yet. He carried a volume back to the Wolsey Apartments, opened a bottle of wine and took out a pencil. Four hours later he was still working on writings from 1529. Holding the open book against his chest, and then holding the mirror at arm's length gave Weatherby shoulder cramps after only thirty minutes. So he rigged a stand like an easel on a table top and placed the opened book on it. Then he placed a mirror on a stand on the desk. If he found if he adjusted the angle of the book and the mirror, he could see the letters in the correct order leaving his hands free to write. What a damnable nuisance. The old goat probably never read his own writing, he thought.

Based on his reading Weatherby concluded that Sir Rodney was relatively inactive during the winter months, spending his time reading and doing experiments in his chemistry lab. He had complained often of rheumatism in his joints. The word *artrite*, Latin for arthritis, kept recurring. However, with the coming of spring he had became much more active. He traveled around County Surrey in a horse-drawn cart attending cabals, consorting with witches and casting spells. If his journals were to be believed, despite his advanced age, he hadn't lost his potency. Most of his sexual partners were young country girls purported to be virgins. He paid them six pence per night. When given a preference, he seemed to prefer sleeping with enchantresses and sorceresses, no matter how old, because of their delightful powders and salves, he wrote. His favorite partner was an enchantress he affectionately called the Pythoness. Just the name gave Weatherby several unwanted graphic images that he tried to push out of his mind.

The journal also described several instances of animal sacrifice that seemed unnecessarily cruel. The goat, lamb, or bullock was skewered or shot with poison-tipped arrows or burned while still alive. Weatherby was relieved to find no description of human torture except for a young warlock who was pulled up, apparently willingly, between two birch trees by hooks buried in his shoulders and loins. Weatherby read for eight hours, calling for food as the evening wore on. He found the work tiring but also fascinating. He went to bed with burning eyes and mental fatigue.

In the morning he went to the Great Kitchen for breakfast and then took a quick walk along the Thames to clear his head. When he got back, Amarantha was waiting in his apartment. She gave him a warm hug before sitting down.

"The messenger returned from Ireland at midnight last night," she began. "While there he made discreet enquiries throughout County Kildare. He discovered that Sir Rodney Shrewsbury did, in fact, take residence at his county seat, Straffan house, four weeks ago and was last seen there two days ago. However, he has been peripatetic in the past and he could easily move on."

"I'll leave today for Ireland," Weatherby said. "Sir Rodney had proximity to our crimes, and he is capable of killing. Perhaps as I read more of his journals, I will discover a motive."

"I know you learned a lot on your trip to France, but I hated you being away so long and I worried about you every day," Amarantha said almost plaintively. "I have completed my tasks here, for now. May I come with you?"

"Of course you may," Weatherby said with delight in his voice. "I don't like traveling alone, and you are very good company."

"I'll have Dredge help me with travel arrangements," Amarantha replied.

Weatherby gathered some books and three of Sir Rodney's journals for the trip. With Dredge's help, the two travelers left Hampton by coach at mid-morning. They would travel west to Salisbury first. The coach held six passengers and was pulled by four horses. Fortunately, not many passengers were traveling that day. With a brief stop for dinner, they arrived in Salisbury at 9 p.m. It was late May and the English countryside was warm and in full bloom. Both Amarantha and Weatherby enjoyed the view out the windows as they bounced along the highway. Once in Salisbury, they stopped at a prosperous-looking inn in the center of town, and after eating a savory meal of beef stew, they retired.

The coach to Bristol didn't leave until 10 a.m., so Amarantha and Weatherby arose early, had breakfast and explored the town. Neither of them had ever been to the famous old town located on the plain that was once called Sarum. They explored the old part of town full of limestone and half-timbered buildings with thatched roofs and then focused their attention on the cathedral. It was of pale grey limestone and located away from the town in a grassy park. The inside was spare with lots of windows of clear glass. Weatherby found it very unlike the cathedral at Chartres, which was dark and gloomy inside. They found the church spire impressive, and spent a long time just gazing up at it. It rose from the roof of the church as a square tower with long slender windows and then soared above that in a tapering spire. Weatherby discovered that it was four hundred and four feet tall, surely the tallest building in England.

The ride to Bristol was shorter than the first day's ride and over good, smooth roads. Weatherby flinched when he first climbed aboard as he noticed a lady in a lace-covered yellow dress sitting in the corner. For a moment he was afraid it was Mrs. Fartingdown, the busybody on the Royal Barge. However, as he nodded toward her, he realized that he was mistaken. Amarantha was soon deep in conversation with the lady, a Mrs. Pinkerton from Bristol.

The coach arrived in Bristol, England's third biggest city, in late afternoon. Mrs. Pinkerton had invited Amarantha and Weatherby to spend the night with her so they rode in her carriage to her house overlooking the Bristol Channel. The trio spent the rest of afternoon wandering around her gardens, followed by supper and cards. In the morning, Mrs. Pinkerton had them taken to the harbor so they could sail across the Irish Sea along with fourteen other passengers and a cargo of English barley and lumber. They boarded a three-masted barque named the *Earl of Pembroke*. Dredge had informed them that the distance was one hundred and eighty miles across the Irish Sea, and that the passage would take at least three days.

Amarantha and Weatherby shared a cabin on the main deck. The first day they sailed west along Bristol Channel close to Wales on the starboard side. The boat traffic was heavy and they passed the towns of Cardiff and Swansea. The swell was three to four feet and the sky was blue. As they sailed into a prevailing wind, the sails were backed. Weatherby sat on the foredeck reading his journals. Amarantha found two ladies to visit with and did needle point. The meals were simple but tasty food that focused on things from the sea such as cod, plaice and cockles. The fourteen passengers sat at one long table and conversed congenially. In the evening Seamus and Ran sat on the afterdeck, wrapped in blankets while they watched the sky fill with stars. The wind died after sunset but their ship was still making way. Both talked about their wishes and dreams and their hopes for the future.

The ship rounded St. Govan's Head and then St. David's Head before turning north along the coast of Wales, where the *Earl of Pembroke* added sail and picked up speed. By the middle of the third day, the ship stood off Dublin, but a strong westerly wind blew toward the vessel, preventing it from reaching the docks. The captain tacked the ship to the north and then to the south slowly drawing nearer to land. Finally at 5 p.m., the hawsers were tossed from the *Earl*, securing her to the chocks on the dock. Rather than staying in Dublin, Weatherby and Amarantha took a coach to County Kildare. They didn't have their land legs yet after three days of pitching on the Irish Sea, but they didn't want Shrewsbury to escape when they were so close. The arrived at 11 p.m. and checked into the Two Sisters, a small hotel, down the hill from Straffan House. Once settled in their rooms, they went into the public house on the ground floor, which was packed with locals. They decided to separate so they could pump more of the locals for information. After each got a pint of ale, they started buying drinks for the indigenous population and talking about Sir Rodney Shrewsbury. The village people were taciturn at first, but after a little alcohol they became much more talkative. Amarantha learned that Sir Rodney had been at Straffan House for the past four weeks, his longest visit in years. Weatherby learned that there were loud parties involving women imported from Dublin almost every night. Over all, the town's people found Sir Shrewsbury an eccentric but someone who was good for the locality as he bought goods and provided jobs. Exhausted, Weatherby and Amarantha stumbled up to bed at 1 a.m., still a little unsteady from their ocean voyage.

# CHAPTER 57

Early the next morning, Weatherby and Amarantha arrived at the dark green front door of Straffan House. The butler took their cards and disappeared for fifteen minutes.

"Please, return at 2 p.m.," he said in a formal voice after reopening the large door just a crack.

Amarantha and Weatherby walked back arm and arm down the hill.

"We have enough time to go into Dublin, rather than waiting in this little village," Amarantha suggested.

"Great idea, Ran. I will hail a hansom," Weatherby replied as he waved his arm.

As they rode into Dublin, Weatherby was impressed by the number of small, poorly built houses that lacked even chimneys. They debarked in the center of town and walked to Trinity College, founded about forty years earlier. It had three small buildings and a large parade ground in the center. As they walked about, Weatherby estimated that ten or twelve thousand lived in Dublin, making it about the size of York.

"This is a poor, undeveloped city for the capital of a country," Amarantha remarked as they crossed a muddy street.

"I understand that the rest of the country refuses to accept the rule of Dublin and that leads to fighting all around the capital," Weatherby replied.

He hailed a carriage and had them taken to Bullock Castle on Dublin Bay. A kindly monk took them on a tour.

"The structure was built in the thirteenth century by the Cistercian Monks," the friar intoned as he led them up the steps.

Weatherby enjoyed historical lectures of this kind, but Amarantha found them boring.

"The Castle was meant to guard the coast against marauding pirates," the monk continued.

Bullock Castle itself consisted of two stout limestone towers each with a fanciful stepped stone design along the top. Both tourists were out of breath by the time they reached the top.

"What a spectacular view," Weatherby said as he gasped for breath.

The bay and then the Irish Sea lay before them with the golden, morning sun shining across it. To their right and left was a sinuous green coastline dotted with villages. Peat smoke rose lazily from the holes in the roofs of many cottages. Suddenly, both travelers were very hungry. They thanked their guide and gave him two Angels for his trouble. They found a tavern near the Castle, where they ate steaming shepherd's pie washed down with a chocolate-flavored black ale.

When they arrived back at Straffan House at the appointed hour, they were shown into an elegant drawing room full of delicate furniture and rich hangings. Weatherby noticed the walls were a pale green with rich cream baseboards and wainscoting. The chairs were finely constructed with subtle carving and rich yellow upholstery. Amarantha thought it showed a woman's touch. Weatherby noticed a three-quarter view painting of a man in a rich black suit hanging over the mantel. He nudged Amarantha and lifted his head toward the painting. Once they were seated a slender white-haired woman entered and greeted them both.

"I am Sir Rodney's niece, Miss Colleen Shrewsbury, and I manage Straffan House for my uncle, as he is often away," she said sitting daintily on the very edge of a chair. "What business do you have with him, if I may ask?"

"We are from Hampton Court Palace," Weatherby began tentatively. "And we have some valuable property that we believe might belong to Sir Rodney."

"How kind of you both to come so far," Miss Shrewsbury replied. "Perhaps you could give me the items and I might show them to my Uncle."

"I'm afraid our instructions from our King, Henry VIII, are to show these items only to the purported owner, your uncle," Amarantha replied smoothly, falling in with Weatherby's deception.

"Unfortunately, he is surveying some of his remote lands with his overseer and won't return before mid-day tomorrow," Miss Shrewsbury replied.

"Thank you for you time," Weatherby said as he rose and Amarantha followed his lead. "May I ask about the remarkable painting over the mantel?"

"Yes," Miss Shrewsbury replied. "It is by William Cork and it is a portrait of my uncle, Sir Rodney Shrewsbury."

"Thank you for your time," Weatherby said with a slight bow.

The butler escorted them to the large front door. As they walked down the hill, they tried to assess what they had learned.

"I think Colleen is lying," Amarantha said.

"About the painting?"

"No, about her uncle."

"I think you are right. After all, she is related to Sir Rodney."

"So either Sir Rodney is there and hiding or he has already decamped."

"How large are his holdings?"

"The book I read in our library suggests that his family owns 4,000 hectares."

"I own some small farms in Scotland and their deeds are in hectares. So, my overseer tells me that there are two hundred and fifty-nine hectares per square mile. How many square miles does Sir Rodney own?"

Amarantha furrowed her brow and did the arithmetic in her head twice, "Roughly fifteen square miles," she replied.

"So he could hide anywhere on his vast property or in some witch's clavern in Dublin, Ran, and we would never find him."

"We came a long way to confront Sir Rodney. I hate going home empty-handed," Amarantha said in a discouraged voice.

"This is a dirty, primitive, poor excuse for a country, Ran. I think it's time to bribe some people with the King's money."

"Let's go back to the Two Sisters and see if the tipplers want to talk," Amarantha suggested as she walked in that direction.

As Amarantha and Weatherby entered the windowless taproom of the Two Sisters, neither of them could see for a few minutes. They stood near the door, letting their eyes adjust. As soon as they could see shapes, they moved slowly toward a table of drinkers. Amarantha picked a young working man and bought him a drink while she batted her eyes in his direction.

"I'm a Welsh girl who got lured here by an older gentleman," Amarantha said, remembering that the Irish hate the English. "I was wondering. Could you help me find him?"

"Is it a wee bit of help your needing, lass?" the workman said in a thick Irish brogue.

"What's your name?"

"Erin Garmagh."

"Could you help me find Sir Rodney Shrewsbury?"

"Aye. I live in the village and know the lot."

"Have you seen him recently?"

"Aye. He was here himself, Thursday last."

"Is he still in the area?"

"I can obtain that for thee."

"It's worth three Sovereigns to me."

"I'll check on that man there and be back afore nightfall."

Weatherby had begun talking to a distinguished-looking man in a rich doublet. He turned out to be the local solicitor who had helped Sir Rodney Shrewsbury on several occasions with altercations involving his neighbors.

"He's a scoundrel, that," the solicitor said vehemently.

"I know he has been at Straffan House these past weeks," Weatherby said. "And I'm hoping he is still here."

"I believe that he is," Solicitor Joyce answered.

"We have come a long way to interview him. Is there any way to know if he is at Straffan House?"

"He's a shifty devil, but I can probably help you with that."

"I would be eternally in your debt." Weatherby said with relief in his voice.

"I will meet you back here at 8 p.m. for supper with an answer," the solicitor replied.

"I will treat you to that, if I may."

The solicitor rose and left the Two Sisters.

The pub was packed with drinkers. Weatherby and Amarantha went to a private table beside the fireplace to compare notes. It seemed as though they had two moles that would search for Sir Rodney; however, they wouldn't have an answer for at least two hours. They walked to a restaurant in the village called the Wild Rose and ate a leisurely dinner. They started with Dublin Bay prawns followed by roast venison and cabbage. Then they both had Irish apple pie with heavy cream. When they were finished eating, the investigators strolled back to the Two Sisters through the cluttered and dirty streets of the village.

The solicitor that Weatherby had spoken with was sitting at the bar when they walked in. Weatherby made the introductions.

"I talked with two people who give me scuttlebutt. They both think that Sir Rodney left Straffan House the day before yesterday. He took four suitcases with him, suggesting that he would be gone for weeks or perhaps for good. No one on the wait staff at the house heard him say where he was going."

"Thank you for your help," Weatherby said as he tried to give Solicitor Joyce a stack of coins.

The barrister declined and left. Weatherby and Amarantha ordered pints of the dark, local brew that they had come to favor, and waited. An hour later, Erin Garmagh entered.

Without preamble he said, "That man there left Straffan House two day ago. He waren't come back soon."

"That is what we heard, also," Amarantha said in a discouraged tone. "Have you any idea where he went?"

"Aye. Tis' him I be thinking is in Dublin," Garmagh replied as his brogue got even thicker.

"Do you have any idea where in the city?" Weatherby asked.

"Aye. He does be going to a knocking shop along the river."

"Do you know its name?" Amarantha queried.

"Aye. The Silver Cloud."

Weatherby handed Garmagh a stack of coins and got up hurriedly. As soon as he and Amarantha got to the street, he hailed a hansom, gave him the name of the Silver Cloud and offered extra coins for a fast trip. The roads from Kildare to Dublin were rutted and narrow, but the driver didn't let that stop him. He took Weatherby at his word. Both passengers were thrown around in the coach even when hanging on with both hands. The driver came to a halt on a rundown street of buildings in poor repair. However, the Silver Cloud was a stately two-story building of red brick with well manicured landscaping around it. A liveried doorman in white gloves stood on the steps.

Weatherby initially planned on going into the Silver Cloud acting like a customer, but he couldn't figure out a way to peek into the parlors and the various rooms to find his quarry. Instead, he decided to send Amarantha in and have her pretend that she was applying for a position as a strumpet. Hopefully the madam would show her around and she could peek into the parlors and bedrooms looking for Sir Rodney. Amarantha was wearing an attractive, slightly low-cut dress and he felt that she could play the part convincingly. Always a willing participant, Amarantha sauntered up the walk swinging her hips, and pinching color into her cheeks.

# CHAPTER 58

Weatherby got out of the hansom and sat on a bench under a tree in front of the upscale house of ill repute. He expected Amarantha's visit to take a couple of hours, so he didn't grow concerned until over three hours had passed and it was 11 p.m. At that point, he began to look at his clock more often, staring intently at the male patrons coming down the wide steps of the house. Suddenly, Amarantha burst through the door, walking as fast as she could in her tight dress. She ran over to the tree where Weatherby was sitting.

"I'm pretty sure that Sir Rodney was in one of the back bedrooms with two young trollops," Amarantha said breathlessly.

"Are you sure?" Weatherby replied.

"No. But I saw his picture at Straffan House and I have a feeling that it was him," Amarantha said. "He was pulling his clothes on when I left and has a horse drawn carriage out back."

'Let's go," Weatherby said grabbing Amarantha's hand.

They ran to their hansom and raced to the back of the bawdy house. As they rounded the corner an older man jumped into a two-wheeled carriage. Weatherby's hansom had the advantage of being under way, but the vehicle they were chasing had the benefit of being lighter and having only one passenger, who was also the driver. Weatherby recognized the vehicle as being a fast conveyance called a calash. The driver whipped his horse and headed away from the river. The hansom fell back initially, but then began to gain on the calash. Just as they were getting close, the two-wheeled vehicle made a sharp right turn. One of the hansom horses kicked over its traces on the turn, and the driver had to jump down quickly and readjust the harness.

"What makes you think we are chasing Sir Rodney?" Weatherby asked as he was jostled around inside the carriage.

"When the Madam offered me the job, she said that a lot of prominent and wealthy men visited her establishment. I asked specifically about Sir Rodney Shrewsbury. She replied that he was a frequent customer and a big tipper. Then she raised her head over her shoulder to imply that he was upstairs right then."

In a narrow part of the road, the hansom slowed briefly behind a loaded wagon. When the road widened, it sped past. Looking out the window, Weatherby saw an approaching barouche pulled by one white horse lose its wheel. The slender, iron-rimmed wheel came rolling toward the hansom and clattered against the side before falling in the roadstead. Weatherby looked out again. He hoped that the small black horse pulling the calash might be tiring. Weatherby's driver pulled closer, but just as they were about to come along side, the smaller carriage made an abrupt left turn. The larger hansom had to slow considerably to make the awkward turn. Once around the corner, Weatherby could see that the calash had gained a half a block. Weatherby was surprised by all the traffic since it was now almost midnight. Over the next several blocks, the hansom once again pulled closer. Derelicts ran across the road in front of the hansom twice yet the driver didn't slow at all. The road now was slightly uphill and the two-horse carriage seemed a little faster. Then the calash turned to the left once again onto a wider busier street. The lighter, smaller vehicle maneuvered between the wagons and pedestrians more agilely, and gradually began to pull away. Weatherby looked at Amarantha as she clung to two leather straps inside the coach as it lurched and twisted.

"Are you all right? Should we stop?" he yelled in her direction.

"Of course not. I want to catch the blighter as much as you do," Amarantha yelled back as her hair fell down in her face.

Suddenly, the hansom screeched to a halt throwing them forward, on top of each other. They unscrambled themselves, opened the door and stepped down onto the roadway. A large wagon pulled by oxen and filled to overflowing with a load of barrels had pulled in front of them and completely blocked the roadway. The calash disappeared down a hill.

"Sorry, Your Lordship," the driver said as he struggled for breath.

"You have nothing to be sorry about, good Sir," Weatherby replied. "You almost had him. Your horses are spent and we will never catch him now. Once your horses are rested and watered, please take us to the docks."

When they arrived at the wharf, Weatherby rewarded the driver handsomely. As luck would have it, the *Earl of Pembroke* had arrived that evening and would sail on the morning tide. The driver carried their luggage aboard and placed it in their usual stateroom on the port side. On the voyage from Bristol the port side had taken most of the spray and should be on the leeward side going back. Weatherby and Amarantha went to a dockside inn for supper and a few hours sleep.

The trip back across the Irish Sea was faster thanks to the prevailing wind at the ships stern. Before boarding Weatherby and Amarantha rested and read and talked about Sir Rodney.

"I'm quite sure that Sir Rodney committed the murders at Hampton Court," Amarantha said. "He was at the Palace when they were committed, he had the means in his laboratory and he is a known murderer."

"You may well be right, Ran," Weatherby replied. "But the three victims barely knew each other, and we have established no links between them. What was Sir Rodney's motive?"

"I think he simply enjoyed the thrill of snuffing out three young lives and then getting away with it," Amarantha replied. "He's laughing at us, just like he did when he outran us in Dublin. He didn't have a driver for that speedy carriage, he drove it himself. Despite being an old man, he outwitted us."

The trip back across the Irish Sea was faster, thanks to the prevailing wind. When the *Earl of Pembroke* docked in Bristol, Mrs. Beverly Pinkerton's carriage was waiting for Weatherby and Amarantha. They spent two days at the widow's home on the bay. They spent the evening at entertainments for her friends and neighbors followed by cards. During the day, they rode noble horses from her stable. Sometimes they rode in the hills, but mostly they rode along the shore. They were on hard sand beaches, so they galloped and cantered along the edge of the sea. The riding was so idyllic that Amarantha suggested staying a couple more days.

"I can't imagine anything more wonderful, Amarantha," Weatherby said with a smile. "However, the murderer is still loose. We had a great holiday, but now there is work to do."

The next morning Weatherby and Amarantha took a coach back to Salisbury and then the next morning traveled back to Hampton Court Palace. Dredge awaited them as they entered the Base Court. He seemed to have truly missed them both. He was very animated, talking fast and quickly, and took both of their suitcases from them.

"What has happened in the twelve days we were gone?" Amarantha asked as the three marched to Amarantha's apartment and then to the Great Kitchen for some food.

"Surprisingly little," Dredge began. "Dr. Wickham was found dead in his apartment shortly after you left. The apothecary thought he died of heart failure brought on by overwork during the epidemic."

"So we don't have to add him to our list of murder victims?" Weatherby said in a joking tone.

"Most definitely not," Dredge replied seriously. "I spent several days cataloguing the raw materials in Sir Rodney's laboratory. However, analyzing the residue in his beaker and flasks proved the most revealing. He had large quantities of lead, aqua regia, and unusual stones from other parts of the world. He was working on a universal solvent, a panacea or substance that would cure all diseases, and transmutation of the elements. Being venal, his main effort was to change lead into gold. He had journals full of the various experiments that he tried."

"What about poisons?" Weatherby asked.

"I've just begun working on a shelf full of opaque glass bottles in fantastical shapes," Dredge responded. "I wondered if they might contain poisons. I fed a drop of a green liquid from a dusty red and purple bottle to one of the mice in our laboratory, and he convulsed and died within a minute. I also found a hollow ring that could be used to secretly slip poison into a drink. The evil and conniving Lucrezia Borgia had a similar ring."

"We need to know if any of his poisons are related to the one with the aroma of bitter rose that took Anna Maria Wimbledon's life," Weatherby replied.

"I will have more answers in a week," Dredge said as he poured himself another cup of tea.

"I suppose a quiet interval at the Palace was normal after the agitation and panic associated with the sweating sickness."

"Except for Richard Weston! I forgot about the Master of the House when you asked if anything happened while you were gone."

"At last some gossip," Amarantha said with relief in her voice.

"Well you know how little we see him," Dredge began. "He's such a recluse. Then just after you left for Ireland, he held a very public and emotional service in the chapel for the Palace residents who died in the epidemic. Of course, the service was conducted by a priest, but Weston spoke before and after the service. Attendance was mandatory, and then we all walked to the common grave east of the Palace where all the bodies were buried for a benediction."

"That sort of display is very out of character for him," Weatherby replied thoughtfully. "The Chancellor warned me that Weston might break apart at any time."

"The next thing he did was even more shocking," Dredge said excitedly. "Just two days later there was a mandatory assembly in the Clock Court. When we gathered there, Weston spoke about the evil of employees stealing food from the Palace and selling it in town for money. Then he had a young chambermaid dragged into the Court and tied to a plank. He proceeded to tear her shift off of her back and lashed her naked back with a leather whip. Her screams reverberated from the walls. Then unbelievably, he had her turned around and lashed her breasts and belly. Fortunately, she fainted, but the blood from the lash stained her buttocks and legs. Two of the guards carried her away, and Weston turned to the crowd and looked at us with a lustful and demonic glare."

"Your description gives me the shivers," Amarantha replied.

# CHAPTER 59

Weatherby was glad to be back in familiar surroundings, and he slept soundly. The next morning he continued his work on Sir Rodney's journals. Meanwhile, Dredge worked on analyzing the cache of poison he had found, and Amarantha catalogued the clothing and other items discovered in the hidden rooms. Weatherby wondered about Sir Rodney's new whereabouts. He decided to use the King's network of paid informants to try to discover his current location. He wrote a note to the Chancellor and enclosed a page detailing all that he knew about Shrewsbury and sent it off. He requested that possible sightings be reported to him by fast courier so that he could follow up before the suspect moved. Weatherby also asked that Sir Rodney's assets throughout the realm be seized in an effort to hamper the suspected killer's movements. Although, he supposed that Shrewsbury's Irish holdings would continue to give him the resources he needed to indulge his every whim.

With a little investigation, Weatherby had discovered that Sir Rodney was not only a patron of the Silver Cloud but also the owner. He was sure a house of prostitution was looked on as a respectable enterprise in Ireland just as it was in England. When Amarantha had applied for a job at the Silver Cloud, she was told if she worked hard and developed return visitors that she might make as much as fourteen Angels or seven Sovereigns a week.

Weatherby was reading the journal for 1514 in a mirror when a messenger knocked. Once in the room, the man turned toward Sir Weatherby.

"They have found a body in the village, Your Grace," the messenger said. "And they asked me to fetch you."

"That's a job for the constables and outside my jurisdiction," Weatherby said without hesitation as he continued to translate the Latin words he saw in the mirror.

"Yes, Your Grace. However, the constable thinks the victim was a resident of the Palace, Sir, and requests your assistance."

"Oh, very well," Weatherby replied in an exasperated tone. "Where is the body?"

"I will take you there, Sir."

"I will need some time to assemble some instruments. Wait by the Great Gatehouse."

"Very well, Sir."

Weatherby walked quickly to the laboratory and informed Dredge, so that he could assemble the tools they would need. As he continued on to the Great Gatehouse, Weatherby reflected on this new turn of events. He now had four unfortunate murder victims and only one suspect, who he was quite sure wasn't even in the country. Once this news reached the Chancellor and through him the King, he felt it likely that he would lose the job that he had so enjoyed for the past five years. His excellent reputation for solving cases was being tarnished. Long ago he realized, as few did, that murderers were a dimwitted, careless, prevaricating lot, which typically made snaring them child's play. His current quarry had none of those characteristics.

Once Dredge arrived, the messenger led the investigators across the bridge and into the village of Hampton. They walked along High Street and beyond the bounds of the village. The courier led them to a tumbled-down cottage with an old thatched roof and crooked windows. Both Weatherby and Dredge recognized it immediately as the gambling den where Dredge had lost seven Sovereigns playing a rigged dice game. Two of the constable's men were lazing around the entrance talking. Weatherby and Dredge entered the dark, dank, smelling cottage and asked for the Constable.

"I understand that perhaps someone from the Palace met his end here," Weatherby began, hoping it wasn't true or at least that if it was true it was someone he didn't know well.

"Yes, Your Grace," Constable Claude Wilson said, bowing slightly. "We have a feeling that he is one of yours."

A body was slumped over one of the dice tables with the victim's face lying in a pool of dark red blood. As he lifted the victim's head Weatherby noted that the dead man's throat was deeply cut in a jagged line. Dredge handed Weatherby a cloth which he used to wipe the clotted blood from the dead man's face. As Dredge approached with a candle, Weatherby looked into the man's still-open eyes.

"By Jove," Weatherby exclaimed. "I believe this is Nathaniel Philbrick! Let me quickly sketch the scene so that we can move the body outside to get a better look."

Dredge had already set up the easel. He placed twelve candles near the body as Weatherby took out a charcoal and began to sketch the scene with large rapid strokes. While he drew, he talked to Constable Wilson.

"Nathaniel was a talented glazier trained near Venice on the island of Murano," Weatherby began. "The most luminous glasses in the world comes from that small island. I don't know why he came back to England, but one winter night in a Greenwich bar he got in a fight over a woman. He stabbed the other man who then inconveniently died."

Weatherby stepped back to examine his sketch and be sure he hadn't missed any details.

"Philbrick went to the Tower for the murder and, by all rights, he should have rotted there," Weatherby mumbled, mostly to himself, as the constable had walked away. "But when Henry took Hampton Court from Cardinal Wolsey, he needed talented artisans for his grandiose building project. He combed his kingdom for artisans and Nathaniel Philbrick's name came up."

Weatherby motioned for the body to be moved. Two of the constables carried the corpse to the front of the house and dumped it unceremoniously in the weeds. Dredge turned the body over. Weatherby took his large glass magnifying glass out of pocket and knelt down next to the body. He checked for the four *mortises,* just as he had with each of the three murder victims. Then he made a sketch of the gaping neck wound that now looked like a ghoulish maroon toothless smile.

Weatherby stood up and said, "It is indeed Nathaniel Philbrick, the master glazier, and *rigor mortis* is moderate. I believe he died at around 2 a.m. I would like to take the body to my laboratory for further examination."

The constable's men placed the body in a wagon and departed under Dredge's direction.

"Is this death akin to the three murders at the Palace?" the constable asked.

"Ah, that is the true question, my good man," Weatherby said. "I am unsure, but I will think long and hard on it."

Weatherby ambled back toward the village lost in thought. When he walked through the Clock Tower, he sought out Amarantha and then Warder Chertsey.

"I need access to Nathaniel Philbrick's quarters," Weatherby said to the Warder.

"Follow me," replied Chertsey.

He lead them on a convoluted course to the east and then into the old gallery along the Knot Garden, talking as he went.

"Most of the master craftsmen have rooms in this area. This gallery was built by Wolsey in 1514," Chertsey said as he stopped at a darkly stained oak door.

He took a key from a ring on his sash and opened the lock. The room was dark and musty. Amarantha went to the window and threw back the drapes. The light revealed a chamber that was cluttered with clothing, glass-blowing tools and stacks of parchment paper, covered with designs for glass windows, hangings and ceilings. Shards and samples of glass in every color of the rainbow were everywhere.

"Be careful, Ran, there are a lot of sharp objects in this room," Weatherby cautioned.

Many books were scattered about. He wondered whether Nathaniel Philbrick had a split personality—part barroom and gambling den brawler, and part esthetically talented artisan. He suspected that the two sides battled fiercely for his soul, and that in the end the lawless brawler had triumphed.

"We will need help to sort and catalogue everything in this room," Weatherby said. "Amarantha see if you can get Dredge and the two assistant librarians to help us after lunch."

Before getting started, Weatherby and his workers gathered in the orchard for a relaxing meal. The trees were well leafed-out and provided shade against the warm summer sun. Small apples, peaches and pears were already developing on the branches above them. They had a large salad of fresh endive, followed by an onion and beet salad flavored with vinegar. The main course was fire-roasted woodcocks filled with bread and sage stuffing. Three bottles of French red wine completed the feast. Weatherby ordered a daryole for dessert, even though it was his least favorite sweet. A small card was buried within the cheese cake inviting Weatherby to pay a visit. It was signed by Ellen Iverson. She was a person he truly liked even though she had berated him brashly about his visit to local house of prostitution during their first encounter. He vowed to visit her the next day.

The dark abode of the late Nathaniel Philbrick was a sharp contrast to the warmth of the orchard. Weatherby set Judith Scotson and Margaret Sedgwick to cataloguing and arranging all of the books in the room. Before starting, they had the books carted to the library so that everyone might have more room. Warder Chertsey was given the unpleasant task of picking up and discarding all of the soiled and torn clothing that lay on the floor, the bed, and the bureau. Having seen Weatherby angry previously, Chertsey did not complain out loud.

# CHAPTER 60

"I want to arrange the glass by color and then by shape if that seems appropriate," Weatherby told Dredge. "Of course, I want you to look diligently on the pieces for any of the linear A or linear B writing that has been frustrating us."

"Yes, Sir," Dredge replied. "I estimate that there are thirteen hundred scraps of glass in this small room. It may take a while."

"I will begin going through this huge stack of parchments," Weatherby said in a resigned tone. Many were designs for glass windows and structures, but others were covered with writing. "Ran, I want you to search the nooks and crannies of this room for a hidden diary or anything else he didn't want us to find."

Weatherby arranged a candelabrum, took out his magnifying glass and started perusing parchments. He soon realized that Philbrick had been an inspired designer. The drawings showed intricate designs and diverse colors yet always had a congruent wholeness that was very pleasing to the eye.

Warder Chertsey finished first. All the other investigators worked into the evening and then adjourned to the library for a cold supper. They were all hungry, but after they had eaten a bit they began to share information about the day's discoveries.

Judith Scotson spoke first, "We have catalogued half of the books alphabetically by author. Many are works of history and many are volumes of fiction. What we are finding is very prosaic. Unlike Sir Rodney's library, there is nothing about astrology, necromancy or torture."

Next Weatherby reported on the parchments. "Most of the pages are covered with exquisite designs for glass windows, as I said. However, some have notes about people who live in the Palace and a few mention townsmen. They tend to be quite insightful and personal. I suspect those rough notes were transferred to another volume like a diary."

"I have searched most of the room and haven't turned up a diary," Amarantha volunteered.

Weatherby's countrymen were compulsive and diligent diarists, and that men were as afflicted with the need to write as women. He strongly suspected that Philbrick had such a treasured tome, and that they only needed to find it.

"It doesn't sound like we found much after a long day of searching."

"I found something," Dredge said. "I just don't know what it is. Philbrick had weights on the floor attached to two letter straps that go to pulleys in the ceiling."

"How very strange," Amarantha said.

"I believe I know what it is," Weatherby replied. "It sounds like one of the torture devices that were used during the Catholic Inquisition in Spain to obtain confessions. The rack is more widely known, but with the device you are describing the person's feet are anchored to the floor and then his hands are strapped behind his back and tightened over a pulley anchored to the ceiling. As the victim is lifted off the ground he either confesses or his shoulders become dislocated. I believe this evil device it is called a *strappado*. We need to look for references to it in his books and journals."

"Perhaps he used it like Anna Maria's hair shirt to inflict self-mortification," Dredge suggested.

"Perhaps, but it would be difficult or impossible to use if both hands were bound behind your back," Weatherby retorted.

"I suggest one of your inductive experiments to solve the issue," Amarantha replied in a taunting tone.

"Aren't you a quick study, Ran," Weatherby replied. "Of course I agree, but remember it is Galileo Galilei's method and not mine. Let's gather in the victim's room in the morning at eight of the clock to continue our investigation."

The hour was late, but Amarantha and Weatherby took a bottle of wine to her apartment to drink while they read. They had a fire laid for the friendliness and cheer it brought to the room. It was late May and the nights were deliciously warm so the fire was no longer needed for warmth. Amarantha read a book of Italian plays recently translated into Dutch. Weatherby was working on a new treatise by his mentor, Anton van Leeuwenhoek, about his latest discoveries with the compound microscope. This essay was also in Dutch, which vexed Weatherby. He had to interrupt Amarantha frequently so that she might translate a word or a phrase. Eventually, Amarantha's head began to nod over her slender leather volume, so Weatherby politely excused himself.

At eight the next morning, Weatherby and Amarantha gathered in Philbrick's dark apartment. Dredge had obviously been working for a couple of hours already. He had sewn together a life-sized leather man and filled him with grain so that he had a realistic weight. Weatherby helped him anchor the dummy's feet to the floor with the weights. Then they strapped his arms behind his back, and pulled on the strap raising the leather man's arms toward the ceiling. The strap traveled several feet over the pulleys before the arms assumed an unnatural angle to the body.

"How could Philbrick do this by himself?" Weatherby asked.

"He could have held the rope in his bound hands and inched it down between his fingers tightening it," Dredge replied thoughtfully.

"Perhaps," Weatherby replied, but he was unconvinced.

"Or he could have only strapped one arm at a time and used the other arm to tighten the rope."

"True. However, he was a bully and a murderer," Amarantha said. "He inflicted pain and suffering on others, not on himself. Why wouldn't he just bring a victim here from time to time and torture the man or woman by tightening the rope and then releasing the rope for his own pleasure?"

"The victim would scream," Dredge retorted.

"This part of the Palace is sparsely populated, and all he would have to do is put a strip of linen in his sufferer's mouth," Weatherby offered.

"I think we need to test Dredge's two ideas about self-mortification," Amarantha said.

"The dummy is very well done and must have taken hours to build, Dredge," Weatherby said. "But I think we need a real person to test your theories."

Dredge stood up immediately and moved the replica aside.

"I admire your pluck," Weatherby replied. "But I am afraid your skeletal abnormalities would prejudice the results."

Amarantha moved toward the *strappado*.

"I will not allow you, Ran," Weatherby said quickly. "To be picked up by your delicate arms. I am the one that needs to be strapped into that infernal machine."

Weatherby removed his doublet and stepped forward. Dredge placed the leather sleeve connected to the rope around his boss's left wrist and handed the other end of the rope to Weatherby. He inched his fingers up the rope, but the weight of his other arm soon stopped his progress. He found that if he held the rope in his teeth between pulls, he could put uncomfortable pressure on his arm, but without having his other arm bound, eventually his left arm rotated laterally and extended easily toward the ceiling.

"When only one arm is bound the anatomy of the shoulder joint defeats the pain this device can inflict," Weatherby concluded.

Next he put both of his hands together behind his back. Then Dredge put the leather straps around both wrists and Weatherby swung his body back until he grasped the rope between his fingers. He worked his way up the rope with first one hand and then the other, pulling the rope through the pulley. In that way, he pulled both hands up some, but the weight of his arms soon overcame the strength of his hands.

"I can't apply enough pressure this way to even give me a twinge of pain," Weatherby observed. "Give the rope a pull please, Ran."

Amarantha stepped forward and grasped the rough fibers of the rope with both hands and pulled.

As he winced, Weatherby said through clenched teeth, "Now that hurts my shoulders, and also my back."

Amarantha quickly released the rope, and Dredge unbound Weatherby's wrists. Weatherby turned to his journal and quickly recorded the results of the experiment with a quill dipped in ink. He included two quick sketches. After he was done, they went to the Wolsey Apartments where Weatherby had ordered a large breakfast. They helped themselves to scones with grape jelly, bacon and eggs and small fresh oranges that had come from the Orangerie at Whitehall Palace. Once they had eaten a bit, Dredge spoke up.

"I found three references to *strappado* in our library last night," he began. "It was sometimes used on unbelievers but mostly it was used on the Catholics' own pious friars to make them confess to heresy and blasphemy. You mentioned the weights on the legs. They could be increased so that the legs as well as the shoulders became dislocated when the rope was tightened. Then some sadistic torturer in rural Spain found that if the body was raised off the ground and dropped suddenly, the pain was even greater. This was called *squassation*."

"How horrible!" Amarantha said.

"I'm recollecting something about one of our previous victims, Dredge," Weatherby remarked. "Bring me the autopsy report on the third murder victim, Gregory Townsend, if you would."

Dredge limped off toward the laboratory. While he was gone, Amarantha and Weatherby made a date for a ride for the next afternoon. Both thought the balmy June days were too wonderful to spend them totally indoors. When he returned, Dredge handed Weatherby the large leather volume of autopsy reports. He leafed through the pages quickly.

"Here it is," He said excitedly. "Townsend's right shoulder was dislocated. At the time we attributed it to the fall from the tower, but I wonder if it wasn't the *strappado*."

"So you believe that Nathaniel Philbrick murdered Gregory Townsend!" Amarantha exclaimed.

"Not necessarily. But he may have tortured him before his murder. I never felt that one person, even a person as strong as Clarence Stevens, could have carried the Reverend to the top of the Great Gatehouse and flung him off the parapet, but Philbrick could have been one of the accomplices."

"Philbrick was a slight man. I don't think he was strong enough to even help lift a body," Dredge said.

"We must return to Philbrick's room and find his diary so we can respond to these inconsistencies," Amarantha said as she arose.

# PART 7

# CHAPTER 61

Weatherby walked from the Wolsey Apartment through the Clock Court and across the Base Court. After he walked through the Great Gatehouse, he turned right toward the Outer Court, pondering that the Outer Court housed most of the operations that stank and employed fire that might spread to the rest of the Palace. Not a winning combination. The Office of the Greencloth, where accounting was performed, was also housed there for reasons that Weatherby didn't understand. He continued on toward the Confectory.

He peered through the upper half of the Dutch door that led into the Confectory. As usual, Ellen Iverson was cooking a steaming pot of something delicious. He was relieved to see that she looked fully recovered from the episode of sweating sickness. Today she was stirring a large vat of daryole with a long wooden paddle. Her face dripped with sweat, and a strand of hair stuck to her forehead.

"Come in here this instant, Doctor Weatherby," Ellen yelled out. "I haven't had a chance to thank you properly for saving me from the sweating sickness."

"You are most welcome," Weatherby replied, opening the door. "Even though we got off to a rough start, you are one of my favorite people at Hampton Court. I was quite worried about you when you presented at the Great Hall with the signs of the disease."

"That's because I'm old and fat."

"From the large wet circles under your arms and your sweaty face, I'm wondering if the dreaded sweat hasn't returned," Weatherby said in jest.

"I'm just fine. Come and sit. I have fresh gingerbread husbands."

"We always have these hurried talks while you try to fill the endless sweet tooth of the Palace inhabitants. Today I want to take you for a leisurely lunch in the village."

"What a lovely offer! Let me finish this pot of daryole and we can go."

Ellen pushed the burning pieces of wood off to the side and spooned the sweet, cheesy mixture into small dishes. She took off her apron and hung it on a peg by the door. They walked out of the Outer Court away from the Palace, past the Office of the Greencloth, the Jewel House, a scalding house, a poultry house, a rush house, a baking house, and a wood yard. Weatherby noted that they all were built as frame buildings, not the beautiful rich red bricks of the Palace. All were located away from Hampton Court itself, Sir Moulton had explained, because they were noxious-smelling or a fire danger. Weatherby's favorite was the Office of the Spicery. Whenever he walked by, the smell of drying thyme and lavender filled the lane outside.

Weatherby and Ellen Iverson walked out the far end of the Outer Court and started across the bridge to town. Weatherby observed that stirring and lifting pots of desserts had left Ellen with strong arms, but she was rotund, and her legs were not nearly as strong. She also had a slow, waddling gait that made him wish he had called a hansom. He had never crossed the Thames so slowly, so he studied the cat-o'-nine-tails along the banks and observed the small dull colored dauber ducks. They labored down High Street to the Lamb and Flag. The stores which had been closed after the epidemic of sweating sickness were now well stocked and open. Even though she came to town rarely, Ellen knew the cook at the Lamb and Flag well. She ordered her favorite dish—chicken and dumplings, with peas and onions on the side. Weatherby, still full from breakfast, settled back with a tankard of ale.

"How is your big-city murder investigation coming?"

"As you are well aware, it isn't worth a fig. Now I even have a fourth corpse to account for."

"I heard about that devil, Nathaniel Philbrick. He never should have been let out of the Tower, you know."

"You are quite right, as usual, although his designs were truly inspired."

"What makes you think his death is related to the other three?"

"He was a Palace resident like the others, and each of them had a different means of death as did he. Did you know his throat was cut?"

"Yes, very deeply I heard, but I think your murderer was very careful to place the bodies, almost theatrically, at Hampton Court. Nathaniel was found in a rundown gambling cottage."

"You must have thought a lot about these crimes."

"I like a good mystery as much as the next busybody."

"Philbrick was one of my suspects in the Gregory Townsend murders."

"Yes, but we both of us know he wasn't strong enough to carry out the deed."

Weatherby nodded and ordered another tankard of ale.

"You are smart, thoughtful and well connected, Ellen," Weatherby mused. "So where do you suggest I look for this killer?"

"Your pursuit of Sir Rodney Shrewsbury is very appropriate. He is rich, smart and vicious. It sounds like you almost caught him in Dublin."

"Amarantha and I got within twenty feet of him twice before he slipped away in his speedy calash. He was lucky."

"Or perhaps craftier. The other problem is his wealth. You have the considerable assets and resources of King Henry behind you. However, even though he was born a bastard, Sir Rodney is one of the richest men in Ireland, and more unscrupulous than you will ever be."

"As long as he stays in Ireland, I can't use the King's men to reach out and grasp him. I have to hope he will be drawn back to the gambling dens and fleshpots of Southwark. Perhaps he will long for his younger days as a wastrel in Naples."

"You might get lucky, but never forget he is a master of disguise. I sat next to him in the Chapel a few months ago. He was dressed as a virginal young woman with modest taste and elegant clothes. His mannerisms with handkerchief and parasol were unfailing feminine. Admittedly, something about her, or him, seemed slightly off to me. So I studied her for two hours during a long Latin mass when I had nothing better to do. Ultimately, I was shocked to realize who she was. His very unusual green eyes gave him away. After the service I leaned over and spoke to him but got no response, of course, because he couldn't disguise his voice. To be sure, I followed him at a distance after the service, and he went back to his secret rooms by the North Cloister."

"Have you seen him since then?"

"No. Leastwise not that I could recognize."

Weatherby wondered if, for the first time in his life, he was up against a criminal smarter than he.

Weatherby ordered another ale.

"I need to visit with you more frequently, Ellen," Weatherby mused. "Do you know anything about the dark-skinned man that Anna Maria's roommate saw go into the dead girl's room?"

"Yes. You asked me to look into that a while ago. He is an Arab and practices a religion called Muhammadism. He speaks little English and is an itinerant who keeps to the southern part of the realm. He sells fine gold and jewels while pursuing a certain class of genteel women. If he ever tarries anywhere, it is in York."

"What a lot of useful information. Does he have a name?"

"That is the most puzzling part. He never gives his name. When people speak of him they call him the Levanter."

"He seems tangled up with Miss Wimbledon in a way I don't fully understand yet. I must see if I can't track him down to question him about Anna Maria."

Weatherby and Ellen Iverson walked out of the Lamb and Flag into the bright sun. He hailed a hansom to speed the return trip. Once in the carriage, he thought about their dinner conversation.

"For me, the murder of Anna Maria Wimbledon is the most disturbing of the three," he mused. "Townsend was a scoundrel who used religion to manipulate simple people. William Suffolk was a misanthrope and a thief. By comparison Anna Maria seems so young, so beautiful and so innocent."

"Looks can be deceiving," Ellen replied. "You never had the pleasure of speaking with her. She had a beautiful voice, and she was thoughtful and kind. If she was attractive in death, then she was strikingly beautiful in life. However, she wasn't innocent. I told you about the girl's dormitory at the Palace and how the young swains got in. Anna Maria knew how to use these lads while letting them believe that they were using her. She developed her own following and was good at withholding her favors if she wasn't rewarded with some rich or precious bauble."

"So that explains why she had more jewelry and finer clothes than the other librarians."

"Yes, but I want to emphasize that she was always subtle and demure. She could bat her long eyelashes better than anyone I ever met. It took me four years to realize that she often had six or seven young gentlemen in her stable at one time."

"Could you ever link her to William Suffolk or Gregory Townsend, or even Nathaniel Philbrick?"

"No, but that is a very interesting question. I will ask my sources."

The hansom arrived back at the Palace. After she slid across the worn leather seat, he helped her down from the carriage. As he walked to his apartment, he tried to catalogue what he had just learned. Unfortunately, he wasn't sure he was any closer to solving his mystery.

# CHAPTER 62

Weatherby strolled to his laboratory. Dredge was busy working on the poisons that he had retrieved from Sir Rodney's lab. Dredge lay down a flask he had been heating over a charcoal fire and washed his hands thoroughly.

"This diabolical man has a collection of the most deadly poisons I have ever come across," Dredge began. "And remember how many I have seen. You sent me to work with one of the top conjurers in London, and she showed me her most lethal poisons and potions and how to deliver them to an unsuspecting victim. Many were truly frightening and led to agonizing deaths. For weeks after that, I was suspicious of everything I ate and drank. I also studied the methods of the Borgia family. In addition to Lucrezia, they had a Pope in the family. The clan solidified its position and multiplied their power by poisoning their adversaries."

"Didn't many of the most lethal poisons come from Italy?" Weatherby asked.

"Yes, mostly because they had practiced the black art for centuries. They had learned from the Greeks and especially the Egyptians, who were masters. Yet, Sir Rodney's collection isn't a descendant from any of these lines. Plus, his potions are far more deadly than any I have previously experienced. You noticed how carefully I washed my hands after handling the flask."

"Do any of them have a fragrance like the bitter rose smell that we found in Miss Wimbledon's stomach?"

"I'm afraid not."

"Keep working," Weatherby said as he walked out of the lab. "But be careful with those diabolical potions."

Weatherby went to the Wolsey Apartment and wrote the Chancellor a long letter about his pursuit of Sir Rodney Shrewsbury. He also felt obligated to write about the death of Nathaniel Philbrick and explain why he didn't feel, at this point, that this new case was related to the other three deaths. Weatherby fervently hoped that the Chancellor and the King were busy with matters of state and had no time to think about their poor detective's desultory progress. He also perused three letters from European universities that unfortunately offered no useful suggestions about the Linear A and B scripts.

As he sorted through the rest of his mail, Weatherby wondered if the proprietor of the dilapidated cottage where Nathaniel's body was found might be of help in solving the latest murder. Weatherby couldn't remember his name, so he walked back to the laboratory, where Dredge was still analyzing poisons.

"Who was the manager of that ramshackle cottage where they had that crooked dice game?" Weatherby asked.

"The one you almost killed with that dagger? He went by Manchester, but I'm not sure if that was his given name or his Christian name."

"Where did he live?"

"I heard one of the other regulars say that he lived with a woman in Teddington."

"Teddington had a corrupt sheriff for decades, who attracted all manner of shylocks and cutpurses to the village. It's not surprising that he should choose to live there. I believe we should pay him a visit in the morning."

Weatherby found Amarantha in Philbrick's lair searching for his diary.

"It is a beautiful summer afternoon and I think we deserve a ride," Weatherby said.

"What a sterling idea!" Amarantha replied. "I will change my clothes and meet you at the stables."

"Bring something warm. I'm bringing a new telescope so we can observe a total eclipse of the moon this evening."

Weatherby left for the stable to be sure the horses were ready. Once mounted, the two riders rode to the north where the houses and farms were the sparsest. It was a hot sunny afternoon, and most animals were resting in the shade except for an occasional fox or hedgehog. Amarantha and her small black mount led the way through a beech forest, complete with piles of brush to jump. She rested her head almost on the neck of her horse as the animal leaped forward, folding his front legs as he rose into the air and landing smoothly. Weatherby's roan was an adequate jumper, but neither the horse nor the rider were as smooth. Weatherby was using the new saddle he had ordered in London, yet he still landed with a jolt. It was too hot for horse and rider not to work up a sweat. Both riders stopped near a pond to let the horses rest and drink.

"I wish the summer lasted all year on this foggy northern island," Amarantha opined.

"We would be as lazy as the Italians if it were. Taking three-hour siestas every afternoon."

"I believe I could adapt to that. Here every grape, grain of wheat and piece of fruit has to be grown during a four-month period."

"You've never been to Italy, have you? When we finish this bloody case I would like to take you. You would appreciate all the art and architecture, in Florence particularly. It is quite small and packed with treasures."

"I shall hold you to that," Amarantha said as she remounted her horse.

She took him on a wild ride through a large wood with glades, hillocks and several tall obstacles to jump. Weatherby used to fall back three or four horse lengths on these wild runs, but now he stayed within one length. As the light faded, they stopped in a meadow and ate a cold supper of salmon and peacock and drank two bottles of Sicilian wine. As the evening progressed and the shadows lengthened, Weatherby took the parts of his telescope from the saddlebags. He assembled the brass tubes and lens before the light faded completely, and then they sat back to wait for the moon to rise. Weatherby showed her Venus and Jupiter through the telescope while they waited for the lunar orb.

"Besides the earth, there are four planets, Venus, Mars, Mercury and Jupiter, that circle the sun. They were all observed by Galileo Galilei when he first searched the heavens with a telescope," Weatherby said. "He even discovered four moons just like our own oyster-white companion around Jupiter. I'd show them to you but my telescope isn't that precise yet."

Finally, the sky to the east brightened and a white sphere as big as a dinner plate rose majestically above the trees. Once the moon had cleared the tallest branches, the upper corner began to turn progressively brown until over the next hour the whiteness had changed to a rusty red—the blood moon. The telescope made the lunar orb several times larger.

Amarantha stared at the surface of the distant structure that through the lenses looked like it was above the next meadow.

"It looks like it suffered from the pox," she said as she looked at the round grey circles of all sizes that covered the topography of the moon.

"It looks to me as though something has crashed into the surface, like pebbles thrown at a firm pudding."

"That seems very improbable, Seamus, you can see how empty the sky is around the moon."

"I'll give you that, but how would the moon get a pox?"

"That seems pretty obvious, from the cow that jumped over it, of course," Amarantha replied in jest.

As the night air cooled, Weatherby in his greatcoat sat with his back against a tree, looking at the moon. Amarantha sat between his legs with her head back against his shoulder. He wrapped his arms gently around her. They talked about nothing in particular. How perfect this is, Weatherby thought, as he made his grip just a little firmer on the woman that he loved. Once the eclipse had run its course, Amarantha fell gently asleep. For the next hour, Weatherby didn't move until finally numbness from hip to toes forced him to stir.

Gently he roused her and stamped his feet until the feeling came back. They rode back slowly through the big woods and the meadows, and then through the small woods to Hampton Court. At night the countryside was alive with foxes, badgers, weasels and hedgehogs. Each hurried into the shadows as the horses approached. Weatherby dropped Amarantha at the Great Gatehouse and then took both horses to the stable. When he arrived at his apartment, he checked the watch around his neck. It was two thirty of the clock. When he first went to bed Weatherby was too excited by the evening to go right to sleep. He read poetry by Boccaccio and fell asleep with the slender volume on his chest.

In the morning, Dredge knocked loudly on Weatherby's door.

"What is it?" Weatherby said in a deep, husky voice.

"I have another rocket for you to try, Your Grace."

Weatherby had been afraid the knock was about Sir Rodney or Philbrick. When he heard it was about his pet project of rapid travel, he leapt from bed.

"Let me put on some clothes," he called back.

When he opened the door Dredge showed him the new features—more powder and a lead-foil lined rocket body completed by a longer copper nozzle at the bottom.

"So the increased powder is to propel the heavier body and stronger nozzle."

"Exactly, Your Grace."

Weatherby walked with Dredge to a large field east of the Palace and placed the dowel in the ground at a forty-five angle. Then without ceremony he lit the fuse, holding his watch in front of his chest so he could time the event. A spark flared at the base of the rocket, and Weatherby feared an explosion would follow, just like the first time, however, the flame steadied and the rocket started across the field. It quickly traveled four hundred yards and came to rest in at an angle in a quince bush. Dredge and Weatherby both ran to it.

"The flight took seven seconds," Weatherby said in an elated voice.

"The missile is still intact. Next time, I think we can include an unwilling passenger," Dredge replied.

# CHAPTER 63

Still buoyed by the success of his experiment with rockets, Weatherby went to the Great Kitchen for a large breakfast. Then he walked to the library to check on Judith and Margaret. They had Sir Rodney's journals arranged in small piles on a large oak table.

"Dating these journals by year has taken us days," Margaret began. "Sir Rodney seems to have cared little about the years, and many lack numerical dates."

"We have a year of authorship for less than a quarter of them," Judith added.

"I was hoping you two could find the volume for 1530, the year I am most interested in, but clearly I will simply need to do more translating and reading," Weatherby replied as he picked up four of the dusty volumes.

He carried the volumes to the Wolsey Apartment, set up his mirror and began translating the Latin. Sir Rodney spent a lot of his time in the smaller villages of the county consorting with witches and seers, Weatherby noted. He also attended ceremonies that featured pagan dancing and animal sacrifice. He wrote extensively about every solar and lunar eclipse and the appearance of comets. Weatherby dated two of the journals by comparing eclipses to astronomical texts written in the past twenty-five years, but they were for 1519 and 1526. While he was thumbing through a journal, Weatherby mused on the backward writing, ancient languages and linear code that his murder suspects and victims used. He suspected he was dealing with a cluster of inhabitants who had something to hide. However, he found Tudor society suspicious and secretive. He mused on its origin. Certainly, once the Romans stopped persecuting the Christians in 500 AD, societies became more open and trusting. Even during the Crusades, all of Europe cooperated against a common enemy. Weatherby thought that English xenophobia had flourished in the past hundred years, spurred on by the clergy. Most sermons that he heard or read in the paper decried foreigners, if not neighbors, as instruments of Satan. Distrust was the currency of the day.

Weatherby was busy translating a third journal when a courier arrived. The King's men had seen the dark-skinned man that Ellen called the Levanter at an inn in York. Weatherby promptly decided to take Dredge to interview Manchester in Teddington and then to go on to York and try and waylay the Levanter. Weatherby walked to the laboratory and found Dredge working on a new and improved missile.

"We need to take a trip to the east," Weatherby said. "Can we leave in the morning?"

"Yes, Your Grace," Dredge replied, putting his new rocket aside.

"I will meet you in the stables at seven tomorrow morning." Weatherby walked out of the lab.

He found Amarantha and had a quiet dinner with her in his apartment. They read together by the fire for a few hours before retiring.

In the morning, Weatherby on his tall roan and Dredge on his pony rode across the bridge in the dewy morning, conversing amicably as they rode. The road was in good condition, and they arrived in Teddington in two hours. Weatherby was something of a hero there for ousting the crooked sheriff who had terrorized the residents for years. Weatherby asked the new sheriff where he might find a man named Manchester.

"He lives along the river," the sheriff said. "He has a bad reputation. I'll ride out to his hovel with you."

The three rode through the village and then along a trail that ran along the river to the west. The hovel looked unoccupied, but the sheriff dismounted and rapped on the door with a cudgel. After several minutes, an unshaven man in a dirty nightshirt answered the door.

"What!" Manchester yelled.

"Clothe yourself and come out here quickly so we can talk," the sheriff said sternly.

After a few minutes, Manchester came out squinting followed by a grey-haired woman in a dirty brown dress and no shoes. Without saying a word, the woman walked down the path toward town.

Recognizing Weatherby and Dredge, Manchester said, "What is it?" in a semi-civil tone.

"We found a mutilated corpse in your gambling den in Hampton six days ago," Weatherby began. "And before you tell me you don't know anything about it, I want you to know I like you for this crime."

"I didn't kill Philbrick," Manchester responded.

"If you can't tell me a story I believe, right now," Weatherby said, "I will send you to the Tower, where the Beefeaters will slowly torture you until you will say anything they want. You would confess to committing adultery with Catherine of Aragon just to stop the pain."

Manchester thought about Weatherby's words for a few minutes and then began to speak slowly, "That prick Philbrick came a gamblin' at the cottage three or four nights a week. He was drunk an' always causin' trouble. Takin' angels from his waren't worth it."

"What happened six nights ago?" the sheriff asked.

"Philbrick staggered in drunker then ever. He's losin' worse than usual about midnight when a wizened old codger comes in and starts playin'. He takes money from everbody, but most from Nat."

"How many gamblers were in your den?" Weatherby asked.

"Mayhap a dozen."

"What next?" Dredge asked impatiently.

"Suddenly thar' was a fight at a table between Philbrick and the old guy," Manchester said. "Nat reached across the table to punch 'im. The codger reached in his sleeve pulled out a thin silver dagger and sliced Philbrick's throat quick as could be. The old man wiped the blade on the dead man's sleeve and walked out cool as a cucumber."

"Did you recognize the old man?" Weatherby said.

"I never seen him afor' in my life," Manchester answered.

"If your story checks out, you'll keep your freedom," Weatherby said as he mounted his stallion.

As they rode back Weatherby turned to Dredge and said, "I just wonder if that old man wasn't Sir Rodney Shrewsbury."

"I hadn't thought of that," Dredge said in a surprised voice. "The codger he described certainly seems vicious enough."

After riding by the sheriff's office, Weatherby and Dredge said their goodbyes and continued riding west. The roads continued to be dry and firm. They spent the night at the Palace at Richmond. Henry VIII also was building there, but the Royal residence was much smaller than Hampton Court. In the morning the two horsemen got an early start toward York. They rode through open woods and well-tended farms. They stayed at a roadside inn for dinner, to sleep, and to rest their horses. The next day they rode north from early morning until evening. A long afternoon ride brought them to the gates of the ancient city of York as the light was fading. York Minster, the cathedral, was eerie and somber in the fading light. They stayed at the Prince's Inn in the center of the old city. Weatherby sent out three paid informants in an attempt to locate the dark-skinned Levanter. Weatherby and Dredge went to the dining room for tankards of ale and a rich dinner of roast beef. Weatherby hoped to hear from one of his snitches that night, so he stayed up late drinking and gambling a little, but no one sought him out. Ellen Iverson had told him that she had heard that the Porcelain Peacock in York was the best bawdy house in the realm. Weatherby considered going, but then retired, fatigued after a long day of riding.

Weatherby was awakened at seven by one of his snitches seeking payment.

"What do you want, Slug?" Weatherby asked sleepily.

"I want my angels, Your Grace," Slug said. "I have found your man."

"Where is he?"

"In a large house on the north side of town with some of his countrymen."

"You need to show me before I will pay you. Have the stableman saddle our horses."

Weatherby sent a message to Dredge and dressed quickly. The two travelers rode beside Slug to a large half-timbered house several blocks away. Weatherby paid Slug and the two investigators settled down behind some brush across the street so they could observe the house. Nothing happened for the next two hours, but then traffic into the house became steady. Respectable, well-dressed women came to the building in carriages and stayed about an hour, none of the residents came out.

"Perhaps the women are buying jewels," Dredge suggested.

"Or they could be up to some other nefarious thing. I want you to follow the next lady that comes out and ask her about that house. I'm hoping one of the residents comes out so that I can speak with them. Lacking that, I will pay a visit to the house and see what I can discover."

Dredge left a half hour later, and Weatherby waited another thirty minutes before crossing the street and trying the door which he found unlocked. Weatherby walked tentatively down the dark and narrow front hallway until he noticed a door ajar on the left side. He walked through the door into a totally dark room. As soon as he entered he noticed a strong pungent smell, and immediately he felt dizzy and weak.

# CHAPTER 64

Weatherby suddenly felt a rope tighten around his neck, and he was propelled out the back door of the house. His vision was blurred, and he was dizzy. He tumbled down a set of stairs and suddenly blacked out. When he awoke much later, he had a fierce headache. He felt a swollen, mushy area on the back of his head. Apparently he had been struck from behind after staggering down a stairway. He was in total darkness as he lay on the damp earth. Was he underground? Slowly, he felt the rest of his body for any other injuries and found none. He carefully wound his watch so that if he found a shaft of light he would know the time.

As he became more lucid, Weatherby began to explore his environment with his hands. The floor was dirt, and there were several side passages that he would explore later. The walls were made of large field stones mortared in place. On one end of the room a stone stairway ascended to a stout iron door.

On one wall was a waist-high shelf holding two urns. He opened one and smelled bread. He was hungry, but much thirstier. He checked the other urn and found it full of cool water. He scooped up some of the chilly liquid in his hands and raised it toward his mouth. Just as he was about to drink he smelled the scent of bitter roses coming from the water. He dropped the water onto the floor and wiped his hands thoroughly on his doublet. He was sure the bread was also poisoned, so he didn't touch it.

Without food and especially without water, Weatherby decided he could live three to four days without finding a way out. With his new deadline in mind, he began to explore his tomb actively looking for a possible escape or a tool he could use pry the door open. He explored each of the side passages from the floor to as high as he could reach standing on his toes. In the last side channel, he found a damp, moss-covered wall. With a source of water, he realized he could survive in misery for many days. He began licking the water off of the dripping wet moss. When he had slaked his thirst, he sat down on the driest part of the floor and slept fitfully.

Time passed, but without concept of light or dark, Weatherby found he couldn't keep track of the days. To pass the time, he thought about who his captors might be and worked on his vexatious murder cases. He found a loose stone near the stairway, and began banging it against the iron door as a signal to anyone that might be looking for him. Despite his fierce hunger, he knew the damp moss was keeping him alive.

As time went on, his thinking dulled and he moved more slowly. Although he smelled nothing, he wondered if poison fumes were being pumped into his prison. He was in an airtight chamber so he also wondered if the air contained in the cavity was being exhausted. A few hours later he was too weak to stand and couldn't complete even a simple thought.

He was only vaguely aware when a strong shaft of sunlight struck his face and two vague forms bent over him.

"Seamus, Seamus!" Amarantha shook him.

Weatherby couldn't speak, but knew that Dredge was nearby. Next he was lifted by some strong men, carried up the stairs and laid in the grass. Once in the fresh air, he recovered quickly.

"Where am I and why are you here, Amarantha?" Weatherby said in a loud whisper.

"You were imprisoned here in York," Amarantha said sadly. "Dredge sent a messenger for me the first day you were missing."

"How long was I underground?" Weatherby asked as his mind continued to clear.

"Six long days, Your Grace," Dredge replied.

"Dredge is the reason you were found, Weatherby," Amarantha said. "But let's move you someplace more comfortable before I explain."

They placed Weatherby on comforters in the back of a wagon and drove him to the Prince's Inn where they placed him in the largest and best room. He was ravenously hungry but ate only a little soup at first. He had treated starving men who had been lost at sea in Scotland, and when first found, gorged themselves to ill effect. Instead he slept in the large feather bed for eighteen hours straight. Amarantha roused him every four hours for a glass of sugary tea. When he finally awoke, he felt refreshed and fully alert, except for aching muscles.

"Tell me about the search and how I was found," he said.

"It was Dredge. He is the one who ran the operation," Amarantha replied.

When Dredge arrived, he described the last six days. "I followed the young lady as she came out of the house as you asked me to. She went to a large structure on the edge of town. I talked with her. She had gone to the house to try and find an emerald ring. When I finished my interview and arrived back to house, it was quiet. I waited there for you for five hours and then knocked on the door. I asked the person that answered the door about you and he denied seeing you."

"Was it the Levanter we were looking for?"

"No, this person was quite short and fair. When it started to get dark, I went back to our Inn hoping you were there. But when I awoke and there was still no sign of you, I sent a courier for Amarantha and contacted the King's men. We began a door-to-door search that lasted for the next five days with no results."

"I'm surprised you didn't give up."

"I would never have given up, Your Grace, without an answer," Dredge replied in an emotional voice.

"What finally broke the case open?"

"Your pencils."

"What are you talking about?"

"You dropped a trail of pencils that led right to your dungeon."

"I don't even remember doing that."

"You dropped a pencil every fifty yards or so, as you were led to your place of imprisonment. If I had seen the first pencil right away, I would have found you in an hour. As it happened, after five days of frustration, just as I was losing hope, I stumbled across it as I was walking aimlessly with my head down."

"Thank you for finding me, Dredge," Weatherby replied earnestly. "Now we need to find the person or persons behind this. We need to analyze the bread and water in the dungeon. Perhaps you can work on that Dredge. Amarantha, I want you to send a courier to Hampton Court and query Ellen Iverson as to who might have been absent from the Palace since Dredge and I left."

Weatherby's assistants left to work on their assigned tasks. As he dressed, Weatherby pondered who might have been behind the kidnapping. His first prospect was the mysterious Master of the House, Richard Weston. He was diabolical enough to carry out such a plot, but probably lacked the skills. His next candidate was the deposed Sheriff of Teddington, who certainly hated him, but the Sheriff lacked the finesse shown by his captors. His third candidate was Sir Rodney Shrewsbury. He was smart enough, rich enough and evil enough to have planned the multilayered abduction. So, Weatherby sent a courier to Ireland to confirm Sir Rodney's whereabouts.

Weatherby walked unsteadily down the stairs to the restaurant for a bowl of chicken vegetable soup with dumplings. He was so hungry; he thought it was the best-tasting food he had ever eaten. He slowed his eating and savored every bite. When he was done, he assembled the King's men who were still in town and went to the white, clapboard house where he was abducted. The King's men dragged four people out of the house. One was an elegant young woman who had been looking for jewels. Weatherby asked her two questions and let her go. Next, he interviewed an older woman who was the housekeeper and cook. She reported that seven men lived in the house and all were itinerant jewel merchants.

"What do these men have in common?" Weatherby asked.

"All the young men came from the east," she replied.

"I'm particularly interested in a jeweler that visited Hampton Court in County Surrey every few weeks. Do the men have different territories?"

"Yes they do, and they talk about them all the time at dinner," the cook replied. "The one named Ishmael works the counties west of London."

"Has he been here recently?"

"Why yes. He was here seven days ago."

"Have you seen him since?"

"No."

"What does he look like?"

"He is the tallest and darkest of all the jewel merchants that live here."

Next, Weatherby interviewed the two Arab drug merchants who had been found in the house—but both claimed to speak only Arabic. He considered torturing them, but suspected that the little information gleaned wouldn't be worth the time, so he threatened their lives and let them go.

# CHAPTER 65

Weatherby had every right to burn the house down, and was about to give the order. Instead, he took pity on the cook and ordered the King's men out of the rooms with their bundles of dry straw and away from the house. Weatherby and Amarantha mounted up and began the long ride back to Hampton Court. Dredge's pony was just too slow for the one hundred and eighty-mile trip, so Weatherby sent Dredge ahead by carriage. Weatherby thought about stopping in Suffolk on the way back to apprise the Earl of Suffolk about his murder investigation; however, a look at the map showed that Suffolk was far out of the way to the east.

Amarantha and Weatherby rode hard and long the first day through the flat country of the midlands, getting all the way to Coventry before stopping at a roadside inn. The next day they completed the ride to Hampton Court. They left their exhausted mounts at the stable around eight p.m. After two long days of riding, for the first time in their lives, Amarantha and Weatherby had seen quite enough of each other and each retired to their own apartments to eat and rest alone.

Weatherby had just finished eating his supper and drinking two tankards of ale. He was nodding off on his sofa in front of the fire, despite his sore muscles, when there was a loud knock on his door. Damn it to hell, he thought. What can the serving girl want now? He slowly unfolded his long legs and walked stiffly to the door.

"What is it?" Weatherby said irritably through the door.

"Open up. It is I," Sir John Moulton said in a loud, agitated voice.

Even in his sleepy state Weatherby noted that Moulton used the nominative form of the pronoun following the verb 'to be'. He doubted that more than two other people in the Palace had such precise grammar. Straightening his doublet, Weatherby opened the door.

"Good evening, Sir John," Weatherby said in a hearty voice. "What can I do for you on this quiet evening?"

"I was most disturbed to hear of your travail in York, Seamus," Moulton said as he took a seat. "You were very lucky to escape alive."

"Yes," Weatherby replied. "I owe my life entirely to my diligent and resourceful amanuensis, Bradford Dredge."

"In any case, welcome back. I'm sure you are extremely fatigued, but I have a matter that cannot wait."

"Proceed." Weatherby stifled a yawn.

"You know that modern-day Druids are my avocation. Dredge found out about one of the most diabolical of their young witches when he was searching for poisons."

"Yes. As I recollect, her name was Hepsibah."

"You are correct."

"But what makes this so urgent?"

"This is the thirteenth day before Kalends, or the eve of the nineteenth day of June."

"I'm still not following you."

"I'm sorry to be so abstruse. Monday is the longest day of the year, the summer solstice, and it is the highest of holidays for the Druids. They built Stonehenge to mark it, and any Druid worth his salt will be there at sunrise Monday morning."

"So you think I might find and question Hepsibah there," Weatherby replied excitedly.

"Not I, we. I can observe, catalogue, and sketch more Druids there in one day than I can track down in the other three hundred and sixty-four days of the year."

"If I recall correctly from plotting the course of the sweating sickness from the east, it is seventy-two miles from here to Salisbury."

"You are precisely right. It would be any easy day's horse ride; however, given your recent incarceration and fatigue, I recommend a coach-and-four. I believe we should leave at eight a.m. in case of a breakdown or trouble on the road."

"I'll be waiting at the Great Gatehouse tomorrow morning at six sharp, Sir John," Weatherby said as he walked his guest to the door.

Weatherby decided he would take Dredge along for technical assistance and to carry supplies, so he sent a note to the servant's sleeping quarters. Then he took a nostrum and he slept soundly.

When the two investigators appeared at the Great Gatehouse an elegant carriage pulled by four matching bays awaited them. They set off westward on a wide, smooth road. Weatherby and Moulton talked of architecture while Dredge slept. By dinner time, they had covered over half the distance and stopped at a roadside inn for a warm meal. Moulton drank more ale at a faster rate than the other two travelers combined.

During the rest of the ride, Moulton slept and Weatherby studied two books about Stonehenge that Dredge had brought along. The first volume came from Sir Rodney's library. Weatherby wondered if the vicious trickster would be at the celebration, and if so what his disguise would be. This book reported that Stonehenge was built before the dawn of time. The huge stones were estimated to weigh twenty-five tons each. Several similar sites, probably built for religious purposes, had been found throughout the British Isles, but Stonehenge was the largest and best preserved of all.

The second book reported the Arthurian legend of the construction of the monument. In this legend, the circle had been built in Ireland by giants who brought the healing stones from Africa. The wizard Merlin had directed its removal to England. The King sent Arthur's father, Uther Pendragon, Merlin and 15,000 knights to Ireland to retrieve the rocks. They failed to move the stones with ropes and force. Then Merlin alone, using skill and gear, easily dismantled the site and sent it over to Salisbury plain.

The second half of the trip went quickly and they arrived at the Salisbury Inn at five p.m. After a large supper, the three moved out to Stonehenge to camp for the night. Dredge went to Sarum plain first and set up camp on the west side of the circle. He pitched two canvas tents and lay blankets and pillows on the ground inside. Sunrise was to be before five on the morning of June 21st, and the three wanted to be ready. When Weatherby and Sir John arrived at camp they sat around a fire, talking and sipping whiskey.

"I have a much easier job than you, Seamus," Moulton said. "I am given a plan developed with the architects, and then I build it."

"Yes, but sometimes you don't get your materials in a timely fashion, or your workmen do shoddy work," Weatherby replied. "And the King always has a deadline—a birthday, wedding or christening, and you must be finished before that day dawns."

"This is true," Moulton said after giving it some thought. "But it's not as bad as your situation. You've been working for eighty-one days, traveled to three countries, not to mention all over England, and you haven't incarcerated anyone."

"Thanks for reminding me. All my fifty other murders were solved within a fortnight. The person or persons who committed these crimes is much smarter and very devious."

"How is this lack of resolution sitting with Chancellor Cromwell?" Moulton queried.

"Surprisingly well. I write him frequent long letters about our industry and downplay the lack of solution. I suspect he and the King are preoccupied with the new treaty they are trying to sign with the Low Countries. I can only hope the negotiations with the cantankerous Dutch last for a few more weeks." Weatherby yawned and said, "I think I'll retire."

He rose and walked toward his tent. He lay down on the blankets Dredge had arranged for him and was instantly asleep. It seemed only minutes later that he was awakened for the predawn ceremony. Remnants of the Druids from England, Wales, and Ireland had been dancing and celebrating all night. A large circle of worshippers, naked except for ribbons in their hair, held hands as they stepped and kicked around a large central bonfire. Witches with wild hair, dressed in fanciful leather garments decorated with suns, moons and comets, prayed at the base of the large tilting Heel Stone. Priests took turns sacrificing goats, lambs, and calves on the altar stone. Sharp knives glistened in the fire light as they slaughtered their innocent bleating victims. It was rumored that human sacrifices were being carried out in a nearby glade.

Over everything drifted an eerie pale of smoke from twenty different fires. Music from tambourines, drums and an occasional high, reedy flute also filled the black night air. Even though he was still fatigued from his recent incarceration, Weatherby wondered how he had been able to sleep at all. Dredge brought the two gentlemen large cups of hot tea. As Weatherby blew across the hot liquid, the sky began to lighten to grey in the east. The tempo of the dancing and music increased. Weatherby looked across the circle of sarsen stones toward two massive vertical stones topped by an equally massive lintel. In the center of the perfectly square frame, formed by the three stones with the earth at the bottom, was a shorter stone with a slender point on its top. The sky had lightened to a yellow-orange as the dancing became more frenzied. At four fifty-eight, by the watch around his neck, Weatherby caught the first glimpse of the sun. It rose a large fiery red ball through the misty morning. As it climbed higher, the sun was centered perfectly on the slender point of the stone in the center of the picture frame.

"Sir John. Come quickly," Weatherby shouted as he pointed at the orb.

Moulton looked at the alignment and gasped.

""This is no coincidence," Weatherby remarked. "This ancient monument is a very precise solar observatory!"

# CHAPTER 66

Weatherby called for his easel and chalk pencils. Dredge set the parchment in front of his employer and Weatherby began to draw rapidly. He quickly sketched the trilith with a chalk rod placing the pointed stone at the center. Then he drew the blood-red sun above the point.

"I need to make additional measurements to confirm my theory about the precision of this observatory," Weatherby said. "I want you to measure the distances, Dredge, between the stones and the circle of vertical timbers."

"Let us go find Hepsibah," Moulton called out excitedly.

The sky was brighter now, and the stones were turning grey. A long black shadow still extended from each vertical stone. The dancing and drumbeating continued unabated with a pair of Druids at almost every stone. The females were pinned against the rocks by leather-fringed males who were embracing them. One couple caught Weatherby's eye. The woman was tall with grey hair and a full body. The man ravishing her was shorter and older. He had been wearing a goat's mask on his head but with the vigorous activity it had fallen back onto his shoulders. The woman had shed a long black costume covered with gold comets which lay at her feet as she rose on her toes with each thrust. Both the man and the woman seemed lost in their own pleasure. Weatherby saw something around the goat man's eyes that looked familiar. Even in the faint light, he thought he recognized the face from the oil painting at Straffan House.

"I believe that is Sir Rodney Shrewsbury," Weatherby said. "Let's detain him."

They moved quickly toward the goat man, but just as Weatherby was about to grab him, the man twisted away from the woman, pushed her toward Weatherby and slipped behind the massive rock. Weatherby pushed the old witch aside roughly and ran along the side of the rock. Unfortunately, a large group of revelers were dancing in a frenzy right behind the stone. Weatherby found it difficult to push the celebrants out of the way. The small man was lost in the throng.

"I believe that was Sir Rodney rogering that old witch," Weatherby said as he tried to catch his breath.

"It wouldn't surprise me if he was here," Sir Moulton said. "It is everything he likes—sacrifice, necromancy, theatre and debauchery. You won't stumble on him again. Let's find Hepsibah."

"There are several hundred Druids here. How will we ever locate her?"

"I made enquiries after you went to bed last night. She and her clan are camped by a grove of trees to the north."

Moulton led the way. They had to dodge dancers and musicians as the celebration had not abated. After fifteen minutes, they arrived at a camp.

Moulton asked for Hepsibah in a language Weatherby didn't understand, and they were directed closer to the trees. Both men stopped in front of a lithe young woman who stood with feet apart and her arms akimbo. Her body and face were covered with a dull maroon paint that gave her an unworldly air. She had large breasts, a flat stomach and small hips. Gold cutouts of the moon and stars adorned her torso. She chanted with a passion that could only be heard when the two men were very close to her.

The witch stared at Weatherby as he spoke, running her hands slowly over her sides and thighs and giving him a piercing look of desire. She took Weatherby's arm and guided him further into the glade. Moulton wandered off to catalogue the Druids at the solstice. Hepsibah tried to pull Weatherby's body against hers, but he resisted partially because of the thick reddish paint. They came to a clearing and both sat down on a stump. Hepsibah spoke in a strange, guttural language.

"I don't know that language," he said in a loud, slow voice. "Can we speak English?"

"Blimey yes," the witch replied without taking her large black eyes off his face.

"Are you Hepsibah?"

"Some call me that."

"I have been looking for you."

"And I for you also," she replied in a breathy voice as she pushed her body toward him.

"I seek some information and I will pay you for it."

"I will give you what you need, but then you must give me what I yearn for."

"I have come all the way from Hampton Court to talk with you. I need a special poison for a very important religious man who is vexing me. It must leave no trace. I am told that you are a master at concocting subtle potions."

"I have skill with deadly elixirs and love potions. Please drink this if you wish for me to help you," Hepsibah said in a husky voice as she handed Weatherby a small, shapely blue glass bottle filled with liquid.

Weatherby touched the bottle to his lips and then expertly poured the liquid down his sleeve before handing the bottle back. His lips became numb, and when he looked back at Hepsibah he felt an intense wave of craving for her, stronger than any such yearning he had ever had before. He started to lean toward her. His hands went to her slender hips and then slid up her flanks. He had never felt such a soft yielding flesh, rather like thick rich pudding. He moved his arms around to her back and moved toward her face. Despite the paint her features were regular and beautiful, especially her large coal-black eyes.

Waves of longing flooded through his belly and legs. When his lips touched hers, he felt a tingling that spread over his face. Her tongue was slender and long, and the end was forked like a snake. She explored every part of his mouth with its flicking tip. She had pulled his body close and unfastened his doublet. Suddenly, Hepsibah sucked all the breath from him and he started to faint. She pulled him forward as she fell back on a blanket covered with the design of a writhing red dragon. She freed him from his clothing and pulled him on top of her slender body. He started to move over her body with his weight on his elbows when a flash of sanity broke through the potion. With a great effort he forced himself to see the juicy young witch as a dry, shriveled old crone. He rolled away and lay on his back, panting on the cool, soothing earth. Her hand went immediately to his shoulder and her mouth to his lips, but now the spell was broken. What would have happened he wondered if he had drunk the entire potion?

He covered himself and kissed her because she had information he needed.

"I want you, my tempest. You are the most sensual creature I have ever seen or imagined." And this part was true. "But I want to come to you on my own. Free without your elixir of love, and I will please you in a thousand ways."

Hepsibah pulled her head back like a snake retreating from prey and looked hard at him with her deep, black eyes.

"We will meet at your den in Wycombe, in a week," Weatherby said as he sat up and offered her his hand.

Hepsibah nodded and flicked her tongue.

"However, before that meeting, I need to dispose of an enemy," Weatherby continued. "You must help me. I have heard of a subtle but deadly poison that smells faintly of the bitter rose. Do you know it?"

"Yes. I concocted it when I was only twelve from deadly nightshade roots, laudanum, belladonna and a concentrate of rose oil to disguise the bitterness. I tested it on a ten-year-old playmate, and she was dead before supper. She had strong convulsions and vivid hallucinations before she passed."

A chill passed through Weatherby, but he kept his face expressionless.

"Perchance, you have some with you?" Weatherby asked blandly.

"No. Druids are forbidden by the priests from bringing poisons to the summer solstice. There are too many nasty feuds between the witches and warlocks. They are a proud and vengeful lot, and this gathering is a perfect time to settle scores. When they realized that deaths were becoming common among the celebrants each year, the wise witches stopped eating while they were here. They would only drink from a fast-flowing stream without using a cup. The ban on poisons now gives the community a measure of safety."

"Your English is excellent," Weatherby remarked.

"I study those around me and learn what I must to have power over them."

"Did you ever give someone a sample of the bitter rose poison?"

"Only once, about two years ago. When you come to tease me until I beg you to consume me, I will tell you who I gave it to."

Hepsibah pulled Weatherby's face toward her and gave him a long, wet, open-mouthed kiss before standing and walking barefoot into the forest. Weatherby noted that her back, buttocks and calves were just as perfectly formed as every part of her front. Was this the residual of the potion he wondered, or something else?

(Readers over fifteen may go to my web site, www.BooksByHooks. com, for another version of this chapter)

# CHAPTER 67

After rearranging his disheveled clothing, Weatherby walked back to the circle of stones which was now in full daylight. The revelers were slowing down and adjourning to nearby tents and wagons to sleep after the night-long celebration. Weatherby soon caught up with Moulton.

"This is considerably bigger than last year's fête," Moulton said. "The government keeps saying that the Druids have been stamped out, but I think not. I've recorded thirty-three new names this morning to my comprehensive list of Druids. I now have over six hundred names."

"Why do they trust you?" Weatherby asked.

"I have the approval of their leaders, and I've been doing this for five years without breaking a confidence. But where have you been?"

"I was seduced by a red-painted hellion. She gave me a potion that made me desire her as I have never desired a woman before. It was appalling."

"It couldn't have been all *that* bad. Despite the paint, she had the figure of a goddess and the face of an angel," Moulton protested. "Have you seen how much public pairing is going on in this five-acre plot? I wouldn't mind probing her."

"She is a bright, manipulative and clever witch, Sir John. She killed a playmate when she was twelve just to see if a new poison she had concocted worked. You are thinking with your cock, my friend."

"Don't you ever want to risk it all on one event or adventure? Don't you ever want to push all the Sovereigns to the center of the table before one roll of the dice? You said yourself that you experienced the strongest physical desire you had ever felt for a woman. You experienced the epitome of desire and then rejected it. Why?"

"I suppose I was afraid that she would ensnare my soul like the devil did in Dr. Faustus."

"An opportunity like that comes only once and if you seize it you can remember it and replay it for the rest of your life. Tell me where you saw Hepsibah last."

"She was in the glade to the north."

The seventy-year-old Master of the King's Works hurried off in a frenzy of lust. Weatherby searched out Dredge and found him near the stone circle sketching the sarsen stones and making caricatures of the Druids.

"I was afraid I had lost you," Dredge said, looking up from his easel.

"I got tangled up with Hepsibah."

"That voluptuous maroon witch?"

"The very one. She gave me a potion, which I broke, eventually, but more importantly she knows about the poison that smells like bitter roses. What happened to you?"

"I struck up a conversation with a pair of dwarf twins that were just my size, and one thing led to another. I feel great!"

"After you break camp, I want you to locate Sir Moulton in the north glade so we can start back to Hampton Court."

"Yes, Your Grace," Dredge replied.

Weatherby went to check the placement of the stones and the two circles of timbers on the inside. He noted the dagger and axe-heads carved into some of the stones. Next, he measured the diameter of the inside of the stone circle and found it was exactly a hundred Roman feet. The rest of the monument was laid out precisely in Megalithic rods, which were 6.9 feet long. Therefore, other stone circles and monuments from Brittany to Scotland that used this same unit of measure. Weatherby realized that the ancients who built Stonehenge had an advanced knowledge of geometry and astronomy and were highly skilled surveyors. Dredge found Weatherby measuring among the stones.

"The carriage is loaded, Your Grace," Dredge called out.

Weatherby climbed in after brushing the dust off of his leggings. Moulton was already curled up in a corner.

"Sir John, thank you for suggesting this most productive outing," Weatherby began. "Did you find the exotic Miss Hepsibah?"

"Yes, but when I tracked her down she had found another partner."

"Dredge and I were both amazed at the level of public fornication."

"The Druids have a priestly caste, like most religions, and offspring conceived during the solstice are believed to be hallowed by birth. They are taught a love of the sun, the moon, oak trees and mistletoe by their parents, and are then given to Druidic priests at age eleven. The Druids aren't concerned about who the mother or father of the child is, just the time of conception."

All three travelers curled up as best they could in the lurching coach and slept after their strenuous night. The driver raced across the rolling countryside. They stopped at an inn in Basingstoke for a late lunch and drove on to Hampton Court. Although tired from the trip, Weatherby searched out Amarantha. She was in the library helping the assistant librarians with Sir Rodney's journals.

"Fie on these damnable journals!" Amarantha shouted throwing a journal down.

"Unfortunately, those pages may contain the key to these bloody murders," Weatherby replied.

"We have spent weeks poring over the volumes," Judith Scotson remarked. "And they remain as obscure as when we first looked at them."

"I'm taking all of you to supper in town," Weatherby announced.

The three women walked across the bridge arm in arm, laughing and talking with Weatherby just behind. Everyone felt better after a tankard of ale. Weatherby told the ladies about his trip to Stonehenge with Sir John. He focused on the costumes, music and structure of the monument, speaking about each in detail. He told them about the importance in Druidic culture of being conceived on the summer solstice and the amazing amount of mating it provoked at Stonehenge. Weatherby embellished dramatically the rising of the blood-red sun over the marker stone of the shrine. They ate roasted peacock and artichokes and drank more ale.

After dinner, Weatherby suggested cards. The table was cleared, and they were brought a deck of tarot cards. They played taroccho for a penny a hand while laughing, teasing each other and drinking. Then Weatherby proposed a game of charades.

"Gleek, taroccho, charades," Amarantha said. "For a serious person, you certainly know a lot of games."

"Charades is a new word game from France that I just heard about, but have never played," Weatherby replied. "It should be perfect for literary types, such as you ladies. One person selects a word such as conundrum, breaks it down into syllables and then gives a clue for each syllable. For example, the third syllable-'drum' collects company, the first syllable 'co' is company, the second 'nun' shuns company, and the whole amuses company. Do you understand the example?"

All three ladies nodded their heads enthusiastically and clapped.

"Then I will go first," Weatherby replied. "The first syllable—with antipathy to the French prides himself whenever they meet on sticking close to his jacket. The second has many virtues, not the least that it gives its name to the first, and the whole may I never catch."

Judith, Margaret and Amarantha all looked puzzled.

Then Amarantha spoke, "The first has to do with clothing which I think is 'doublet' and the second gives its name to the first, so I believe the answer is 'doublet double'."

"But the clue about the whole word is 'may I never catch'. How does that fit?"

"Wearing a 'double doublet' even on the coldest day would make one too warm to catch a cold."

"Yes. I see," Weatherby replied. "Here is an alternate answer. My first is 'tar' as a French-hating English sailor. My second, which gives its name to the first, is 'tar'. Its virtues are many including, waterproofing, preserving wood, making dyes and patching. Then my whole, which may I never catch, is the dreaded 'Tartar', the Mongol warrior."

Each of the dinner mates drank ale and contemplated the answers so far.

Then Amarantha spoke up, startling everyone, "I have one! My first is an actor's failure, my second an actor's approach to his audience, and my third is an actor without words. My whole is a theatrical entertainment."

"You are a quick study, Ran," Weatherby said with admiration.

"I think your third syllable is the easiest and it is 'mime'," Margaret said quickly.

"Your first paragraph, an actor's failure, is 'maul, slam, scorn, or trash," Judith added.

"Except none of those work with 'mime'," Weatherby suggested. "How about 'pan'?"

"Then the second, an actor approach his audience, is 'to'," Judith said "And the word is 'pantomime'."

They all laughed and clapped. Margaret and then Judith proposed their own words for the group.

More ale and conversation finished the evening, and they walked back across the bridge arm in arm, chattering happily. After the long ride from Stonehenge followed by a long evening of drinking Weatherby went to sleep easily, but he awoke at 3 a.m. cold and covered with sweat. His recurring nightmare had been more vivid than ever. In his dream, he rode through the fen on his white horse as the three charging spirits on black horses came closer than ever, just before the baby crawled out of the woods into his path. Weatherby could feel the horse's breath on the back of his neck. As he turned his head, he recognized the face of the first wraith: Sir Rodney Shrewsbury. Weatherby tried to go back to sleep in hopes that he could recognize the other two faces, but when he drifted off they were shrouded in darkness. He awoke again and got out of bed, changed his sweaty rail and went back to sleep as soon as his head struck his feather pillow.

# CHAPTER 68

The next morning, Weatherby slept late and stumbled to the Great Kitchen for breakfast. Then, rather than checking his mail in the Wolsey Apartment, he went back to the library to crack Sir Rodney's journals once and for all. His first theory was that the older journals would have ink that had faded, so he arranged the books in that order. The most faded journal was dated 1485, written when Shrewsbury was only eighteen years old. Perhaps he was on to something. He picked the next three most faded journals, but none had dates. The fifth most faded tome had a date in it of 1524. Weatherby concluded that fading had to do with exposure to the sun and quality of the ink rather than age.

His next hypothesis was that the quality of the handwriting would deteriorate with age as the writer grew impatient or lazier and perhaps developed a tremor. He used the volume of 1485 as an example of early writing and compared it to the volume of 1524 by searching for the same words. He was just starting to get some sample words when a messenger broke into the library.

"I have an urgent message, Sire, from the Sheriff of Teddington," the messenger said as he struggled to catch his breath.

"What, pray tell, is the problem?" Weatherby replied in an irritated voice.

"He needs you help with a gambler named Manchester," the messenger replied, still not fully recovered.

"Zounds! I am *not* the constable for the entire bloody county of Surrey!" Weatherby shouted angrily. "Now be gone or I will put you in the stocks."

"Sheriff Tucker said you might be unwilling to help."

"I'm not unwilling. This matter has nothing to do with me, you fool. I got Sheriff Tucker his current well paying job. He is at my beck and call, not I at his. You have five seconds to leave, as my patience is at an end!" Weatherby shouted as he flung a large leather-bound book at the messenger, narrowly missing his head.

The messenger backed quickly toward the door with both his arms in front of his face and just as he went through the heavy glass doors he shouted back, "He thought I should mention the name of Miss Judith Scotson!"

"Light-minded idiot! What has this got to do with Miss Scotson?"

"Manchester is holding her hostage in his house by the river," the messenger replied.

"Run to the stables and have them saddle my roan post haste!" Weatherby ordered.

He had been with Judith less than twelve hours ago, and suspected she was safe somewhere in Hampton Court, but didn't feet he could take a chance. He ran to the stable and when he arrived his horse had just been saddled. He threw the stirrups down off the horn, leapt into the saddle and spurred his horse toward Teddington. He left a message for Dredge telling him of his whereabouts. Weatherby arrived in the village in less than forty minutes. He had been to Manchester's hovel before concerning the Nathaniel Philbrick murder, so he knew where he was going as he rode along the ill-kept lane along the south side of the river. The sheriff and his men were crouched behind logs and bushes thirty yards from the hovel.

"What have you got here, Sheriff Tucker?" Weatherby said as he slid from his saddle and reflexively crouched down.

"It's that crazy gambler, Manchester," Sheriff Tucker replied in an exasperated tone. "Usually he is so drunk that he ain't much trouble, but today he's holding a hostage and he gots a crossbow. He already wounded one of my men!"

"What does he want?"

"The crazy fool says he's wantin' a fast horse and a hundred gold Sovereigns to let the lassie go unharmed," the Sheriff replied.

"Well I've got the horse," Weatherby offered. "Let me write a note you can take to the Bank of Teddington for the Sovereigns and here is my watch for collateral."

"Are you lettin' him go, then?" the Sheriff asked incredulously.

"Are you totally crazy? I just want to get close to him."

Two of the Sheriff's men galloped to the bank in the center of the village for the gold coins. While he was waiting, Weatherby called into the house.

"Manchester!" Weatherby yelled into the hovel. "I am Sir Seamus Scott Weatherby, and I work for King Henry. We have met before, and I am here to resolve this problem."

"I want me money!" Manchester yelled back in a surly voice.

"I can arrange that, but first I need to know that Miss Scotson is all right."

"She is sitting right next ta me!"

"Yes, but I need to talk with her before we proceed."

Weatherby heard some rustling and shuffling.

"Seamus!" Judith yelled out.

"Are you all right?"

"I'm tied up with a thick rope, and I had a gag in my mouth, but otherwise I am unharmed."

"I'm very glad to hear that you are unhurt, Judith," Weatherby said. "If you were to let the young lady walk out of your house right now, Manchester, we could resolve this little problem without your spending even one day in jail."

"I don' trust ya'!" Manchester replied.

"We have interacted twice before, and everything that I have told you has come to pass. Therefore you have no reason to mistrust me. Isn't that true?"

"Yah, but I ain't letting her go."

The Sheriff's men had returned from the bank, and handed the gold coins to Weatherby.

"I have your money and a fast horse," Weatherby replied. "I'm sending the Sheriff and his men away now so you and I can make an exchange."

Weatherby motioned the Sheriff and his men back, and then walked toward the door of the hovel. He pushed open the door and walked into the gloom. Judith was sitting on a broken chair with her hands tied behind her back and a rope around her torso. Weatherby walked over to her and looked into her eyes.

"Are you still unscathed?" Weatherby asked Judith as he leaned over her and placed his hand gently on her back.

"Get away fum' her!" Manchester yelled.

Weatherby took several steps backwards and opened the bag of Sovereigns, tipping it so that Manchester could see the gold.

"May I sit down?" Weatherby said as he eased into a stained leather chair without waiting for an answer. "How can we affect this exchange?"

"Lay the money on the floor along with yer' frog sticker and walk yonder. Then I will let the wench go."

"That won't work for me," Weatherby said gathering up the gold and standing up. "I've met all your demands fully and promptly, Manchester, and now you are acting in bad faith. I shall turn this over to the Sheriff."

Manchester said nothing as Weatherby sauntered toward the door. Once outside, the King's Detective motioned for the Sheriff to move close to the hovel again.

"Manchester is being uncooperative, even though he made no new demands," Weatherby said. "Could you shoot a pair of flaming arrows through the broken windows?"

"What about your librarian?" the Sheriff said.

"I slipped her a small knife, and her ropes are already cut. I can get her out of there safely," Weatherby said in a reassuring voice.

Two of the Sheriff's men bent their longbows and fired two flaming arrows into the tinder-dry hovel. Weatherby heard scurrying in the house, and then all was quiet.

Weatherby turned and spoke to the Sheriff, "Give me ten minutes, and then storm the front door with four of your men. Have them make as much clatter as they can. I will try to slip Judith out the back door."

When Weatherby heard a clamor from the front, he quietly opened the back door and slipped into the building. The floor creaked under Weatherby's feet, but the sound was drowned out by the men at the front door. When Weatherby motioned Judith stood up quietly and walked toward him. He wrapped his arms around her and guided her quickly to the back door. When she stepped outside, Manchester, turned and fired a bolt from his crossbow at Weatherby. Despite the close range, the bolt missed Weatherby but pinned the sleeve of his doublet to the frame of the house. Weatherby extracted his dagger from its sheath and quickly cut his sleeve free. He stepped outside and found Scotson standing close to the doorway in shock. He moved her quickly away from the building.

As he rounded the corner of the hovel, Manchester burst through the Sheriff's men and mounted Weatherby's horse. Without thinking, Weatherby handed Judith to Sheriff Tucker, jumped on the Sheriff's strong black horse, and galloped after Manchester. The felon headed east through the village and on toward Kew. Weatherby soon passed the four Sheriff's men and their spent horses. He wasn't sure whether he was angrier about losing his good roan horse or his newly made black leather Italian saddle with silver hardware. As he entered a large grove of beech trees, Weatherby caught a glimpse of his horse and picked up his pace.

When he got closer to Manchester, Weatherby tried whistling at his mount. When his roan was grazing, he always came promptly to his master's whistle. To his surprise, in response to the whistle, the big roan slowed, then stopped and lowered his head to crop the grass. Despite Manchester switching the horse and digging his heels into the horse's side frantically, the horse would not move. Weatherby pulled alongside Manchester.

Manchester said, "What will you do with me?"

"This is my third run-in with you, you wretched scum." Weatherby spat at him. "By all rights I can cut your throat right here and leave you to bleed to death. You are far more trouble than you are worth."

# CHAPTER 69

Weatherby tied Manchester across the saddle of the Sheriff's horse like a sack of potatoes and rode back to Teddington. He left the prisoner tied to the horse and went inside to speak to the Sheriff.

"I captured your felon. He is outside on your horse," Weatherby said as he entered the Sheriff's office. "Send him to the Tower. Where is Miss Scotson?"

"My men took her to the inn," the Sheriff replied.

Weatherby mounted his own horse and rode to the inn where Judith was just finishing lunch. On the way he stopped at the bank to return the gold Sovereigns in exchange for his prized watch.

"Thank you for saving me from that appalling man, Seamus," Judith said as she kissed Weatherby on the lips.

"What were you doing in his hovel?"

"My brother Roderick has a gambling problem and owed Manchester twenty-one angels. I was trying to reason with the proprietor of the gambling den to resolve the debt."

"I tried that once with Manchester," Weatherby responded. "But he only responds to threats. He's on his way to the Tower, so you won't have to worry about the angels."

"I can't thank you enough."

"May I arrange a carriage to take you back to Hampton Court?"

"Can't I ride with you? It would be a lot faster," Judith said in a coquettish voice.

"Of course you may. Let's go."

Weatherby helped Judith up onto the roan just behind his saddle, and then he mounted. She pressed herself into his back and wrapped her arms around his waist as he pointed his horse toward Hampton Court. As they rode, the gentle pressure of Judith's hands felt good on Weatherby's chest. He could feel her breasts pressing against him through his linen shirt. It was a warm afternoon and as they both perspired the two layers of cloth between them became less of a barrier. Weatherby had always found Judith appealing in an undefined way—perhaps it was her warm brown eyes and her abundance of brown hair that curled softly. They talked about Hampton Court and Anne Boleyn.

"Let's switch places," Judith said halfway home. "I wasn't planning on riding today, and the horse's rump is chafing my thighs."

Weatherby stopped and dismounted. He offered his hand to Judith, and as she dismounted she stumbled against him and kissed him again. It felt soft and wonderful and full of possibility. Judith removed her gown-like dark red kirtle so she would be cooler and packed it in a saddle bag. Her white chemise was moist with perspiration and clung to her body, hinting at her breasts and a patch of darkness at the summit of her legs.

She mounted quickly and Weatherby pulled himself up behind her, pressing against her back. One hand rested naturally on her left thigh, and his other arm circled her upper torso lifting her breasts. Judith took the reins with authority and pointed the rangy horse toward home. Gradually, Weatherby's hand drifted up from her thigh and toward the center of her body until his fingers nestled between the top of both of her legs and the base of her belly. After a few miles of riding she lifted herself in the saddle and at the same time spread her knees so his fingers descended and were trapped between her strong legs. She moved his right hand up onto her left breast. She rode contently like that the rest of the way back to Hampton Court. Just before they entered the stables, she stopped and moved his hand between her legs with her hand before letting out a soft moan. She turned and kissed him on the mouth before dismounting and slipped her kirtle back on. Once in the stable yard, Weatherby jumped down and then raised both hands toward Judith. She put both hands on his shoulders and dismounted into his arms giving him a fourth, longer and considerably wetter kiss.

"Thank you for a delicious ride," Judith said as Weatherby took her arm. "I only hope we can do it again soon."

The two of them ran into Amarantha as they walked across The Clock Tower.

"It sounds like I missed all the fun," Amarantha began. "What ever possessed you to take on that conniving gambler all by yourself, Judith?"

"I suppose I thought I could outsmart him or charm him, or both," Judith replied.

"I ordered a supper for us in the orchard on this perfect warm summer evening," Amarantha said taking both of their hands. "But first I have a surprise for my two dear friends."

Amarantha led them back to the stables and into one of the unused stalls. She roused a long-legged puppy from the straw. He was rough coated, with yellow fur and dark grey ears and muzzle. He licked Amarantha's face enthusiastically.

"What have we here?" Weatherby said tousling the puppy's ears.

"My da' always had dog when I was a child," Amarantha mused. "And I decided I needed one."

"His paws are huge!" Judith remarked, picking up a floppy paw.

"What sort of dog is it?" Weatherby asked.

"It's an Irish Wolfhound pup that I purchased from a Cambridgeshire itinerant," Amarantha replied proudly. "He will weigh nine or ten stones, and will be almost three feet tall. I'm going to teach him to hunt."

"That doesn't sound like you at all, Ran," Weatherby said and then added jokingly, "Check her for a fever, Judith."

"What is its name?"

"I thought about calling him Seamus, then I decided to call him Sporter. He's awfully cuddly despite his spindly legs. He's smart too."

Amarantha returned the puppy to his bed of straw, and Judith, Amarantha and Weatherby walked leisurely out to the orchard. Amarantha had arranged an elegant dinner of poached pike with dill, followed by stuffed game hens and grilled vegetables. Amarantha had arranged for several bottles of iced champagne, newly arrived from southern France. The light yellow bubbly liquid went particularly well with the pike.

After supper, Weatherby wandered over to his laboratory to check on Dredge. The two hadn't spoken since their return from the bacchanal at Stonehenge. Dredge was writing a letter to the dwarf Druid twins he had met on Sarum plain.

"I may need a few days off," Dredge said looking up from his writing with a leer on his face. "If they were to invite me for a visit."

"Of course. Unless we are in hot pursuit of a murderer," Weatherby replied with a smile.

Weatherby had trouble thinking of Dredge as a sexual being because of his gross physical deformity, but he realized that perhaps the dwarves were a perfect fit.

"I believe you had quite an adventure today, Your Grace," Dredge said changing the subject.

"Right-o. Damsel in distress, don't you know," Weatherby replied.

"And Miss Scotson, is a very appealing young woman, if I may say so, Sir," Dredge retorted in a mocking tone. "Not to mention that she's taken by you."

"What are you talking about?"

"Whenever I'm with Amarantha and Miss Scotson, Judith always comments on how handsome and smart she finds you to be. She seems quite smitten by you," Dredge said a bit warily. "Certainly, you've noticed."

"Actually not. But she was quite forward on the ride home from Teddington, now that you mention it."

"Now you are also her hero, Your Grace," Dredge said, reflecting on yesterday's event. "You saved her from that filthy, violent cad."

"I wish you had been with me today. Judith and I were both very lucky."

Weatherby related the events of the abduction and rescue in lurid detail, casting himself as the hero. It was a bright spot in his ongoing and frustrating murder investigation. Then Dredge poured Weatherby a glass of port.

"I did follow up on Manchester's story about the death of Nathaniel Philbrick when I returned from Stonehenge," Dredge offered. "Two other gamblers that were there that night confirmed his story of the old man who cut Philbrick's throat in a flash. So Manchester was telling the truth, even though it doesn't matter now that he is in the Tower."

"I think the killer was Sir Rodney. Did either gambler give us any more details about the slasher?"

"One said the man was only five feet tall, slender and had curly white hair. The other said he cheated at dice and had piercing, cold blue eyes. Both are gamblers and probably cheats, but each commented on the quickness and steadiness of the old man's hands. Neither saw the knife until after Philbrick's throat was deeply cut and blood was gushing out."

"As I told you, I believe I saw Sir Rodney Shrewsbury at Stonehenge for the summer solstice," Weatherby replied. "His disguise had slipped off while he was shagging some old witch. Prior to that, he had to be in York to arrange and supervise my imprisonment. Also, when Amarantha and I were in Ireland, he was in Dublin. I want you to make a map charting his movements and let's see if we can't snare him."

"Yes, Your Grace," Dredge replied. Weatherby walked back to his apartment, but found it hot and close feeling after several warm summer days in a row. He took a book and walked into Hampton and sat at a table near the door of the Lamb and Flag with a tankard of ale.

After about an hour someone came to the edge of the table and said, "What are you reading?" It was Christopher Dickinson, master mason.

"Sit down," Weatherby said enthusiastically. "I haven't seen you in weeks. I wondered if you had been transferred to another project."

"No. I'm still laying bricks here at Hampton Court. How is the murder investigation going?"

"Not well. I'm afraid."

"Am I still a suspect?"

"Yes, I suppose so," Weatherby said. "As is every person in the realm, but others more evil and conniving that you have floated to the top of the pond since we last talked. Sit down and let me buy you a drink."

# CHAPTER 70

"Our building for Henry VIII is so extensive that we are having trouble making enough bricks in our own brickyard." Dickinson opined. "We have contracts with yards in Escher and Weybridge but sometimes the bricks aren't well fired and just crumble."

"It doesn't seem to my untrained eye that construction is lagging," Weatherby replied after a large swallow of ale.

"We are just finishing the Boiling House and Larding House off the Fish Court to the north of the Base Court."

"That's right next to my apartments. I can hear the work sometimes."

"But the work on Cross Court to the west of the Knot Garden has slowed for lack of good bricks," Dickinson mused.

"Will the work at Hampton Court ever be done?"

"Yes. But the plans I have seen will take another five years to complete if Henry lives."

"He's only thirty-nine, and he could live a long time. Except for his jousting wound and increasing weight, he seems to be in good health."

"May he outlive both of us," Dickinson said, lifting his tankard. "So that the peace of the realm continues."

The two talked a while longer and then walked back to Hampton Court while enjoying the warm summer night. Weatherby slept soundly until 3 a.m. when he awoke in a sweat. It wasn't his usual nightmare however, but a full color, lurid, erotic dream about the young witch Hepsibah. She had been much in his thoughts and daydreams for the past three days. Weatherby thought it might be a residual effect from the Druid's love potion he had barely sipped. He went back to sleep, enveloped in warm thoughts of pliant, engulfing female flesh.

In the morning Weatherby had breakfast with Amarantha and Dredge in the Wolsey Apartment. Dredge brought his map showing the presumed whereabouts of Sir Rodney Shrewsbury.

"What are your conclusions about Sir Rodney?" Weatherby asked.

"We have him in Dublin, then far to the north in York, and then back to the far west at Stonehenge," Dredge replied. "Despite his age, Your Grace, he is very mobile. I suspect he travels alone in that two-wheeled calash that you observed with a very strong horse. From your and Amarantha's description, he can't weigh over nine stones."

"I suspect you are right, Dredge," Amarantha mused. "The carriage is very lightly built and the wheels are large but with slender spokes. A good horse can pull a hundred and twenty-six pound man all day with barely a rest."

"Add his disguises into the mix, and it's no wonder we haven't snared him," Weatherby replied. "I will send another description to the King's men. Perhaps they will stumble across him.

After eating, Weatherby went to the Wolsey Apartment to check his mail, and Amarantha went to walk Sporter. Seamus was discouraged to see a large stack of epistles on Wolsey's large walnut desk. Most was dross or outdated. There were more negative replies had come in about his linear writing, and a long, chatty letter from Father Lawrence Croceus was in the pile. Weatherby was amused to read about the Catholic intrigue in Paris and the struggle to produce illuminated manuscripts. The letter took his mind off his current list of unsolved problems.

On the bottom of the pile was an official-looking letter from Whitehall Palace. Weatherby was worried it was a reprimand from Chancellor Cromwell about the interminable murder investigation at Hampton Court. Weatherby ripped the letter open impatiently. He was disappointed to see it was an elegantly written invitation to Henry the VIII's birthday party at Whitehall Palace on June 28th. He threw the parchment on the floor as he realized that no excuse would exempt him from the fête. The visit of the Royals to Hampton Court had been a massive waste of time, and now he would have to travel to London for the party. He was still trying to craft an excuse when a servant burst into the apartment.

"There has been an accident, Your Grace," the servant shouted. "A new wall has fallen."

"Where?"

"The new Cross Court, Your Grace."

Weatherby jumped up and followed the servant. The new walls were built up fifteen or twenty courses at a time and then allowed to dry for three or four days so the mortar became strong. When Weatherby arrived in the Knot Garden, a pile of collapsed bricks lay next to the fallen boards of the scaffolding. Three workers lay on the gravel path two with obviously broken arms and one with a broken leg. Since Dr. Wickham died, Weatherby was the only physician at Hampton Court.

Weatherby sent a servant to have Dredge bring splints and strips of linen. He gave each man a dose of laudanum from his medical bag, and when the supplies arrived he straightened the broken bones with the assistance of a burly workman and applied the splints. Three additional workmen had been partially buried in the fall of masonry, and their fellow laborers dug them out quickly. One had a large contusion on his back, which Weatherby cleaned and Dredge dressed. The second was not so lucky. He had several broken ribs and a broken collar bone. After some laudanum, Weatherby wrapped the broken ribs with slender, tight strips of linen and sent the man to rest. It took twenty minutes for the masons to remove the bricks that covered the man at the base of the scaffold. His pelvis and arms were crushed. His face was purple, and he wasn't breathing. Weatherby applied stimulation and smelling salts with no response before sending the unfortunate man to the morgue. He checked with Christopher Dickinson—the masons had hurriedly laid twenty-five courses of bricks the day before, and then last night had been too cool for the mortar to set properly.

That night after dinner Weatherby summoned Dredge to the Wolsey Apartment.

"I need to visit Hepsibah to find out who she gave the bitter rose poison to," Weatherby said, "and I want you to accompany me within the hour."

"Yes, Your Grace."

The two met in the stable and headed to Wycombe, a ride that took ninety minutes. They got directions to Hepsibah's camp in the woods south of town. The buildings were all made of natural logs and sat in a tidy clearing.

"I want you to stay out of sight," Weatherby instructed. "I may be gone as long as twenty-four hours, but if I haven't reappeared or given you a sign by then, come in and get me."

"Yes, Your Grace," Dredge replied, concern in his voice.

Weatherby rode to the center of the camp and dismounted. After tying his horse he walked to the largest building. He was greeted as if he had been expected and ushered into a large room complete with a fire burning in the center. The walls were hung with bright tapestries showing fantastic beasts and witches. He stated his business and was shown into a smaller sitting room. Hepsibah came in almost immediately, wearing a thin green silk floor-length gown embroidered with gold thread. The material was almost transparent and pressed against her thighs and bosom as she walked.

"I see you've come about the bitter rose poison, just as you said you would," Hepsibah said as she hugged him and rubbed the front of her body sinuously against his.

"Who did you sell it to?" Weatherby asked.

"First, you must do something for me."

"Yes?"

"I want you to take the potion that you avoided so cleverly last time by pouring it down your sleeve and spend some private time with me so that I may know you."

Weatherby had thought that the witch might suggest something like that, and he had thought about just having her arrested and tortured. However, the merest brush of the potion on his lips had held powerful sway on his senses and filled him with an intense unknown pleasure. He wished to try it again.

"Very well."

"Then go with these young witches."

Two slender young women wearing red leather shifts and sandals took his arms and escorted him into a room filled with steam. In the center was a large tub of hot water. The young witches removed his boots and slowly detached the rest of Weatherby's clothing. All three entered the tub. They washed every inch of him and then perfumed his body and oiled his hair and combed it back. They placed a rich purple robe on his shoulders that reached to the ground and took him to Hepsibah. She admired his body. While the two witches held his arms firmly, she probed his mouth with her forked tongue. Then she took the familiar blue glass bottle and emptied it into his mouth. She gently stroked his neck until he swallowed.

Weatherby felt a wave of carnal desire start in his chest that then spread into his loins. He approached Hepsibah, but was gripped again by the two young witches and constrained in a prone position by wide purple ribbons on a large velvet bed. Once he was restrained, he felt someone sucking each of his toes and running their lips over his calves and then thighs. Next she knelt over him while touching his buttocks and back with her strong supple hands. He struggled against his bonds wanting to turn over, but the restraints were too tight. Finally, he relaxed and enjoyed the kisses and caresses.

Hepsibah knelt beside him and clapped her hands twice. Somehow he was lifted several feet into the air and flipped onto his back—again restrained, but Hepsibah was close beside him. Later he had a memory of full, pillowy tissue, a taut undulating belly, compliant lips and a curved configuration pressed against various parts of his body. The whole experience was the most intensely erotic and pleasurable of his life, but blurred by the potion.

Dredge found him outside the compound the next morning tired and slightly dazed. "Are you all right?" Dredge asked.

"I have never felt so satisfied in my life," Weatherby moaned. "My organs feel totally obliterated. Does that make any sense?"

"No, Your Grace," Dredge replied. "Let me take you home."

(Readers over fifteen may go to my web site www.BooksByHooks. com for another version of this chapter)

# PART 8

# CHAPTER 71

Dredge had worked as Weatherby's amanuensis for five years. He admired his employer's intelligence, discipline and focus. He always called Weatherby Your Grace in his presence but otherwise he called him SS, short for Seamus Scott. He had never seen SS as addled as he was right now. He didn't know what to do. Then he remembered an elixir that Weatherby had given him yesterday for just such circumstances. He pulled the vial from his inside pocket and unstoppered it.

"Drink this, Your Grace," Dredge implored.

Weatherby downed the syrupy, bitter tasting, tincture. At least he is compliant, Dredge thought. After sitting on a stump, his boss seemed less shaky and more alert.

"Let me help you onto your horse," Dredge said as he helped Weatherby stand and mount his horse.

Dredge pointed them toward home. As they rode, Weatherby slowly seemed more like himself. He asked questions about the last twenty-four hours which Dredge, of course, was unable to answer. He changed the topic to the things he did know.

"I have built a more powerful new rocket, Your Grace," Dredge began. "I reinforced the body with another layer of glued paper and drilled holes in the copper cone at the base to lighten the structure and allow more air at the burning gunpowder."

"Let's test it as soon as we have a sunny day," Weatherby replied. Then abruptly changing direction he said, "What happened to me back there?"

"I believe you fell under the spell of a powerful young witch," Dredge said softly.

"I went there with a purpose. What was it?"

"She promised you the name of the person she gave the bitter rose poison to."

"Right now the whole twenty-four hour period is a blur of soft touches, mounting pleasure and then intermittent feelings of bliss," Weatherby said wistfully. "But I'm sure I asked Hepsibah about the poison. Just before I left the lodge, I remember one of the witch's naked assistants placing a paper in my pocket."

Weatherby pulled an intricately folded, purple paper from the inside pocket of his doublet. The inside was covered with stars and comets drawn in silver ink but in the center it said, *Rosa Acerbus* or bitter rose in Latin and below some scrolling lines appeared the letters, '_SH____'. Most of the letters were blurred by sweat. Weatherby planned to pass the soft purple paper to Dredge, but just before he did it he felt warmth in his chest and a twinge of desire. He threw the paper onto the ground. Weatherby dismounted and picked the paper up with the tweezers in his pocket. He placed the paper in a folded piece of parchment and then washed his hands thoroughly.

"The note implies that Ishmael was the favored one who was given the bitter rose poison, but the paper is impregnated with Hepsibah's love potion so be careful with it," Weatherby said in measured tones. "When we get back to the laboratory, see if you can analyze it."

Weatherby on his tall roan and Dredge on his short pony rode the rest of the way back to Hampton Court in silence. After dropping his horse at the stable, Weatherby sought out Amarantha for dinner. They took cold vegetables and chunks of ham out to the rose garden with a bottle of Rhenish wine.

"Where have you been, Seamus?" Amarantha asked.

"I had to get some information about the poison that poor Anna Maria Wimbledon was given," Weatherby replied.

"Were you with that slut Hepsibah again?"

"Yes. She is the only mortal I've ever found who knows about the bitter rose poison."

"But you *spent the night* with her."

"She is smart and doesn't yield information readily."

"So you were plying her with questions about poisons the entire night?"

"Well not exactly."

"I hate that you pressed your body against hers at Stonehenge and then spent the night with her at Wycombe."

"Are you jealous, Ran?"

"What if I am?"

"I just never felt that from you before, my darling."

"I am no one's darling," Amarantha frumped.

"I'm just a man, you beautiful thing, and men unlike women have sexual needs that must be satisfied. I learned that about myself when I was seventeen, and as a doctor I've seen it over and over again. Pent-up sexual desire leads men to behave badly, and congress with a willing woman or a visit to a bawdy house can set them right with the world for a half a Sovereign or less. Why do you suppose there are so many houses of ill repute? I suppose I'm deeply flattered that you care," Weatherby said as he gave her a tender hug.

Not to be put off, Amarantha retorted, "Those fancy establishments like the White Swan keep unfortunate girls and women with no skills off the streets and out of debtor's prison. That and the worry that otherwise respectable women might be attacked in the streets are the only reason male officials turn a blind eye toward them."

"We've never talked about this before. I had no idea you were so vehement."

"Don't get me wrong. You work, talk and play with women as equals, unlike nearly every powerful man and our society as a whole, but in the sexual area you are clearly prehistoric. The women I know well are surprisingly like men in the sexual arena with much the same desires and feelings, but we all hide it in society for fear of being ostracized."

Weatherby look a drink of Rhenish wine and said, "You've given me something to think about, Ran. I'm sure this wonderful topic will come up again. I'm going to go to the library and work on those accursed journals."

As he walked there, he reviewed the approaches he had tried to date the journals—ordering them by degree of fading, relating them to comets and shooting stars, having his assistants look for numbers that might be dates—none had worked. The problem was that Sir Rodney, unlike most compulsive Tudor diarists, didn't put a front page on each journal giving the writer's name, location and date. Weatherby decided to read the last paragraph of one journal and then see if he could match it to the first paragraph of one of the other tomes. He had liked puzzles since he was small and that was reason he was a good detective, however, he had to admit that the tortuous nature of his current case was vexing him.

When Weatherby arrived in the library he was cheered by the assistant librarians, Judith Scotson and Margaret Sedgwick. Margaret made him a cup of tea and Judith gave him a warm kiss that reminded him of the erotic ride they had made from Teddington. Then Weatherby sat down and spent six hours looking at the frustrating journals. At the end of the day, he felt no further ahead in unraveling Sir Rodney's copious writing.

Weatherby sought out Sir John Moulton for some relaxing dinner conversation. He found Sir John hunched over a plan in his construction shack. The King's Surveyor was puffing his pipe furiously and swearing.

"What seems to be the trouble, Sir John?" Weatherby asked.

"The length of this gallery is off three inches and I've added it six times," Moulton said in an exasperated voice.

"Here give me the numbers. I'm quite good at arithmetic," Weatherby said taking a pencil out of his inside pocket.

Weatherby added the series of numbers twice. "It's forty-six feet, seven inches."

"Thank you," Moulton said. "Let's eat!"

The two men walked across the bridge and through the village to The Lamb and Flag. They sat in the heavily timbered public house in the front of the inn and quaffed several tankards of ale. Moulton had a lot of questions about Hepsibah, which Weatherby answered to the best of his ability. Eventually however, he got bored of the subject.

"She is a very shapely and erotic witch, Sir John," Weatherby finally said to close the subject. "I never had such feelings of passion and fulfillment because of the potion she had me drink. But regretfully, the entire twenty-four hours is a blur and I can not give you a coherent accounting of it."

"I'm sorry to hear that. I already told you that for me, more than half the pleasure of an assignation is reliving it in my imagination later. I can imagine the scent of a woman with all its complex elements. No two smell the same. I can remember the texture of a nipple I touched thirty years ago."

"You are quite a sybarite, Sir John. Why don't you approach her yourself? She is only seventeen and sometimes doesn't know her own mind."

"I'll stop ruminating about her. I have a fifteen-year-old chamber maid that I'm seeing who is very willing."

"Good for you. How are the King's various projects coming along?"

"The finishing touches on the Great Hall are going well and the gallery off of the Knot Garden is back on track after the wall fell down. The Bayne Tower is complete and turned out to be quite handsome I believe."

"Will you be relocating to another Palace?"

"Probably not. New plans for the Great Close Tennis Court and the Queen's Apartments are arriving weekly. I could easily be here another three or four years if the King lives."

"And I will still be here then trying to solve my confounded murderers," Weatherby opined.

# CHAPTER 72

The two adjourned to the dining room for oyster chowder and roasted duck and drank three bottles of wine with their supper. Fresh strawberries in cream were served for dessert. By the end of the meal both were tipsy. Just walking straight took both men's full concentration and their speech was slurred. Just before the bridge over the Thames, a small patch of dense woods narrowed the road. As they entered it, something white and ethereal floated eerily over their heads. Both men stopped and instinctively leaned against each other as they looked up. Weatherby drew his dagger. Then they heard the approach of horses' hooves, and three black stallions galloped abreast toward them with riders in long black gowns. At the last possible moment, the horses divided around the frightened men and cantered over the bridge.

"God in heaven," Moulton whispered.

Weatherby's heart slowed and the two men walked across the bridge, both discussing what they had seen. When they reached the Palace side of the bridge, Amarantha and Dredge jumped out of the bushes.

"Did you see those horsemen?" Moulton asked.

"On this quiet night, what, ghostly horsemen on charging black steeds?" the two said together before they burst out laughing.

"I see," Weatherby said slowly. "This was an elaborate ruse by you two tricksters. I apologize for them, Sir John. They have often done this to me on All Hallows Eve, but never in midsummer."

Three of the four were now laughing on the dark, quiet banks of the Thames and Moulton soon joined in.

"How did you do that ghost?" Weatherby asked Dredge.

"Just a sheet stuffed with rags on a wire," Dredge replied smugly.

"And the horses?" Moulton asked.

"I remembered a nightmare Weatherby told me about three months ago where he was being chased by three black chargers," Amarantha said. "They only had two black horses in the stable, so we had to paint the third gelding with bootblack."

Even though he was still drunk, Weatherby broke in, "This is the way my staff displays their displeasure about the day and night I spent with Hepsibah. They know that in future before I disport with the voluptuous young witch, I will think twice and probably be more circumspect in the degree of contact I have with her. You see, even though they won't say it, they think that I behaved shabbily and they are probably correct."

They had reached the Great Gatehouse and each of the four headed off to bed. Weatherby slept fitfully. An execution was planned for the next day, and Weatherby ordered a hearty breakfast.

Manchester was to be hanged at noon in Teddington, and Weatherby wished to question the abductor one last time. Reports were that he had been quite brave during his brief sojourn at the Tower. He had withstood the rack, the *strappado* and the burning of his feet with stoicism. However, he had been sentenced to hang anyway for abducting Judith Scotson.

Weatherby went to the stables where his roan was already saddled. Amarantha was holding the reins of her small black Arabian. A drawing and quartering, or a hanging was a social event as popular as Christmas or Easter in Tudor England. Amarantha would shop at the stalls set up on the edge of the crowd to sell food, crafts and clothing. The two crossed the bridge across the Thames and then turned east. They rode side by side on the broad flat road and talked amicably.

As they rode into Teddington a crowd of two thousand or so had already gathered and the flags and banners gave a carnival atmosphere. Amarantha went to an inn for tea while Weatherby went to the jail. Manchester sat in a small cell, devouring a large meal. The jailer let Weatherby into the cell.

"I want to ask you some questions," Weatherby said without preamble. "Given your situation, I hope you will answer truthfully."

"Unh," the prisoner grunted with his mouth full of food.

"Did you recognize the man that slit Nathaniel Philbrick's throat at your gambling den?"

"Aye."

Pulling a parchment out of this pocket with a visage drawn on it, Weatherby said, "Is this the man?"

"Aye."

"If you don't stop eating, I will have your precious food taken away and they will stretch your neck despite a great rumbling in your belly."

Manchester had been eating with his fingers. He wiped them on his filthy doublet.

"That be Shrewsbury," He mumbled. "He gambled at the hut over the yars. Big stakes un' wee bit o' luck. Lots uh fights un' knifin's."

"Did he ever talk about William Suffolk or Gregory Townsend?"

"Nuh."

"How about Anna Maria Wimbledon?"

"He jabbered about her and her ripe twat."

"So you think he lay with her or only imagined it?"

"Beats me."

Suddenly Weatherby was tired of this stupid, vile, troublesome man and he quickly stood up and left the jail. Amarantha was at a nearby inn and they both walked to the slight hill where the gallows were located. Weatherby estimated at least four thousand people were now present. Children ran to the front and their parents jostled each other to get a better view. Most were eating, talking and laughing like a day at the fair. Amarantha stopped to look at some books that were for sale.

An hour later, an old solid-wheeled wooden cart approached with the unfortunate Manchester manacled to a post in the bed with his head hanging down. When they saw him the crowd cheered. The cart was drawn slowly by a beaten-looking mule. The throng parted to allow the condemned man to pass. Stopping at the gallows, he was led up the steps with his hands bound behind his back. A priest approached and Manchester knelt and prayed. A stout rope was placed around his neck and he was maneuvered over the trap door.

The hangman had control over the swiftness of death once the body was dropped. A large winding of rope around the central strand pulled tight under the condemned man's ear, made a swift painless death more likely. This had not been done for Manchester. A fall of ten to twelve feet assured enough acceleration so that the jerk at the bottom broke the vertebra just below the skull and severed the spinal cord. Manchester would only fall five feet.

The Sheriff read the charges and the sentence. The crowd cheered. The hangman opened the trapdoor, and the body fell a short distance insufficient to break the criminal's neck. Manchester's feet kicked the air and his mouth gasped for breath. His face turned purple. He lost control of his bladder and bowels but the agonizing kicking continued. Weatherby was disgusted at the prolonged, amateur job the hangman had done. He turned away and blocked Amarantha's view as well.

"Such barbarism!" Amarantha exclaimed.

"The King condones it as entertainment," Weatherby said sadly as he took Amarantha's arm and walked quickly through the throng.

"He also hopes to educate his subjects about the punishment for misbehavior. What a tawdry spectacle."

"Thank fortune you and I would be beheaded if we committed some unspeakable crime. At least it would be fast."

The two had reached their horses, mounted, and pointed them toward home. They rode side by side silently as they left Teddington. Then, Amarantha brought Weatherby up to date on her investigation of the Master of the House.

"He had been gone this last month," Amarantha began. "With business at Whitehall and Canterbury. But now he is back and he is the most guarded man I have ever met. He has resumed his assault on my virginity, but I am coy and teasing as usual."

"Perhaps in a moment of weakness he will reveal a secret to you," Weatherby said.

"I suspect he would be more compliant if I pleased him with my hand. He always seems to have an erection."

"You know how abhorrent I find that," Weatherby replied. "But if you must, just don't let him see you naked, and avoid intercourse with him at all cost. If it comes to something like that I would rather beat the information out of him."

"If only we could find Sir Rodney or Ishmael. Then none of this subterfuge would be necessary."

"Perhaps Ellen Iverson will have some new clues. I'll talk with her when I get back. Now let's talk of pleasanter things."

"Have you ever seen a summer day lovelier than this?"

"No. I have a glade I want to show you," Weatherby said nudging his horse off the trail with Amarantha following.

He stopped his horse in a grassy glade and tied both mounts to a branch. He walked to the edge of the glade where a gentle stream splashed pleasantly into a deep blue pool. Weatherby peeled off his sweaty doublet, linen shirt, hose, boots and loincloth and stepped into the warm water. Amarantha followed two steps behind him shedding her clothing as she walked toward the edge. As the water reached his waist, he turned and offered her his hand. He guided her into deeper water as he gazed on her full breasts, white stomach and triangle of tangled red hair. They floated across the pond joined by one hand as they chatted amicably. On the far side of the pool a large patch of bright yellow marsh marigolds shimmered and small green heron fished warily.

As the sun weakened Amarantha felt a shiver. Weatherby helped her up onto the grassy bank and rubbed her dry with his linen shirt. Once they were clothed, they rode back to Hampton Court refreshed despite their memories of the botched hanging.

# CHAPTER 73

Weatherby and Amarantha spent the rest of the afternoon and evening in the Wolsey Apartment sorting through mail and reading like an old married couple. They retired early. In the morning he took some breakfast on a tray to the Confectory. Ellen Iverson was already making tarts and a large pot of cherries in sugary syrup boiled merrily on the fire. Ellen spread the food on a nearby table and warmed Weatherby's biscuits before spreading a thick layer of butter and jam on them.

"I heard the hanging was a great success," Ellen said.

"If you mean it drew a big crowd," Weatherby replied, "then yes. But it was a botched job by an inexperienced hangman with kicking, gasping and the release of bodily fluids."

"That executioner isn't inexperienced at all," Ellen retorted. "He's been sending people to hell for a decade."

"Why did he do such a shabby job then?"

"He is a gambler and was always in debt to Manchester. You remember when Dredge had his problem with dice. Manchester always treated his marks badly. The hangman did that agonizing death just the way he wanted to do it."

"Zounds, Ellen. I really need to talk to you more often. Why can't you just tell me how to find my murderers so I can go back to my comfortable apartment in London?"

"Exactly so. Why would I want you to go? You may be the only person at Hampton Court that is smart enough to appreciate my cleverness."

"I most certainly do! Now you need to tell me where to find Sir Rodney."

"Despite his resources and deviousness, I'm surprised you haven't brought him to ground yet."

"Thanks for your confidence."

"I would look close to his lair here at Hampton Court. He is old and no longer agile. He must rely more and more on his disguises and sleight of hand rather than speed. I suspect he was at the hanging yesterday and you looked right at him without recognizing who he was."

"What about Ishmael?"

"I believe that is what you call the dark-skinned one who sells precious stones. He should be your first objective. He isn't as smart as Sir Rodney, and he must trade regularly to sustain himself. You know the cities where he has contacts. He has to visit those cities no matter how surreptitious. I've seen him and can help you make a sketch."

"How could I get along without your help?" Weatherby said as he grabbed a warm cherry tart and took a bite of the flaky crust.

"You couldn't," Ellen concluded as Weatherby went out the Dutch door of the Confectory.

He went to the library to check on Margaret and Judith. They were still working on Sir Rodney's fifty-seven journals. Margaret had found a small number at the bottom of pages numbered by multiples of thirteen and thought it might be a hidden catalog. However, after checking the rest of the journals it didn't pan out. Since their intimate ride from Teddington, Judith always placed a hand on Weatherby's arm or shoulder. When they were completely alone she touched the back of his neck lightly.

Weatherby and Amarantha would be leaving in the afternoon for the King's birthday party on June 28th the fourth day before Kalends of July, so Weatherby spent the rest of the afternoon with Dredge in the laboratory. He was still analyzing poisons from Sir Rodney's lair and was impressed by their variety and potency. He hadn't stumbled across the bitter rose poison yet. He was still trying to crack the Linear A and Linear B codes used by Anna Maria Wimbledon and Henri de Lèves. Dredge constructed a large table top pattern twenty-six boxes on a side with the letters of the English alphabet along the columns and the symbols of the codes along the rows. By placing a numbered block on one of the squares, he could initiate a substitution and then proceed in a pattern by adding subsequently numbered blocks. So far hundreds of substitutions had not yielded any readable text, just a rare random word.

"Take the easel and some paper over to the Confectory so I can sketch a likeness of Ishmael," Weatherby said.

"When you get back from London I want to try out the more powerful missile I built," Dredge said as he took the rocket down from a shelf. "I thumbed through some Chinese books on fireworks and borrowed ideas from some of the pictures. Almost all their designs have angular cardboard pieces like fish's fins glued on the sides to prevent wobbling, so I added two sets to our rocket."

"I like the bright red color you painted it."

"She also has a sister," Dredge replied as he took down an identical three-foot-long blue rocket.

"I have time, and it's a windless day. Let's fire one now."

"Let me get a passenger," Dredge said as he reached into a cage full of mice.

They walked to a large grassy meadow south of the Palace. Dredge had built a v-shaped launch pad out of two boards that he had driven into the ground.

"The rockets were getting too heavy for that stick we were using as a launcher and this way the rocket will go up at precisely forty-five degrees," Dredge remarked.

He loaded the mouse into the chamber below the nose cone and laid the rocket in the v formed by the two boards. He lit the fuse and both men stepped back. Nothing happened at first, but then after a hissing sound, a thin burst of white fire poured out of the base of the rocket and the tube moved up the launcher and took off into the humid blue sky. The fins did make the projectile travel straighter. It streaked across the field and landed softly in the grass. Weatherby measured the distance at five hundred and thirteen feet, with a flight time of five seconds.

"You boosted the speed, Dredge," he said excitedly. "Your red rocket went seventy miles an hour. At that rate, I could travel to London in fourteen minutes. How I would love that."

"That will never happen for humans, Your Grace," Dredge replied. "God wouldn't allow it."

"You mark my words," Weatherby replied vehemently. "Sometime people will be able to go that fast even if you and I don't live to see it."

They both reached the undamaged rocket lying in the soft grass at the same time. Weatherby opened the capsule and extracted the mouse.

"He doesn't look any the worse to me," he said. "Observe him for a couple of days and if he shows no ill effects, release him as a reward."

They walked back to the laboratory, very pleased with themselves. Weatherby walked to the Water Gate where Amarantha awaited the trip down river. A chambermaid had loaded both of their luggage for the King's birthday and a picnic basket. The elegant red and gold barge cast off and the oarsmen moved the craft into the center of the Thames. The craft was loaded with Palace residents going to the King's party. Richard Weston was aboard wearing a rich velvet doublet and shoes with large buckles. Weatherby motioned Amarantha toward him so she could flirt and pump him for information.

Weatherby sat along the starboard side so he could observe the wildlife along the shore. He recognized the man in the next seat as Clyde Lowery, William Suffolk's former assistant.

"How have you been?" Weatherby asked.

"Well. I got promoted to Will's position and have been busy making panels of glass for windows and door," Lawrence replied. "You've seen how much building is going on. Sir John Moulton thinks windows add elegance even to a kitchen or closet so we are shaping and leading glass seven days a week."

"Have you thought anymore about who might have wanted William dead?"

"Not really. I told you before that he seemed perfectly happy at Hampton Court the first year and a half and that suddenly things changed. He had trouble making friends and finding girlfriends, but it was more than that. His belief system seemed to change in a way that he never revealed to me. Suddenly he was dour, brooding and preoccupied. Perhaps he developed a relationship with another man. He had no success with the women at the Palace, everyone saw that. Then the shame of it became too much for his partner."

"Is there a lot of homosexuality at Hampton Court?"

"The usual amount among the clerics, I suppose but not among the construction workers. They fill the two whorehouses every night. That's what would make such a relationship between two men so shameful."

"It an angle I haven't explored," Weatherby replied thoughtfully. "I'll check it out. Have you found any pieces of glass with writing on it?"

"No. I looked at one piece of yellow glass with a suspicious line on it but it turned out to be just an irregular crack."

Amarantha and Richard Weston seemed to be having a disagreement and Weatherby moved over close enough to hear their conversation.

"I am certainly not going to do that!" Amarantha said.

"But it is such a perfect opportunity to stay together at the Savoy Hotel, my darling," Richard said in a soothing voice.

"I have fittings and makeup appointments before the King's lunch tomorrow, Richard. I have to have the waist taken in and bosom let out," Amarantha replied, touching Richard's arm. "I will see you at the luncheon."

She winked as she walked past Weatherby.

# CHAPTER 74

The barge pulled into Tower dock at seven. It was light and the western part of London still bustled, taking advantage of the long summer day. The streets were full of carts, horses and pedestrians. Dust was everywhere from traffic on the unpaved avenues. Weatherby hailed a hansom and helped Amarantha aboard before giving directions to his apartment in Threadneedle Street. Mrs. Pansy was waiting with some cheese and a glass of wine. The travelers had time to clean up before her stuffed pork roast was ready. After they ate they sat under a gas lamps and Weatherby read erotic stories and tales of love from *The Thousand and one Nights* out loud to Amarantha.

In the morning both dressed in their finest summer clothes for the King's birthday luncheon. Amarantha wore a long light-blue silk dress. Whitehall Palace near London Bridge was in the center of the city and didn't have the vast grounds for gardens and orchards that Hampton Court did. The meal was served at hundreds of tables set in a large courtyard. King Henry and Anne Boleyn were an hour late. Weatherby wished he were spending the warm summer day at home in Surrey. The King wore a black and white doublet with slashes along the sleeve that showed gold material underneath. The style featured broad, padded shoulders for men and when combined with Henry's prominent belly gave him a massive appearance like a lazy old bull that had gone to fat. Weatherby had read that as a young man Henry had a thirty-five inch waist, which was now, he estimates, in the mid-fifties. Ladies fashions were to appear as petite as possible. Anne's dark blue silk dress featured a French hood, a low-cut bodice and a very small cinched waist.

If placed on a balance and weighed, Weatherby suspected it would take four Annes to balance one Henry. In fact, the size difference was ludicrous. The King looked like a large brown beehive with Anne a tiny bluebird flitting around it. More like grandfather and granddaughter rather than King and Consort, he thought. Weatherby's mind moved on to wool-gathering as the toasts and the many courses of the luncheon dragged on. The most popular dish was huge pie crusts carried in by two servants. When cut open, they released flights of small song birds. A orchestra of thirty players sat just to the left of the King. They played 'The Kynge's Ballade' and other tunes that Weatherby recognized. Just before the second dessert of berries in a sweetened whipped cream, Weatherby was handed an envelope from a liveried servant. It read:

Sir Seamus Scott Weatherby, MB

He tore it open. He was commanded to appear before the King at three that day. He passed the note to Amarantha who quietly shook her head. Both rose from their seats and after a brief bow toward the Royals, took their leave.

Once they were alone, Amarantha said, "What is that about?"

"The interminable murder investigation I'm conducting within the confines of one of the King's Palaces without any resolution in sight."

"But that is so unfair. The three of us have worked tirelessly on every possible clue and lead."

"To what result, Ran?"

"Think you should show the King a sketch of Ishmael and Sir Rodney and ask his help in locating them."

"That is a capital idea. I will do that if I get a chance to speak before he discharges me."

Amarantha went with Weatherby to find paper and charcoal in the unfamiliar castle and then Weatherby found a quiet corner to draw. He arrived at the Privy Chamber fifteen minutes early and was shown in just as the tower clock struck three. His Monarch was on time for once in his life, Weatherby thought sardonically. The King and Chancellor Cromwell sat behind a broad oak table with a clerk off to the side. The clerk's quill scratched annoyingly on a large piece of parchment. Weatherby bowed low.

"The King is displeased with your investigation of the tragic deaths at Hampton Court Palace," Cromwell intoned. "He demands an explanation, now!"

"I have solved over fifty murders for the King in the past five years, yet none is as complicated and vexatious as this current case Your Majesty," Weatherby said with his head still bowed low.

"I don't give a damn about five years ago!" The King roared. "I want the murderer in the Tower so that he can be tortured before I put him to death!"

"You have been richly rewarded for you past successes," Cromwell said in a more soothing tone. "How can we make this right?"

"My staff and I will redouble our efforts beginning tonight if I may beg to be excused from our Monarch's birthday celebration."

"So be it!" Henry roared back. "You have a fortnight."

"Thank you, Your Majesty," Weatherby replied. "But I must find these two men and break them. Indulge me with a month if it please, Your Highness," Weatherby continued as he placed the two sketches on the oak table. "My I have your excellent servants look for these two men?"

"Agreed." The King responded in a resigned tone. "You are almost as recalcitrant as the Dutch."

Weatherby backed out of the Privy Chamber with his head still bowed. Amarantha and Dredge were waiting just outside and he motioned them into a deserted bay window before giving them the news. It was too late in the day to take a barge back to Hampton Court. The three decided to visit the inns and brothels of London in hopes of finding Sir Rodney or Ishmael. Dredge and Weatherby took the disreputable and more dangerous Southwark side of town and Amarantha visited the more genteel establishments around the Tower. They agreed to meet at the center of London Bridge at two a.m. Weatherby and Dredge caught a hansom to the center of Southwark and then split up. Weatherby worked east toward Greenwich. Lots of people were out on such a warm summer night. The public houses were poorly lit and it took time after ordering a tankard of ale to check all the inhabitants without looking obvious. In the second inn, Weatherby saw a slight older man that looked a lot like Sir Rodney in the gloom. As he worked his way toward the man, the resemblance seemed even stronger, and then the man spoke in a heavy Italian accent. The rest of the bawdy houses and inns were crowded with revelers that bore no discernable likeness to the two suspects. When Weatherby arrived, footsore and tired on the bridge, Amarantha and Dredge were already waiting.

"Any luck?" Weatherby asked.

"I struck up a conversation with one slight East Indian, but he isn't our man," Amarantha said while Dredge just shook his head.

They caught a hansom back to Threadneedle Street and fell into bed exhausted. In the morning they caught the early barge back upriver and arrived at seven in the evening. Weatherby went through his mail hoping to find something that would break open the case, but he found nothing. Sometimes when he was puzzled he sought out a quiet place, usually outdoors, where he could relax and just think. He walked south of the Palace and sat against the trunk of a large beech tree. First he let his mind just wander and then slowly he brought it into focus. He drifted off to sleep for a bit. When he awoke he was certain he was dealing with a small cabal, perhaps as few as three people, that his murder victims were being used by them and that the motive was religious and subversive. Now all he had to do was find one of them. If he could identify one of them, he probably could make that person incriminate the other two.

As he was walking back to the Palace, a chamber man approached with a note from Ellen Iverson saying that Ishmael had been seen in Reading the previous day. It was eight-thirty, a little too late to start a ride, so he dined with Amarantha and Dredge and went to bed early. Weatherby left early the next morning. A rainstorm during the night had wet the roads, but at least they weren't slippery. Reading was a medium-sized town twenty-three miles to the west. Weatherby arrived in Reading, muddy and a little saddle-sore by late morning. He sought out a room in the Wheatsheaf Inn where he could change, and then expressed an interest in buying jewels to the owner and was directed to a house on High Street in the old part of town. He rode a fresh mount into the city past a large monastery with moss-covered walls. The building he sought was a white clapboard house on a side street that reminded him of the house where he had been drugged in York. No one came to the dark green painted door after several knocks so Weatherby entered. If he smelled anything amiss he planned was to hold his breath and flee. He remembered the strong pungent smell that has weakened him before he was put in that appalling dungeon. He had no desire to repeat that experience.

He walked down a hallway with empty rooms on each side and then into a kitchen. He had a feeling of *déjà vu*. A woman was bent over a large pot of boiling stew, throwing cabbage and leeks into the mix.

"Pardon me. I was hoping I might buy some rare jewels," Weatherby said. "Is there someone here who might be of assistance?"

The woman looked up and Weatherby recognized her immediately as the cook from the house in York.

# CHAPTER 75

"What are you doing here?" Weatherby exclaimed.

"I work fur one of them stone salesmen, Master," the woman replied.

"I arrest you in the name of the King as an accessory to his servant's imprisonment," Weatherby retorted, reaching for her arm.

"What servant? What imprisonment?" The woman shrieked back. "I ain't no criminal. I ain't done nuffin'."

She pulled her hands back and silently crossed himself.

"What's your name?" Weatherby demanded.

"Mattie Dunn."

"Where's Ishmael?"

"Upstairs, sleepin', last I knowed."

Weatherby turned and bounded out of the kitchen and up the stairs, taking two step at a time. He threw open each door as he went down the hallway. In one room darkened room he found a bed with rumpled covers. The blankets were still warm and a small blond woman lay huddled in the covers.

"Where is he?" Weatherby shouted.

The woman pointed to the door with a pale, slender arm. Weatherby ran to a nearby window and saw a man running toward the monastery. Weatherby bounded back down the stairs and out the back door. He ran across the yard and toward the buildings of the monastery. The walls were of grey limestone quarried from the nearby Berkshire Hills and covered now, four hundred years later, by moss. The outline of the building and moss created shadows a man could hide in, Weatherby noted. He sprinted past the abbey and looked down High Street into the town. He saw no male running. Weatherby decided that Ishmael had ducked into monastery. Reading Abbey contained hundred of relics including the hand of Jesus' disciple James. What a bizarre hiding place for an infidel, Weatherby mused. The interior of the abbey was very dark with many hallways and heavy oak doors with round iron handles. He slowed his pace and began to check each room and cubby along the way. Chanting monks in brown burel robes with hoods walked deliberately up the hallways. Ishmael could have stolen a robe and Weatherby looked for a tall, slightly built brother of which there were few. He spoke to those over five feet tall and waited for a response in the King's English.

Weatherby had heard that Reading Abbey was one of the most prosperous abbeys in the realm and from the size of it could easily have held several hundred monks. He found the Keeper of the Keys and explained that he was looking for a Mohammedan. Guards were soon placed on all the exits and Weatherby continued his search with the help of two monks. After two hours of searching for the infidel all the monks that weren't guarding exits gathered for a simple lunch of soup, bread and prayer.

Refreshed and rested Weatherby and the two monks resumed searching. The sanctuary was full of many small side altars and tombs on stands. The only light came through tall but narrow stained glass windows. Most of the glass was a blue color that was beautiful but admitted little light. Each of the monks carried a candle. Weatherby found the dust disturbed under the tomb of Constance of York along one side of the narthex. Further behind the white marble tomb he found a worn brown sandal unlike the style the monks wore.

"The infidel was wearing sandals," Weatherby said picking up the footwear. "I saw them on his feet. Where could someone go from here to hide?"

"Down into the treasury under the apse, I expect," one of the monk's replied as he led them in a new direction.

The stairs spiraled down into the damp dark under the altar. Each stair tread was worn into a gentle curve by the tread of thousands of feet over the centuries. The damp smell reminded Weatherby of the dungeon where he had been held captive. He fought down a faint feeling of panic. Even with candles the three searchers stumbled against tombs, old candlesticks and broken statues. The older monk was in the far corner of the tomb when someone exploded past him. Weatherby stretched his arms out instinctively and brushed the person but couldn't hold him.

The slight figure sprinted into the darkness and then onto the stairs. The iron gate at the top of the limestone stairs slammed shut. The three searchers moved as one toward the stairs and clambered to the top where the gate had been locked.

Weatherby banged into the bars in frustration. The smaller monk worked his hands through the bars and eventually undid the lock, but precious time had been lost. All three raced instinctively toward the town side of the Abbey. It would offer the narrow streets and old buildings where Ishmael could hide. The monk guarding the narrow limestone arch that opened toward the town was still dusting himself off.

"Where did he go?" the older monk asked breathlessly.

The guard pointed toward the old part of Reading. The monks were not allowed to accompany Weatherby. He said a hurried thank you and headed into the first dark street. The old half-timbered buildings loomed over the narrow road and shoppers walked from shop to shop buying foodstuffs and house wares. Where to begin? He decided to make a quick trip the length of the street to see if any of the businesses might catch the eye of a Muslim jewelry merchant. Most of the shops were uncluttered, making hiding difficult, and none had an eastern theme where Ishmael might find a willing friend until the very last shop on the left. Its hand-painted sign said, 'Levantine Trader' and the small space was filled with oriental chairs, Persian rugs and brass pots. Weatherby slipped through the door and began searching behind the chests and trunks. The dark-skinned proprietor walked toward him.

"May I be of help?" the owner asked politely as he bowed slightly.

"Have you seen this man?" Weatherby asked as he pulled a folded piece of paper from his inside pocket.

"No, Your Grace."

Weatherby thought the proprietor answered a little quickly without really looking at the visage on the paper. He brushed past the owner and walked quickly toward the back door. As Weatherby approached, Ishmael jumped out of a tall wooden cabinet and raced for the back door. Weatherby knew the slender man was younger and faster. As Ishmael gained distance across the dark field behind the establishment, Weatherby pulled his dagger and threw it at the escaping Muslim. Though the knife was too heavy and thick-handled for a throwing knife, he managed to hit Ishmael's shoulder, cutting him but not sticking in his flesh. In a few more strides, the jewel salesman had disappeared into the night.

Weatherby walked back into the store and rested briefly in a wicker chair. He walked down the street and reported the man he was looking for to the bailiff on duty at the constable office. The bailiff was suspicious at first.

"This here station is undermanned, Your Grace," the bailiff whined. "En we's won't be a much help."

"Then I need your name and I need to speak to your Sergeant," Weatherby replied sternly.

"I be Cecil, but thar' ain't no Sergeant jus' now," Cecil said in a disheartened voice.

Weatherby spun on his heel and walked out of the constabulary, slamming the door behind him. He was deeply disheartened. The King had given him thirty days, and he had just wasted one solid day on an important suspect without getting his hands around the man's scrawny neck.

Men Weatherby's age often lost their mental edge and sought less-demanding occupations. He had already lived eight years longer than the average Englishman. He checked his mental powers daily with feats of memory and puzzles. He thought his mental powers were undiminished, however he wasn't as young as he once was and twice during this investigation suspects had gotten away because he wasn't fleeter of foot. As he walked back to the Wheatsheaf Inn, he considered spending the rest of his days as a small town surgeon in rural Scotland. Then he remembered vividly how much he had hated it when he tried it after medical school. He drank some ale and ate a hearty supper of roast chicken before falling into bed completely exhausted with aching calves and a dense black cloud still hanging just above both of his ears.

In the morning he felt little better, but mounted his friendly roan after the horse snorted his approval when he first saw his master. Weatherby rode out of the courtyard of the Inn and into a dense fog. The ride home was necessarily slow and he arrived at Hampton Court in the afternoon. He sought out Amarantha and described his discouraging day in detail while she massaged the muscles of his shoulders and back. She listened without comment to his long tale of woe.

When he was finished talking she volunteered, "You need to employ another assistant, Seamus. You already have beauty and diligence on your side in Dredge and me, but you need a muscular young gazelle. I will find one for you, but right now I want you to come with me."

Amarantha blindfolded him and took Weatherby's hand. She led him to the second floor of the Bayne Tower. She had received permission from the Master of the House to use the King's large heated bath. She ushered Weatherby into the steamy room adorned with a hundred candles. She took off his clothing and then removed the blindfold. She helped him over the side and into the steaming bath and left, leaving a fresh fluffy robe behind.

# CHAPTER 76

Weatherby soaked in the steaming water for two hours. He let his mind wander, and slowly his frustrations and discouragements fell away like wilting rose petals. He wrapped himself in a robe and walked to his apartment for a night of deep dreamless sleep. In the morning the world seemed brighter, and he met with Dredge to review his amanuensis's progress.

"The deciphering of the two codes-Linear A and Linear B is at a standstill, Your Grace," Dredge reported. "None of the learned texts on deciphering codes have been useful. I have applied all the formulas they write about from the simplest to the most complex, and all I get is pages of gibberish. The Italian states have a long history of devious communication, and a clever Duke or Bishop would often develop a completely new code for an important project. So we may have a totally unique system of writing that has never been used before. Both of our encoders wrote lots of text, particularly Anna Maria. The only practical code would be one with simple enough rules that they could be memorized."

"Unless the rules are recorded somewhere," Weatherby replied. "Like at the beginning of Miss Wimbledon's diary."

"I spent extra time looking at the first three pages of foolscap," Dredge said. "I even had the librarians separate and count each symbol. I concluded that the beginning was neither a table for decoding nor a set of rules for enciphering the text."

"What about the learned professors that we queried?"

"We sent samples of the text to most of the major European universities," Dredge responded in a discouraged tone. "As you know, the professors of Linguistics didn't recognize the writing and had few suggestions about where we might search for answers."

"We need a fresh approach to this problem," Weatherby mused. "Take a sample of the writing to Sir John Moulton and Hepsibah and see if they have any ideas. I'll mail a sample to Dr. Angus McKenzie at the University of Edinburgh. He isn't a linguist but an eccentric professor of necromancy and the occult. Perhaps his bizarre turn of mind that might just help us."

Richard Weston, the Master of the House, had called an emergency meeting in the Great Hall for ten a.m. Weatherby resented almost every meeting called by the authorities but particularly those called by Weston. He had a trivial side and, as the Chancellor had written, had developed an egocentric and uneven turn of mind. Weatherby found such public gatherings irksome. He went at the last possible minute and sat far to the back of the Hall, hoping that at some point when Weston began to drone on and on, as he always did, that he might sneak out without being noticed. Weatherby estimated that almost every one of the three hundred permanent residents of Hampton Court was there. Weston was fifteen minutes late. When he arrived he ascended the dais immediately. Three religious men in ecclesiastical robes followed him. He grasped the podium, turned toward his audience, and began to speak.

"We are here for the trial of Seamus Scott Weatherby, former Doctor of Medicine who has been accused of being a warlock," Weston intoned.

Weatherby had been drifting off to sleep until the mention of his name startled him awake. He wasn't even sure he had heard Weston correctly, but Dredge, Amarantha and Sir John Moulton were moving to him quickly.

"Did you know about this?" Dredge asked.

"Of course not!" Weatherby replied in a disdainful voice. "I certainly wouldn't wander into one of Weston's obnoxious gatherings unprepared."

Weatherby's mind raced. No one knew about his real indiscretion with Hepsibah at her lodge in Wycombe. The only time he had been seen with her was at the solstice, and she had initiated all the fondling and kissing. Perhaps this trial was because Amarantha hadn't yielded to Weston and he was striking back at her employer. The real problem was that the punishment for being a witch or a warlock was death by hanging. Weatherby considered trying to get a postponement, but he was afraid such a tactic might make him look guilty to residents of Hampton Court whom he saw as his greatest allies.

"Please repeat that last infamous and scurrilous lie, Mr. Weston!" Amarantha shouted out from the back of the room.

"Careful, Miss Thompson, or as Weatherby's associate you may be accused of being a witch as well!" Weston said.

"I am a licensed barrister, a graduate of the University of Utrecht, and Sir Weatherby's designated counsel!" Amarantha said in an aggressive voice. "Withdraw your charge against me immediately, or I will declare this proceeding null and void!"

After a lengthy pause as Amarantha glared at Weston, he said, "I withdraw the charge against you. Please read the charges against the accused!"

One of the portly bishops in a long red silk cassock and matching miter with two ribbons down his back stepped forward and began to speak.

"Louder!" Several people in the back rows shouted.

"The accused is charged with consorting with a witch, having sexual congress with a sorceress, casting spells and giving innocent Christians potions that have turned them toward the devil," the Bishop said in slow, measured tones.

"Sir Weatherby denies all those charges and will prove each one false," Amarantha replied boldly. "Call your first witness."

"The court calls Jonathan Tibbits," the bailiff cried out.

Tibbits shuffled forward with his head bowed. After being sworn in, the Bishop questioned him.

"Tell us what you saw, young man," the bishop asked.

"I attend the solstice at Stonehenge yearly to sell ale, and I saw Sir Weatherby embraced by a naked young witch covered in red paint," Tibbits replied.

"Anything else?"

"No."

Amarantha jumped to her feet and said, "Who initiated the contact?"

"I'm not sure."

"Had you been drinking?"

"Well, yes."

"In your inebriated state, isn't it possible that the witch embraced Weatherby as he happened by?"

"Yes."

"Next witness," Amarantha said brusquely.

A woman named Annie Butcher was called up and sworn.

"Tell us what happened to you Miss Butcher," the Bishop said.

"After the sun rose, I ran across Sir Weatherby, and as he greeted me I had a stirring in my loins which I believe was the work of the devil."

Without giving the Bishop a chance, Amarantha asked the first questions, "As I understand the ceremony, Miss Butcher, people were coupling everywhere without shame, which might have given you some ideas, might it not?"

"Yes, I suppose so."

"Did Sir Weatherby offer you a potion, stare into your eyes, or touch you in any way?"

"No, he didn't."

"You are dismissed, Miss Butcher," Amarantha said brusquely. "I would also like to request that all charges be dismissed against my client due to lack of evidence."

"Sit down Miss Thompson!" Weston bellowed. "This is not your proceeding. Please bring out our star witness."

A tall, well-dressed man with a hood over his head was led out.

"This is your star witness?" Amarantha said sarcastically. "Have him take off his hood so we can look him in the eye."

"He is of the highest character, but his identity must be kept secret because he is also a witness in another capital case," Weston said. "Tell us your story, Mister X."

"I saw the accused at Stonehenge. I saw him have intercourse with a witch named Hepsibah. I saw him take a potion from the sorceress and give it to a fine Christian woman who then tore her hair and clothes and shortly later fornicated with a nearby reveler."

"You are a liar, Sir!" Amarantha shouted. "How long have you been a professional witness and how long have you been a perjurer?"

"I—I—I, am not a l—liar!" the witness yelled through his mask.

"You are in someone's employ," Amarantha yelled. "Who is it?"

"Only for the capital case!" the masked man yelled.

"Sit down!" Amarantha shouted. "Your testimony can be bought, and you aren't even honest enough to look Sir Seamus Weatherby in the eye while you are telling these lies! So much for your star witness, Weston."

"And I suppose you have a witness of impeccable character, who was there, and can refute what the last gentleman just said," Weston said smugly, because he knew that neither Weatherby nor Thompson had any foreknowledge that a trial was going to be conducted.

The Master of the House was confident that they wouldn't have any witnesses, let alone a good one.

"The defendant calls Sir John Moulton, Surveyor of the King's Works," Amarantha called out in ringing tone.

She wanted no delays or missteps as a sign of uncertainty or guilt.

"Would you like to wear a shroud over your head, Sir Moulton?" Amarantha said sarcastically.

"I would not," Sir Moulton replied. "I want to be able to look into the eyes of my interrogator."

"I understand that you were Sir Seamus Weatherby's constant companion on the trip to Salisbury for the Summer Solstice."

"That is correct. In fact I am the one who suggested and organized the trip," Moulton said with pride in his voice.

"Tell about his interaction with the young witch, Hepsibah."

"Weatherby had never met her before. She was very taken by his stature, and visage, and being totally naked she approached him and kissed him and then touched herself in a most lascivious way."

"How did Sir Weatherby respond to that?"

"He was taken aback and drew away."

"What about a potion?"

"I saw Hepsibah offer him a small, blue, stoppered bottle which he sniffed and then he touched a slight amount to his lip, like the man of science that he is, before returning it to her."

"He was constantly in your sight?"

"Yes," Moulton lied without hesitation.

"Did he offer a potion to any man or woman at Stonehenge?"

"He did not."

"Was he the instigator of any lascivious or lubricious behavior?"

"There was much licentiousness about, but he was not."

"I have no further questions," Amarantha said in conclusion. "Your witness."

"Has Sir Weatherby paid you for your testimony today?" Weston asked in a defeated tone.

"Zounds, my good man!" Moulton shouted running up to Weston and putting his face just inches from the Master of the House. "I'm of a mind to thrash you!"

Moulton rained blows down on Weston's head with his fists as the Master of the House covered his face with both hands and retreated.

# CHAPTER 77

Amarantha thought that Moulton's behavior bordered on the outrageous, but since it was Richard Weston who was getting pummeled, she stood by passively. Moulton got out of breath after a few minutes, and then she made a show of intervening.

"Stop gentlemen," she said. "It's time to end this charade. I demand the charges be dismissed."

"You are not in charge here, Miss Thompson!" Weston shouted. "I call for a vote on the charges!"

"This court is a sham!" Amarantha replied.

Weston motioned toward the three bishops, indicating that he wanted them to vote. The first bishop in a purple cassock held up a black card indicating a vote of guilty. The crowd, which had been well-behaved, erupted in shouts, jeers and whistles, suggesting that the vote was rigged. Weatherby had the support of nearly all of the Hampton Court employees. He was an unknown at the Palace until the dreaded epidemic of sleeping sickness. He had personally saved the lives of dozens in the audience, who thanked him daily, and apparently they had told their acquaintances about him. Dredge motioned Weatherby to the back of the Great Hall during the disorder.

"Your horse is saddled and outside the back door of the Great Hall," Dredge said in a soft voice. "If the next bishop shows a black card you will be found guilty and sentenced to hang. You must ride your horse across the Base Court through the Great Gatehouse and then head to the southwest where the population is sparse. Don't stop under any circumstances until you have ridden for five hours as fast as your horse will carry you. You should be in Winchester. Stay at the Lincoln Inn, but don't show your face and eat in your room. One of us will meet you there and slip you to Southampton and then onto a ship to France."

"Thank you, Dredge," Weatherby replied. "You are a good and loyal employee and friend."

The Sergeant at Arms had restored order in the Great Hall. Weston motioned to the second bishop who was dressed in red silk. He rose and slowly exposed the card which he had hidden in his sleeve. It was on edge to most of the audience and they all rose from their seats as one. Gradually the bishop turned the card to the audience. It was white! The crowd erupted again. Now they were not only shouting but throwing pieces of wood, vegetables and scraps of parchment at the podium. The warders took out their truncheons and swung them at anyone in reach who was standing. There were too few enforcers, though. They could subdue only a quarter of the crowd and as soon as they left one area the Palace residents, men and women alike jumped back up, stood on their Benches, waved their arms and shouted. The warders began to clear the crowd from the Great Hall. Amarantha realized that an empty hall would make Weatherby standout and likely prevent his escape. She walked to the podium.

"Order! Order!" Amarantha called out in a loud voice as she motioned with her hands for everyone to sit.

Very slowly the noise began to abate and the group in the front began to sit down. After fifteen minutes, a modicum of order was restored although a murmur of voices continued.

"The fate of Sir Seamus Scott Weatherby will be determined by the final card," Richard Weston intoned.

The third ecclesiastical dressed ominously in a black silk cassock stepped forward and very closely removed the card from behind his back. It was white. Weston hadn't made his case, and Weatherby was innocent. The crowd erupted again even more raucously than before and the warders made no attempt to control them. They clustered around Weston and the bishops to protect them. Moulton, Dredge and Amarantha gathered around a bemused Weatherby. They took a hansom to the Lamb and Flag and Moulton ordered ale for everyone.

"How could the Master of the House have planned such a thing without our knowledge?" Dredge asked. "We have a network of informants and friends living throughout the Palace."

"I have no idea," Weatherby replied. "You three were magnificent *ad libitum*. Had you planned it, I don't think you would have done a better job."

"You escaped, Weatherby, by the skin of your teeth," Moulton said with relief in his voice. "However, we must utterly destroy Weston immediately by any means legal or illegal. How shall the four of us go about this?"

"It won't be easy. Weston has some connection to the King that Chancellor Cromwell has only alluded to. I will enquire by letter today. However, you, Moulton, continue to amaze me. I believe your quote is from Job, he lamented, 'My bones cling to my skin and to my flesh, and I have escaped by the skin of my teeth. All my intimate friends abhor me.' At least I'm not in that terrible spot! You don't even strike me as religious, Sir John."

"I'm a very Old Testament individual. An eye for an eye," Moulton responded. "Let's just take him without any niceties."

"It would be delicious to poison him with one of Hepsibah's odorless concoctions," Amarantha mused. "I could deliver it myself if Weston hasn't decided I'm *persona non grata*. He has a good brain but when he's with me he usually doesn't think with that. I may be able to flirt my way back into his good graces particularly if I dress in some dishabille."

"I appreciate your willingness to dupe him," Weatherby replied. "But I don't want you to ever be alone with him again. In fact, that is an order. He is too vindictive and unstable. He may also know a lot about or murders, and eliminating him might deprive us of valuable information and clues. I wish I had had one more chance to talk with Philbrick before his throat was cut."

"Amarantha remains your best entrée to cracking Richard Weston," Moulton said thoughtfully.

"I can hide close by when they are together and protect her from him," Dredge declared.

"I think that is our best plan." Weatherby replied. "Now let's stop focusing on the Master of the House and celebrate my narrow escape from getting my neck stretched!"

They all raised their glasses and toasted Seamus.

"Just one other comment about that sham court," Moulton said in a slurry voice. "Where did Weston get those three crooked clerics? Clearly, they had been paid to convict you and could not quite do it because of Weston's pathetic case."

"I suppose they came from the smaller dioceses and needed the money," Weatherby replied. "I believe the one in black was from Kew. I recognized him from a case I did there three years ago. In any case I think it is time we solved these murders. I want you, Sir John, to look at the infernal diaries of Sir Rodney Shrewsbury if you can spare some time from your building projects."

"Of course," Moulton replied.

"I want you to use your maps and charts, Dredge, to find Ishmael for me," Weatherby continued. "We need to locate him and then bring him to ground. I also think Hepsibah knows more about our suspects than she has told me. I admit that I lack a little focus when I'm around her." Weatherby's drinking companions all giggled. "Perhaps you can get something useful out of her, Amarantha."

Weatherby ordered more ale, and all four were lost in their own thoughts for awhile. Eventually they wandered out of the dark public room of the Lamb and Flag into the bright sunshine and walked across the Thames and back to Hampton Court. Weatherby went to the Wolsey Apartment to write a letter to the Chancellor and look thorough his mail. Amarantha arrived a few minutes later with her dog Sporter, who was several inches taller, and a young man in tow.

"This is Tad," Amarantha began. "He is your new employee and will go on investigations with you. As you can see, he is strong and fleet of foot."

"Can you be relied upon, young man?" Weatherby asked in a serious tone.

"Yes, Sir," Tad replied tentatively.

Weatherby swung his left fist toward Tad's jaw and the young man reached up and grabbed the fists inches short of its target.

"Very good!" Weatherby replied. "Introduce him to Dredge. He can help him in the lab when we aren't rousting about the countryside."

Weatherby had Ellen Iverson brought to the Wolsey Apartment and she was waiting outside. Amarantha ushered her in.

"I've never been in this part of the Palace afor," Ellen began as she looked about. "It's quite elegant."

She ran her hand lovingly over the fabric of one of the velvet-covered chairs.

"Sit down," Weatherby said with a motion of his hand. "I want know what you heard about the mock trial."

"The stablemen, chambermaids, cooks and butlers love you to a person," Ellen began once she was seated. "They are suspicious of persons with titles and are often treated dismissively by them, but you saved many of them from the sweating sickness."

"Did you have any forewarning of the trial?"

"No I didn't. As you know. Weston is guarded in his manner, but I have people in every part of the Palace. I just finished talking with three of my contacts. The bishops were from Kew, Basingstoke and Oxfordshire and we think that he planned in Kew so that he could spring it on all of us. I must say how happy I am, Sir, that you were acquitted."

"Thank you, Ellen, but we must clip Weston's wings, and I want your help."

# CHAPTER 78

Amarantha spent the afternoon planning her visit to Hepsibah's lair in Wycombe. She took Dredge and Tad along for protection. Dredge told her all about the witch's lair made of logs that was located deep in the forest. There were several small windows that were covered cheaply with stretched linen. Dredge gave Amarantha some small sacks of gunpowder mixed with a chemical that burned red when lit. If anything untoward happened, Amarantha needed to light the small sack near a window.

Once she was packed she went to Weatherby's apartment for an intimate dinner. He had said that it was what he most desired after his narrow escape of the morning. When she arrived, he opened a bottle of wine from Gascony. After sampling the wine they were served mussels in a garlic-flavored chicken broth.

"I was very lucky this morning, Ran," Weatherby said. "I could easily have been convicted and hanged. While all that was going on, I decided dying would be dreadful, but it would be heartbreaking not getting to see and work with you every day. I'm bad at expressing feelings, but I've treasured every moment we have spent together. I don't want that to end."

They made a large pile of the sharp black shells after they ate the chewy pink meat inside.

"I love the things you say to me sometimes, Seamus," Amarantha replied. "Do you remember the day you seemed to be accusing me of being unfeminine about the needlework?"

"Yes."

"Then when I complained you said the nicest things about me that anyone has ever said."

412

"I'm sure I wasn't very elegant. As you well know, I'm usually facile in conversation unless I am with a woman that I truly care about."

"You mean like Geneviève?"

"I'm sorry I ever mentioned her to you, Ran. She is just part of the *demi-monde* as class of women meant for entertainment of every kind both mental and physical. They are taught to do wonderful tricks with their hands and their mouths that I had never even thought of. You know enough French to know it means 'half-world' that is someone who doesn't belong to the 'whole-world.' We don't have anything like it in England. However, one doesn't fall in love with a courtesan, and I am certainly not in love with Geneviève. I told you that when I faced death his morning I was saddened by all the times I wouldn't get to spend with you, not her."

"It's just that her only purpose is to please you when she is with you and I have a lot more responsibilities."

"Exactly true. She couldn't possibly do all that you do, Ran."

Weatherby gave Amarantha a warm, firm hug before they sat down to a heron pie flavored with thyme. They talked casually and aimlessly through the next three courses and then ate a bowl of lignonberries and cream. After supper, Weatherby read Amarantha a Scandinavian saga. After an hour of listening, she stretched and yawned.

"I'm going to retire," Amarantha said. "Dredge and I need to leave early in the morning for Hepsibah's lair. Why doesn't she ever get tried for what she clearly is, a witch?"

"I've wondered about that, and I believe there are two reasons. First I'm sure she bribes the local constable and bailiff, and secondly, everyone is afraid of what she might do to anyone that was even cross with her, let alone tried to arrest her. They see her as powerful and ruthless and they may be right. She used the bitter rose poison to kill a ten-year-old playmate just to test the concoction. Be very careful of what you eat and drink there. Her potions are tasteless and very potent. Dredge thinks the food is less likely to be tainted than the drink and he will give you several little bottles of oil that you may drink surreptitiously to blunt the effect of the drugs."

"And why am I going to visit her in her own lair again?" Amarantha wondered out loud.

"To learn more of what she may know about the murders, Ran," Weatherby reminded her. "But you don't have to do it. I already exposed you to that madman Weston. You've done more than your share."

"I'm half teasing, Seamus," Amarantha replied. "I will enjoy the challenge, and I want to match wits with her and also see why you find her so irresistible."

Weatherby walked Amarantha to the door of her apartment and gave her a warm goodnight hug.

"The librarians and I will focus on the Shrewsbury diaries while you are gone," Weatherby said. "I'm tired of having so many loose ends."

In the morning Amarantha and Dredge left before Weatherby awoke. He ordered a breakfast of berries, cream and scones for the library and began working on Sir Rodney's diary.

"I can frame the question we must answer in one sentence," Weatherby said as he sat down with tea and a bowl of cloud berries. "Which of these infernal, dusty old books is about the year of our Lord 1530?"

"We have found dates written as numerals in eight of them and you have found comments about comets and eclipses that you can time precisely in five more," Margaret Sedgwick remarked. "That leaves forty-four volumes that could be about the year 1530."

"We tried ordering them by style of writing, fading of the ink over time and fashion of binding with no success," Weatherby mused. "But Shrewsbury had to have a way of referencing what year a volume was written, or they would be useless to him as source documents. We know from his lair that he is acquisitive and messy but I very much doubt he is disorganized."

"How would you code your books if you were an overly smart, diabolical, aged Oxonian?" Judith Scotson asked as she ran her hand seductively over the front of Weatherby's thigh.

"He may have gone to Oxford, but I suspect he became infatuated by the Druids and their dark power before college," Weatherby reflected having trouble ignoring the pleasant sensation from his leg. "We have fifty-seven volumes which we believe span about forty-eight years. Therefore, Sir Rodney began journaling in 1482 when he was fifteen. What is the earliest volume we have identified?"

"1486," Margaret replied.

"So what was his system for secretly ordering his precious diaries, ladies?"

"I think he hid a letter or a symbol in a specific part of each volume that would be easy for him to find and hard for us to find," Judith suggested.

"So do I," Weatherby replied quickly. "But what and where?"

"Sacred numbers to the Druids are three, seven, and fifteen," Margaret remarked.

"Let's each take a volume and look," Weatherby suggested as he picked up one of the dusty volumes. "Let's try the obvious pages first."

Each counted pages from the front and looked at those that would have been numbered three, seven and fifteen. Judith found a little mark in the corner of her volume on page fifteen, but finally decided it was nothing.

"Let's multiply them and see if anything shows up," Weatherby offered. "We've already looked at nine, but let's try forty-nine and two hundred and twenty-five."

After a few minutes searching, Margaret slammed her volume down and said, "I didn't find anything. I think these diaries are abstruse and maddening. I'm sorry you ever found them!"

"They contain a wealth of valuable information, Margaret," Weatherby replied. "Try three times seven times fifteen. That includes all three of their sacred numbers."

"How much is that?" Judith asked as she stroked Weatherby's arm.

"Umm. It's three hundred and fifteen," Weatherby replied after a pause.

"Fie me!" Margaret shouted out. "There is some numbers in the lower left hand corner. I think it says 9151."

"I've got one too!" Judith called out. "Mine says 3251."

"That's it. You have discovered the dates," Weatherby said excitedly. "They are just backwards, like the rest of the writing. Check the one that we decided was from 1527. That was the year of the comet."

Judith rushed to the pile of books and opened the one that they had decided was from 1527. She opened it to page three hundred and fifteen and read out loud, "7251."

"We have broken the system of that craven old man, Librarians!"

All three reached for the pile of uncatalogued books and turned frantically to the same page.

After fifteen minutes Judith said, "This is the one."

Weatherby confirmed that the date was for 1530, written backwards in the lower left-hand corner.

"I want to read this volume right now," Weatherby said. "Order food and wine and get some fresh sheets of paper and lots of ink and I will translate the significant material he wrote for you."

Weatherby set up his mirror and candle arrangement on the table while Judith and Margaret collected writing implements. He began laboriously translating the backward writing made legible by the mirror. Weatherby's Latin had gotten much better since he started translating the journals. In fact, he now found grammatical errors in much of Shrewsbury's writing. He read a couple of pages while Margaret and Judith looked on expectantly.

"This is probably from the fall probably of 1529," Weatherby said. "He's dividing his time between London and a witch's lair near Oxfordshire."

I'm going to skip forward some pages. He studied the writing for another hour.

"Now it's Christmas, and he's at a bacchanal in Winchester," Weatherby said. "He does go on and on about his conquests."

He skipped a large bunch of pages.

"Now he's on a tour of witches lairs along the Welsh border," Weatherby said. "It seems to be February judging from comments about the weather and the lack of vegetation. He just poisoned three minor officials that he didn't care for. They did nothing more than speak ill of him."

Weatherby wondered how that active old *roué* have time to do all this writing backward in a foreign language.

# CHAPTER 79

Weatherby retired at midnight, planning to spend the next day translating the journals. Early in the morning he had food sent to the library and resumed the laborious task of translating the backward writing from Latin to English. He found descriptions of botanical specimens, long diatribes on the Catholic Church and images of the dress and behavior of his various witch consorts. Shrewsbury took a trip to Straffan House, his county seat near Dublin, and then came back to Hampton Court in late March, just before the murders began.

Weatherby found a description of the bludgeoning of William Suffolk and marked that spot in the journal. Shrewsbury gave a detailed description of the wound that killed the young architect and then a surprisingly detailed description of the King's investigator. Shrewsbury wrote that Weatherby was overly concerned with details and wouldn't be able to see the bigger picture necessary to solve the crime. So far Shrewsbury's assessment was accurate, Weatherby thought ruefully. Shrewsbury must have been in the Great Kitchen that night. Perhaps he was disguised as the kitchen maid that served Weatherby tea.

Weatherby began a diligent search of the pages before the description of the head wound. Sir Rodney wrote about potions and one included laudanum, but he often did that. He also described creeping around the Palace, but Weatherby realized that that was also common as his rooms were hidden off a dark little-used hallway. He didn't describe the murder itself as he had the death of the three petty officials near the Welsh border. Weatherby now knew that Sir Rodney was in the right place to commit the murder and that he was by nature a murderer. Why hadn't he described the actual act?

Weatherby recollected that Anna Maria Wimbledon's body had been found two days before Nones, on April 3rd. Weatherby spent the afternoon laboriously reading the text following Sir Rodney's description of the William Suffolk's laying out in the Great Kitchen. Shrewsbury went to Wycombe for a Druidic dance after the first murder and had an orgy with Hepsibah and one of her assistants, Griselda. Weatherby wondered if she was one of the young witches that bathed and restrained him when he was recently at Hepsibah's lair. Sir Rodney could certainly have gotten the bitter rose poison then. Hepsibah didn't remember giving it to him he recollected, but Shrewsbury was very capable of stealing it.

On the day of the murder Shrewsbury met with Anna Maria Wimbledon, but he also met with the ladies of the Green Cloth, Ellen Iverson and Christopher Dickinson. Weatherby could find no written evidence that Sir Rodney poisoned the beautiful young librarian! Also, Hepsibah had said that she had given the bitter rose poison to Ishmael, and Sir Rodney reported no meeting between them.

Weatherby tried to skip ahead nine days to two days before the Ides of April, because that was the day Gregory Townsend was murdered. It was difficult to find April twelfth, and Weatherby floundered around a bit in the journal. After a supper break he decided to translate the whole section from two days before Nones to two days before Ides. There had been little to transcribe so far, and Margaret Sedgwick had gone on to other work in the library, but Judith Scotson had remained at Weatherby's side. She touched his arm or leg frequently, and once when they were alone and squeezing through the narrow space between the table and the book shelves, she had pressed her ripe body into his and kissed him full on the mouth. It had been a pleasantly warm, wet sensation. They sat side by side late into the night reading and writing by candle light.

When he got to the twelfth of April, Weatherby discovered that Sir Rodney had decamped from Hampton Court. He had Griselda sneak out of Hepsibah's camp and the two of them had taken a trip to the south coast in Sir Rodney's four-wheeled barouche. It was a slower but more comfortable carriage than Shrewsbury's infernal two-wheeled calash that Weatherby and Amarantha had chased all over the streets of Dublin. Sir Rodney and the wilful Griselda ended up fighting. She had used her long nails to gouge Shrewsbury's face, and they rode home for two days without speaking. In any case, Sir Rodney had been far away from the Palace when Townsend was flung from the parapet of the Great Gatehouse. Sir Rodney Shrewsbury might well have killed William Suffolk and Anna

Maria Wimbledon both, but he didn't kill Gregory Townsend. Weatherby had never liked the slight, old man for that crime anyway. His experiment with the hog's carcasses confirmed that at least two large men had done in the Protestant minister. Weatherby thought that the likeliest suspect for that crime was the violent glazier Sir Rodney had already dispatched Nathaniel Philbrick.

It was three in the morning and Weatherby's eyes burned and his muscles ached from hunching over the diary and reading in the mirror. Judith was asleep next to him with her head fallen forward on her folded arms. He gently shook her shoulders. Her face had deep red creases from the imprint of her sleeves.

"It is nearly three," Weatherby said in a whisper close to her small pink ear.

She reached her hand toward him and said sleepily, "Come and sleep with me. I'm cold, and need the warmth of your body."

"Not tonight," he said gently as he kissed her softly on the forehead.

Weatherby stumbled off to his apartment on stiff legs. Amarantha was spending the night with the treacherous and diabolical Hepsibah. He prayed that his assistant was safe. He woke during the night, not to his recurring nightmare, but to thoughts of Amarantha Thompson. Was she in danger? Finally, he got up as sleep eluded him. During the whole forenoon he fretted about her while shuffling through papers in the laboratory. He tried to draw a plan of Hampton Court, but got the proportions all wrong. He would have to ask Dredge to do it, as he was much better at such things. At noon he got an urgent message from Dredge telling him to come to Wycombe as quickly as possible.

As soon as his roan was saddled, Weatherby set off at a gallop to the east. He had made the trip often enough to know that it would take ninety minutes, but by pressing his steed he arrived in less than an hour. He went directly to the small inn in Wycombe. Dredge and Tad were waiting for him.

"We found Amarantha early this morning wandering aimlessly outside Hepsibah's lair," Dredge said in an anxious voice. "We put her on her black Arabian but she became more and more disoriented. I was afraid she was going to fall from her saddle; we doubled back here so I could put her in a bed. Then I sent Tad to fetch you."

"She may have caught a disease," Weatherby said. "But more likely she was poisoned by that arrogant witch. Let me examine her."

Amarantha lay supine in the bed in her riding clothes. Weatherby removed them carefully and placed her under the covers. She made no response to his ministrations or to any of his verbal requests. She appeared to be in a deep vegetative coma, like someone who had received a severe blow to the head. He checked her skull carefully, but found no marks or bruises. Her breathing was deep but only six breaths per minute. He screwed together the two parts of his wooden, tubular stethoscope and listened carefully to her heart. The 'lub-dub' sound was soft but regular, but her heart rate was one hundred and sixty-six. He considered a number of drugs and poisons that killed by first depressing mental acuity and also acted on the heart. His first thought was deadly nightshade, known locally as naughty man's cherries. It contained a chemical called belladonna, translated as 'beautiful woman' because the Egyptians knew that a drop in the eye dilated the pupil. Weatherby pushed back Amarantha's lids and observed large pupils with a very narrow blue iris. He called for Dredge.

"Go quickly to the local apothecary and ask for an American herb called pilocarpine," Weatherby said in an urgent voice as he turned back to his patient.

He regretted putting Amarantha into the hands of the vindictive and erratic witch. Amarantha hated being coddled, so he treated her like a colleague, forgetting sometimes how precious she really was to him. He looked in his bag for a stimulant and made a poultice of tea leaves that he placed on her chest. Her breathing had gotten even slower. He had nothing to lose, so he sent Tad off with a note demanding that Hepsibah reveal what poisons she had used. Weatherby had read that Egyptian courtesans carried drops of belladonna with them on their liaisons to renew the illusion of limpid pools, so fortunately the drug was short-acting. He simply had to support Amarantha through the most intense effects of the drug and prevent any further exposure to naughty man's cherries. He suddenly decided to check her mouth carefully and found a small cloth packet filled with a powder tucked inside her cheek. Weatherby removed it gingerly. Hepsibah had deliberately placed a dose of belladonna there to prolong the poisoning! Weatherby rinsed Amarantha's mouth with cool water. Unfortunately, her coma seemed to be deepening toward a profound and fatal collapse.

# CHAPTER 80

Weatherby had received a sample of a potent new stimulant, coca, from a colleague at the University of Edinburgh. It was from the tips of the leaves of a low-growing bush that grew in the mountains of America. Weatherby had meant to try it on animals, but hadn't had the opportunity. It was reported to be quite potent. He chewed the leaves some to soften them and then placed three or four in Amarantha's mouth. After a few minutes she was still in a coma, but she began to move her limbs a bit. Weatherby knew that Dredge had only been gone a few minutes but it seemed like an eternity.

"I found the apothecary," Dredge said as he burst through the door. "He had just received a batch of pilocarpine leaves. I had him grind some in a mortar and pestle."

Dredge handed Weatherby a small leather pouch. Weatherby was unsure of how to deliver the antidote.

"Make a poultice of some of these leaves," Weatherby said to Dredge. "While I blow some of the powder into her nose.

"Will that work?" Dredge asked.

"I have no idea," Weatherby said in a frustrated tone. "But I can't get her to swallow a nice hot cup of tea made of the leaves with sugar in it, now can I?"

Weatherby blamed himself for Amarantha's current state, since he had sent her on this investigation and he knew he was taking his frustration out on Dredge. If she recovered, he resolved to treat her more deferentially as he blew powder into her nose through a wheat straw. He pulled a chair up to Amarantha's bedside and placed a cool, wet cloth on her forehead. The morning was hot, and the mistress of the inn brought Weatherby a glass of lemonade. He reflected on the time limit the King had placed on his investigation and tried to recall how many of his thirty days had elapsed all ready. Seven? He wasn't any closer to a solution of these vexatious murders and he wasn't sure where to turn next. In any case, Amarantha Thompson's recovery would be his first priority. He looked at her closely. She seemed to have small random motions in her hands and face, and her pulse had slowed to a still very fast one hundred and fifty.

Through the afternoon Amarantha remained the same. Weatherby ate a light lunch at her bedside and then Dredge relieved him for an hour so he could take some fresh air. Almost against his will, he went to the paddock, jumped on his roan, without a saddle, and rode quickly to Hepsibah's lair. No one was about. He kicked the door open and walked across the first large room that had had a fire in the middle. In the next room he saw that the furniture was disordered and jars were scattered about. The third room was dark, and he could see little. As his eyes adjusted he saw that the two young witches we twined around each other sleeping on a pallet in the corner. Weatherby shook them roughly.

"Where is Hepsibah?" he shouted.

The two hugged each other in fright and said nothing.

"Where is she?" Weatherby said even louder.

The two slender proto-witches hugged each other harder, and turned their faces away from Weatherby. He bent down and wrapped both of his arms around the two of them and sat them up.

"She went into the forest on foot this morning to gather herbs and then she planned to decoct them at her outdoor fireplace," the dark-headed witchlet said as she stroked Weatherby's arm.

The blond witchlet pressed her body against Weatherby before saying, "We used to make potions in the big room, but often we got dizzy and saw things."

Weatherby extracted himself from the two and walked through a door in the corner of the room. The bright light blinded him at first, but he could see smoke rising from behind a hill just in back of the lodge. He walked there quickly through a carpet of blooming wildflowers. Hepsibah stirred a large black pot with a wooden paddle. She wore a shapeless black gown, and it all looked like a memory from his childhood when his parents had threatened him with a witch if he were bad.

"What have you given Amarantha?" Weatherby shouted over the crackle of the fire.

"I see you've come back for more, my sturdy inamorato," Hepsibah replied as she approached him, her black eyes flashing.

"You've drugged my precious assistant, Hepsibah," Weatherby said as he took a step away from her. "And I need to know the ingredients of the potion."

"Come here and lie with me and then we can discuss it," Hepsibah said as she sank down onto bed of fragrant pink and white flowers.

"No. I need to know how you poisoned her and I need to know now," Weatherby said pulling the witch upright. "She had fallen into a coma."

"I have no need to harm her," Hepsibah replied. "I simply wanted to loosen her focused consciousness with a few hallucinations. Take the packet out from her gums, and the effect should wear off quite quickly."

"I already found the poisonous sachet." Weatherby twisted Hepsibah's wrist. "What in God's name did you put in it?"

"I rather like that twisting thing you are doing," Hepsibah purred. "It was an innocent mix of hyssop, Hypericum or St. John's wort, and belladonna with a touch of vinegar to speed the effect."

"What is the antidote?"

"I don't study such. I look for herbs which prolong ribald pleasure and induce days of hallucination."

"You are beautiful, but also smart," Weatherby said changing tactics. "I believe you know the antipodal remedy even if you don't employ it."

"Come and lie with me just for a few minutes, so I may taste your flavors again," Hepsibah said as she untied her robe from her neck and let it fall open.

Weatherby considered beating her for the answer, but she seemed to enjoy pain and could not reveal the location of her antidote, so reluctantly he took off his doublet and lay down beside her. The flowers that were crushed under them gave off a sweet aroma. He kissed her and ran his strong hands over every part of her body, but his anxiety about Amarantha was growing. Hepsibah had relaxed onto her back and moaned softly between kisses.

"Please help me now, and I will return as your slave for a fortnight," Weatherby lied.

The witch rose languorously from the ground leaving her black robe behind and walked into her lair. Weatherby followed, noting her perfect shape. She opened a drawer full of small bottles, and after a little searching selected a small brown one.

"Place five drops of this in each ear," Hepsibah whispered to Weatherby as she pressed her nakedness against him.

He kissed her briefly and unceremoniously and ran out the door. He jumped on his horse and sped back to the inn. Dredge was still sitting beside Amarantha's bed looking worried.

"You were gone longer than I expected, Your Grace," Dredge said.

"I decided to try and talk Hepsibah out of the elements in the potion and then try for an antidote," Weatherby replied although he was still out of breath. "And I got both!"

He waved the small brown bottle in from of him. He shook the bottle and unscrewed the dropper and gentle placed ten drops under Amarantha's tongue.

"Hepsibah said I should put this in Ran's ear, but as a physician I know she has a much richer blood supply under her tongue."

After administering the antidote he gently closed her mouth. The patient hadn't changed in the last two hours, for better or for worse. Neither Dredge nor Weatherby wanted to leave their colleague's side, so they dined in her room. They spent the evening talking about the suspects, Ishmael and Sir Rodney. Dredge had done some more rocket experiments in his spare time and he told his boss about the results. They decided to split the night. Dredge would stay with Amarantha from eight until two a.m. and Weatherby from two until eight in the morning. Weatherby retired in one of the upstairs bedroom. He was awakened from a deep sleep by Dredge.

"Is it 2 a.m. all ready?" Weatherby asked.

"No, Sir it is only twelve-thirty of the clock," Dredge replied. "But you must come and see."

They both bounded down the stairs to Amarantha's room. She was sitting up in bed and seemed to be completely back to her normal self.

"What am I doing here?" Amarantha asked as she stretched.

"You were drugged by the conniving Hepsibah," Dredge replied.

"I'm glad you're better, Ran," Weatherby said. "I feel totally responsible for exposing you to such danger."

"You had no way of knowing, Seamus," Amarantha replied. "You seem to slide in and out of her clutches with ease."

"Pun intended, I'm sure," Weatherby said dejectedly.

"Yes, but at least we had a sister-to-sister talk before she slipped me the potion," Amarantha said. "And she claims she only gave the bitter rose poison to Ishmael, and before that to one old witch from Anglia."

"Good work, Ran," Weatherby remarked. "But it still wasn't worth it. Now get some rest."

Weatherby and Dredge left Amarantha's room and retired for the remainder of the night. In the morning, Amarantha felt fully recovered and full of energy so the three colleagues rode back to Hampton Court laughing and talking as they went.

# PART 9

# CHAPTER 81

When they arrived back at the Palace, Weatherby sent Amarantha to her apartment to rest. Then he took Dredge to the library and showed him his translations of Shrewsbury's journals for the days of the murders.

"He's not shy in his journals," Weatherby noted, "even when he commits a crime. For example, he brags about the three innocent petty officials he poisoned to death on the Welsh border. However, during April of this year, he seems strangely reticent. It's almost as if he had a premonition that someone would discover and then laboriously translate his writings."

Weatherby handed Dredge several pages of translations in Margaret Sedgwick's hand and let him study them. After an hour of quiet study, Dredge turned to a particular page.

"I believe he is writing for an audience here," Dredge said as he pointed to the last part of one page. "It's the day that Anna Maria was poisoned and isn't candid at all about what he is doing. The other passages you showed me just seemed to stream out of him. This one is stilted."

"I had the same feeling," Weatherby replied. "I can't believe I've been tricked again by that old man! We have all worked so hard to understand and translate his writing."

"I believe that is a question you will have to ask him yourself, when you run him to ground," Dredge said as he lay the parchment on the table.

"He is a master of disguise and I suspect he has been very close to me many times, not just when his headdress fell off at Stonehenge."

"We must intensify our search for him."

"I already have all the King's men in England and his supporters in Ireland on the lookout."

"I suspect we will have to find him ourselves."

"Visit Ellen Iverson and see if she has any clues. I believe that the Village of Hampton is having a fair. I will take Ran with me if she is up to it. It will have big crowds, which are perfect cover for that weasel Shrewsbury."

Weatherby walked to Amarantha's apartment. She was just getting up from a nap and was bored from rest and confinement.

"I haven't been to a village fair in years and I would love to go!" she said.

"We will have a good time but we're also looking for Sir Rodney," Weatherby replied.

"Sounds like a perfect combination to me," Amarantha said as she picked up a parasol to protect herself from the sun.

They walked across the Base Court and through the Great Gatehouse and toward the river. Weatherby took Amarantha's arm protectively. The water in the Thames was at a mid summer low, but the water still sparkled in the warm sunlight as swallows swooped under the bridge and robins called from the river side trees. The fair was held in a large field to the north of the town. As they approached, Weatherby heard the murmur of the crowd and saw long pennants of every color attached to tall saplings. Hampton only had about twelve hundred residents, but it wasn't unusual for a fair to draw five or six thousand people.

The edge of the field was lined with colorful canvas booths and the back of an occasional wagon. There was an island of booths in the center of the field. Minstrels wandered among the fair goers playing lutes and flutes. Groups of children in their best clothes ran in every direction. Near the entrance to the fair, a butcher was roasting an ox on a spit and the smell filled the air with the juicy aroma of succulent meat. At the entrance booth Weatherby paid the five-penny admittance fee for both of them. Amarantha always worked the booths at a fair in a clockwise direction and Weatherby fell in along side, even though his inclination was to proceed counterclockwise.

At the first booth Amarantha bought a circular wall hanging made out of wheat stalks with full heads of grain, she selected a tightly knit snood for her beautiful hair at the second booth. Weatherby sensed a major shopping spree fueled by Amarantha's recent escape from death.

He settled in to watch the crowd for persons of interest. He noted that the local prostitutes had abandoned their houses and were flirting with the farmers, especially single ones, using their warm smiles and batting eyelashes. Weatherby watched more than one strumpet lead her customer into the nearby woods to complete their transaction. Many of the wives banded together into groups and locked arms as they talked and chatted. Amarantha was haggling over a piece of wool that had been dyed red. She kept unrolling it and holding it up to her arm and then putting it back and mentioning another price.

Weatherby spotted a person dressed as a young woman that made him suspicious. Something about her deliberate toe-out walking looked masculine to him. He followed her for a while and noted that when she went into a booth she didn't speak, but made her wishes known with hand gestures. Finally, he arranged to bump into her gently.

"I beg your pardon," Weatherby said as he looked hard at the little upturned face for signs of facial hair or heavy makeup.

The girl curtsied slightly and said, "Not at all, Your Grace," in a clearly feminine voice.

Weatherby backed away. He rejoined Amarantha who handed him another purchase. They stopped for some of the spit-roasted beef and ate it standing there while the warm, flavorful juice ran down their chins. Weatherby offered his handkerchief when Amarantha was finished. She walked back to the cloth seller for a third time as his eyes idly followed a group of men crossing the field. They were all richly dressed and dark-skinned. Something about the second one from the right looked familiar. The person looked like Ishmael. Weatherby followed the group about ten yards behind them. He could hear they were talking excitedly in a foreign tongue. They all turned into a large tent that was selling cheap jewelry. Weatherby went up to the table and pretended to study a ring. The language the men were speaking was rapid and seemed eastern in origin. Weatherby tried to see the face of the man he thought resembled Ishmael, but he had gone to the back of the tent behind a curtain. Weatherby waited as long as he could for the suspicious man to show himself. He remembered how quick a runner Ishmael was from chasing him through the Abbey and the town of Reading. He realized he should have brought Tad, but Weatherby thought he might encounter Sir Rodney at the fair, not Ishmael. Weatherby circled back and found Amarantha haggling for ribbon. He stood by patiently. When she was done, he guided her away from the crowd.

"I haven't had any luck with Shrewsbury, but I think Ishmael might be here," Weatherby said in a soft voice.

"I'm sorry I've been of such little help," Amarantha replied. "I just got swept up in the shopping. What can I do?"

"Walk with me to that large green canvas jewelry booth over there and help me get a close look at one of those swarthy men."

Amarantha took Weatherby's arm and they sauntered in that direction. As the evening progressed the light was fading despite torches and bonfires and the crowd was growing. A large number of people, mostly women, had crowded into the green booth and several were actively bargaining for brooches and necklaces. Unfortunately, he man Weatherby was interested in was not at the table making sales.

"I am going to get a look behind that curtain," Weatherby said. "Slip behind the tent and make sure he isn't standing back there. I showed you a drawing of his face after I was imprisoned in York. Do you recollect it?"

"Yes," Amarantha replied as she headed in that direction. "I wish we had brought Tad."

"Or even Dredge. I had the same thought earlier."

Amarantha moved off, and Weatherby elbowed his way slowly up to the right side of the table so he could see behind the curtain. The curtain blew gently in a mild breeze offering Weatherby could occasional glimpse of the space behind it. Three men stood talking in the corner. The tallest one, that resembled Ishmael, was standing between the other two men. Weatherby just couldn't be sure if it was him.

Rather than giving up Weatherby stepped behind a fat woman looking at a necklace, placed both of his hands on her ample buttocks and pushed her forward. She fell heavily onto the table, pushing it back and unbalancing the salesman who was helping her. He stumbled into the curtain, pulling it down, and revealing the three surprised men in the corner. The tallest man looked directly at Weatherby. It was Ishmael! Weatherby moved forward, leapt onto the table and then into the back of the booth. Ishmael turned, pulled a small dagger, slit the tent from top to bottom, and sprang out of the back of the booth.

Weatherby was close behind. He burst through the opening to find Amarantha sprawled in the grass.

"Are you hurt?" Weatherby said.

"No. That dark man knocked me down and fled into the forest."

Weatherby went only a few yards into the dense woods, before realizing that he wouldn't be able to find Ishmael in the darkness. Instead he returned to help Amarantha.

"Let me walk you home if you are able," Weatherby said, taking her arm.

"I just have a scraped elbow," Amarantha said as she leaned on her companion.

Weatherby took another look at his disheveled, uncomfortable, but brave companion and called for a hansom to take them both back to Hampton Court.

# CHAPTER 82

Weatherby walked Amarantha to her apartment and hugged her goodnight. Then he sought out Warder Chertsey. Eight of the King's militia were passing through and Weatherby asked that they be assembled in the Great Kitchen. He brought a sketch of Ishmael from the laboratory.

"A man who committed a murder here at Hampton Court was seen at the Hampton village fair this evening," Weatherby began. "I want you to search northeast and southwest of the Palace for him. He is five feet eleven inches tall and darker skinned than this drawing shows. His name is Ishmael, and he is very quick. He is armed with a small dagger and may have as many as four friends who will help him fight back or escape. Report back here at nine in the morning, and good luck!"

After the militiamen had departed, Dredge and Chertsey looked over the maps with Weatherby. He had only eight men to deploy, and knew he couldn't search in every direction. Weatherby had picked the northeast because it was toward London where the population would provide anonymity.

"This suspect is a creature of villages and towns," Weatherby began. "He will be most comfortable hiding there. However, there is a chain of villages toward the southwest that could offer protection."

"If only we knew how he traveled," Dredge said.

"Ishmael moves from place to place too quickly to walk, so it has to be by horse or carriage."

"I have never seen him using either," Weatherby mused. "But jewels aren't heavy or bulky and a horse would give him a lot more mobility."

"Let's just hope the militia finds him," Chertsey concluded.

Weatherby went off to bed.

In the morning, he sought out Amarantha and took her to breakfast.

"How are you feeling, Ran?" Weatherby asked.

"Just a little sore. I wish I could have stopped him for you."

"Believe me, he is as slippery as an eel. I have been around him several times now and he has always eluded me," Weatherby said as he ate his favorite breakfast of ham and eggs.

After they had finished eating, the chamberlains announced the arrival of Father Lawrence Croceus. Weatherby had met the friar from Nottingham on a carriage ride to Southampton, and the two had carried on a lively correspondence since. Croceus knew about the Linear A and Linear B codes and had spent some time trying to crack them. Weatherby had his guest shown to the Wolsey Apartment. Never a tall man, Father Croceus had grown more corpulent thanks to the fine food in Paris. A flight of stairs made him short of breath for several minutes.

"How goes the murder investigation?" Croceus asked.

"Poorly," Weatherby lamented. "After three and a half months of work, I still have three corpses and no one in the Tower for any of them. The King has given me an ultimatum that, despite our best efforts, will result in my being sacked very soon."

"You'll just have to live in Paris. Then we can meet regularly for dinner and attend the theatre."

"I certainly won't have the funds for that."

"I have no funds, but manage to live quite well," Croceus replied.

"But you are a vassal of the mighty Catholic Church which collects one out of every five farthings the populace earns here in England. As we both know the believer is told to give ten percent of everything to his church. Plus the church owns vast lands and whole towns that generate millions of additional sovereigns in rent each year."

"You have a point," Croceus said thoughtfully. "I suppose you'll just have to become a priest."

"No disrespect intended, Lawrence, I like the economics of the Church but not its theology."

"You are an idealist, Seamus. I'm quite sure that many of my fellow priests are nonbelievers but they enjoy the music, the orderly life and not having to do physical labor. Also, we get to labor in the cathedrals—the most sumptuous places in Christendom except for some Palaces, like Hampton Court."

"You will just have to help me solve these cases so I may continue in the King's employ."

"Very good. Let me see your documents and I will give you the answer."

Weatherby began pulling books filled with parchment off the shelves and handing them to Father Croceus. Weatherby was explaining what he knew about William Suffolk's murder when a militiaman broke in.

"We came across the man you call Ishmael heading to London about two of the clock this morning, Your Grace," the man said in a loud voice. "We turned him back to the west, and then lost him for about two hours during the darkest part of the night. We spread out our search pattern, but the four of us were pretty sure he had eluded us. Then, as it began to get lighter the man on the far right picked up a trail and called us over there with his horn."

"Was it him?" Weatherby inquired.

"Yes, Your Grace, it was. Some of the fibers from his doublet got torn off in the brambles from time to time. We followed him back to the edge of Hampton. Then we lost him near the Flag and Lamb."

"The other four militiamen that searched to the west will be back in an hour," Weatherby said. "I want all of you to continue your search for this felon. I will have Warder Chertsey send some additional men to help you. Report back to me this evening."

"Very good, Your Grace," the soldier said while bowing and backing out of the room.

Weatherby summoned Chertsey and had him send six additional men to join the search. With Dredge's help, Weatherby looked over the maps of Hampton and the surrounding countryside. It was apparent that a lot of abandoned buildings in the area and dense growth along the river would provide good cover for their lone suspect. Weatherby had a pack of dogs sent out from the stable to join in the search. Then he took Amarantha to the Library and read her the parts of Sir Rodney's journal for 1530 that he had translated. He reminded her that the date of each of the fifty-seven journals had been found by him, with Judith and Margaret's help, on page three hundred and fifteen of each volume.

"I may be missing something, Ran," Weatherby said as he pulled down the large leather volume. "All of Shrewsbury's writing, even his description of his murders and rapes, seems very frank. Yet during the time frame of the three murders here at Hampton Court, he suddenly becomes coy and tangential. Let me read you some more."

Weatherby began reading pages from the journal for the spring of 1530. After a couple of hours of reading, Weatherby caught Amarantha stifling yawns politely behind her hand.

"Am I boring you?" Weatherby asked.

"It's not the most engaging thing you have ever read to me," she replied gently.

"What am I missing?"

"I think that Sir Rodney, like most of us, writes his recollections a few days after the events, and he knew that you would find his journals. He took your measure in the Great Kitchen the night you examined William Suffolk's body on the trestle table. He knew that as a doctor of medicine you would know Latin, and that you were compulsive enough to translate the backwards journals once you found him."

"Why didn't he simply destroy his diaries?"

"That would spoil the game he played with you in the Great Kitchen and with both of us in Dublin. Don't you remember? He could have left our heavy hansom in the dust in his light little calash, but keep in mind he stayed just out of our reach. I don't think you ran across him accidentally at the summer solstice either, or even that his head piece was dislodged by his vigorous thrusting. He's playing cat and mouse with you—and the mouse, Sir Rodney, wants to stay just out of the reach of the swipe of a large, clawed paw."

"Fie me! I should have asked you sooner, Ran."

"Perhaps, you aren't thinking too straight in the Library since Judith is playing touchy-feely with you all the time."

"I think that that is a bit of an exaggeration, Amarantha."

"I am not blind, Seamus, and everyone knows how she feels about you," Amarantha replied petulantly.

"While I may, like any man, respond to an occasional caress. I have turned down her advances several times, and I will continue to do so. You are so much more intricate."

"Thank you, I think," replied Amarantha, somewhat mollified.

"Let's find Father Lawrence and Sir John and go to the Lamb and Flag for supper and some serious drinking."

Amarantha put away the journal they had been reading and the two went in search of drinking companions. When the quartet was assembled they walked across the bridge into Hampton talking and laughing. Weatherby bought the first round of ale. The tavern was full of local merchants and farmers relaxing after a long day of work. Moulton gossiped about the King and Anne Boleyn.

"I hear that Henry isn't able to meet with his council, he is so besotted with desire for Anne," Moulton said. "He will be forced to visit a war on some poor country if she doesn't surrender her maidenhead."

"Fie. She is no virgin, Sir John," Lawrence volunteered. "I used to hear confessions in Nottingham, and young country girls are ridden harder and sooner than a stylish mare."

"Don't forget that Anne went to the Netherlands when she was twelve. Then she and her sister Mary were in France getting educated until Anne was twenty, Father Lawrence," Amarantha volunteered.

"And you are saying that the French are less licentious than the English, Madame?" Croceus said derisively. "I live in Paris now and I find them, if anything, more so."

"She has seen too many reputations sullied to be careless about such matters," Moulton said as he ordered another round of ale.

"There is even an allegorical poem by Sir Thomas Wyatt called *Whoso Lists to Hunt*, Sir John," Weatherby interjected. "That tells of Henry's unsuccessful pursuit of an unobtainable and headstrong Anne."

The four were ushered into the dining room for a dinner of roast duck with broadbeans and turnips. Sir John ordered three bottles of red wine from the Canary Islands. In the midst of their revelry, an off-color joke by Father Lawrence was interrupted by an insistent militiaman.

"We have cornered your suspect, Your Grace," the tired soldier said to Weatherby.

# CHAPTER 83

"Where is he?" Weatherby said as he jumped up, throwing his napkin on the table.

"He is at Hampton Court Palace, Your Grace," the militiaman said.

"Where, my good man?" Sir John asked.

"He has barricaded himself in the Great Gatehouse."

The four diners quickly exited the Lamb and Flag and took a hansom back to the Palace. The militiamen stood around the bottom of the Great Gatehouse and looked up.

"Where is he?" Weatherby asked.

"In the room at the top of the left tower, Sir," the militiaman replied.

"Well, bring him down here immediately!"

"It is not that easy, Your Lordship. He has barricaded himself at the top and has filled the stairway with broken furniture and lumber from the upper rooms."

"Take your men and tear the furniture down, now!"

"If we move a stick of it, Sir, he says he will throw himself from the parapet. You do want him alive, don't you?"

"Yes. We must keep him alive at all cost."

"Then we will stand down and await your orders, Your Lordship."

Weatherby conferred with Sir John, Amarantha, Father Lawrence, and Dredge, who had just joined them. Amarantha thought they should keep Ishmael busy talking while the barricade was quietly dismantled. Sir John thought his men could build a tower in secret, and then roll it up to the Gatehouse. Father Lawrence thought an athletic boy could scale the back of the tower and surprise and subdue the dark-skinned man.

Weatherby answered them all in one statement. "Too noisy. Too slow. Too dangerous."

He had Dredge make a large paper cone so that he could talk to the captive who was five stories in the air.

"I work for the King and I am prepared to let you go free in exchange for some honest answers from you," Weatherby lied.

"Agadh," Ishmael called back.

"He has to know English. He's been in the country for several years," Weatherby replied in a disgusted tone. "Why is he speaking Arabic?"

No one had a good answer. Finally, Warder Chertsey spoke up.

"I don't believe it's Arabic, Your Grace," Chertsey said in a soft voice.

"Well, what the hell is it then?" Weatherby demanded.

"I believe it is Druidic."

"What does it mean?" Weatherby, Moulton and Amarantha said in unison.

"It means no."

"In that case I like Lawrence's idea the best," Weatherby said. "Get me a slender, acrobatic young man and a long rope, quickly."

Dredge scurried off to collect a stable boy and a line. Weatherby turned back to Chertsey.

"How is it that you know the Druid language?" Weatherby asked.

"Well sir, despite Cardinal Wolsey's influence, over the years we have had some Druids working in the Palace," Chertsey replied softly. "It was necessary to know a little to converse with them, Your Grace."

In a short time, a lithe young stable boy arrived, and Dredge put a long coil of hemp rope over his shoulders and explained what they wanted the lad to do. Weatherby handed the lad a small dagger which the young man tucked in his belt. Dredge led the climber into the Base Court after Weatherby gave him specific instructions. Then Weatherby went back through the gate to distract Ishmael. He began talking in long monologues to Ishmael through the megaphone without even waiting for an answer.

In a few minutes the young man came around the front of the left tower of the Great Gatehouse at the fourth-floor level, moving confidently. He worked his way up over the brick work toward the fifth floor window and then placed both hands on the window sill. He pulled himself up and pushed the upper part of his body through the window. Just as he got one foot on the sill, Ishmael must have seen him and lurched forward, pushing the climber. The lad lost his grip, his arms and legs cart wheeling as he fell eighty feet to the cobbled driveway. His body bounced once and then lay still. Weatherby and Dredge hurried over to the stable boy, but he was dead.

"I didn't foresee that," Father Lawrence said. "This is all my fault."

"Don't be ridiculous, Croceus!" Moulton yelled. "The crazy Muslim or Druid, or whatever he is, did that, not you!"

Weatherby asked that the body be taken away. A small piece of wood, with a piece of parchment wrapped around it, floated down and landed near Amarantha. Dredge handed the parchment to Chertsey who studied it by candlelight for several minutes.

"I think it says he will kill himself at midnight to appease his gods," Chertsey reported.

"It is now eleven-twenty, and we need another plan quickly," Weatherby remarked as he refocused on the problem. "Moulton's tower will take too long to build. All we have left is Amarantha's frontal assault. Let's get started."

"Perhaps we could stun him or disable him with one of our rockets, Your Grace," Dredge suggested.

"That's a capital idea, Dredge," Weatherby said excitedly. "How many do you have?"

"Three."

"Send Tad to fetch them!"

"Wouldn't a carronade shot work just as well?" Moulton asked.

"Firstly, I'd be afraid the ball would kill him outright. And secondly, this is a peaceful Palace. Have you seen our armory? We don't have even one cannon or a mortar, let alone a carronade."

Weatherby continued to talk to Ishmael through his megaphone while they waited. Soon another note floated down. It had 'Fi coelio' written on it. He handed the note to Chertsey.

"It simply says, 'I believe'," Chertsey replied. "I think he's getting his courage up to jump."

Tad arrived walking gingerly with the three rockets cradled in his arms. Dredge took one and placed it on its launcher, and then got down on his hands and knees to check the angle. He aimed for the large open window on the fifth floor of the Great Gatehouse. He signaled that he was ready. Weatherby sent ten men into the stairway to start removing the broken furniture and lumber, and then nodded at Dredge, who lit the rocket. The fuse sputtered, and then a cone of flame propelled the rocket up the launcher and toward the window. Its course looked good until it got close to the window, and then it struck the diamond-shaped stone work just above the opening.

"You have two more chances," Weatherby remarked nonchalantly.

"I won't need them. This one will go through the window," Dredge said as he picked up another rocket and placed it on the launcher.

This time, Dredge lay down on the ground and sighted up the launcher tube and adjusted it slightly. He placed the second rocket in the cradle of launcher and without fanfare lit the fuse. It sputtered a little, like the last one, and then a loud sound came from the rocket as it accelerated up the launcher and rose toward the window, going through the upper left corner of the aperture and into the room. Three seconds later an explosion could be heard from the room and smoke billowed out of the window.

Weatherby signaled for his ten man crew to remove the obstruction in the stairway. It seemed like an eternity, but it took them only twelve minutes to clear a path. Weatherby bounded up the stairs with Moulton and Amarantha behind him. The door at the top of the stairs wasn't even closed, but dark grey smoke billowed out of the room. Moulton and Weatherby grabbed panels of wood and fanned the smoke out of the area.

Ishmael lay in the corner of the room on a pallet. Amarantha thought he was dead. Weatherby went to his side and felt for a pulse which was thready but present. When he took his fingers away from the captive's wrist, a large sheet of burned skin came off. He seemed to be burned over most of his body where charred flesh was exposed below burned clothing. He shook the burned captive gently and spoke to him in a low voice at the same time.

"Are you Ishmael?" Weatherby asked.

The victim's eyes fluttered open and he nodded his head yes.

"You are badly burned and will meet your maker soon," Weatherby asked. "Do you believe in Mohammed the prophet of the Arabs?"

The burned victim vigorously shook his head no.

"Are you a Christian that needs to confess your sins?"

Again, the victim shook his head.

"Do you believe in the celebration of summer festival of Lughnasadh and Lugh the God of the Druids?"

Ishmael nodded his head vigorously and murmured something that Weatherby didn't understand.

"Say it again."

The murmur was louder this time. Warder Chertsey had joined the group in the upper room and spoke.

"He is speaking in Druidic again," Chertsey said in a soft voice. "He says that he needs to confess his trespasses."

Ishmael spoke in a low voice.

Weatherby caught an occasional word—*seadh*, *cretim*, and *agadh* but had no familiarity with the language.

After a time Chertsey leaned away and said, "He has confessed to a series of robberies and two rapes."

Weatherby noticed irregular breathing and said, "He will die soon. Ask him if he murdered William Suffolk with a hammer blow."

Chertsey spoke haltingly to the burned victim and then all noted that Ishmael nodded his head yes. Ishmael began to jerk and twitch violently.

"Ask him if he murdered Anna Maria Wimbledon and Gregory Townsend," Weatherby said excitedly.

Chertsey leaned close to the dying man and spoke in the Druidic tongue. At first, Ishmael didn't seem to answer, but finally he made a sound followed by some gurgling just as his breathing stopped.

"Yes! He says he committed both of those murders also!" Warder Chertsey said with relief in his voice.

# CHAPTER 84

Weatherby examined the burned body for any sign of life and found none. As he stood, he felt a wave of elation that the three murders were solved. Amarantha wrapped her arms around him.

"Well done, Seamus. You have found the murderer and he has confessed," Amarantha said in a lilting voice interrupted by coughs from the smoke.

Moulton shook Weatherby's hand in congratulations as they all left the acrid air of the small room.

"Thank you, Sir John, but I could not have done this without the diligent good work and risk taking of Amarantha and Dredge," Weatherby said as he slowly descended the stairs.

Dredge aasked his men to take Ishmael's body to the laboratory so Chertsey's men could clean the room in the tower of the Great Gatehouse. Sir John suggested a celebration, but it was one a.m. and Weatherby thought Amarantha looked tired.

"I need to post a report to the Chancellor tonight, Sir John," Weatherby said. "Let's arrange a gala luncheon for tomorrow."

Weatherby walked across the Base Court and through the Clock Court to the Wolsey Apartments. He took out writing implements, a fresh bottle of ink, a new goose quill and a small piece of parchments. He liked the smell of ink and the rough feel of parchment as he began to write:

To the Privy Council especially Lord Thomas Cromwell, Chancellor

Right honourable sir, with my most humble and dutiful thanks for your Lordship's forbearance toward me at all times, my servants and I make bold to present you with excellent news that the heinous murderer, late of Hampton Court Palace, has in the extremity of dying confessed to the murders of three innocent subjects of the King who resided in his elegant Palace. I beseech you to present this news to his Worship, Henry VIII, our noble King and preserver of the faith.

Your honour's most dutiful bound obedient servant,
Seamus Scott Weatherby, MB Edinburgh
This 5th day of August 1530

Weatherby sealed the note with red wax he had melted in a candle flame, and stamped it with his signet ring. It was now two a.m., but he summoned a courier to carry it post haste to Whitehall Palace.

He considered spending the night in Judith Scotson's willing arms, but decided the impulse was just a combination of excitement followed by extreme fatigue and he rejected it. Weatherby walked wearily back to his apartment and fell into bed with his clothes on. Despite his fatigue he awoke at three thirty in a cold shivering sweat. His nightmare had recurred. He had awoken, as he usually did, just as he was about to trample the baby in the white nightgown as it crawled into the path of his horse. He had looked back as the breath of three charging stallions burned his neck. The last time he had the terrifying dream, he recognized the face of the first hooded rider as Sir Rodney Shrewsbury, and this time he recognized the second rider as Ishmael. However, the third rider's face was obscured by the hood and the shadows. Weatherby shivered, but not from the cold, when he realized that despite bringing Ishmael to ground, Sir Rodney Shrewsbury was still loose, and according to the dream a third man was involved.

Weatherby changed his nightshirt and walked across the dark, deserted Palace to Judith Scotson's room. He tapped softly on her door and she opened it. She motioned him into the room. He slid wordlessly into her warm bed. She untied her nightgown at the neck, and let it fall to the ground before climbing back into bed, and wrapped her arms around Weatherby. He was instantly asleep.

In the morning, Weatherby was surprised to wake up in Judith Scotson's feather bed. She was still asleep. He lifted the cover and looked at her full rich body, and then he slid out of bed and walked back to his apartment. He had a full morning ahead of him. First, he wanted to perform an autopsy on Ishmael, and then he needed to coordinate the arrangement of a gala luncheon for everyone that had helped him solve the case. When he got to the laboratory, Dredge had the body laid out naked on the zinc table. Next to Ishmael's head was a row of sharp, clean, autopsy tools. Both proctors noticed severe burning of the skin over seventy percent of the body. His genitals were normal except for enlarged testicles on both sides. On cutting them open, infection was evidenced by the presence of pus. Weatherby made his usual large y-shaped incision over the chest and abdomen, and then Dredge sawed through the ribs. The internal organs showed no serious diseases. There was little evidence of alcohol abuse or malnutrition. The liver, pancreas, spleen and stomach were normal in size, and Dredge took small samples to examine under the microscope. The brain examination was also normal.

"Except for his venereal disease and the burns that killed him," Weatherby said wiping his hands, "this was a normal, healthy young man. What a waste."

"Perhaps Leeuwenhoek's microscope will reveal diseases that we can't perceive," Dredge replied.

"It won't explain why he turned to murder," Weatherby said over his shoulder as he left the laboratory.

Weatherby headed to the Great Kitchen to plan his celebratory luncheon. He checked the freshness of the fish, meat and vegetables. Then he went to the orchard to make sure that the tables and chairs were in place. He went to his apartment and changed into better clothes and then went back to greet his guests. Once everyone was seated they had a fresh salad course, followed by salmon, dill and cream. Then there was duck in a cherry sauce and a spectacular platter of lamb served with mint. Weatherby made sure everyone had as much champagne as they could drink. After a pause, a variety of desserts were served. When everyone was uncomfortable from eating too much, Father Lawrence Croceus rose and used his ample belly as a resting spot for his glass. He gave a flowery, twenty-minute toast in praise of Seamus Scott Weatherby. Father Lawrence included boyhood tales and adventures with the constable in London that neither Amarantha nor Dredge had ever heard. When he was finished, he lifted his glass and the audience gave a loud, 'Hear! Hear!'

Weatherby was embarrassed by the flowery toast filled with all manner of praise, but rose and lifted his glass to talk about every person that helped him during the past four months. He spoke about

Ellen Iverson, the librarians, Christopher Dickinson, Sir John and even Warder Chertsey. He asked Dredge to stand while he recounted his many accomplishments, finishing with the story of the amazing rocket. Then he turned to Amarantha.

"She is simply the best assistant a man can have," Weatherby began. "She survived two illnesses during this investigation, one of which was brought about by the evil witch Hepsibah. In addition to being a red-haired beauty, she is smart, diligent, supportive, intuitive, and eager to accomplish any task she is given. Here's to you, Amarantha Thompson! You are a treasure!"

Weatherby raised his glass and the guests followed.

"This is my last toast!" Weatherby said after banging on his glass with a spoon. "To the memory of Anna Maria Wimbledon, William Suffolk and Gregory Townsend. May they rest in peace!"

The guests lingered in the warmth of the orchard after the speech-making enjoying the conversations and the remaining champagne. Dredge surreptitiously pulled out a pencil and paper and began listing tasks he needed to do before they all moved back to Threadneedle Street in London. Amarantha thought about asking for time off to visit a sister in Kent. As the guests began to wander off, Weatherby suggested a meeting in the Wolsey Apartment. The three gathered there fifteen minutes later.

"This has been our longest case, and I'm sure both of you are ready to move on," Weatherby began after each had a cup of tea. "While we have solved the murders, we have not captured that rascal Shrewsbury, nor have we solved the plot that underlies the whole crime. There is a plan or a design behind these events that we have not yet illuminated. I'm not willing to decamp and then get called back here in a fortnight because of some new revelation. Dredge, I want you to start a new journal entitled *Death by Design*, and each of us will enter the part of the master plan that we can see. Amarantha, please list all the places where we know that Sir Rodney has been, and give it to Dredge so he can make a map we can study for clues."

Amarantha and Dredge swallowed the rest of their tea and headed off to work on their new assignments. Weatherby checked his mail in the hope he could find something that would help him solve the Linear A and B codes. He found nothing. He was pleased that he had found the murderer, but he had unanswered questions. He took out a quill and parchment and listed the unresolved issues:

1. Sir Rodney Shrewsbury. Where was he? Did he know Ishmael? Did he impregnate Anna Maria?
2. Richard Weston. Was he just crazy or more malevolent?
3. Linear A and Linear B code. If he managed to solve one, the other would open like a nut hit with a hammer.
4. What religious crime was de Lèves executed for?
5. What was the design behind these three murders?

He decided he must answer these questions, no matter the cost in time and treasure.

# CHAPTER 85

Weatherby felt expansive as he sauntered through the Clock Court and across the Base Court to the Outer Court where so many things were prepared for the Palace. He visited the Office of the Green Cloth and then swung into the Confectory. Ellen Iverson was stirring a bubbling pot of caramel and heating chocolate over a fire to make a batch of candy.

"Thank you for the tasty luncheon," she began. "It's unusual for us commoners to be invited to a fête."

"You are welcome. I thought I might catch you napping after so much food and drink."

"I already rested," Ellen said as she motioned to a pallet next to the fireplace. "You must be very pleased with your accomplishment; but you didn't come here just to be social."

"I suppose not."

"What is still troubling your restless, probing mind?"

"Oh, there are many dropped threads and unanswered questions remaining in this case, but the one that looms largest is the whereabouts of Sir Rodney."

"He has always been as slippery as an eel in muddy water. Even when it isn't necessary he likes to obfurskate."

"You mean obfuscate."

In any case, I already told you that I believe he is very smart, obscenely rich, and twisted. What ever do you want with him? You have your confession."

"I want to know about the relationship between him and Ishmael and if he was the mastermind behind the whole evil plot. One of the worst things about murder is that we don't have to see the victims each day crying, 'murder most foul and unjust.'"

"You've gone as far as Ireland to find him, but he is like the children's toy, the cup and ball. If the string is very long the dark wooden ball can circle far from home, but it always comes to rest again in its polished wooden cup. The cup for Sir Rodney is Hampton Court."

"But it was the possible presence of Sir Rodney that drew me to the Hampton village fair, and I didn't see him."

"You know, as well as I do, that doesn't mean he wasn't there," Ellen said haughtily. "He is a master of disguise and can disappear into thin air. I once saw a performance by a magician that was certainly Shrewsbury. He made a plump, white goose disappear. If you find him, it will be close to the Great Gatehouse."

"Thanks for the advice. By the way, I slept with Judith."

"I know."

"I was tired, lonely and cold. We didn't couple."

"I know."

"Now, how could you possibly know that?"

"The chambermaids change the sheets on her bed and then come here for tarts, no pun intended. You would be amazed at who is sleeping with who."

"Whom," Weatherby said as he went out the Dutch door of the Confectory with a large candy in his right hand.

"Come back and I will tell you," Ellen called out, thinking that Weatherby was asking a question, not correcting her English.

Weatherby went to the construction shack to look for Christopher Dickinson. The master carpenter was working on a roof in the Queen's apartment.

"Could we talk privately?" Weatherby yelled up toward the scaffolding.

"Yes, of course," Dickinson replied.

He swung down easily after tucking his hammer in his belt without using any of the steps.

"Let's walk to the Knot Garden for privacy."

"I still have questions about Ishmael and Sir Rodney," Weatherby began, wanting to mention Richard Weston too, but thinking that would not be prudent. "I know you mentioned homosexuality the last time we spoke."

"As I told you, that was mostly amongst the poor monks who have no outlet besides sodomy."

"What about Ishmael?"

"He was a lover of women of every size and shape. He rarely drank, but once at the Lamb and Flag after far too much ale he bragged of having had three women that day and the prowess for two more. He was uncircumcised, of course, being a dark-skinned infidel. That made him exotic and very appealing to a certain type of woman."

"Did he consort with the women of the Palace?"

"Yes, he bragged of sleeping with Anna Maria Wimbledon, Margaret Sedgwick and particularly Peggy Ealing, Anna Maria's roommate."

"What about Sir Rodney?"

"He was the most perverted human I ever met. He liked old witches and their priapic potions best, but everything seemed to arouse him. If someone caught him locked together with an animal I wouldn't be the least surprised."

"Yes, my good man, but what about sodomy?"

"I caught Sir Rodney in Peggy Ealing's bed with George Boleyn, Anne's brother. Everyone knows that George leans toward men and boys. They were both quite naked and barely gave me a glance before they resumed their embrace."

"Do you think they had a relationship?"

"I find that very doubtful. Nothing about Sir Rodney was very constant."

"If you were looking for Shrewsbury where would you look?"

"There is something about this area, Surrey County, that draws him back again and again, and that surprises me. Somehow, I picture him more at home in the fleshpots of Southwark across the river from London. However, there is a Lady Elwell who resides in Kew that he has been seen with him over the years, and of course he has that large apartment at Hampton Court you found behind the secret wall."

"Thanks for the information. You know a lot of the tittle-tattle at the Palace."

"I make it my business to watch and listen."

Weatherby walked from the Knot Garden to the Wolsey Apartment to look over his mail. He was reading a letter from Monsieur Favier in Chartres when two men dressed in the King's livery, green and white vertical stripes with a red rose embroidered on the chest, knocked on the open door. Weatherby knew the green and white uniform had been the emblem of the house of Tudor since 1485. They walked into the apartment carrying a small wooden chest bound in iron.

"Your Grace," the shorter Yeoman of the Guard said, bowing low. "From our noble Monarch, King Henry."

The taller yeoman set the chest on the desk and handed Weatherby a small brass key. Upon opening the lid, he found the coffer was filled with hundreds of shiny, gold sovereigns. While not easily amazed, Weatherby could not believe his eyes and gazed speechless at the shiny pile of stamped metal.

"I believe you will find there are seven hundred pounds in the chest, Your Grace," the yeoman said. "And he sent this to you also."

The second Yeoman handed Weatherby a leather pouch as he bowed deeply. Inside, sealed with the King's own ring was a deed to a two-hundred hectare farm in the fertile southern part of Scotland. Weatherby took two sovereigns and handed one to each yeoman as a vail, or tip. After they left, Weatherby sat in his chair amazed. A loyal serving man worked all year for four or five pounds and he had just been given a hundred and fifty times that. The King's generosity was stunning. Apparently, the Monarch had been deeply concerned about the murders that occurred in his favorite Palace of the sixty some he possessed. Weatherby sent for Amarantha and Dredge.

When they arrived, Weatherby showed them the deed first and then the pile of money.

"I'faith!" Amarantha exclaimed.

"God's death," Dredge yelled as he looked into the chest that shimmered in the candlelight.

"None of this would have been possible without you two," Weatherby said in a grateful voice. "I want each of you to have a portion of it. I will secure yours, Dredge, with my barrister so as not to tempt the gambling gods again. I'll place yours in the account you have in the Bank of Cardiff, Amarantha. There is only one stipulation on these gifts. If you try to use the money to retire early, I will rescind every ha'pence. You are both too valuable to lose over a few thousand farthings."

Weatherby opened the secret wooden panel Thomas Wolsey had built behind his desk and put the gold in the compartment protected by two locked iron doors. Then he replaced the keys around his neck, next to his bulky watch.

"I call for a celebration at the Lamb and Flag!" Dredge called out.

"I most heartily agree!" Weatherby remarked. "Let's find Dickinson, Moulton and Father Lawrence."

The group met in the Clock Court then walked through the Base Court and through the Great Gatehouse and into a warm August afternoon. Amarantha recognized immediately that she was too warmly dressed and unlaced the bodice of her dark blue kirtle, removed her arms from the top, and let it fall down over her skirt. Weatherby always watched the movement of her body especially when she removed clothing. Soon he was sweating also, so he took his doublet off and carried it over his arm. The pace of the group was particularly slow due to Father Croceus's corpulence, but it was a fine day and everyone in the village of Hampton was about. It was such a rarely beautiful day that few people were in the public room of the Lamb and Flag. The six celebrants drank their first two tankards of ale quickly and began laughing and talking loudly. Without any instruction, Amarantha and Dredge knew that they should be discreet about the actual amount of the largesse that the King had given to his humble servant, Weatherby. Each had calculated separately all the goods and lands that their mentor could by with his treasure.

# CHAPTER 86

With more ale, the group became even rowdier. Two prostitutes wandered in from the White Swan. Moulton quickly invited them to Weatherby's table and bought them some ale. Soon, Dickinson and Moulton were playing a game of touch and kiss with the two girls, each taking a turn closing their eyes. One of the trollops had such a low-cut bodice that at one point her ample breasts fell out to approving cheers from the five men. Sir John got a handful before it was tucked safely away. Each of the attendees had a chance at making a toast. Unfortunately, Father Croceus went first and his comments and stories went on for more than forty minutes. Each toast was delivered in a voice that was slower and slurrier than the last. Weatherby ordered a platter of wild mushrooms and roasted rabbit to combat the drunkenness of his companions. He spoke last.

"This would not have been possible without the help of each of you," Weatherby began. "We make a great team. I will remind the King, when I thank him for his generosity, for the part each of you played in solving these heinous crimes. To our judicious, caring, generous, and powerful Monarch, Henry VIII!"

The party broke up shortly thereafter. Dickinson and Moulton headed to the White Swan with the two trollops, convincing Father Lawrence to go with them. He claimed that he had never been to a house of ill repute and he was curious. Amarantha, Dredge and Weatherby moved into the dining room for a more substantial meal of, roast venison with leeks and cabbage.

Unfortunately, their meal was interrupted by a confrontation. While they were eating, Weatherby had noted a couple sitting quietly along the far wall. The woman appeared to be in her thirties, but her manners seemed suspicious to Weatherby. The motion of her hands seemed too large and emphatic for a woman. Weatherby set his fork on the edge of his plate and wandered over to the couple's table.

"I'm Sir Seamus Weatherby and I believe we have met," he said politely to the woman. "What is your name?"

The woman's companion took offense and jumped to his feet.

"I don't care who you are! Bugger off!" the man said in a slurred voice that suggested too much to drink.

"Sit down and shut up, my good man," Weatherby said, as he pushed the man down into his seat. "I was speaking to the lady."

Dredge came over to the table and Weatherby opened his doublet so the man could see his dagger.

"What is your name?" Weatherby said again.

"I'm Annabel Wyatt from Windsor," the woman said in a high, clear, obviously female voice.

So it wasn't Sir Rodney Shrewsbury in one of his best disguises.

"I humbly beg your pardon, Madame," Weatherby said as he bowed and backed away from their table. "Allow me to send you a bottle of Rhenish wine."

The two companions went back to their table to finish their joint of juicy venison. When they were finished eating, they walked home, still slightly unsteady from drink.

In the morning, Dredge continued to work on his plan to move the laboratory back to London. He estimated that packing would take five days, the transport two days by ox-drawn cart, and once there, the unpacking another five days. Weatherby slept in. He hadn't felt so relaxed in months. He had a large breakfast delivered to Amarantha's apartment. She was still in her nightgown. Her thick auburn hair was disheveled, and one shoulder was bare. He found her more beautiful like that, than when she was coiffed and highly made up. They ate companionably and talked about the things they most wanted to do when they returned to London.

During breakfast a courier brought Weatherby a message. One of the King's sergeants had seen a man in Richmond the day before that he thought was Sir Rodney Shrewsbury. He seemed to be visiting or living with a small group of apostate nuns and monks who lived in a chapter house in a nearby wood. Weatherby had his horse saddled and this time decided to take Tad along on the ride east. Weatherby had never spent as much time on horseback as during the Hampton Court case, and he relished it. He liked interacting with his mount and getting out in the countryside. He found it a good time to think. The chapter house was to the west of Richmond, and after asking directions, Weatherby found it.

On approaching the stone building, Weatherby noticed rubbish in the yard, a broken window, and tiles that had fallen off the roof. Usually religious orders kept their properties well repaired and tidy. Weatherby thought. He approached the first monk that he saw.

"Good day, Father," Weatherby called out. "Where might I find your superior?"

"She's usually in the cloisters drinking ale by now," the monk replied in a surly fashion.

Weatherby dismounted and walked into the cloisters scattering loose, scrawny chickens before him. A monk lay on a bench, deeply asleep and snoring loudly. Weatherby walked into a number of rooms until he found one containing a large barrel of ale. Next to it sat a fat nun in a dirty habit, holding a tankard. She seemed half asleep.

"Who's in charge here?" Weatherby asked sharply.

"I'uum da mudder superur," the nun replied in the slurry voice of a drunk.

"Have you seen this man?" Weatherby said as he held a sketch of Sir Rodney up to her face.

"Looks faamiller, famililer," the nun replied as she tried to focus her gaze on the parchments.

Weatherby walked out in disgust and finally found a monk using a hand mill to grind barley into flour. He asked the same question.

"Yes, he has been living here for the past fortnight," the monk replied. "And sleeping with one of the young nuns."

"Where might I find him?"

"He has been staying in the prioress's house. She can't drag her fat, drunken form that far from the barrel of ale anymore."

Weatherby walked outside the cloister and toward what was once a lovely two-story stone house with leaded glass windows. Half the windows were broken and shutters hung by a nail. Weatherby motioned Tad inside and followed without knocking. Upturned chairs and broken furniture lay about, but he saw no one in the dark room. He walked up the wooden stairs slowly and as quietly as possible, but each tread squeaked. As he neared the top he could peer across the floor toward a large four-poster bed where he heard the slow, steady breathing of more than one sleeping person.

As he stepped up onto the second to the top tread, his shin pushed against a wire and a large, heavy armoire fell from the ceiling blocking the door. Weatherby cursed, and he and Tad pushed against the armoire with both of their shoulders. It didn't budge. They redoubled their efforts grunting as they pushed but without success. Weatherby had a vision of Shrewsbury, in the bedroom, leaping from bed, pulling his pants on and sliding down a back gutter to run into the woods. He sent Tad to get a timber to pry the armoire away from the door while he ran down the stairs and out the back door. It was worse than he had expected. A small man in a nightshirt was disappearing into the woods on horseback. Unfortunately, Weatherby's roan was tied up at the cloisters eighty feet in the wrong direction. Undeterred, he ran to his mount, untying the reins as he leapt into the saddle from the wrong side of the horse, spurring his mount into the woods. He guessed that Shrewsbury had a two-minute lead on him.

Weatherby had solved a case in Wales two years ago where a man had murdered his brother. The murderer's alibi had been that he was at a tavern a mile away when the act was committed. Dredge and Weatherby had run fast horses over good trails, using Weatherby's new Italian watch to time the beasts, and discovered that the rider could easily have gone a mile in two minutes.

The trail was narrow with lots of turns and low-hanging branches. Even worse, were exposed roots that could trip even a sure-footed horse. Weatherby rode for twenty minutes before coming to a fork in the road. He brought his mount to a halt and peered down each branch. Weatherby was about to take the left fork, when far ahead to the right he saw a small patch of white in the woods. As he plunged down that path he realized that Shrewsbury was taunting him again by halting his steed out of reach but not out of sight. Weatherby plunged ahead, but the path became narrower and twisted, slowing his progress. After another hour of riding without a sighting, he gave up and turned his horse back toward the chapter house.

Once back, Weatherby questioned the nun that Sir Rodney had been sleeping with. She confirmed that he had been staying in the prioress's house for a fortnight, but was often away during the day. At times he had returned with potions that the two of them heated over a fire and then swallowed. He had always kept his horse saddled with reins lightly tied at the back door.

After a quick dinner in Richmond, Weatherby and Tad began their ride back to Hampton Court after a quick dinner in Richmond. Seamus had been outwitted and made a fool of by Shrewsbury again, and he was dejected. He always met Sir Rodney on his own ground. He decided that he needed to lay a trap to lure Shrewsbury to a location where he, Weatherby, had control. As he rode he began to think of a suitable location and an irresistible piece of bait.

# CHAPTER 87

Weatherby ate an early supper with Amarantha in the Knot Garden where he vented all of his frustrations about Sir Rodney Shrewsbury on her. Mostly, he hated that he had been outsmarted by the wily old professor, again. By all rights, the old codger should have been caught in bed at the chapter house. After all, he was asleep in bed with a nun when Tad and Weatherby fell upon him.

"You seem to have become his *raison d'être,*" Amarantha remarked.

"I just want to get my hands around his scrawny little neck. So he will think I'm going to squeeze the life right out of him."

"I can't imagine he is afraid of death at his age. I suspect his real fear is of being bored."

"I am always walking into his traps and now I want to lay one for him myself. I want to use that old ruined manor at Oatlands, the one that has a ghost, and is thought sacred to the Druids. I might use Hepsibah as the bait."

"You would subject the woman of your dreams to that kind of risk?" Amarantha said sarcastically.

"She has fallen out of favor with me since she poisoned you."

"She did that simply so you would have to beg her for an anecdote and she would get to feast her eyes on your physiognomy again," Amarantha remarked petulantly.

"I believe you mean antidote, not anecdote."

"No, I meant anecdote. I thought she would want to give you a short personal account of her recent adventures."

"In any case, she will be my bait, and I will make her cry out in discomfort until Shrewsbury comes to save her."

Amarantha was tired, so he walked her back to her apartment. Then, after tucking two condoms in a pouch for protection, he walked across the bridge to the White Swan. He had needed a woman all week, and now he thought it was interfering with his concentration. He picked a young redhead named Holly, so that during the act he could pretend he was with someone else. When he was finished, he wasn't tired, so he went to the Lamb and Flag. He expected to see Dickinson or Moulton or one of the other artisans that he had come to know, but none were there. He ordered a tankard of ale and then saw Peggy Ealing, Anna Maria Wimbledon's old roommate, sitting alone by the fireplace. Weatherby took his tall ceramic tankard and walked over to where she was sitting.

"I haven't seen you in weeks, Peggy," Weatherby said in a kind voice as he sat down next to her.

"Months, actually," she replied, placing a hand gently on his forearm. "With all the new building at Hampton Court, Chancellor Cromwell sent me to Italy to buy furniture and paintings for King Henry. I just got back yesterday."

"What a nice time of year to be there."

"Actually, I was in Naples and it was muggy and smelly, with many fatal cases of malaria—that is the Neapolitan word for bad air. Additionally, an unescorted woman is in constant danger in the southern provinces. I had to hire a traveling companion to pretend to be my aunt."

"I'm sorry for that. Have you recovered from the tragic death of your roommate?"

"Only in part. I still awake frequently from nightmares about her death. She was so young and vibrant."

"I hope my abrasive interviews right with you after her body was found didn't make things worse for you."

"What you told me made more apprehensive. I couldn't sleep. However, I wasn't completely honest with you. It was the worst day of my life. I was not at my post, so I wasn't able to help her in any way. We had been roommates for eight years and were very close; I was hiding in a deserted room in the long gallery with my lover. I was so involved in my own passion that I wouldn't have noticed if the sky fell. I had been swallowed by my growing love for a man, even though I knew he had other women. I had just taken his handsome dark face in my hands, turned it toward me and called out, 'Ishmael, Ishmael'."

Weatherby felt as though he had been struck by lightning. Perhaps Peggy Ealing was lying, but why? With those two words she had firmly and irrevocable established the Muslim's alibi, posthumously. Weatherby threw some coins on the table and with a mumbled goodbye, walked quickly out of the Lamb and Flag and back to the Palace. He had Dredge and Amarantha awakened and sent to the Wolsey Apartment. He told both of them what Peggy Ealing had said.

"Weren't we going to interview her again a third time after the terrible death of her longtime roommate?" Amarantha asked.

"Yes, but the Chancellor sent her to the Italian States to buy furniture, so we couldn't have talked with her again," Weatherby said by way of explanation.

"What if she is lying?" Dredge said.

"It is possible, but I can't understand what her motive would be," Weatherby replied.

"She loved the philandering, dark-skinned alien, and she's trying to preserve his reputation even though he's in paradise," Amarantha said.

"His Muslim heaven is rivers of wine and dozens of willing virgins as sexual partners and his Druidic heaven isn't much different," Weatherby corrected. "As an infidel to the ways of Mohammed, Peggy can't affect his paradise no matter how much she loved him. No, I think we have to reconsider what we believe about the murders. Someone else may have murdered Miss Wimbledon, and perhaps Ishmael killed no one. However, I saw him nod when I asked if he had killed William Suffolk."

"I don't see how a false confession helps Ishmael's afterlife," Dredge replied.

"Stop packing for London, Dredge," Weatherby said. "We need to re-evaluate our situation. Let's collect our evidence and documents on each of the three deaths and meet in the laboratory in one hour."

It was three a.m. but all three investigators hurried out of the Wolsey Apartment as they constructed a mental list of the evidence they wanted to review. Amarantha identified the most with Anna Maria Wimbledon, so she reviewed the materials they had collected on the beautiful young woman. Dredge reviewed the death of Gregory Townsend, the lay preacher, and Weatherby gravitated toward William Suffolk.

When they gathered in the laboratory, Weatherby had a large pot of tea delivered to keep them awake.

"Let's start with the last murder and work backward," Weatherby suggested. "Gregory Townsend's body was found three days before the Ides of April. You have investigated his murder, Dredge. What can you tell us?"

"We never thought that one man could have killed Townsend," Dredge replied. "He was clearly thrown from the very tower in the Great Gatehouse where Ishmael died. If you recall, when we experimented with the hog carcasses, we decided a minimum of two burly men were necessary to throw the body from the parapet. When we autopsied Ishmael, despite his height, he only weighed ten stones which means in reality couldn't have been one of the murders."

"But he could have ordered the murder and hired two oafs to carry it out," Amarantha offered, stifling a yawn.

"Yes, but all his friends and colleague are Levanters like himself," Dredge volunteered. "It would take six of them to hurl a body."

"He could have hired some simple farm boys, but they would have confessed by now to save their skins," Weatherby suggested. "I now think the chances of Ishmael having killed Gregory Townsend are small. I'm more suspicious of Sir Rodney or even Richard Weston. Shrewsbury could have lured some oafs from Kew to do the killing by offering them gold, then using more sovereigns to have the first oaf kill the second before he poisoned the second and took all the gold back. Call on the Sheriff of Kew in the morning, Dredge, and see if any farm hands are missing."

"What makes you suspect Richard Weston?" Amarantha asked.

"Ever since my spurious trial, I've been more suspicious of him," Weatherby replied. "He could have used a couple of ne'er-do-wells from the undercroft, and then paid them to leave the county."

"Richard hasn't been talking since I embarrassed him at your trial," Amarantha mused. "But, he may be sexually frustrated enough to talk with me again. I'll give him a try."

"Just be very careful, Ran," Weatherby said. "Don't let him get you alone in case he wants revenge."

"I'll watch my step."

"What about Anna Maria Wimbledon?"

"You risked your spotless reputation by spending the night with that witch Hepsibah.to find out who she gave the bitter rose poison to, and I thought the note she gave you had Ishmael's name on it."

"It wasn't quite that simple," Dredge replied. "The writing on the purple paper was badly blurred by perspiration. The only clear letters were S and H. It seemed most likely that it was part of Ishmael's name; however both of those letters occur in Shrewsbury's name also. Someone needs to talk to Hepsibah again. I don't think it would be safe for you, Your Grace, or for you, Amarantha. I'll visit her later today after I stop in Kew."

"We've got a lot to do," Weatherby said. "Let's get some sleep."

Amarantha and Dredge willingly trudged off to bed. Weatherby wrote a quick note to Chancellor Cromwell about the latest developments in the convoluted murder investigation and enquired about returning his reward of gold sovereigns, at least for now. He also went into detail about his plans to tease the truth out of the remaining suspects in the case.

# CHAPTER 88

In the morning, Dredge set off early to visit the sheriff at Kew and to then talk to with Hepsibah. Amarantha arose early to track down Richard Weston at breakfast. It was the perfect opportunity to meet him in a public place and gauge his feelings for her. Weatherby had nothing urgent to do, so he slept in, finally awakened by Sir John Moulton loud pounding on Weatherby's door.

"Get up, you layabed!" Sir John shouted. "I need your help!"

Weatherby staggered to the door in his night rail and opened the heavy wooden door a crack.

With eyes still half closed, Weatherby said sleepily, "What is it?"

"There is a man in my construction shed, and I can't get rid of him."

"With all your burly young workers? Have him thrown out in the road."

"I could," Moulton said. "But there is something compelling about this dirty old man. He has a presence. That's why I came to seek you out. I need your astuteness."

"I'll be happy to quiz the old codger," Weatherby replied as he threw on some clothes and stepped out into the hall. "But we both know you are smart enough to solve this conundrum on your own."

Weatherby and Moulton walked to the ram shackled construction shed set in one corner of the Clock Court. When he walked through the door, Weatherby could immediately smell the strong, sour, smell coming from the old man. He must not have washed in months, Weatherby thought. The man was huddled in the corner of the shed. He had a long white beard that was stained brown around his mouth and he was dressed in rags, but his blue eyes were alert and engaging.

"Who are you?" Weatherby asked.

"I be Taliesin, the descendant of Myddin Wyllt, the wizard you know as Merlin," the old codger said in a strong sonorous voice. "The wizard who made Stonehenge."

"Yes, we both know who Merlin is, but you look more like an itinerant stumblebum, my good sir. Perhaps you could show us some of the powers you inherited from Merlin."

"I have nothing to prove to you, you young whippersnapper," Taliesin replied, turning his head away from Weatherby.

"True, but just to humor me on this fine summer morning."

"I have power over astrology, dreams, languages and fertility," Taliesin answered.

"Fair enough. Tell me as an astrologer about the powerful eclipses of the sun that effect crops and political fortunes."

"Actually, a solar eclipse is the triumph of earthly desires over reason and occurred in 1512 and 1515."

"Yes. I am aware of those and of the disastrous crop of the latter year that caused thousands of serfs to die, but what about future eclipses? If you are really a wizard, surely you can predict future eclipses."

"They will be in 1564, 1583, and 2008. Do you want me to fill in the others between those last two dates?"

Weatherby had been reading an astronomical text by a Spanish monk who calculated eclipses, and he knew that additional darkenings were indeed predicted for '64 and '83.

"I hardly think we need concern ourselves with the year 2008," Weatherby replied.

"Personally, I plan to be around to watch it from a mountain top in the new world. Would you like to know more about your nightmare, or more appropriately night *stallion* and the three wraiths on charging black steeds?"

Weatherby was shocked. He was sure he had never mentioned his recurring nightmare to Moulton. How could this smelly old man possibly know about it? Weatherby summoned Warder Chertsey and ordered the wizard bathed and barbered before he was fed. Then he motioned Moulton out of the construction shed.

"He may not be a wizard, but he has powers," Weatherby murmured. "Once he is clean, I should like to question him some more."

Weatherby went to the Great Kitchen and ate a large breakfast of bacon, eggs and fresh bread with butter. Then he went to the library to check on the solar eclipse dates. There Weatherby learned Taliesin had been absolutely correct about 2008. He was anxious to talk with the wizard some more. On a whim, he grabbed Anna Maria Wimbledon's presumed diary in Linear script A, which was laying on the table. They met in the Wolsey Apartment. The old wizard looked considerably better after shedding his rotten, filthy clothes and having been bathed, shaved and powdered.

"You've been having this recurrent nightmare for seven months," Taliesin said without preamble. "And you can seldom go back to sleep after having it. Do you want me to interpret it for you?"

"Yes."

"The three wraiths chasing you are the murderers of Hampton Court. Therefore, you are looking for three reprobates. The baby in the long white nightgown that crawls in front of you represents something new," Taliesin replied. "It could be a new love, a new trade or a new level of consciousness, but it is something fresh in your life, and you are struggling against it."

Weatherby was impressed enough that he handed the wizard the large parchment volume in his hand.

Taliesin took it in is his gnarled old hands, opened it and began to read.

"This is the sacred diary of Anna Maria Wimbledon begun in April of the year of our Lord, fifteen hundred and twenty-eight. All other volumes steeped in hypocrisy and cant have been destroyed by fire," Taliesin read in a steady voice.

Weatherby jerked the volume from the wizard and slammed it shut.

"What do you think you are doing?" Weatherby shouted out.

"I thought you wanted the text translated, Your Grace," Taliesin replied. "Was I just to admire the penmanship?"

"So you claim to be able to read this volume written in an obscure language I call Linear A?"

"Of course."

"How is that possible?" Weatherby blustered. "I have sent samples of this text to fifty or sixty scholars and linguists all over Europe, and not one of them can identify it, yet you claim to be able to read it fluently. Explain that to me, now."

Taliesin made no immediate reply, but instead fixed his intelligent blue eyes on his inquisitor clearly enjoyed Weatherby's consternation.

"First of all, I am a wizard," Taliesin said. "And secondly, this is a language called Old Ogham, or the Celtic Tree Alphabet that I learned as a child. The Druids were an oral culture and suspicious of the written word, but sometimes writing was necessary. You simply sent your enquiries east to the wrong part of the world. You should have sent your epistles to the uncultured west. There are small pockets of Druids and Celts that still use this language in the remote parts of western Ireland and the Hebrides."

"We decided that each set of lines represented a letter in the alphabet," Weatherby replied. "But we were still unable to decipher the code."

"That is because the beginning of writing in Old Ogham is noted by a feather mark," Taliesin said pointing to the first symbol. "Then the writer, you said her name is Wimbledon, told me to skip the first three letters and then read only every third letter to decipher the message. Three was a sacred number to the Druids."

"I will supply you with food, drink and anything else you require for the next few days, Taliesin," Weatherby said. "If you will translate this tome, I will have the assistant librarians transcribe everything you say."

"Very good, Your Grace, then send me a willing woman," Taliesin said. "When do we start?"

"I will have you taken to the library with this precious book," Weatherby replied. "So you still have your generative powers despite your age?"

"I'm only seventy-eight, Your Grace, which is quite young for a wizard, and I fathered a son two years ago, thanks to a potion I invented myself."

Taliesin left with a chamberlain. Weatherby sat down at Cardinal Thomas Wolsey's large evenly-grained oak desk. Since he had fallen from grace, Weatherby thought, Wolsey had been stripped of nearly everything, his many opulent palaces, most of his titles and even the magnificent black sarcophagus he designed for his own burial. For now, he remained Bishop of York, however, and lived in the rainy north with his 'wife', Joan Larke.

Weatherby thought about giving Taliesin some Linear B writing from the unfortunate Henri de Lèves, but he was sure now that it was a simple variant of Old Ogham, and that the wizard could read it easily. He would bide his time and thank his good fortune that at last the codes were broken. Weatherby sent a chamberlain to the White Swan to fetch a trollop for Taliesin. He went in search of Amarantha. He found her in the orchard having tea. The apricot and pear trees were full of ripe fruit now. The apples were still green but already the size of leather tennis balls. Flocks of orioles and robins busily pecked at the fruit.

"How did your little *tête-à-tête* with Weston go?" Weatherby asked as he sat down and Amarantha poured him tea.

"He seems to have no memory of me abusing him at your bogus trial," Amarantha replied in a surprised voice. "And he is just as forward about desiring me as he always was. I wonder if we aren't seeing a slow descent into lunacy."

"What could he tell you about our major suspects?"

"He knew all about Ishmael, but I couldn't divine if they were friends or enemies. He admired the jewel broker's way with women and tried to emulate him."

"What about Sir Rodney?"

"I'm even surer, now, that he knew about Shrewsbury's apartment here at the Palace, and I have the feeling that the two of them spent some time together over the years. I wouldn't be surprised to learn that they were in cahoots the next time we talk."

"You don't sense any danger when you are around him?"

"I don't think he has any memory of the shellacking he took at your trial. After a few kisses, he is putty in my hands."

"I don't even like to think about that," Weatherby said shaking his head.

# CHAPTER 89

A chamberlain rushed up with a note for Weatherby, who ripped it open and read the contents.

"Sir John has been attacked," Weatherby said in a shocked voice. "He was taken to the Lamb and Flag. We need to go there to minister to him."

Amarantha and Weatherby hurried to the laboratory and gathered a large black bag full of medical supplies then they called for a hansom. When they arrived at the inn, Moulton lay on a scarred, trestle table in the first room moaning. He was so bloody that at first Weatherby couldn't tell where his injures were. He had Amarantha cut his clothing off while he instructed a serving maid to bathe the victim in half water and wine to prevent infection. Palpating his friend's limbs, Weatherby found no broken bones. However, once his clothes were off it was clear that Moulton had fifteen or twenty lacerations on the front of his body. Many were superficial, but one at the base of the neck and one across the upper thigh were deep.

After washing their hands in wine, Amarantha and Weatherby went to work sewing up the gaping flesh with needle and thread. Moulton was conscious but confused. Weatherby had him drink a tankard of ale through a hollow piece of straw.

"Who found him?" Weatherby asked.

"I did, Your Grace," a man standing in the shadows volunteered. "He was a lyin' by that old thatched house that waar a dice den. I tripped 'or 'im."

"Did you see anyone else?"

"Nuh. I 'spect he waar thar the night."

"Will you go back there, my good man, and search for the weapon that did this?"

"Aye," the peasant said as he departed.

Weatherby turned toward Amarantha and said, "I'm afraid this happened because Sir John is my friend. The real killers are still on the loose, and this is their way of reminding me of that. I want you and Dredge to be extra careful."

"Who did this?" Amarantha asked.

"The deep wounds are on Sir John's left side. So, a right-handed person attacked him. He has wounds on the underside of his forearms, so he was awake when this happened and defended himself. Perhaps he was slipped a potion first to slow him down. Judging from the superficiality of the cuts, the attacker need not have been strong. It might even have been a woman."

"But, you have already decided who you think did this, haven't you?"

"Yes. I believe this is the work of Sir Rodney Shrewsbury."

Amarantha moved up to Sir John's head, touched his cheek and said softly, "You were beaten and left for dead, but Weatherby and I are here now, and we will nurse you back to full health."

Moulton's eyes opened and focused on Amarantha's angelic face.

"Who did this to you?" Weatherby asked.

Moulton shook his head slowly from side to side and took another sip of ale.

"Was it Sir Rodney Shrewsbury?" Weatherby continued.

Moulton raised his eyebrows but didn't utter a sound. It was clear to Weatherby that he must come after Shrewsbury quickly with everything he had. He had picked the ruined manor at Oatlands for his ambush, because it was small enough that he could control the grounds with a small number of men. He considered using Hepsibah as bait; however, he had seen both of them at the summer solstice. They had not been together at the mystical moment when the huge, red ball of the sun rose over the marker stone, so he deduced that they weren't all that close. He decided to use the old witch Bozalosthtsh that Shrewsbury preferred apparently because of her special, ancient potions. Weatherby had Dredge write a note in his flowing hand sending the militiamen to capture Bozalosthtsh and bring her to him.

Sir John seemed to be improving. Dredge arrived on his pony after his visiting Hepsibah.

"I came as soon as I heard," Dredge said as he tried to catch his breath. "Will he be all right?"

"Yes, but I'm afraid, as I told Amarantha, all of this is my fault," Weatherby said dejectedly. "I think this vicious beating was a message to me."

"Tell me how I help repay the scoundrel."

"First tell me what you learned from Hepsibah."

"She and her young assistants were as seductive as ever. But when I pinned her down, she wasn't sure who she had given the bitter rose poison to. I think she takes a little too much of her own potions. She remembers a visit, but thinks it might have been Ishmael, Weston, and Sir Rodney together, if you can image that. Her memory is a blur, just like your last visit with her."

"I suppose she was taking some of her own philter at the time, and she wrote the name so we couldn't read it. Even though it's not very helpful, I appreciate your making the trip," Weatherby said dejectedly. "Go to the laboratory and draw up a detailed plan for capturing Sir Rodney once we lure him to Oatlands."

"I don't have any drawings or measurements of the manor house, Your Grace," Dredge replied after a moment's thought. "I will get some supplies and a fresh pony and ride over there this afternoon. If I camp at the ruin I should have everything ready in two days."

"Take Tad with you. He can help with the measuring stick and drawing materials."

"I have a new measuring string that I copied from an Italian tool book that I will show you sometime. It is twenty-seven yards long when it is at room temperature and dry. I have marked each yard with red ink and each foot with black ink. It will make measuring a site much faster than with the five-yard rod we have used before."

After Dredge left, Weatherby helped load Sir John into a wagon so he could be transported back to the Palace. Weatherby had supper brought to Sir John's apartment, and he and Amarantha ate together quietly at his bedside while the Surveyor of the King's Work slept. The two took turns sitting with their friend through the night. In the morning Moulton, while very sore, seemed much better. When he was fully awake and had eaten some breakfast, Weatherby pulled a chair up to his bedside.

"What happened the night before last, Sir John?" Weatherby asked.

"I was walking home late from the White Swan, as I often do," Moulton began. "I was weary and my vision was blurred, but no hansoms were about and I was just trying to get home. Suddenly, I got so dizzy that I sat down on the side of the road by the bridge. I thought the feeling would pass in a minute, but it didn't. I vomited, but it didn't make me feel any better. Then someone approached me from the side, and without a word cut my thigh. Several more slashes followed quickly, and I lost consciousness. I don't remember anything after that until you and Amarantha started sewing up my wounds."

"Who did this to you?"

"I don't know. I believe it was just one person, and that he was male and not very large. But, I never saw his face."

"Could it have been Sir Rodney?"

"Yes. I did see my assailant's hands. His skin was wrinkled and had brown spots. It could have been Shrewsbury, but why would he do this? I don't even know him."

"He must know that we are friends and I believe he was sending me a message," Weatherby said as he rose from his chair. "I will check on you later today."

Weatherby returned to the Wolsey Apartment to work on his plan to capture Sir Rodney. There were thirty of the King's militiamen in County Surrey, and he sent a message to their sergeant asking all of them to bivouac one mile east of Oatlands Manor. He planned to use them, first, to construct a trap for Shrewsbury, under Dredge's direction, and then to set it.

Weatherby checked through his pile of mail and found two recent sightings for Sir Rodney. Both were from stews across the Thames from London. Weatherby knew the location of both of these houses of ill repute and realized that they were only four blocks apart. As he finished reading these reports, a militiaman came in dragging an old woman dressed in black. Despite her age, she had smooth skin and perfect teeth.

"Here's your witch, Your Grace," the soldier said as he pushed her roughly down onto the wooden floor. "We also captured her two young warlocks."

"Are you the witch they call Bovalosh?" Weatherby asked as helped the old lady up.

"My name is Bozalosthtsh. Why have I been dragged here?"

"You have been accused of casting spells upon Anne Boleyn's cousin and preventing her from conceiving," Weatherby lied.

"I have done no such thing, Your Grace," Bozalosthtsh said vehemently

"I've a mind to send you to the Tower and torture the truth out of you! I'm going to have you confined overnight without food or water and we'll see in the morning if you are more compliant."

Weatherby walked to Sir John Moulton's apartment and found his friend sitting up, smoking a pipe and studying a parchment plan.

"You look much better, friend," Weatherby remarked.

"I feel much better!" Sir John replied. "Anyway, I was tired of lying in bed. I must tell you, I think Amarantha did a better job of sewing me up than you did, Doctor!"

"Next time I'll let the barrister do the whole job, and I'll just apply leeches and bleed you mercilessly," Weatherby replied sarcastically after looking at Amarantha's even stitching.

# CHAPTER 90

That night, Amarantha and Weatherby had a leisurely supper of wild game featuring woodcock, duck and venison. They agreed not to talk about Shrewsbury or any other controversial subject. Instead, they visited about books and music. Amarantha was reading about Giotto. She was thinking about his Arena Chapel in Padua that was decorated with forty frescoes depicting the life of the Virgin Mary. Perhaps, when the case was over, she would go to the Italian States and see it in person. Weatherby was studying the music of Josquin de Près, a Flemish composer. He had just received a score for a motet, *Praeter rerum Seriem.* He imaged the melody in his head, and he hoped to play it with someone soon. After dinner, they both went to the library to see how Taliesin's translation of Anna Maria's diary was coming. Taliesin sat on a cushion wrapped in a multicolored robe like an eastern pasha. Margaret and Judith were sitting on both sides of him and they were writing.

"How is it coming?" Weatherby asked.

"Well. He has translated more than half of the volume," Judith said as she handed Weatherby a tall stack of papers.

"How is he holding up?" Amarantha asked as if the wizard weren't there.

"He is very robust," Margaret replied. "But the constant sexual innuendo is tiresome."

"What have you discovered so far?"

"The unfortunate woman was a devout Catholic, despite her proclivities, until she was twenty-eight," Judith began. "Then two years ago she got involved with a dark-skinned Arab that will mostly likely turn out to be Ishmael. She added him to the stable of men that gave her valuable gifts for the services she provided for them. However, this time she didn't keep her partner at arm's length. She fell in love."

"This reminds me of her roommate, Peggy Ealing's story," Amarantha replied. "So they both were madly in love with the same man?"

"I agree," Judith said. "The difference is that Peggy kept her religious beliefs, and Anna Maria changed and became a zealot for her new beliefs. Her lover was not a Mohammedan as you might suspect, but rather a Druid."

"Due to oppression most Englishmen think the Druids have been extirpated, but, in fact, many still exist in County Surrey as well as Ireland and Scotland," Weatherby said. "How did her religion change her life?"

"We don't know yet," Margaret replied. "We have only translated through the fall of 1529. We have several more days of translating to do."

"Thanks for your hard work, all of you. I will send a bottle of wine," Weatherby said as he and Amarantha left the library.

After a calming walk around the orchard, Weatherby and his associate retired.

In the morning, after breakfast, Dredge returned from Oatlands Manor.

"The remains of the Manor were in much worse shape then I had been led to believe," Dredge said as he sat down wearily and took a large cup of tea. "So the plans went quickly. The only area appropriate for constructing a trap is the grotto, which is bigger than the Undercroft here at Hampton Court. I will draw the plans for Oatlands Manor this afternoon."

"I never thanked you properly for your work on the trip to Chartres, Dredge, or your excellent work with the rocket that delivered Ishmael to us," Weatherby said.

"I consider myself lucky to be in your employ, Your Grace," Dredge replied. "You treat me as your equal in more respects than anyone else would, and I am thankful for that daily. Speaking of that, I want to show you something I have been working on."

Dredge led the way to the laboratory and spread a large, detailed parchment architectural drawing of Hampton Court Palace on the zinc-covered table.

"If you draw a line from the location where we found Anna Maria Wimbledon's body in the third floor of the Bayne Tower, to where we found William Suffolk's body in the new construction in the Chapel Court, it measures one hundred and thirty-five feet," Dredge said, laying a straight edge on the plan. "And sacred numbers to the Druids are one, which symbolizing the sun and unity; and three, symbolizing earth, sky and sea."

"What about five?" Weatherby asked.

"It is perhaps the most sacred of all," Dredge replied. "It represents the five provinces, north, south, east, west, and center. Also the fifth letter of the Ogham alphabet is the white poplar called the tree of life."

"In that case, look, if we make a line from Anna Maria's body to Gregory Townsend's remains, the distance is again one hundred and thirty-five feet!" Weatherby said as he moved the straight edge. "And, finally, the distance from victim one, William Suffolk, to victim two, Miss Wimbledon, is also one hundred and thirty-five feet, completing an equilateral triangle."

"I don't think that happened by accident!" Dredge shouted. "I believe that means that all three were killed by the same person."

"Or at least that the killers had a common goal," Weatherby mused. "I also recollect that all three of their heads were pointing to the center of the triangle! Bisect each angle and draw a line to the center and show me where they meet."

Dredge measured the angles carefully with a brass compass and drew thin lines using the straight edge. He made a small red x where the lines met and stepped back so Weatherby could observe his work.

"The spot is on the south central side of the Great Hall," Weatherby said. "I believe we have to excavate there."

"Sir John Moulton will never allow it," Dredge replied. "His carpenters just finished laying a beautiful, tight-jointed oak floor on that side of the Hall."

"I'll talk with him. It's just possible that two fine people and a mountebank lost their lives because of what might be buried there. Get your fancy Italian measuring string, and let's find the spot."

Dredge and Weatherby went to the spot where Anna Maria's body had been found and measured one hundred and thirty-five feet. Then they did the same for the other two victims. With some adjustments, they found the spot in the Great Hall where the three lines met. Dredge marked the spot with a large brass chess piece.

"Now, with Tad's help I will draw up my plans for Oatlands Manor," Dredge said as Weatherby walked toward the door.

Weatherby met Amarantha in the Knot Garden for a plate of cold chicken with assorted cheeses and mixed greens. They polished off two bottles of French white wine while they ate and talked.

"You seem to be feeling better about your cases," Amarantha observed, before she filled her mouth with a large sip of the tasty golden liquid.

"Yes. I feel we are making some progress, albeit slowly," Weatherby observed. "I wrote Chancellor Cromwell about our setback right after Peggy Ealing's revelation, and offered to send the money back, but I haven't received a reply."

"I think the government has all they can handle, given their current disagreement with Spain," Amarantha observed.

"Much of that has to do with the battle of Gavinana, where the Spanish captured Florence and put the Medici back in power," Weatherby mused. "I'm just glad they are busy with faraway events right now."

"I think the symmetry of the bodies that you and Dredge found is amazing," Amarantha said. "What will you do next?"

"I need to get Sir John's permission to dig up his beautiful new floor, and Dredge says that it won't be easy."

"Perhaps I should ask him. He likes me, you know."

"I'll say. He admires beautiful women, and he already informed me that you did a better job of sewing him up than I did."

"I'll go speak with him now." Amarantha arose and placed her linen napkin on the table.

Weatherby went back to the library for the afternoon to look over the shoulders of the translator. Dredge interrupted him early in the afternoon with a plan for the ensnarement at Oatlands Manor. After a few modifications drawn in pencil, Weatherby approved it. Dredge and Tad headed west with Shrewsbury's favorite witch to deliver the plans to the militiamen. Now, with the plans in place it would take time before they could spring the trap.

Weatherby and Amarantha walked to the Lamb and Flag for dinner. A sudden rainstorm blew up just after they crossed the Thames, and they took cover in a doorway. They pressed their bodies together in the small space to avoid soaking their clothing. They talked and laughed while the drops hit with such force that they bounced back up off the ground, looking like the tines of a pitchfork. Once the rain slowed, Weatherby held his cloak over Amarantha's head as they hurried to the Inn. Once there, they joined the two sisters from the Office of the Greencloth for drinks and dinner. After the sisters left, Weatherby asked Amarantha about her meeting with Moulton.

"He said 'no' at first, but after some flattery and flirting he finally agreed," Amarantha said as she placed her hand on top of Weatherby's. "He wants you to mark the spot with a red x."

The two rose to leave. The rain had stopped and they walked amicable back to Hampton Court hand in hand. The August night was now cool from the rain shower. The air was full of a fresh, clean smell.

"Shall we go for a ride on the morrow?" Weatherby asked.

"What a lovely idea," Amarantha replied softly.

Before retiring, Weatherby remeasured the distances from each of the three bodies and marked the spot where they intersected in the Great Hall with a red velvet 'x.'

# PART 10

# CHAPTER 91

After a hearty breakfast, Amarantha and Weatherby walked to the stable. Sporter, Amarantha's Irish wolfhound was brought out by a stable hand and sat beside his mistress. Amarantha's small black Arabian mare was saddled, and whinnied in anticipation of a ride. Weatherby's large roan stood silently in his new black Italian-style saddle. Once they were both mounted, they headed out of the stable area at a walk. They agreed to ride north into the deep beech woods and rolling meadows. They had first ridden there month ago when they were caught in a sudden hail storm. Both remembered their intimate embrace when they had gotten dangerously cold from the hard rain followed by sleet. But neither of them had ever spoken about it. It was hard to remember the aching cold that quickly spread into their core on this warm summer day.

As usual Amarantha led the way on the trail. Few farms or houses lay to the north and because of the lack of habitation they spooked hedgehogs, hinds, and even a stoat. The shady woods were pleasanter than the open fields, where the sun beat down, through clear skies. They rode quickly without talking for the first two hours, and then they jumped large piles of downed limbs and small streams. Amarantha stopped before each obstacle suggesting a way to get across, before she spurring her mare forward ahead of Weatherby.

At lunch time they stopped at the edge of a field where there was dappled shade. A chambermaid had packed cold salmon, cucumber salad, beets, and fresh bread with two bottles of white wine. Amarantha and Weatherby ate their fill and then stretched out on a blanket and napped. Weatherby was awakened he thought at first by a pesky fly. Then he looked across the field and saw a man moving through the underbrush.

The man was dressed in olive drab, homespun clothes color and had painted his face in splotches of brown and green. The figure was clearly meant to blend into the underbrush. Weatherby had never seen anything like it before. He spoke softly to Amarantha.

"Don't move," he whispered. "But look across the field by that small oak three."

"All I see is trees and shrubs," she whispered back after looking in that direction.

"Keep looking."

After ten minutes of staring, Amarantha said, "I don't see anything, Seamus. I'm worried about you. You are seeing Sir Rodney everywhere. That woman you embarrassed at the Lamb and Flag because you thought she was Sir Rodney in disguise is a perfect example of your obsession. There is nothing over there but shrubbery. I think you need to take a rest."

Amarantha put her head down but Weatherby stared at the edge of the clearing for another twenty minutes.

"Now," he whispered.

A shaft of light reflected from the bushes, perhaps from the lens of a spyglass, as the sun sank a little lower into the west. Now Amarantha saw the man.

"Fie, me!" she said out loud. "You have an exceptional pair of eyes only exceeded by that clever bastard's disguise. I'll walk a few steps to the side and pretend to make water, perhaps the removing of my kirtle and baring of my legs will draw his attention, and you can crawl to your horse and run him down."

Amarantha made a show of standing up and stretching her arms. Then she walked a few yards away from their blanket and began to remove her outer garment. Weatherby crawled back toward the horses on his elbows, and after untying the reins jumped into the saddle and spurred his horse across the field. His big roan was halfway there before the disguised figure put down his spyglass and noticed the approaching rider. He turned and ran into the woods crashing down a hill to a ravine dense with wildflowers and bushes.

Soon Amarantha, in her shift, was at Weatherby's side and the two explored the stream at the bottom of the ravine, first on horseback and then on foot. Amarantha's dog Sporter worked in tight circles around them with his wet black nose on the ground. After two hours of searching they had not turned up a footprint or a thread of cloth.

"If his back is as well disguised as his front, he could be right next to us," Amarantha said. "I'm very surprised that Sporter can't locate him."

"Shrewsbury has spent years consorting with witches and learning their tricks. He's probably as invisible to Sporter's nose as he is to our eyes. I'm sure he is so close that we could trip over his scrawny little frame."

They both realized that they weren't going to catch the wily professor. His spying had taken the fun right out of their ride. They turned their respective horses reluctantly back toward the Palace.

"At least Sir Rodney is nearby and not in Ireland or Wales," Weatherby mused.

"When will Dredge have your mousetrap completed at Oatlands?"

"He has thirty men at his disposal and I told him to work them day and night. I'm hoping he will be ready soon."

Weatherby and Amarantha dropped off their horses and Sporter and spent the evening reading. Shortly after ten, Weatherby received a terse message from Dredge saying that all was in readiness at Oatlands.

Weatherby was reading by candle light when Sir John Moulton stopped by.

"Much as I didn't want to, my friend, I had my workers pull up that beautiful oak floor in the Great Hall," Moulton began as he sat down.

"Did you find anything?" Weatherby asked excitedly.

"Yes and no. I had the workers stop when we got down two feet, just as something strange came into view. I didn't want a half dozen workers to know what was there, so I had them cover the hole with a tarp. Let's go finish the job now."

The two men gathered four candelabra and walked across the Base Court to the Great Hall. Moulton had left two shovels propped against the wall. They both began to dig, but almost immediately something slimy and wet appeared in the bottom of the hole. Moulton set both shovels aside. He handed Weatherby a small knife and both dug the soil away from the buried mass. They freed each side and then Moulton lifted the wiggling mass out of the hole. It smelled of reptiles and the earth. It was eighteen inches in diameter and consisted of a vast number of serpents twisted into an artificial knot held together by their saliva and slime.

"What on earth is this?" Weatherby asked in a voice full of astonishment. "Could it possibly justify three murders?"

"Absolutely!" Moulton responded vehemently. "It is a *Gloine nan*

*Druidh,* known as Druids' glass. I have read of it, but never thought I would see it."

Moulton carefully pulled the vipers away revealing a many-sided egg-shaped structure of isinglass ribbed with pure gold.

"It possesses the most extraordinary virtues!" Moulton remarked. "If you touch it, you will have astonishing good fortune."

Weatherby took the slimy ball and held it aloft for several minutes.

Early the next morning Weatherby asked Ellen Iverson to spread the word that a witch named Bozalosthtsh had been abducted and was being tortured at Oatlands. Then Weatherby rode west to the ruined manor house where Dredge proudly showed off the modifications he had made. Then they both worked on hiding the tools and scraps from the work that had been completed. Dredge laid out the plan on a scarred oak table, after Weatherby stationed the militiamen in the surrounding woods. He divided the men into groups of three and four hidden at each point of the compass. If the quarry was sighted, one man was to alert the group next to them so they could join in. Then the remaining soldiers were to give chase.

Weatherby thought it might take days for Shrewsbury to appear. He wanted screams to emanate from the grotto where Bozalosthtsh was bound and held. He didn't have the stomach to have the old harridan beaten for days, and he didn't think she would survive it. Instead he hired two old women from the village of Oatlands and paid them handsomely to sit near the witch for twelve hours each day and scream every few minutes as if in terrible pain. Dredge set up a cot for Weatherby in a small closet off the grotto; however, the detective found he could only stand the screaming for couple of hours before he was forced to go outside.

For the next two days, nothing happened except a long hard summer rain that soaked everything. By the third night, Weatherby was in foul mood. He hadn't been sleeping well on his makeshift cot, and he was having his nightmare every night. That night he drank whiskey to help him slumber and fell into his cot exhausted about eleven-thirty. In the middle of the night a small scraping noise awoke from a deep sleep. He had been deeply asleep. As he rubbed the sleep out of his eyes, he saw some figures around the witch, tugging on her ropes. He leaped out of bed and ran toward the figures on unsteady legs.

As Weatherby approached two young witches were cutting the thick ropes that wound round and round Bozalosthtsh's body. They turned toward him with slender daggers raised. Weatherby recognized them as the young twin witchlets from Hepsibah's lair. They were developing magical powers, but were only fifteen years old and each weighed around seven stones. Weatherby was so much sturdier that he held off one twin while he took the knife from the other and pushed her roughly to the floor. Her knife blade cut Weatherby superficially on his shoulder before he grabbed the witch's forearm and twisted it behind her back. Her forearm was no bigger than the handle of a whip, and he easily overpowered and pushed her down as well.

Dredge came in and fell upon the figure on the other side of the Bozalosthtsh. Weatherby moved quickly around the foot of the bench where the old witch was tied and reached for the third assailant. However, the man twisted out of Dredge's grip and dove under the bench where the bait was restrained. Weatherby saw the man's curly head of white hair as he sprinted for the door, and he was sure it was Sir Rodney Shrewsbury. Despite his advanced age, the culprit was quite agile. Weatherby ran after him. Near the end of the grotto, the hallway forked into a large branch and a small one. The larger branch was seven feet wide and curved gently to the left before coming to an abrupt dead end. The narrow branch was only eighteen inches wide thanks to an arch of stones ordered by Dredge, but after a series of turns, led out of the grotto and opened onto the back of the ruined manor.

Cleverly, Sir Rodney picked the smaller passageway, and by the time Weatherby squeezed around the turns the villain was disappearing into the woods toward the east. Weatherby blew a whistle he carried around his neck to alert the sleeping militiamen, but he was afraid that his elusive quarry was about to escape again.

# CHAPTER 92

Weatherby and three of the militiamen rode to the east searching for the wily villain. It was a moonless night, and the shrubs and bushes were still wet from the day's soaking rain. They looked assiduously for footprints, broken branch and scraps of clothing that had been torn off. They returned to Oatlands Manor two hours later, cold and discouraged. Weatherby sent the remaining militiamen off in a fan-shaped search pattern to the east in the hope of stumbling upon Sir Rodney. Dredge helped Weatherby out of his wet clothing and built a fire in the fireplace.

"I can't believe that infernal old man has outwitted us again," Weatherby discouragingly as he took off his wet clothing. "How did he know which fork to take?"

"Perhaps he was just lucky, Your Grace."

"Or maybe he paid one of our workmen for a copy of the plan."

"Yes, that may be more likely. Anyone without foreknowledge would have taken the wide corridor at the fork, just as we planned, and would be in irons right now."

Weatherby lay down on his cot still shivering despite being covered by a pile of blankets. He fell asleep wondering what his next move should be. Two hours later, Dredge awakened him.

"The militiamen who were stationed to the west of the Manor have captured someone they wanted you to see," Dredge said.

Weatherby dressed quickly and stepped into the room where Bozalosthtsh had been bound. Two soldiers held a slight old man with wet clothing and scratches on his face. His head was covered with curly white hair. Weatherby recognized him immediately from the portrait at Straffan House. It was Sir Rodney Shrewsbury, himself!

"Welcome to Oatlands, my good sir," Weatherby said sarcastically. "Get him out of those wet clothes, but keep a grip on him at all times until he is in irons. I don't want him to get pneumonia before I have him tortured. As soon as you have him in ankle and wrist irons, bring him back to me. In the meantime, put my branding iron in the fire."

Shrewsbury caught Weatherby's eye and smirked before he was roughly taken away. The guards brought him back in dry, ill-fitting clothes and irons and pushed him onto the floor in front of Weatherby.

"I'm prepared to make the rest of your life an unending misery, Sir Rodney," Weatherby began. "However, if you give me the information I need I might be persuaded to let you go back to Ireland for the rest of your days, even though you don't deserve it. So tell me, who murdered William Suffolk, fifth son of the Earl?"

"Ishmael murdered him, as everyone knows," Sir Rodney replied.

Weatherby took his red-hot branding iron out of the embers and held it a quarter of an inch from Shrewsbury's left cheek.

"I demand civil answers from you," Weatherby yelled as he move the iron even closer to the pale pink skin of Sir Rodney's face.

"I don't recognize your authority, Scotsman," Sir Rodney replied. He moved his face against the iron and his skin began to sizzle. "I am richer, smarter and more nimble than you. I have been in your grasp a dozen times in the past four months. I toyed with you in Dublin during that chase in my calash. I could have sped away and left you in the dust at any time. It took the help of thirty some men to capture me. I was even there the first night you came to Hampton Court and examined the carcass of that worthless architect. I took your measure then and found you wanting!"

"Who murdered Anna Maria Wimbledon, you cur?" Weatherby spat at the old man.

"I don't find your threats particularly frightening, and am under no obligation to answer you."

"Put him in the blind passage off the grotto for the night," Weatherby ordered.

Once Sir Rodney had been dragged out, Weatherby sat down with Tad and Dredge and passed around a flagon of ale.

"I would like to send that murderer to the Tower," Weatherby said. "So that I can extract a full confession from him, Dredge. However many of the gaolers are vicious and nearly half of the prisoners sent through the Traitors' Gate die from the effects of torture before they can be drawn and quartered."

"Perhaps we could send him elsewhere," Dredge replied.

"When I visited the bishop of Winchester a year ago, he was torturing Protestants," Weatherby reflected. "Perhaps we should send Sir Rodney there. He has spent a lot on equipment. I know he has a rack, thumb screws, and a strappado like the one we found in Philbrick's room. It was appalling. He was torturing three peasants when I was there to save their souls. Two of them were women. He has a machine called the scavenger's daughter, which I had never seen before. It consisted of an iron base plate and two semi-circular bows. The bows were fastened tightly across the poor victim's back, holding her in a crouching position. It worked quickly. She confessed to consorting with the devil while I was there."

"I will send Shrewsbury there in the morning, Your Grace, if you will write a note to the bishop," Dredge replied.

"I want him guarded at all times by our ten best men," Weatherby said. He dismissed the rest of the King's men and then rode leisurely back to Hampton Court to seek out Amarantha.

"Dredge and I captured Sir Rodney!" Weatherby ejaculated as soon as he saw her.

"What good news!' Amarantha replied grasping both of his hands.

"Actually we just got him by the skin of our teeth," Weatherby replied more humbly.

"I bet you were successful because you had Tad."

"Actually, he slept through the whole thing. The militiamen stumbled across him at the last possible minute. We were searching to the east and had moved most of our men there, and he had doubled back undetected to the west."

"Where is he now?"

"I sent him to Winchester to be tortured for answers. He had the nerve to say that he had been within my reach a dozen times in the last four months. He even mentioned that carriage chase you and I were in in Dublin."

"I told you I thought he was toying with us when I wondered if you had become his *raison d'être*. But at least you captured him. Let met treat you to dinner at the Lamb and Flag."

Amarantha and Weatherby walked arm in arm across the bridge to the village. The inn was filled with noisy shopkeepers and farmers. Weatherby always found the buzz of human conversation stimulated his appetite like a hungry bee returning to the noise of the hive. Amarantha ordered pheasant, and they ate and drank into the afternoon.

After they had drunk a little too much ale, Weatherby turned to Amarantha and said, "I'll ride over to Winchester this afternoon to supervise the interrogation. Would you like to come along?"

"I believe I won't," she replied. "I am appalled by torture, as you know, and believe it should be outlawed in any civilized country."

"I know your position, and in general I agree with you. I just can't conceive of another way to break this arrogant old man. He may well not volunteer anything, you know. When I threatened him with the branding iron, he rested his cheek against it without flinching. He seems impervious to pain, and I can't imagine that at his age he is afraid of dying. I don't believe there is another person on the earth that he cares about."

"What about Hepsibah or Bozalosthtsh?"

"That is a very good point! He came all the way to Oatlands Manor to rescue her."

"I don't suppose you know where she is any more?" Amarantha asked.

"But of course I do. That is a brilliant idea. I will have her sent to Winchester post haste."

The two walked back to the Palace. Along the way, Weatherby told Amarantha the amazing story of *Gloine nan Druidh*.

"That is a fantastic story!" Amarantha chortled. "I believe you are making the whole thing up as you are wont to do."

"By God's blood, it is the whole truth!"

"Prove it, then."

Weatherby marched Amarantha to Moulton construction shack and walked in after knocking.

"Sir John, show this unbeliever what we found the other night," Weatherby said.

"By all means," Sir John said, resting his pipe on his drawing table.

He handed a plan to Christopher Dickinson as he walked out and led the way to his apartment. Once there he locked the door behind and pulled the treasure wrapped in blue velvet from a chest under his bed. Wordlessly, he handed the shiny globe to Amarantha.

"My God!" Amarantha exclaimed. "This is truly preposterous."

"Hold it high for a few minutes, and it will bring you good fortune," Sir John instructed.

Amarantha lifted the globe skyward and held it there until her arms tired.

Weatherby hugged Amarantha goodbye and went to the stable for his horse. It was four p.m. he noticed by the watch around his neck, but he had only fifty-two miles to go and the summer evenings were still long and warm. He let his horse set its own pace and arrived at Winchester Cathedral just after nine.

# CHAPTER 93

The monks made him a dinner of dark bread and a thin vegetable soup. Weatherby was shown to a monk's cell where the only objects in the room were a large crucifix on the wall and a narrow pallet. Weatherby pulled off his riding clothes, hung them on the crucifix, and was instantly asleep. In the morning the monks awoke him at five, and served him a breakfast of hard black bread and water. When he finished eating, he walked to the large treasury under the cathedral where the dungeon and torture chambers were located. Since Martin Luther's teachings had spread, the bishop needed larger quarters for torture. He had forced unrepentant Protestants to dig out the area under the nave before he burned them at the stake, always fueling the fire with Lutheran bibles and recently cut wood so the fire would burn slowly and inflict the maximum amount of pain and accompanying screams before the apostates went to hell. He found Sir Rodney Shrewsbury hanging from the wall by iron clamps tight around his wrists. His feet were just four inches of the stone floor, so when he flexed his feet he could briefly lift his body and relieve the pain in his arms.

"Good morning Sir Rodney," Weatherby said in a cheery voice. "I can have you down from there and on your way in twenty minutes."

"In exchange for what?" Sir Rodney said back in a tired voice.

"Just some simple, honest answers," Weatherby replied in a soothing voice."

"Let me down and I will tell you everything I know."

"No. It doesn't work like that. Tell me the answers first, and then you will be let down."

"Perhaps I'm not ready to yield."

"Have it your way then. Tomorrow we will, shall we say, move on to some more vigorous and exquisitely painful torture. I will see you then."

"Mayhap I will be more talkative then."

"Tomorrow may well be the last day of your life. For if you do not talk, you will be of no further use to me. I have had more than my fill of your disguises and skulking about. At that very moment, you become more useful to me dead than alive. Where should I send your wretched, bony corpse?"

"Just contact Bozalosthtsh or Hepsibah, and they will fetch my remains and pack my body in sweet herbs."

"Actually, you can tell Bozalosthtsh yourself."

He motioned for the jailer to bring her in. He had her outfitted in rags and had her body smeared with charcoal and filth. She wore iron ankle and wrist bracelets that were connected to chains that were far too heavy for her. She clanked loudly on the flagstone floor as she walked.

"What have they done to you, B?" Sir Rodney asked.

Bozalosthtsh only cried out in reply. The jailers put the witch on the rack, tying her arms to the top rung and her feet to the lowest and then pretending to tighten the drum as if they were stretching her. Even though no stretching occurred, she shrieked even louder. Sir Rodney set his expression and made no reply. The Bishop's men took the witch off the rack and hung her by her hands from the wall. One guard pretended to slash her with a sword while the other sprayed pigs' blood on her body. She was twenty-five feet from Sir Rodney, and he couldn't tell that she wasn't actually being cut. He looked at the old witch with a pained expression and turned his head toward Weatherby.

"Cut her down! She never hurt anyone!" he yelled. "I will tell you anything you want to know."

Shrewsbury was promptly cut down and placed on a bench with his elbows on a table. Weatherby offered him a tankard of cool, fresh water. Sir Rodney gulped it down greedily, spilling almost half on the table. Weatherby was confident that he knew who killed Gregory Townsend, so he started with that question.

"Who killed Gregory Townsend?" Weather asked in a stern voice.

"Ishmael, with the help of two of his Levanter friends," Sir Rodney replied after a long pause.

"And who killed Anna Maria Wimbledon?"

"As you know, it was also Ishmael."

"Liar!" Weatherby yelled as he stood up. "I know that isn't true."

Weatherby motioned for the guards to string Sir Rodney from the wrist clamps so his feet were off the floor. A moan escaped from Sir Rodney as he was lifted up despite his attempt at stoicism. Weatherby sat down at the table dejectedly. After a few minutes, Bozalosthtsh came and sat beside him. She had rubbed the pigs' blood off of her body.

"You have a problem, Your Grace, and I have one too," she said in a soft voice. "But I may be of some assistance."

"How is that?" Weatherby asked archly.

"I wish to be free again, but you will not release me unless Sir Rodney talks. I know him well, and he will not talk of his own free will."

"What is your solution?"

"I have a truth potion with me that might give you the answers you need. In exchange for it, Your Grace, I would like my freedom."

"I am willing to try it. Bring it to me."

"There is only on difficultly."

"And what, pray tell, is that?"

"It usually works, but sometimes it is fatal."

"I will take that risk for him," Weatherby replied. "Bring it to me and you may be on your way."

Bozalosthtsh returned with a worn leather bag and extracted a bright blue powder that she handed to Weatherby.

"It must be inhaled," she said. "It works within minutes, and if it is fatal, it is also quick."

Weatherby took the potion and released the witch. He decided she had been as cooperative as she could be. Weatherby had the guards hold a heavy cloth over Sir Rodney's nose and mouth. After a minute, he had the guards remove it and place the bright blue powder under his nostrils. The entire potion was sucked into the Rodney's nasal passages. Then Weatherby had the guards unclamp his hands and lay him on a table. He glanced at his watch.

"Who killed William Suffolk?" Weatherby said in a loud voice near the professor's ear. There was no answer. Weatherby repeated the same question over and over for the next several minutes. Then Shrewsbury's eyelids began to flutter, and he spoke suddenly.

"I killed William Suffolk with a workman's mallet," Sir Rodney said in a barely audible voice. "I wore my stilts and a long black robe to frighten him into submission first."

Weatherby wanted to ask a dozen other questions about Suffolk, but he needed to act quickly, so he moved onto the next crime.

"Who killed Anna Maria Wimbledon?" Weatherby intoned.

"What a loss! That beautiful Druid princess who would soon bear us a child for sacrifice!" Shrewsbury said in a loud voice as his agitation increased.

Then Sir Rodney began to lose focus.

"Who killed her?" Weatherby shook his captive violently.

Shrewsbury looked right at Weatherby.

"Sir Richard Wes . . ." he began.

Then his breathing stopped, his lips suddenly turned the bright blue of the potion, and his eyes rolled upward. Weatherby stood. His muscles ached from the desire he had to get the information about the murderers before his detainee succumbed. Suddenly, he felt very relaxed. Weatherby told the guards who to contact about the body. Then he had his horse saddled and rode back to Hampton Court. It was late afternoon, and the shadows were long. Seamus had been pushing Amarantha toward the Master of the House so that he could learn more about his shenanigans, but now that he was sure that Weston was a murderer, he wanted to be at the Palace and at Amarantha's side.

After riding an hour, the twilight faded and Weatherby slowed his pace straining to see the road ahead. Dark shadows usually turned out to be just that but sometimes they were rocks or puddles. After an hour the moon rose in the east. It was half full and lay over the rich dark sky like a lazy rotund woman in a full white skirt. Weatherby appreciated the blue, white light. He arrived back at Hampton Court at 10:30 p.m. After leaving his horse at the stable, he went to Amarantha's apartment, but found it empty. He went directly to Richard Weston's office. At the entrance, he saw Amarantha's dog, Sporter, lying near the door with its belly slit open. The large, gentle dog was nearly dead and gasping for breath. Weatherby put his handkerchief over the animal's nose and mouth. Then he stroked the wolfhound's head while it took its last breath.

He quietly back away, and found Tad and sent him to locate Dredge. The three of them went to laboratory to assemble a satchel of weapons and tools. Loaded down with the instruments they thought might be of use, they headed back to the Master of the House's Office on the first floor by the Great Chapel.

# CHAPTER 94

As the three men approached the hallway, Weatherby sent Tad to have a chamberlain remove poor Sporter. Approaching the doorway Weatherby and Dredge crept along the side of the hallway. When they got to the door Dredge tried the handle and was surprised to find that the door swung open. Weatherby and Dredge slipped through as quietly as possible. Weston's office was totally dark and didn't seem to be occupied. Weatherby ventured a call.

"Richard. I am looking for Miss Amarantha Thompson," Weatherby called out.

"I have her and she is unharmed," Weston called back after a pause in a tremulous voice from the next room.

"She must remain so, Sir. Or I will personally torment and torture you in diabolical ways that have never been thought of until now for a month of Sundays."

"I'm afraid of pain," Weston wailed back. "But how can I trust you?"

"You and your spies have observed me for the past four months and you know I am an honourable man," Weatherby replied without hesitation. "If I give you my word, it is also the King's word. You will be vouched safe."

"Then come and get her, I offer no resistance."

"This will be easy," Dredge said.

Just as the two stepped forward, a series of steel bolts shot across the room and buried themselves into the oak paneling. One caught the flesh of Dredge's thigh and another tore Weatherby's doublet. Both men retreated to the hallway to light torches and arm themselves. Weatherby picked a short sword, and Dredge a dagger. They found the crossbows that had fired on them were lined up on each side of the room. The two men broke the triggers on each so they couldn't be fired again. Weatherby decided to feign being shot so he staggered through the doorway, falling into the next room as if fatally wounded. Dredge remained at the doorway, cautiously looking in.

Weatherby lay utterly still for several minutes. He had arranged his fall so that he lay on his right side with his torch resting across his leg. He could see that Amarantha was bound and gagged at a table. Behind her stood Weston with a loaded pistol, Amarantha's body was his shield. The pistol shook in Weston's hand. Dredge peeked through the doorway and Weston fired shattering the molding of the door, but missing his intended victim. Weatherby wished he had brought a pistol, even though he would have been afraid to fire with Amarantha so close by. Weatherby knew that Wheelock pistols were notoriously hard to aim even at close range, because of their weight.

Weatherby realized that the only light in the room came from his torch and a candelabrum on the desk. Weatherby would need Dredge's help and he wanted to alert his assistant.

"Richmond prioress's house," Weatherby yelled back into the first room as a coded message.

He hoped Dredge would recall the story of him and Tad charging the upstairs bedroom of the prioress's house where Shrewsbury was bedding one of the young novitiates. Weston fired his shaky pistol again, but missed. Weatherby waited a few seconds to let his message sink in. Then he put his torch quickly on the floor and rolled it around to extinguish the flame. His part of the room darkened. Then he flipped his torch end over end toward the candelabrum. It struck the vertical brass part, knocking the candelabrum to the floor with a clatter, but more importantly it extinguished four of the five candles. The one remaining source of light backlit Weston and it cast Weatherby and the doorway where Dredge would enter into darkness.

"Now!" Weatherby yelled as he jumped up and ran toward the desk.

He knew that Richard Weston would get off one shot before the two of them fell upon him. Weston fired and barely caught Weatherby in the flesh of his left shoulder. The force of the ball turned Weatherby half way around, but he recovered quickly. The noise from the discharge in the small room was deafening. Weatherby temporarily lost his hearing. The two men reached the desk at the same instant, despite Dredge's bowed legs and short body. Dredge pulled Amarantha down onto the carpeting and covered her with his body. Weatherby knocked a second pistol out of Weston's hand and wrestled him to the ground.

"Zounds," Weston yelled as Weatherby pummeled his face and chest with his fists.

"Come over here, Dredge, and help me tie him up!" Weatherby yelled.

They flipped Weston onto his stomach and secured his hands behind his back. Dredge cut Amarantha's bond. Except for a bruise around both of her wrists and a bruise around her neck, she seemed all right.

"How is Sporter?" Amarantha asked. "He tried to defend me during the abduction."

"I'm very sorry to tell you, Ran," Weatherby said in a soft voice as he rested a hand on her shoulder. "He's gone."

"Bastard!" Amarantha yelled as she pummeled Weston with her fists and then kicked him in the side.

"He will pay fifty times over for that. I have requested two of the most diabolical torturers from the Tower. They will conduct the examination with a prolonged and exquisite amount of pain unless every question is fully answered." He turned to Tad, who had just arrived. "Secure him in the undercroft and make sure he is under constant guard."

"Yes, Sir," Tad replied as he roughly pulled Weston to a standing position and shoved him out of the room.

After first making sure Amarantha was all right, Weatherby brought her up to date on events at Winchester.

"Torturing Shrewsbury was just as unrewarding as you thought it would be, Ran," Weatherby began. "Even though the Bishop's men are expert. Sir Rodney would promise to tell all, but the minute I cut him down he would clam up. However, I still had Bozalosthtsh so I pretended to torture her in front of him using lots of fresh pigs' blood, but he was unmoved. She certainly can scream."

"I thought he really cared about her," Amarantha replied.

"I did too," Weatherby said in a puzzled voice. "I suppose it was all an act. In any case, Bozalosthtsh offered me a deal. She offered me a blue truth potion she was developing in exchange for her freedom. I didn't see that I had any choice."

"Did it work?" Amarantha asked excitedly.

"It did. He confirmed that Ishmael killed Gregory Townsend. Then Shrewsbury confessed to killing William Suffolk after donning stilts and a long black robe to frighten his victim. You remember we knew the killer was five feet eleven or taller. The bad part of the truth potion was that after speaking the truth most of the imbibers die suddenly."

"What about poor Anna Maria Wimbledon?" Amarantha asked.

"I asked the devilish conniver about him," Weatherby replied. "And he said Richard Wes . . . Just before he expired."

"So that's why you hurried back here so quickly."

"Yes I was afraid you might be in danger."

"And I was. Richard came to me earlier this evening, and invited me to an elegant dinner with lots of champagne in his office. Unfortunately, I brought Sporter. Everything seemed so pleasant and nonthreatening. The food was delicious and the conversation sparkled. Sometimes recently he has seemed a little unbalanced, but tonight he had no unbelievable stories about his past. Then he must have put something in my last glass of champagne, because I had an irresistible urge to sleep. When I woke up a little, later I was bound in a chair behind his desk. I cursed myself for getting lulled into that position and not tucking a dagger into my kirtle before coming. Then you burst in."

"I rode as hard and as fast as I could, Ran, as soon as the name 'Richard' slipped out of Sir Rodney's dying mouth."

"I've seen Richard shoot before, and he is rather good with those clumsy pistols," Amarantha replied. "Let me look at your shoulder."

Amarantha ripped back the shirt over Weatherby's left shoulder before heading into the other room to wet a clean cloth with wine from the last bottle.

Weatherby looked down as she cleaned the dried blood away and said, "The ball missed the bone."

"Yes, but even a lawyer like me knows that it needs to be sewn shut," she replied as she sent Dredge for some instruments.

"While we are waiting for needle and thread," Weatherby wondered. "What do you think about our investigation? We could end up with three unrelated victims killed by three barely acquainted murderers. It isn't a very satisfying *dénouement*."

"That's why we must torture Richard Weston gradually and slowly so that we extract the maximum amount of information," Amarantha said with real conviction.

"Suddenly, you are a proponent of torture?"

"I'll make an exception for the Master of the House," Amarantha replied forcefully. "He killed my devoted Sporter. I think all three of us should be present for every torture session so that every word can be recorded, and we can sense any changes in his mental state that we can exploit."

Dredge had arrived with boiled needle and thread, and Amarantha cleansed the wound with brandy. She rubbed the torn flesh so vigorously that Weatherby gasped. Then she began quickly sewing up the wound with narrow, even stitches.

"I believe I agree with Sir John," Weatherby remarked.

"How's that?"

"You remember when both of us were sewing up Sir John's lacerations after his beating? You are better at sewing up wounds than I am."

"Now you and I both know I am just a poor barrister without any surgical or feminine skills."

"Ha!"

# CHAPTER 95

Weatherby and Amarantha walked to their apartments as dawn coloured the sky over the Royal Chapel. Dredge made sure they were undisturbed until eleven and then sent a big breakfast to Amarantha's apartments so that they might eat together. After eating, the three planned their assault on Richard Weston. With two of the murderers dead this might be their last hope for answering many questions. Weston was unstable, and they had to be careful not to push him over the brink to madness.

"I think we should let him see all of the fearsome instruments of torture and then let me talk to him privately," Amarantha said. "Perhaps then I can get the answers we need with the promise of help with an escape."

"He needs to see the two men sent from the Tower to mete out the punishment," Dredge volunteered. "One of them is a least six feet, nine inches tall and weighs at least twenty-five stones. He is bald and has a large scar across his cheek. I think he would make Sir Rodney quake."

"Let's get on with it then," Weatherby said as he rose from his chair.

They walked across the Base Court and down into the Undercroft below the Great Kitchen on the north side of the Palace. There, Richard Weston was clasped on the old stone wall by two iron clamps around his wrists. His feet rested on a wooden block so that he stood comfortably. The two warders from the Tower sharpening their blades and testing their equipment in front of him. Weatherby motioned them away as he and Dredge stepped around the corner so Amarantha might speak privately to Weston.

Weston looked frightened. He had spent a long night sitting in his cell and anticipating his painful torture.

Once they were alone, Amarantha said, "There is absolutely no reason for you to be tortured, Richard."

"I hope you are right," Richard replied in a shaky voice.

"You just need to answer some simple questions," Amarantha said. "Such as who murdered Gregory Townsend?"

"That Druid Ishmael killed him." Weston answered.

"And who killed William Suffolk and why?" Amarantha continued.

"Sir Rodney Shrewsbury killed him," Weston said hurriedly. "Suffolk was a Druid convert also brought us messages inscribed on blue glass from the Exalted Master Druid, Henri de Lèves, from France. But Suffolk taught himself the old Ogham writing and wanted to be part of the inner circle and sleep with Anna Maria Wimbledon. He had to be eliminated because the grand master wouldn't promote him and he knew too much."

"Who killed Anna Maria Wimbledon?"

"She was the chattel of the inner circle," Weston began. "We bought her with gold from her lover Christopher Dickinson. Then the three of us impregnated her. We consecrated her as a Druid, and each of her consorts was a Druid, so her baby would be a suitable sacrifice and get all of us into exalted positions in heaven. We planned to sacrifice her offspring on the Heelstone of Stonehenge with a sacred Druidic sword of gold and silver on the night of the winter solstice."

"Why did you kill her then before she delivered your sacred progeny?" Amarantha asked.

"I had no choice, even though I loved her with all my soul. I hated sharing her with Ishmael and Sir Rodney. I had trouble restraining myself from attacking both of them after they spent a night with her. But as her pregnancy advanced, she realized that she had more and more power over us and she threatened to reveal us to the local sheriff if we didn't do her bidding. All of the county sheriffs had been ordered by the King to search out and eliminate the Druids in the realm. Poisoning her was the hardest thing I ever did. I held her in my arms until she breathed her last. My tears wet her neck and the bodice of her gown. I can never forgive myself for doing that. I tried to run away with her to save her, but the network of Druids in Surrey County is extensive and ruthless. They brought us back twice, stripped us, tied us together face to face and then beat us. They said the next time they captured us they would tie us together and run a sacred sword through both of our bodies."

Weston began to shake. Amarantha found a blanket to put over his shoulders. He mumbled words that she didn't understand. She worried he might be losing his fragile grip on reality. Weatherby peered around a column and encouraged her to hurry.

"You have been most cooperative and will be allowed to go free," Amarantha lied. "I simply need to know the name of the Grand Master, the person who controlled the triumvirate of murderers. Tell me who it is. Is it Hepsibah?"

"No, although she is crafty enough and completely ruthless. For now she is too young to bear such responsibility. No. It is someone in our midst who is cleverer than Sir Rodney at disguise, more hidden than Ishmael and more learned in the ways of the Druid than I am. He is the true owner of *Gloine nan Druidh* and because he possesses the Druid's glass he will have the luck to survive and run free while his three lieutenants, Ishmael, Shrewsbury and me will all be dispatched to the underworld. The Grand Master is . . ."

A bolt from a crossbow whistled across the undercroft and pierced the lower part of Richard Weston's neck, pinning his body to the old wooden beam just behind his head, where he sat. His mouth filled with blood, his head fell forward, and his arms went limp. Weatherby, who had been hanging on every word that Weston spoke, jumped up and ran in the direction where the deadly missile had originated. He quickly found the crossbow with spare bolts leaning against a column. There was no sign of the bow man. Next he ran to Weston's side and confirmed his fear that the talkative Master of the House was dead and would reveal no more secrets. Weatherby sat down with Amarantha to review what they had learned.

"I believe that what he said was true as far as it went," Amarantha began. "I was close to him and I could smell his fear. He was truly terrified by the torture he imagined."

"If he speaks the truth, then we have three murderers, Ishmael, Sir Rodney Shrewsbury and Richard Weston and all are dead," Weatherby lamented. "They are the inner triumvirate of the Surrey Druid council, which if Sir John is correct, rules a clan of nearly a hundred Druids. Henri de Lèves was the Grand Master. He sent messages written in old Ogham on pieces of the Chartres' blue glass, and William Suffolk carried the pieces from the south coast of England to Hampton Court. Those messages controlled the actions of the local clan. What is missing is the Master of the local Druids that gave the triumvirate their orders."

"Sir Rodney said that the master was right under our noses," Amarantha offered.

"But who is he?" Weatherby asked.

"Perhaps it is a woman such as Hepsibah."

"She is smart and devious enough for the post but she is still too young."

"What about Ellen Iverson? She is very well connected and smart."

"If she is the master, I have totally lost my ability to judge a sincere character. I'm sure it isn't her."

"What about a man?"

"The names that come to mind are Christopher Dickinson, Nathaniel Philbrick, or even Sir John Moulton," Weatherby mused. "Remember, Weston said the premier Druid was a master of disguise."

"I can interrogate Dickinson," Amarantha said.

"Sir John is very powerful through his appointment by the King," Weatherby said. "I can distract him and have Dredge search his apartment and construction shack."

"But who else are we missing?"

"No one in the village comes to mind except perhaps the head priest of the local Catholic Church," Weatherby replied. "I have met him but I don't know him well. I can speak with him."

"Is there anyone we are overlooking?"

"I don't believe so."

"Let's get on with the investigation."

Weatherby walked into Hampton to talk to the head priest of Our Sacred Mother Catholic Church. Amarantha sought out Christopher Dickinson. Dredge located walked to the construction shed in the Clock Court and finding it empty, searched for evidence that Sir John was the local Master of the Druids. Late in the evening, the three gathered in the Wolsey Apartment for supper. Each reported on his findings.

"I talked with Dickinson for over an hour, and despite many questions got no feeling that he was a Druid, let alone a master," Amarantha said.

"I searched Sir John's construction shack and apartment," Dredge reported. "Even though he studies witches and warlocks, it seems it is just a hobby. From his papers I believe he is a devout Catholic and not a Druid."

"I talked with the Abbot of the local church," Weatherby said. "And I can find no evidence that he is deviant or has any hidden agenda. So all of us drew blanks. We need to approach this predicament from a different angle. Perhaps one of our victims left us a clue that we overlooked."

"I doubt that Anna Maria did," Amarantha replied. "She started out a Christian, but converted to Druidism and carried their sacrificial victim until the very end. Then the triumvirate turned on her, not she on them."

"William Suffolk was also a Christian who became a devout Druid," Dredge volunteered. "He was a supporter that was killed because he knew too much and had begun translating the secret message."

"That leaves Gregory Townsend. Why was he killed?" Weatherby asked.

"Perhaps they needed a third body to complete the mystical triangle around the Druid's egg," Dredge suggested.

"I think it is more likely that the three saw Townsend as a threat because he was converting so many Palace residents to Protestantism," Weatherby mused, "and therefore keeping the followers of Druidism from growing at the Palace which threatened the local balance of power. But he may have been threatened by Weston or Sir Rodney before they killed him, and perhaps he left us a clue before he was thrown from the Great Gatehouse. In the morning let's meet and go through all the evidence we have on him.

# CHAPTER 96

Weatherby slept soundly. He noted with pleasure that he hadn't had his nightmare since the three murderers had been revealed. Early the next morning, the three investigators gathered in the Great Kitchen for breakfast. A large fire blazed in the fireplace. A black stain of soot went almost fifteen feet up the whitewashed wall, evidence of the thousands of fires that had been lit on that hearth. Weatherby had his favorite breakfast of eggs and ham with thick slices of bread warmed in the fire.

When they finished eating, they strolled across the North Cloisters, walked along the edge of the Base Court, and then turned left into the Clock Court. Dredge had already pulled down all the journals, clothing, and bottles that pertained to Gregory Townsend. All three began reviewing the materials that related to Gregory Townsend's murder. Using Weatherby's large magnifying glass Amarantha, studied the victim's clothing. Dredge began examining all the samples from the autopsy that had been preserved in bottles of neutral spirits, while Weatherby read the journal entries written in Dredge's flowery but legible hand. No one spoke as they examined the evidence for the next hour and a half.

Finally, Weatherby broke the silence, "I'm not finding a thing. Perhaps I was wrong and we need to look elsewhere," he said in a disappointed voice.

"The inside of his clothes have some designs sewn in them," Amarantha offered. "But they are all unambiguous Christian symbols."

Weatherby was just about to suggest another line of attack when Dredge placed a small black pebble on the table for all to examine.

"Do you remember this?" Dredge asked.

"I certainly do," Weatherby said. "You found that in Gregory's shoulder by being very thorough when I had lost interest in the autopsy."

"It was very uncharacteristic of you. I was just lucky," Dredge replied. "You would have found it, I'm sure."

Weatherby fingered the pebble. "It has the initials P and C on one side. Let's look in your roster of names for the part and fulltime Palace residents."

Dredge pulled down a large leather-bound volume and thumbed through the pages.

"There are only two people in the Palace with those initials," Dredge offered. "A chambermaid named Patience Conway and a Peter Chertsey."

"Well Patience isn't the Druid ruler, that's a surety," Amarantha said. "Who is Peter Chertsey?"

"That is the Christian name of that obsequious old retainer who is the master of the guards at Hampton Court," Weatherby replied excitedly.

Without another word, they all jumped up and walked quickly to the servant's quarters where Chertsey resided. The door was locked, but Dredge pulled a ring of keys from his pouch and began trying various keys. Soon the door was open, and they burst into the room. Books, clothing, and tools were scattered around the floor and the unmade bed. Chertsey had clearly decamped. Dredge placed a sheet of paper on a cluttered table and sat down to write. Amarantha and Weatherby began sorting through the items and reporting to Dredge what they had found. Amarantha found body padding that would have made Chertsey appear to have an ample stomach. Weatherby found grey and brown cosmetics that would also have aged and disguised the Master of the Guards. The tools consisted of grappling hooks, spy glasses, calipers, and magnifying glasses. Small instruments of torture such as thumb screws and a head squeezer were also in the room.

Books and manuscripts were scattered open and torn around the table and floor. Several volumes related to the black arts, there were manuals of torture, and incriminating writing scrawled in old Ogham.

"He left here in a terrible hurry," Dredge observed.

"Chertsey must have felt you breathing down his neck, Seamus," Amarantha offered.

"He certainly had me deceived over the past four months," Weatherby said in a discouraged voice. "I discussed every aspect of these cases with him like he was a confidant."

"Remember the night we rousted him out of bed at one a.m.?" Dredge queried. "I'm surprised we didn't see something suspicious then."

"That night I was focused on terrifying him rather than looking for clues. I always try to keep my eyes and ears open but sometimes I am just swept along by events."

"Where could he go and feel safe?" Amarantha asked.

"Certainly not to France," Weatherby observed. "His controller, Henri de Lèves, was beheaded in Paris. America wouldn't work. There are no Druid clans there and most of England has become dangerous since Henry began to extirpate the Druids. I suspect the rural areas of Wales or the west of Scotland, where the ancient religion still thrives, would be safest for him."

"We can send a message to King's militia with a sketch of him," Dredge suggested.

"True," Weatherby replied thoughtfully after a pause. "But Henry's men are neither numerous nor reliable in the far reaches of the kingdom. Besides, we have tracked down the three murderers and each has received the ultimate punishment."

"It would be much more satisfying if we had someone to torture," Dredge replied.

"I believe that Weatherby may be correct," Amarantha said sympathetically. "The murderers have been run to ground and dispatched. The rocket attack inadvertently killed Ishmael. Sir Rodney Shrewsbury was killed by the witch Bozalosthtsh, even though she claimed to love him. That conniving sybarite Sir Richard Weston was probably killed by Peter Chertsey, but it was the murder of a murderer, even if Chertsey's motive was to save his own neck."

"Eloquently put, my lovely and intelligent assistant," Weatherby said as he looked longingly at Amarantha. "Pack up our laboratory, Dredge. It's time we headed back to London. I will miss the Hampton Court Palace mightily. However, soon there will be another corpse in another palace, and King Henry will need our help."

Weatherby took Amarantha's elbow and guided her to town for a final dinner at the Lamb and Flag. He requested a private dining room with heavy damask napkins and tablecloths and the inn's finest silverware. He ordered Amarantha's favorite meal of roast beef and Yorkshire pudding served with fresh summer vegetables and two bottles of a rich French Bordeaux wine. They chatted amicably and affectionately through the meal. After the dishes were cleared and they were enjoying a last glass of wine, Weatherby took both of Amarantha's small, shapely hands in his and looked into her beautiful green eyes.

"I love you, Amarantha," he said.

# DEFINITIONS

Abstruse-difficult to understand.

Amanuensis-a literary secretary. 1619.

Apostate-one who has renounced his religious faith or moral allegiance. 1532.

Barouche-a four wheeled horse-drawn carriage with double seats. The riders faced each other. A collapsible half-hood folded like a bellows. 1813.

Calash-a light carriage, often with two wheels. The driver sat up high in front 1666.

Cant-insincere talk.

Comestibles-edibles, usually cooked.

Copse-a wood of small trees.

Decoction-extraction of an essence by boiling.

Dishabille-a state of being only partially or carelessly clothed.

Fen-low lying marshy land.

Hansom-a horse-drawn cab for hire. The driver sat behind and above the passengers. 1847.

Hermaphrodite brig-a type of two-masted sailing ship which has square sails on the foremast and fore-and aft sails on the mainmast, hence the term hermaphrodite. From the word for an animal having both male and female reproductive organs. Dutch 1500s.

Hammerbeam-a short beam projecting from wall at the foot of a principal rafter in a roof, in place of a tie-beam. It allowed an open chamber unobstructed by supporting columns. 1395.

Hectare-a European unit of area equal to 2.4 acres.

Ides-the fifteenth of March, May, July or October in the ancient Roman calendar. The thirteenth day of every other month.

Largesse-the generous giving of gifts, money, or favors.

Mendacious-prone to lying.

Misanthrope-a person who hates mankind.

Mullions-a vertical piece of stone or wood that divides the panes of a window.

Oriel-a bay window projecting from a wall and supported by a bracket.

Osteomalacia-softening of bones due to a lack of calcium.

*Raison d'être*-reason for being. 1867.

Shill-a self-interested promoter.

Stone-a unit of weight in the United Kingdom equal to fourteen pounds.

Supernumerary-somebody extra.

Umbrage-annoyance arising from some offense.

Wraith-a ghostly insubstantial apparition.

# ANACHRONISMS

1. 'Lead' pencil invented 1547.
2. Tobacco introduced to England 1556.
3. Tea introduced to England 1657.
4. Anton van Leeuwenhoek described bacteria using the microscope 1674.
5. Geoffrey Chaucer started *Canterbury Tales* in 1587.
6. Acids and Bases first described by Antoine Lavoisier in 1776.
7. Gabriel Fallopius was born in 1523.
8. Boccaccio wrote the *Decameron* in 1550.
9. Moliere wrote the **School for Wives** in 1662.
10. Richard Lovelace was born in 1518.
11. Word 'rocket' coined in 1611.
12. Rules restaurant founded 1798.
13. Kew Gardens, first building 1631.
14. Rene Hyacinthe Theophile Laennec invented the stethoscope in 1810.
15. First wooden bridge across the Thames at Hampton was built in 1750.
16. Dom Pierre Pérignon, the inventor of champagne was born in 1639.
17. Chocolate was first served in 1657.
18. Galileo Galilei was born in 1564.
19. Tulips arrived in England 1570's.

# ACKNOWLEDGMENTS

I am indebted to Blythe Hoekenga for constant support and encouragement. Three diligent people-Britta Hoekenga, Gretchen Hoekenga and Bob Sanchez spent many hours editing the manuscript. Britta is best at syntax and making my convoluted sentences clearer. Bob is excellent at homophones and diacritical marks. Bob also did an exceptional job of proofreading. All three of them had dozens of useful suggestions-which I was happy to take. Thanks to Brandt Hoekenga for his elegant and attractive cover. June Shaffer helped with my egregious punctuation. Thanks to Pat Conway, Sim Middleton, and Dorothy Webb for their many helpful suggestions, and kind support.

I am inspired by Antonya Nelson.

Simon Thurley's excellent and comprehensive *Hampton Court: A Social and Architectural History,* Yale University Press, New Haven, CT (2003) served as my daily companion and compass.

Kent Rawlinson, resident historian at Hampton Court, was kind enough to read parts of the manuscript and correct several of my architectural misconceptions. He was most generous with his time and knowledge.

Finally, thanks to Hilary Hoekenga, my favorite gadfly, and to Nicole Segura and Marti Hoekenga-Rigg.